By MARGUERITE LABBE

All Bets Are Off
Ghosts in the Wind
Make Me Whole
Other Side of the Line
Playing Ball (Multiple Author Anthology)

TRIQUETRA TRILOGY
My Heart is Within You
Haunted by Your Soul
Our Sacred Balance

Published by DREAMSPINNER PRESS
www.dreamspinnerpress.com

OTHER SIDE OF THE LINE

MARGUERITE LABBE

DREAMSPINNER PRESS

Published by
DREAMSPINNER PRESS

5032 Capital Circle SW, Suite 2, PMB# 279, Tallahassee, FL 32305-7886 USA
www.dreamspinnerpress.com/

Other Side of the Line
© 2015 Marguerite Labbe.

Cover Art
© 2015 by Catt Ford.
Cover content is for illustrative purposes only and any person depicted on the cover is a model.

ISBN: 978-1-63476-584-8
Digital ISBN: 978-1-63476-585-5
Library of Congress Control Number: 2015942798
First Edition September 2015

Printed in the United States of America
∞
This paper meets the requirements of
ANSI/NISO Z39.48-1992 (Permanence of Paper).

For Lynette Michelle, thank you for the inspiration. Caleb and Hal are as much yours as they are mine.

ACKNOWLEDGMENTS

FOR ALL the insights, advice, research help for everything that went into this book, a big thank you to Jamie, Sarah, George, Carole, Mikella, Ella, Vicktor, Lynette, Chris and Keir. If I've forgotten anyone, it's all my fault and I apologize. Any mistakes are all mine as well.

AUTHOR'S NOTE

WE MAY not always understand where another person is coming from, but without compassion we cannot have real communication. Too many have lost their lives. For all the progress we've made, there is still so much more we need to do to support each other. These are only a few:

Trayvon Martin. Rebecca Wight. Michael Brown. Mark Carson. Jorge Steven López Mercado. Tamir Rice. August Provost. Eric Garner. Justin Goodwin. Freddie Gray. Joseph Walker-Hoover. Eric Harris. Lateisha Green. Walter Scott. Rev. Clementa Pinckney. Angie Zapata. Tywanza Sanders. Lawrence King. Rev. Sharonda Singleton. Sean Kennedy. Cynthia Hurd. Michael Sandy. Rev. DePayne Middleton-Doctor. Jason Gage. Ethel Lance. Scotty Weaver. Susie Jackson. Myra Thompson. Sakia Gunn. Rev. Daniel Simmons Sr. Scott Amedure.

Black lives matter. LGBT lives matter.

PART ONE

CHARLESTON, SC— SEPTEMBER 2, 2023

SIXTY YEARS.

The significance of that number still awed Caleb Hudson. In two months, he'd be celebrating having Hal Zimmer as an integral part of his long, wonderful life. It blew his mind and made his chest ache with the weight of sixty years of loving and belonging.

Caleb parked their car under a shade tree at James Island County Park and glanced over at Hal. Throughout all the changes stretched over their lives, Hal had become a vital part of him as much as skin and bone. More even. Caleb couldn't imagine Hal not being in his life. The thought terrified him as they grew older.

All those years spent as friends, then lovers, and finally, after having grandkids, getting married. When he first fell in love with Hal, marriage had been impossible. It was hard enough being of different races, even more difficult because they were gay. Then all of that ceased to matter so much. Which just illustrated the craziness of life. Caleb laughed and reached for Hal's hand as he shot Caleb a questioning look. "I love you," Caleb said.

Hal smiled, his gray-green eyes softening as he squeezed Caleb's hand. "I love you too."

The years seemed to have elongated Hal. The lean lankiness of his body had newer, sharper angles, and his receding hair had gone silver. Caleb tried to picture the sweet-faced, sandy-haired, freckled boy he'd met as a kid, but the image had faded over the years. Now he barely remembered a time before Hal had been in his life, and he didn't want to.

"If you keep looking at me like that, the kids are going to tease us about acting like newlyweds again." Hal's eyes glinted with humor.

"They'd have to get here first, and not one of them has any notion of what it means to start on time." Caleb swung his legs out and braced himself to stand on his stiffened joints. Today it was easy to overlook the aggravation in his building excitement to have his entire family together again.

The late-morning sun heated the air and sank into his bones with a familiar southern comfort. A light breeze promised to keep the day tolerable once the sun reached its zenith. The picnic area was silent, the grills cool, and the meadow empty of playing children. Caleb couldn't wait for the noise and bustle of their family to fill those quiet spaces.

"Let's start with the banner," Hal suggested. "We can worry about the food after we conscript helpers."

"If they're not here by then, I say we go for a walk and leave them to wonder what happened to us," Caleb said, looking out at the low line of bushes obscuring the creek. There had been a time when their entire summer had been spent exploring all the little creeks and wooded areas around Charleston. He wanted to revisit that today with the grandkids.

"I doubt they'll be that late." Hal nudged Caleb with his elbow. "We can sneak away after lunch for an hour."

When they were little that would've been a suggestion for shenanigans, then later on a hint for getting their hands on each other, now it meant they'd probably actually go for a walk, Caleb thought with an inward chuckle. Some people yearned to go back to past days, but even with the nostalgia and reminiscing, right here was exactly where he wanted to be. Right here with Hal, getting ready to greet their extended family, outsiders no longer. Now they belonged to their own community where differences were a matter of celebration.

They pulled out the stepladder and proceeded to string the banner over the large pavilion they'd rented for the day. Hudson-Zimmer Family Reunion. Sixty years of family and friendships. The years stretched back so far… a shining path of memories, some good, some bad, the way of every life, though there had been far more good. Caleb liked to think that when he and Hal moved on, the memory of the obstacles they'd overcome to be together would be an example to their kids. Love sure as hell conquered everything, even if it was a tooth-and-nail, bloody fight.

Charleston itself had changed so much in those years, that old southern belle had on a new dress and attitude as neighborhoods shifted and tourism boomed. Though change could come late to the city, there were times when it seemed like Caleb didn't recognize her anymore. Most of the changes were good, some traditions, though, it had been sad to watch slipping away. The sounds of his childhood, the old brogue of the white gentry, that was unlike any other southern city, the cadence and rhythm of his Gullah side of the family. Still, it had a love of history he didn't think would ever fade, and he was reminded of that every time he walked the Market or down through the historic homes south of Broad Street.

"You're quiet today," Hal said, steadying the stepladder as Caleb climbed down.

"Just thinking about us and our home." Caleb folded the stepladder to return it to the car before the grandkids arrived and decided to play with it.

Hal scratched behind his ear and shot him an amused glance. "That covers an awful lot of ground. Anything specific?"

"No, merely reflecting. We have quite a history," Caleb replied in an offhand manner.

The honk of a horn interrupted them, and they turned to see their nephew's car pull into the lot. Memories cascaded through Caleb's mind of the terrible, rainy night when a seven-year-old Drew had shown up on Caleb and Hal's doorstep to tell them his dad, Caleb's brother, had shot himself. He remembered how worried they'd been when Drew joined the Marines and served in Iraq. Caleb had never understood how much his own parents loved him until Drew came to live with them as their ward.

Seeing Drew now brought that warm wash of pride, love, and a renewed pang. Caleb still missed his brother and regretted not being able to help him with his demons. It was a tragedy that PTSD had never been discussed until long after his passing.

"Hey, Uncle Caleb, Uncle Hal," Drew called with a wave before heading to the trunk of the car. His wife and their two children, Joshua and Abby, came to join Caleb and Hal under the pavilion as Caleb's heart picked up in excitement. Abby ran up for a hug as Joshua followed behind at a slower pace, caught between wanting to do the same and a new teenage aloofness.

"Who are you?" Hal said gruffly, squinting at Joshua with humor flashing in his gaze and a faint smile touching his lips. Caleb hid a grin as Joshua hesitated, his eyes widening. Hal could be such a tease. Joshua flashed Caleb a questioning look and turned back to Hal.

"Pawpaw, it's me, Joshua."

Hal squinted even more and shook his head. "Can't be." He measured a height with his hand, several inches shorter than what Joshua had grown into since they'd seen him last. "My grandson's about yea high. You, on the other hand, look like you could've eaten him for breakfast."

Caleb caught Joshua in a hug. "He's just having fun with you. Give him a hard time about his eyesight, and he'll ease up."

"I heard that," Hal retorted.

"I guess it's good to know all your senses aren't going," Caleb shot back as Hal embraced their grandson.

Drew came up with a loaded hamper and set it on one of the long picnic tables. His broad grin lit up his dark brown eyes as he moved toward them. Caleb found himself checking Drew over, cataloguing changes. He'd recently been to the barber, and the lines on his fade haircut were sharp and new. It was funny how a child could age, have children of their own, but it didn't stop their parents from checking on them.

"Looking good, Uncle Caleb," Drew said, clasping his hand and pulling him close for a hug before turning to do the same for Hal. "You too, Uncle Hal."

"How'd the move go?" Caleb asked as another car turned in and Hal went off to greet them.

"Good. It'll be different now that I've retired from service, but Atlanta's not that far away, so we'll be able to visit more." Drew replied as they both turned to see Hal embrace a tiny white lady with an abundance of graying curls. "Oh wow, Aunt Lily made it too? I haven't seen her since the wedding."

"Hey, Lily," Caleb called with a wave to Hal's only sibling. "We're not looking for any trouble today."

"Then why'd you invite him?" Lily said with a poke to Hal's side.

Caleb couldn't stop grinning as more family arrived. It had been too long since they'd all been together, and family was everything. First Caleb and Hal's other two foster sons, who now had families of their own, arrived and then some of Caleb's cousins. The sounds of shouting, playing children filled Caleb's ears and heart with a steady, happy warmth. Life was good today.

Finally their youngest, and only daughter, pulled into the parking lot as their sons were setting up the grill. Hal shook his head. "Now who's surprised Kendra's the last to get here?"

"Nobody with any sense," Caleb commented and raised his voice for Kendra. "You do realize you're the only child to live in Charleston with us. What took you so long?"

"One word and it starts with a Z," Kendra replied in exasperation.

"Grandpa! Pawpaw!" Caleb straightened at the sound of the high, piping voice and caught Zoe as she hurtled toward them. He swung his littlest grandchild up while she squealed with laughter. "Grandpa! Grandpa! Like my shirt?" She patted the T-shirt they'd all received for the reunion, only she'd covered hers in colored marker spots and stripes.

"I do. Did you decorate it yourself, baby girl?" Caleb asked studying the colorful mess she'd made of herself all before the noonday sun had hit its peak.

"Yep." She grinned, showing a gap between her front teeth, and hugged him hard around his neck. For the love of the good lord, she'd even managed to get colored marker all over the dusky skin of her arms like an abstract tattoo. She leaned precariously out of his arms toward Hal. "Pawpaw!"

Hal scooped her up with a shake of his head. "You have extra spitfire in you today, don't you?"

"Uh-huh." She hugged him, then wiggled and reached for the ground. "Wanna play, k?"

Hal set her down and watched as she raced off to join her bigger cousins who were playing ball in the nearby field. He winced as she dove headlong into the fray, and Caleb echoed the sentiment. "That girl fears nothing."

"That's the truth."

"Hey everyone." Kendra waved to them and set down a wrapped box on one of the picnic tables. "It's so good to see y'all again," she said, hugging each one of her brothers in turn before turning to Caleb and Hal. "Dad, Pops." She dropped a kiss on their cheeks. "Give me a moment," she said and chased after her daughter.

Hal took his hand and gave it a little tug. "Hmmm?" Caleb said. There was a twinkle in Hal's gaze. The same twinkle he always got when he was about to tease Caleb. That at least had never changed. They were the eyes of the oldest friend Caleb had. Of one who had stuck with him through separations, disagreements, and big blow-ups. Damn he loved that man.

"What's so funny?" Caleb asked as Hal's twinkle transformed into an open grin.

"You." Hal slipped an arm around Caleb's waist. "Being with family has always made you the happiest."

"I can't deny that." Caleb glanced up at him. His family started with Hal.

"It feels good to see them all together again, doesn't it?" Hal asked softly.

Caleb looked over the group, a hodge-podge of black, white, and in-between... how things had changed. When they'd met, Charleston was just starting to desegregate, years behind other cities. To go from that, to this... it humbled him. It awed him. Caleb squeezed Hal's waist and smiled.

"Yeah, it does feel pretty good," he replied, as the grill sizzled and the air filled with the scent of roasting meat and oysters, the sound of the grandkids' laughter carried on the breeze from the river. It felt pretty close to perfect.

HAL SAT back with a groan and dropped his napkin on his paper plate. That last bite had been a mistake, but his sister could make the best cobbler, north or south of the Mason-Dixon Line.

"I never could understand how you can eat like you do and still be rail skinny," Caleb said with a shake of his head.

"It's one of my many gifts," Hal replied. He took his husband's hand with a warm rush of affection. He'd never take the simple gesture for granted. Not after so many years of having to disguise it, of having such touches questioned.

He watched Caleb as he savored the last few bites of banana pudding, chuckling as Caleb licked the spoon clean. "Sure you got it all?"

"Hush, you, and let a man enjoy a few indulgences today," Caleb retorted with an amused gleam in his eyes.

Hal had been giving him a hard time all day about being sentimental, but they'd both been doing a lot of reflecting as this anniversary approached. Caleb's face showed none of the exhaustion that came upon him periodically, though the darker bags under his eyes would probably never go away. It worried Hal and made their time together even more precious.

Caleb caught his look and frowned at him. "You'd better not be sitting there worrying about me today. I'm fine."

"You talk as if we've ever stopped worrying about each other." Caleb was just as bad, concerned about Hal's eyesight and always leaving lights on all over the house just because he'd taken that little tumble down the stairs last year. He lifted Caleb's hand to his lips. "Your knuckles are getting ashy."

They weren't really; Caleb was meticulous about using lotion. He remembered a time when he had been a little jealous of Caleb's rich, warm brown tone and despaired that he'd never lose his freckles.

Caleb raised a brow, meeting him stare for stare, but didn't give Hal the satisfaction of rising to his bait. "Since the first day we met, you've given me more cause for anxiety than I have you."

Kendra rolled her eyes and pulled the dark twists of her hair into a ponytail before coming to take their plates. "You two," she chided. Hal remembered the long months of waiting during the surrogacy and then the joy of bringing her home from the hospital, a little bundle of waving fists, wide, dark eyes, and a puff of curly black hair. From day one the boys had been enthralled with her, and God help anyone who ever gave her trouble.

"Name one time I stressed you out when we were younger. I was the calm one," Hal continued to tease, pulling his thoughts away from the memories.

"Don't believe one word he says," Caleb retorted, as their grandkids crept closer. "Your Pawpaw believed a little too much in causes and flag waving, and he didn't always think his actions through, like hopping on a bus for Charleston without telling his parents."

"You did not." Joshua's eyes widened.

"Well." Hal tugged on his earlobe. "I had to come. Your grandpa was going off to war, and I needed to see him before he left."

"Like Dad," Joshua glanced toward Drew who was deep in conversation with his brothers.

"Yes, and I think it was more cause for concern on my part than his." Hal laid a hand on his chest as Caleb shook his head. "I was perfectly safe at college in New York."

Caleb snorted. "I know all about the trouble some of those antiwar protestors got into. Every time I thought about Kent State, I went cold inside worrying about how it could be you if you didn't start watching your step."

"You've done it now, Joshua. You've got them started," Drew called out. "They'll go on nonstop for the rest of the day."

"Not yet. First, let's get the leftovers put away." Hal adjusted his glasses and rose from the picnic table. Once they marshalled all the grandkids into service, cleanup was fast and fun. More than once Hal found himself watching his family laugh and bustle. He truly was as bad as Caleb. They were really all here. They all were a part of his and Caleb's lives. The amazing beauty of reality was enough to make a man ache.

His gaze sought out their children, lingering on each one in turn. "You okay, Uncle Hal?" Drew asked.

"I'm just happy you're all here. Now that you're closer and your brothers are just in Savannah we need to get together more often," Hal said.

"I promise we'll make more of an effort. In fact, I was thinking everybody could come to my place for Thanksgiving." Drew looked around the gathering. "Wow, there sure are a lot of us."

"I know. I swear, your Uncle Caleb has cousins I didn't even know existed."

Drew laughed. "You tried claiming the same thing when they showed up for your wedding."

"Yeah, I'd like to know how they found out. I told Caleb we should've eloped, but he was sure we could get away with a small, quiet ceremony." Hal searched for Caleb as the memory of that long-awaited day still had the power to make his throat close.

"Then you both were deluding yourselves," Drew replied. "If I recall, y'all led the whole family on a two-day party that ended with you, Uncle Caleb, and the grandkids in the Pineapple Fountain."

"Good times." Hal watched Kendra and Lily talk with their heads together under the pavilion. "You know I'm beginning to think Caleb is right. The whole gang of you is up to something," Hal accused, and Drew merely grinned with a shrug.

"We won't keep you in suspense." Drew turned and waved at his siblings. "I think we'd better fess up before they decide to finagle answers out of us. We all know how that'll go."

"Come on, Pawpaw, Grandpa, take a seat," Joshua said, and Hal followed the sound of his voice to find two chairs set out underneath the arbor.

"Ooooohh," Zoe squealed. "Is it time to—"

"Shut it," Abby hissed and tugged on one of Zoe's braids. "It's a surprise."

Zoe clamped her lips together, glared at Abby, and yanked her braid free. "I wasn't gonna say what it was, dummy."

"Be nice," Caleb cut in before the argument could get physical. When the two girls weren't getting along like the best of friends, they were fighting like they meant to draw blood. That's all it took, two words in his deep rumble, and they quieted down. Hal wished it had worked as well on their kids when they were younger, but grandkids were a whole different breed.

He followed Caleb to their place of honor with bemusement. Everybody had been astir for months now, going about whispering and calling them up to ask crazy questions about their history together. He'd even caught Kendra rooting around in their attic one afternoon when they'd come home early from a trip to New York.

"We wanted to do something special for this reunion. After all, in two months you two will have known each other for sixty years," Drew said as he grabbed the wrapped box from the end of the picnic table. "So we came up with a plan, got together, and everybody worked on the surprise, even the grandkids."

Caleb smiled, and Hal ran his thumb across Caleb's knuckles as he looked down at their linked hands with a tender ache. He loved the way they fit together, loved the contrast of their skin tones, loved knowing they'd had all those years together and managed to maintain their closeness, even during the years they'd been apart. Sixty years.... It was hard to believe how much had changed, and yet there had been constants too, like the bond of their friendship. How they both had clung to that anchor. Hal smiled and squeezed Caleb's hand, felt the reassuring press of his fingers in return.

Drew brought the mystery box over and set it on their knees. It was heavy, wrapped in beautiful thick paper and tied with a silver bow. That part had to have been Kendra's work. She always took extra time with things like this.

"Can I help open it?" Abby asked, fingering the paper where it was taped down.

"No, let them do this one," Drew said and tugged her out of temptation's way and onto his lap to watch.

Conscious of all the attention and cameras on them, Hal gave Caleb an amused smile as they tore off the paper and lifted the lid of the box. Inside sat a handmade photo album with a picture of their wedding on the front. Caleb drew the book out, and Hal leaned over to look as he leafed through the pages. There were photographs, letters to each other over the years, notes from old friends commenting on their relationship, and hand-drawn pictures the grandchildren had done. Hal's chest tightened, and his eyes stung. The whole family had gotten involved… the way families should.

"Oh my, will you look at that?" Caleb's gnarled fingers paused on a picture of them from fourth grade. Caleb had his arm around him, his chin thrust out in an expression Hal had often seen on his face, a kind of protective challenge that dared anybody to say anything.

Hal remembered the day a reporter had come to the school to do a story on desegregation. He'd been so caught up in confessing his homesickness to Caleb, leaning into him trustingly, that he hadn't even realized the man was there. The flash of the man's camera had come as a shock.

"That picture sure caused a fuss, didn't it?" Hal said with a laugh. Time had caused the picture to fade and go grainy. He couldn't believe the kids had managed to dig that one up.

"I'd forgotten all about that. I was more worried about James Littleton that year." Caleb mused. "Remember him?"

"How could I forget?" Hal thought back on the little boy with a mean face and meaner mouth.

"Who's James?" Zoe asked, coming over to look at the picture. "Is he there?"

"James was the bully your Grandpa saved me from during my first week at school. Right after I shocked the entire class by shoving my foot so deep in my throat I choked on my kneecap," Hal replied.

Joshua's eyes widened as Zoe giggled at his words. "You embarrassed yourself in class?" he asked. At almost thirteen, the thought of being humiliated at school was the worst horror he could imagine.

"Your Pawpaw didn't just embarrass himself, he upset the teacher so much he barely passed history, and I didn't save him from the bully, he saved me," Caleb said. "First time in my life a white kid ever stuck up for me. We've been friends ever since."

Hal chuckled at the curiosity lighting their grandchildren's eyes. "What happened? Did you get in a fight?" Abby escaped her father, bouncing over to look at the book.

"You don't want to hear any of my old stories, do you?" Caleb asked with a look of feigned astonishment as their adult kids exchanged amused glances.

"Uh-huh," Zoe said with a nod and plopped down on the ground next to Abby. "I love your stories, Grandpa."

"That's because he makes things up to make them sound better," Hal said.

"Not this time. This story needs no embellishment. Let me tell you about how I met your Pawpaw and of some of the crazy times we had as kids." Caleb settled back with a grin on his face. "Now, in 1963, things were very different, and I'm not talking about all those gadgets and nonsense that y'all have now...."

CHARLESTON, SC—
NOVEMBER 6, 1963

CALEB HUDSON sat in the back of the class trying to remain quiet and unnoticeable, which was difficult when he stood out like a dark hollyhock in a field of Easter lilies. He stared at the history book in front of him, thinking of his dad's words. He said the same thing every Monday morning before Caleb headed to Uncle Vern's house in Charleston and then to his new school: "*Be good.*"

Each morning Caleb took the words differently. Some days, he hoped if he behaved, then the other students and his teacher would accept him. Other days, he was sure it meant that if he wanted to keep his skin whole he'd better be good or else. Dad said quite a bit with only a few words, and Caleb had learned to figure out the whole meaning. Today he'd decided it meant he had to have the guts to be an example. But Lordy it was hard. He was only ten after all.

The sound of that Gullah accented voice, the scent of fish on Dad's clothes, and the feel of his hand heavy on Caleb's shoulder filled him with a renewed bravery each Monday to make the walk from his home to his uncle's house. Uncle Vern had stuck his neck out to give him this chance to go to a good school, and if Caleb wanted to be like his hero Henry Flipper, he'd have to hold on. Caleb tried hard to remember Dr. King's speech, but by midweek, his courage started to waver underneath the silent disapproval of his classmates and teachers, and the not so silent cruelty from James Littleton.

Caleb lifted his gaze, and his insides clenched as he found James staring at him. The boy's face twisted into a sneer, his expression dark with promise, and his blue eyes hard with malice. Caleb's stomach soured. James had a mean, thin mouth on him, and though he was smaller than Caleb, his fists were sharp, and he had a fondness for poking Caleb with sticks when nobody was watching. He appeared extra mean this morning, like he'd spent last night thinking up ways to be a jerk today. Unless something distracted James, Caleb was in for trouble later on. He'd have to run out of the schoolyard like a scalded haint if he wanted to keep out of his path.

"Caleb, are you paying attention?" Mr. Gibbons's testy voice cut through Caleb's thoughts, and his gaze jerked back toward his teacher as his cheeks heated. His classmates snickered, James the loudest of them all, while Caleb struggled to recall what Mr. Gibbons had been saying. He did not want to be called in front of the class to recite the discussion.

"Yes, sir. You were giving an introduction to the start of the war and talking about the first shots fired at Ft. Sumter," Caleb said and hoped that was enough. The newest student, Hal Zimmer, gave him a sunny smile, startling the heck out of him. None of the other kids had ever grinned at him in such a friendly way. Hal, with his sandy blond hair and smattering of freckles, was a lone light in a dark space.

"Quite right." Mr. Gibbons didn't press for more much to Caleb's intense relief and his classmates' obvious disappointment. He didn't always remember dates that well, though he was pretty good with names and places.

At the beginning of the school year, Caleb could sense the anger from the others build up like the pressure in the air before a hurricane, and he worried that when the storm came, it was going to be a doozy. By now, though, most of the others had settled on ignoring him, and that was worse than the anger. The anger had frightened him, the shunning left him feeling less than human, and now he was stuck between the ache of being nonexistent and the physical pain of James' attentions.

He wished there were others like him in his class. He hadn't been the only black child to walk into this all-white elementary school this September, but he'd been the only one placed in Mr. Gibbons's fourth grade class. Mr. Gibbons had been none too happy to have him either.

Caleb's teacher paced across the front of the classroom, leaning on his cane, his white hair gleaming in the afternoon sunlight. "Now can anyone name a hero from the War of Northern Aggression?" He paused and focused on Hal in the front row. Hal had just started in their class on Monday, coming all the way down from New York. "That would be the Civil War for those of us who might not understand… given their unfortunate origins."

"Oooohh!" Hal's hand shot up. He talked funny, fast and with a strange high accent. He liked to try to answer all the questions, and sometimes he stared at Caleb too much, but he never seemed mean about it, only curious. At least his eyes didn't slide away as if Caleb's skin was covered in rancid oil, and that made for a welcome change.

Mr. Gibbons looked around the room to see if anyone else wanted to volunteer, and his gaze lingered on Caleb for a moment. Several answers crowded his mind, and Caleb sifted through them trying to think which answer would please him the most before settling on General Beauregard. Still, Caleb remained silent and prayed he wouldn't be called on again. He wasn't too fond of the teacher's method of asking questions. It made him feel small and ignorant.

Mr. Gibbons focused on Hal again. "Well, Hal?"

Hal straightened, his shoulders squaring with pride. "William Tecumseh Sherman."

The classroom fell silent, not a rustle of a page or a rattle of a pencil to be heard. Caleb's mouth fell open as Mr. Gibbons's face turned a mottled red, and his hand tightened on the cane. Hal seemed to sense how deep he'd stepped into it, because he looked around the room, his little freckled face drawn together in confusion.

He caught Caleb's eye, and Caleb couldn't stop himself from grinning. "Amen," he mouthed, and Hal smiled back.

"Stupid Yankee," James snarled under his breath, breaking the quiet. Caleb glanced at him, saw the way his hands had tightened into fists and how his gaze glittered through dirty-blond hair. There would be trouble later on.

Mr. Gibbons pounded the floor with his cane, his bushy brows coming together in a fierce frown. "Sherman was a war criminal," he thundered. Hal turned to face him, his shoulders sagging. "Stand up! Tell me and your classmates why you think a man who burns his way through enemy country, depriving its citizens of food and shelter, should be called a hero?"

Hal stood reluctantly and glanced around at the rest of the class for support that wasn't there. "Umm, I guess that wouldn't be very heroic, sir."

"Do you think a man who tries to break the spirit of a people in the name of conquest should be called a hero?"

"No, sir," Hal said again, his voice even quieter now. He stared down at his feet and flinched when James snickered. Caleb felt the pang of remembered humiliation when he'd been in similar situations. It was mighty painful to be the object of everyone's attention when Mr. Gibbons had his irritation focused on you.

"Speak up, young man! Don't mumble." Mr. Gibbons jabbed his cane in Hal's direction. "I cannot abide a child who cannot make themselves understood. They have no place in my classroom. Answer the question."

"No, sir!"

"You need to reexamine your definition of a hero, now sit down and remain silent until you have something positive to offer." Mr. Gibbons pounded his cane again for emphasis.

Hal dropped into his seat, the nape of his neck turning a fiery red. He remained quiet for the rest of the afternoon, his head bowed, his whole body hunched. Caleb felt another one of those little pangs. He'd been in that same exact position too many times to count, afraid to meet Mr. Gibbons's gaze, and forced to hear the other students whispering about him. It was horrible.

James especially made his opinions about Hal known with several vicious comments pitched low so Mr. Gibbons, with his worsening hearing, wouldn't catch. Hal certainly did hear them and curled in even tighter. Hal was sure in for it now. He probably didn't realize how bad, though. Caleb should be glad James's attention was turned from him, at least for now, but he couldn't help but feel sorry for Hal. It wasn't going to be pretty when Mr. Gibbons released them for the day.

If Caleb was smart, he'd be long gone before that happened. Maybe he'd get a chance to warn Hal to get himself home fast, though that would only delay the inevitable. Sure as the sun rose over the Atlantic, James would make sure to get his licks in whenever he could.

HAL GATHERED his books and stuffed them in his rucksack as the rest of the classroom cleared out. He glanced up, met Mr. Gibbons's stony gaze, and shrank a little more inside. He didn't understand why his teacher got so mad. Maybe he had a granddaddy in the Civil War like Mr. Drake back home. He looked as old as Mr. Drake, though twice as unkind. Mr. Gibbons reminded him of an evil Foghorn Leghorn.

He shouldered the rucksack and trudged out the door, his whole body weighed down from the stress of the day. He wanted to return home to New York and their little town on the river. Everybody here talked funny, lyrical and low, like they had all day long to say something, and it was unnaturally warm for this time of year. There should be frost on the ground and the promise of snow coming. The city was too noisy compared to his hometown, and he didn't know anyone or need to know them if they were going to be as unfriendly as they were today. He had to find his sister and get home before anything else went wrong.

"Stupid Yank." A hard shove knocked him forward, and Hal's rucksack was torn away from him. "Go back north."

Hal spun around to face James and received another shove that knocked him off his feet. He landed on his bum, and his face heated from a new bout of humiliation. Behind the boy, a few of his other classmates had gathered to watch, some openly laughing, some not, but all of them hostile.

"Leave me alone!" Hal scrambled to his feet, scanning the ground for his rucksack, while trying to keep one wary eye on his adversary.

James held it up with a sneer. "This what you want?"

Hal reached for it with uncertain hands. "May I have it back, please?"

"Sure." James shoved the rucksack at him hard enough to make Hal fall again. The air left his lungs from the force of the blow, and his arms remained empty. "Come on, don't you want your stupid bag?" James taunted in a malicious voice as he waved the rucksack in front of him.

Hal stared at his feet, his eyes stinging, afraid to take James up on his offer again. Where were all the teachers? He didn't expect Mr. Gibbons to help, but surely one of the others would notice. Then someone stepped up beside him and held out a dark brown hand. Hal's head fell back as he looked up at Caleb. He'd been the only classmate who smiled at him after Hal had kicked the proverbial hornet's nest in class. Caleb's round face was serious, his jaw set in a determined line as he wisely kept his gaze on Hal's tormentor.

"Stay out of it, boy," James snarled. "Or I'll get you even worse."

Hal took the offered hand and helped himself up, feeling less alone. He snatched his rucksack from James's feet where it had dropped. James looked at Caleb and Hal standing side by side, then back at his cohorts who watched with expressions of astonishment on their faces.

"I'm not afraid of you," Caleb said with bravado, but Hal heard the undercurrent of uncertainty in Caleb's voice. Even worse, James heard it too.

"Yeah, well you will be." James drove his fist into Caleb's stomach. Hal's new friend staggered back, raising his arms to protect himself.

"Yeah, get him." The rest of the kids hooted and cheered James on as he reached back to hit Caleb again. "Mind your own business. This ought to teach you."

Hal couldn't believe they were all ganging up on Caleb, just because he'd come to his defense. Then incredulity and fear vanished as Caleb cried out in pain when James hit him again.

"Leave us alone!" Hal clenched his fists and ground his teeth as a red haze flooded through him. He jumped in, grabbed James off Caleb, and bopped him a good one on the mouth. The shock of the punch reverberated through his knuckles.

"You hit me!" James wailed, and the rest of the schoolyard went quiet. James raised a hand to his bloody lip, staring at Hal in shock and pain. Hal stared back, surprised at his own daring. He wasn't much for fighting, and he felt a little sick, but he couldn't watch James hurt Caleb when Caleb had only been trying to keep him from being pushed around.

Hal's heart raced and his stomach churned as he stepped back so James could get to his feet. Please let him go away. Fear seized a hold of his lungs, making it hard to breathe as the tension rose. Hal didn't want to fight anymore, though he recognized that he would if James attacked either of them again. James turned to his friends for support, only to find them appearing as uncertain as he did.

Hal moved next to Caleb, sure that his legs were about to shake, and he hoped it didn't show. They were in for it now. But James grabbed his belongings with a snarl and raced off as Miss Mathers came into the yard. Relief flooded though him, and Hal clutched Caleb's arm to keep himself steady.

She observed the standoff in the schoolyard with a steely gaze, noting James's swift retreat. "Go on, get home," she said with a shooing motion of her hands and an odd look in Hal and Caleb's direction. The other kids scattered as the hot taste of battle left Hal's mouth leaving him feeling foolish and at a loss. His first week at the new school had been pretty awful, and he didn't know what he could do to make friends now.

"Why didn't you hit him back?" Hal asked in a low voice as Caleb dusted himself off.

Caleb shot him an incredulous look. "Are you crazy? I'd be in real trouble then." He picked up his books, tucked them under his arm, and began walking out of the yard.

"I don't understand," Hal said, but Caleb didn't respond. Hal waited a moment and then hurried after the only kid who had been nice to him all day. He hoped he hadn't offended Caleb by staring at him in class, but he didn't know how to ask if he had. There were no black kids in his little town in New York, and Caleb, with his smooth dark skin and eyes an even deeper shade of brown, constantly drew his eyes.

"Why'd you help me?" Hal asked instead, falling into step beside him.

Caleb paused and looked over at Hal like he didn't quite know what to do with him. "I promised Dad I'd be good. Leaving you alone to get shoved around by James wouldn't be good in his book. Besides, I've been in your shoes, and it's no fun."

The enormity of what happened struck Hal. He hadn't even been in Charleston a week, and he already had the teacher mad at him. Usually teachers liked him. It was probably going to be a long time before anybody would want to be his friend judging by the angry mutters when the other kids left the schoolyard.

"They don't want me here." Hal stared at Caleb in confusion, trying to figure out how it had gone so wrong.

"That's all right," Caleb said, his shoulders stiffening as he thrust his chin out. "'Cause they don't want me here either."

They faced each other by the crowded, noisy street, and then Hal gave him a tentative smile. "You think maybe we could be outsiders together?"

Caleb grinned, a white flash of teeth that erased the unhappiness on his face. "You sure do talk crazy." Hal wasn't sure if he referred to his accent, that many other people had commented on, or his words, but before he could ask, Caleb patted his arm. "Outsiders together… yeah. We could be like those outsiders that go on to do big things even when people say they can't, like Henry Flipper."

"I don't know him." Hal followed Caleb, his curiosity pricked. "What did he do?"

"He was a slave who went to West Point and became a Buffalo Soldier. I'm going to be a soldier like him one day and engineer things like bridges," Caleb said with pride.

"Not me, that's too much work," Hal shook his head. "I'm going to work on a riverboat and go back home to search for Captain Kidd's treasure. What's a Buffalo Soldier?" The miseries of the day fell away as Hal put Mr. Gibbons and James from his mind. Maybe Charleston wouldn't be so bad after all.

CHARLESTON, SC—
NOVEMBER 7, 1963

CALEB SET his schoolbooks on the table and dug into breakfast with a hunger he didn't have most mornings. Today the grits and eggs tasted extra yummy. Uncle Vern came to the table with a pitcher of Tang and a carafe of coffee, sitting across from him with an astonished expression on his kind face.

"Please tell me you aren't growing again," Uncle Vern said as he filled Caleb's glass before settling back with his coffee. "I thought we had a deal. You're allowed to grow just before summer and winter. Otherwise, trying to keep you in clothes and shoes would be an ongoing effort I cannot possibly keep up with."

Caleb grinned and took a drink of his Tang. He loved his uncle, who had opened his home to him and made it possible for Caleb to go to school in the city. How Uncle Vern convinced Caleb's mom to let him go, he didn't know, but he was grateful. Though he was sure it included Caleb coming home on the weekends. Uncle Vern looked like Caleb's mom. They had the same broad-cheeked smiles and large, dark eyes that made them appear younger than they were.

Uncle Vern hummed along to the Beach Boys record playing in the living room. He loved music, and his record collection spanned from classical to jazz to the musicians and singers who were popular today. He'd taught Caleb about them all.

Many people in their family considered Uncle Vern odd for remaining a bachelor, but he was Caleb's favorite uncle out of the whole bunch. So what if he didn't have any lady friends? He worked hard at his law office, and his evenings were busy with gatherings where men came over to discuss politics and make plans for the Charleston Movement. Sometimes they just listened to the radio or records while drinking bourbon and smoking cigars.

Usually the gatherings happened after Caleb's bedtime. Often he stayed up and listened on the stairwell to the men talking. There were times when their conversation about civil rights scared him and sent him back to huddle in his bed with images seared into his head of men in white masks coming to drag his uncle away or fears of having his church bombed or burned down.

Uncle Vern always seemed to know when Caleb had been eavesdropping. If it was one of the scary nights, his uncle would come to talk to him in his gentle voice until Caleb was soothed enough to go to sleep. Last night the conversation had been about the Freedom Voting in Mississippi, and his uncle's friends had been encouraged by the turnout. Caleb wasn't sure what it meant, and his uncle hadn't come to discuss it with him. Caleb figured that he'd ask him tonight, when they had more time for one of their long conversations. Uncle Vern didn't treat Caleb like he was a kid who couldn't understand all the grown-up stuff.

Between the pleasant night and meeting his new friend Hal yesterday, Caleb faced the school morning with more cheer than usual. "I can't stop growing," Caleb replied. "I tried to tell my legs to stop, but since they don't have ears they aren't listening."

Uncle Vern laughed and filled a plate for himself, piling the eggs high. "I guess that would put a damper on it. It's good to see you smiling this morning. I was beginning to get worried. You can be so serious, and I hated sending you off in the mornings like you're going to a battle. What's changed? Has the teacher eased up on you?"

Caleb snorted at that ridiculous thought. Mr. Gibbons was not the kind of man to forgive or forget. So he doubted he could ever expect any leeway from him. Though, given yesterday's scene, Hal might be the target instead of Caleb. He didn't like the thought of Hal going through that either. Yesterday had marked the first time that anybody had stood up for him at the new school. It made him sad to think Hal would probably soon realize that being an outsider with him wasn't nearly as healthy as being on good terms with the rest of their classmates.

"No, Mr. Gibbons is still a skunk." Caleb ate a few more bites of his breakfast and thought about Hal. He was a funny kid with his fast, clipped accent, freckled nose, and earnest way of talking. "A new boy started school this week. He's from New York. I like him."

"I take it he's friendlier to you than all the rest of the kids?"

"Well, he stared at me the first couple days. Then yesterday he said something stupid in class, and Mr. Gibbons went off on him. All the other kids started calling him a Yankee and tried to rough him up after school." James had just been messing with Hal when he'd pushed him around. He liked to make his victims feel stupid and helpless before he started hurting them.

Uncle Vern watched him thoughtfully, taking a sip of coffee. Caleb had never seen anyone love his coffee like his uncle. Some mornings he filled his plate and forgot to eat as he read the paper or went over his daily schedule as he drank cup after cup. Maybe if he ate more he wouldn't be so rail thin. Since he went to all the trouble to make sure Caleb ate, then he should eat some too. Caleb nudged the plate closer to his uncle.

"Tried? Did one of the teachers step in?" Uncle Vern asked with a penetrating look.

Caleb's mouth went dry, and he had a hard time swallowing his grits. His uncle had made it clear he wasn't to start anything with James and his friends. Caleb wondered if he'd consider Caleb's actions a breach of that promise. "Well, I helped him up when James shoved him."

He stole a glance at his uncle who watched him with an unwavering gaze. "James got mad at me for interfering and hit me." His uncle winced, and Caleb hurried to finish the tale before he received a lecture about fighting. "And then, you won't believe this, then Hal punched James and told him to leave me alone!"

"I take it Hal's the kid from New York?" Uncle Vern waited for Caleb's nod. A worried frown lined its way between his brows. "Is he black?"

Caleb shook his head, pushing the rest of his breakfast away. "Nope, he's all white except for his freckles. He promised to be my friend. Do you think he'll keep it?" Caleb hadn't realized how much he wanted a friend until Hal had offered. Sure he had friends on his uncle's street. At home with his parents, he had his brother, Rodney, and the kids he'd known since he was a baby. But he had no one at school. Hal coming to his rescue had opened a whole new world of possibilities to him. He didn't want to lose that and go back to being alone.

Uncle Vern hesitated and offered Caleb a little smile. "Time will tell. Until then, be careful and remember, trust is earned. However, any kid who stands up to James Littleton on your behalf is worth giving a chance to prove they'll keep that promise. Don't you think?"

"Yeah." Reassured, Caleb finished the rest of his drink and carried his dishes to the sink. "I've got to go. Don't want to be late." He grabbed his books and lunch bag, hugged his uncle, and hustled out the door.

"Have a good day," Uncle Vern called out after him. "And please try to stay out of James's way."

Normally Caleb took his time getting to school, hoping to slip in right before the bell. This morning Caleb ran and quickly warmed up despite the morning's coolness. Maybe he could catch Hal before he went into the schoolyard alone.

As he neared, he spied Hal walking hand-in-hand with a little girl. She looked like one of those fancy china dolls Caleb had seen in the toy store. Her blonde hair was fashioned in twin braids twined with ribbons. She wore a pretty blue dress that matched her eyes, and shiny black shoes on her tiny feet.

Caleb slowed to a walk figuring Hal might not want to talk to him with the girl around. He needed to catch his breath and ease the stitch burning in his side. Then Hal saw him, and a grin animated his face. He waved to Caleb as the girl looked over with a curious gaze. She followed along without a fuss as Hal headed toward him instead of the school.

"I sure am glad to see you," Hal said, relief evident in his gray-green eyes. "I think I saw those boys waiting for us on the other side of the gate. They won't mess with me with Lily around would they? She's only seven. I don't want her getting hurt because they're mad at me."

Lily firmed her little chin with an expression of mutinous resolve. She had delicate, fine features and looked nothing like Hal except for the same smattering of freckles. "I'll kick them in the shins if they try. I can take care of myself. I got home all by myself yesterday."

"Yeah, and I got in trouble for it too," Hal retorted. "Caleb, this is my kid sister, Lily."

"Hey, Lily." Caleb waved. "She should be pretty safe. The school would come down pretty hard if they tried messing with someone as little as your sister."

Lily considered him with a cocked head as she pulled on one of the ribbons tied around her hair, undoing the pretty bow. Caleb wasn't sure what to think of the way she studied him. Then Lily smiled, flashing a pair of deep dimples, and handed him the ribbon. "Here you go. I don't want it."

Caleb looked down at the pale blue satin strip with a blink of confusion, trying to figure out what the heck he was supposed to do with it. Hal snatched it back with an exasperated sound. "Mom will fuss if you lose your ribbons again."

"But I don't like them," Lily protested. "They're silly."

Hal wound the offending strip around the end of Lily's braid, ignoring her sulk. He must've had lots of practice because he made a pretty neat bow. "Come on, we're going to be late if you keep messing around."

Lily stuck out her tongue and ran off toward the school. "I don't need you," she called.

Hal shook his head with a sigh. "Girls are trouble. Do you have any sisters?"

Caleb was grateful that he didn't. Lily looked like trouble in pigtails. "Nah, just an older brother." He missed Rodney during the week and wished he'd taken Uncle Vern up on the offer to go to school here too. James wouldn't dare mess with him with Rodney around. But Rodney had refused, and he thought Caleb was crazy for choosing to go to this school. Some days Caleb thought Rodney might be right.

"Do you think Mr. Gibbons would let me sit near you?" Hal asked as they made their way into the schoolyard.

Out of habit, Caleb glanced around to see where the rest of his classmates were. He spotted James and a couple of his pals, but the yard was crowded with the rush of students and there were too many teachers present for them to cause problems. James glared at them, made a rude gesture, and disappeared inside. "He might," Caleb said in response, "though he'd probably make a nasty comment about retreating if you ask."

Hal considered that for a long moment, then shrugged. "I'm used to nasty comments. It's okay if he says yes."

Caleb was blown away that Hal would risk Mr. Gibbons's sharp tongue for the chance to sit by him. It made him feel a whole lot less alone as they entered the school together. Even if Mr. Gibbons said no, it didn't matter. Caleb obviously had a friend.

Their classroom buzzed with conversation and laughter as they came in. The noise died down to whispers, giggles, and furtive glances. James turned around in his chair and shot Hal a vicious look. Caleb glanced at his friend's face, and to his disbelief, Hal stared James down with his chin thrust out. Caleb had to give it to him, Hal was one gutsy white boy, and from James's expression, he didn't know what to do about it. Caleb liked seeing his tormentor at such a loss.

Caleb slid into his chair as Hal marched toward Mr. Gibbons's desk. When Hal passed by James, Caleb feared he would pull one of his mean tricks like trying to trip Hal or jabbing him in the side with his pencil. Caleb didn't even realize he'd clenched his fists until James stole a glance at him and settled back in his chair. His friends looked on in wonder as Hal passed by James unabused.

Caleb couldn't hear Hal's conversation with their teacher, but he couldn't miss Mr. Gibbons's sharp glance in his direction. Caleb was very conscious of the empty seats around him, a painful reminder that the other kids treated him like he had an illness they could catch. He looked down at his hands and told himself it didn't matter if Mr. Gibbons said no. At least Hal asked, and Caleb would be forever grateful to him for that kindness.

Hal slid into the seat next to him, and Caleb's breath caught in surprise and delight. Hal's beaming smile was infectious, and Caleb grinned back at him as the rest of the school year turned in a new direction.

HAL CAME into the schoolyard, clutching his lunch in both hands, his stomach jumping. James and his crew were occupied at the swing set. He could probably manage to sneak by them and hide out in the concrete pipes at the end of the yard. Nobody played out there. But Caleb might not be able to find him either.

He found a bench where he could keep an eye out for James and be in the line of sight of the teacher by the door. He wished Caleb was there, but he had been called to the principal's office just before lunch break. Hal hoped Caleb wasn't in any trouble.

The laughter of the other kids mocked him as Hal pulled out his apple. He wasn't all that hungry. He watched them playing, oblivious to Hal sitting by himself. The few who did notice made faces at him and went on their way. He supposed he should be grateful they didn't point him out to James, but mostly he was lonely. Homesickness rolled over him in a wave, and Hal blinked back tears before anyone noticed. He didn't understand why his family couldn't have stayed in Dobbs Ferry. That was their home, not Charleston.

"Hey," Caleb slid onto the bench beside him, breathless. "I was worried James would corner you before I got a chance to get here."

"Nah, he hasn't seen me. Too busy trying to push girls off the swings." Hal took a bite of his apple, feeling better now that Caleb had arrived. "You weren't in trouble, were you?"

"No, but I was scared, let me tell you. There's a reporter from the newspaper coming to our class today. The principal wanted to make sure that I look happy when he gets here." Caleb pulled out his own lunch as Hal thought his words over.

"That doesn't make sense," Hal argued. He'd never heard of a reporter doing a school happiness report. "Why'd he pull you in the office? He thinks you'd cause trouble?" Hal couldn't picture that at all, Caleb barely said a word in class.

Caleb took a bite of his sandwich and shook his head. "No, the reporter's doing a story on desegregation."

Hal frowned as he contemplated the apple in his hand. He'd heard that word before, during one of Dad's dinnertime tirades. It didn't apply to his school back home, so he hadn't paid much attention. Charleston was very strange with different rules and people. "Desegregation… that's black kids coming to white-kid schools, right?" Hal didn't see any problem, though he remembered Dad did. "Dad says something like…." He screwed up his face, trying to recall his words. "It should be separate but equal."

"But it's not, equal I mean," Caleb said. "The school I was going to wasn't as good as this one. We had to share books in class 'cause there wasn't enough to go around."

"That's not fair." Hal frowned. "I'm glad you're here." He never would've had a chance to meet Caleb otherwise, and he liked Caleb.

"Yeah...." Caleb looked away, lost in thought. "Hey, thanks for talking Mr. Gibbons into letting you sit by me."

"I wanted to." Hal shrugged. "You're the nicest kid in this whole school." That statement only reinforced how different it was here from home. There he never had to worry about being ambushed as he came to class. He had plenty of people to play with during lunch, and when Dad got into one of his moods, he had lots of places where he could go until it all blew over.

"Hey, what's wrong?" Caleb asked in a low voice, dropping his head close to Hal's. "You look upset. Nobody else bothered you, did they?"

"Nothing," Hal muttered, shoving his half-eaten apple back into his bag. He missed New York so much it was like an invisible gnome sitting heavy on his chest. He didn't want to drag down Caleb's day by telling him that he wished he were somewhere else.

Caleb remained quiet, and then he put his lunch aside too. "Hey, we're friends right? For-real friends, not just pretend."

"Yeah, I wouldn't lie about something like that." Hal lifted his head to look at Caleb. He didn't want Caleb to think he was messing with him. He was Caleb's friend.

"Don't friends tell each other what's bothering them?" Caleb asked.

Hal nodded and looked down at his hands as his eyes stung. Talking about it, admitting it, would make it real. They were never going to return home. Not ever. Hal's lower lip trembled. "I miss New York. I want to go back, but Dad says no way and stop whining."

Caleb slipped his arm around Hal's shoulder. "I miss my home too. During the week I stay with my uncle. Sometimes, I miss it so much it makes my stomach hurt."

That admission and Caleb's arm around him made Hal feel so much better. Somebody understood him and didn't think he was a sissy. He leaned into Caleb, taking the comfort given so freely. "You'd like Dobbs Ferry. There's a river to play by," Hal said.

"Not saying Charleston's better, but we have two rivers, and the Atlantic. Maybe some time I can show you them," Caleb offered.

That caught Hal's interest, but before he could say anything Caleb stiffened. He looked up in confusion, expecting to see James and his friends coming in their direction, but instead a man stood before them, lowering a camera. Caleb dropped his arm, and Hal scowled at the intruder. Having a reporter follow them around didn't sound like any fun at all. He could take his pictures during class. He inched closer to Caleb and whispered in his ear. "Want to go hide out in the pipes for the rest of lunch?"

"Yeah." Caleb grinned at him and grabbed his lunch. They bolted for the pipes, going the long way around the slides and by the time they got there, they were breathless and laughing.

"Did you see his face when we ran?" Hal giggled, the misery he had felt earlier all but gone.

"He was so surprised." Caleb peeked out of the tunnel and then hunkered back next to Hal. "He's taking pictures of the school now."

Hal took out his lunch, feeling hungrier after that run. "The principal should've called Foghorn Leghorn into the office instead. He's going to be mighty cranky having some guy take pictures and poke his nose into everything."

Caleb's eyes widened until they were huge with disbelief. "Did you just call Mr. Gibbons Foghorn Leghorn?" He asked in an awed voice.

Hal shrugged as he unwrapped his sandwich. "That's what he sounds like."

Caleb closed his eyes and shook his head, laughing softly. "Picturing him as a rooster might make class funner."

Hal started to eat his lunch, comfortable with the silence that fell between them. He liked having Caleb near.

Caleb stirred his finger in the dirt and dust that had drifted down the pipe. "Can you keep a secret?"

Hal stole a glance at him and saw the seriousness in Caleb's expression. This didn't sound like a little secret. This sounded like a big SECRET, and Hal was immediately interested. He raised his hand and crossed his heart. "I can keep secrets real good. I have lots of them." So did his sister, but Hal figured even saying that would be a giveaway and maybe make Caleb think he couldn't be trusted. So he kept quiet.

"You swear?" Caleb insisted. "It's important."

"I swear." Hal searched for something he could swear on that would let Caleb know he was trustworthy. "I swear on the chance of ever going back to New York." That was big time. If he broke his word, he'd never see Dobbs Ferry again.

"That works." Caleb dug a couple folded pieces of paper out of his pocket. Curious, Hal looked over his shoulder. They were pamphlets of some kind, both with The Charleston Movement blocked out across the top. One of them was a call to action, and as Hal read through it, he felt a calling stir in his chest.

Hal pointed to the other poster. "What's a black list?"

"It's like a boycott, a promise to not go to these stores because they still segregate. Some people I know, they're putting the posters up around town to try to get people to stop buying at these stores until they start treating everyone equal."

Hal searched Caleb's expression. He got the feeling that Caleb didn't just know those people; they were close to him. This was a serious secret. Hal had heard things on the news when Dad watched. People were getting hurt, like bad hurt. People like Caleb.

"Caleb, I triply swear, on my soul, I won't say a word, not even to Lily." Usually, Lily was his secret holder and he was hers.

Caleb grinned and stuffed the papers back in his pocket. "Thank you, 'cause they'd whup me good if they found out I had them." Hal grimaced in sympathy. He knew all about whuppings.

"Do you help hang up these posters?" Hal asked. "Could I do it too?"

Caleb looked at him in surprise and then shook his head with regret. "I'm not allowed. They say I'm doing my part by going to school. But soon I'll be old enough to help."

Hal heard that all the time… when you get older… enjoy being a kid. You couldn't do anything important as a kid. "Well, if I'm still here when we get old enough, I want to help too."

CHARLESTON, SC—
NOVEMBER 22, 1963

HAL TAPPED his pencil against his history book as he crammed for his
Civil War quiz. He was determined to ace it this time. No matter how
hard he'd studied, he hadn't managed to get anything better than a C,
and he dreaded bringing home his quarterly report if it didn't improve.
Granted, Dad had been in a much better mood since he'd gotten that
promotion and they'd moved to Charleston, but Hal didn't think that
would last if he didn't raise his grade up to his usual standard.

He glanced over at Caleb who studied as well, his head propped
up on his hand. These last two weeks would've been utterly miserable
without him. James had tried several times to find one of them alone,
but since they'd taken to going everywhere together, he'd finally given
up in disgust. Hal was sure it was a ploy. James was just waiting for
them to let their guard down, and Hal was not about to let that happen.
No siree.

Caleb caught his gaze and grinned. Hal liked it when he smiled,
that flash of white teeth next to his dark skin. Caleb didn't look like
anyone in his town back home, but Hal realized that the two of them
weren't all that different. They liked school, well the learning part at
least, and talking about books they'd read. They liked being outdoors
and exploring. Caleb had showed him all around Charleston after school.
Maybe moving here didn't mean his life was going to be total misery.

Hal had spent so many hours playing near the Hudson River,
searching for Captain Kidd's hideaway. Those were his favorite memories
of his home. When Mr. Gibbons had called out Caleb Hudson's name that
first day, he had taken it as a good omen. Getting to know him had been
difficult at first. Caleb was always the first one out the door when the bell
rang in the afternoon and the last one in his seat in the morning. But at
least one good thing had come out of his confrontation with James—it had
given him the chance finally to talk to Caleb.

A commotion in the hallway caught his attention, the noise of running feet and a woman sobbing in the distance. Mr. Gibbons made a displeased sound, and Hal concentrated on his book before the teacher noticed his attention had wandered. The noise outside increased as Mr. Gibbons made his way to the classroom door leaning on his cane. The door popped open before he reached it, and their vice principal, Mr. Evans, peered in.

Something was wrong. Hal had gotten to be pretty good at judging the mood of a room, and right now, the nape of his neck prickled. Mr. Evans was pale, and Hal could clearly hear crying in the hallway. It sounded like more than one person. Kids were filing by, quieter than normal, their faces pale too. Hal turned to Caleb and found him staring at the door with an expression of profound unease.

"What is the meaning of this?" Mr. Gibbons demanded in a tone Hal had become all too familiar with. He didn't think Mr. Evans stood a chance, vice principal or not. Gibbons had a voice and manner that could wither a person where they stood.

"Everyone, I need your attention, please," Mr. Evans said. Hal shut his book and edged his chair closer to Caleb as much to reassure his friend as himself. The sense of wrongness grew stronger. Mr. Gibbons must've felt it too because he didn't argue. "President Kennedy has been shot in Dallas."

The silence deepened as a profound shock settled over Hal. He couldn't fathom anybody daring to shoot a president. He glanced at Caleb again, saw the same shock in his dark brown eyes. Hal moved his chair even closer to him.

"We're dismissing school," Mr. Evans continued in the same low, intense voice. "Please go home in an orderly fashion and pray with your families that the president pulls through."

Between the bewildered thoughts stumbling through his brain and the fear that gripped his heart, Hal couldn't break out of his daze. He knew people died and that there was a war going on in a faraway country. He also remembered the fallout shelter Dad had built for them in New York. He wished he were there right now where he had a safe place to retreat to. He didn't understand why people had to hurt each other. Hal struggled with guilt over hitting James even if he'd only been defending his friend.

Caleb patted his hand, and Hal looked over at his anxious face. "Come on. We should get home fast."

Hal shoved his books into his rucksack, not taking his usual care. Even James and his gang were subdued. There would be no threat of retaliation today. "I've got to get Lily," Hal said, shouldering his rucksack. "She'll be scared."

"We can wait for her," Caleb assured him. "I betcha they're letting the oldest grades out first and making sure the little ones have someone at home before they release them."

That made sense to Hal, and they went to the first graders' classrooms. The sound of crying intensified as more students joined in. Hal shifted uneasily from foot to foot. Mr. Evans hadn't said the president died, but the sound of those wails indicated its seriousness. He wondered if the police had nabbed the shooter or if he had run away. Hal shivered. He didn't know how far away Dallas was, but he had the feeling that it was closer than he wanted it to be.

When Lily came out of her classroom and saw him, tears began to roll down her ashen cheeks. Hal caught her hand, and she clung to him, whispering, "Hal, I'm scared." She'd be mad over that admission later, and seeing his little sister so upset spurred him out of his own shock.

"It'll be okay. Come on, Mom will be waiting for us." Hal glanced at Caleb. "We can walk you home first." Caleb's uncle lived in the opposite direction of their house, but Hal didn't think it would delay them enough for Mom to worry. "Is that okay?" he asked Lily and she nodded.

"You don't have to," Caleb said, though his anxious expression had not eased one bit. He kept hunching his shoulders like he did when he wished to be smaller and invisible. Hal noticed him doing that in class when the mood had turned tense because James whispered mean things or Mr. Gibbons got worked up over current events. He had a much greater understanding of what got people so worked up, thanks to his many conversations with Caleb.

"We want to, don't we, Lily?"

Lily's tears had ceased though she continued to cling to Hal's hand like she was afraid he'd let her go. "Uh-huh." Lily's curls bobbed as she nodded again. "I don't want to go home. Not if Dad's mad."

Hal hadn't thought of that, and a lump of ice dropped in his stomach as they made their way outside. Maybe Dad was stuck at work and hadn't heard the news. The chaos in the schoolyard belied that wish. Parents were converging on the building, some looking so upset that Lily began to cry again.

As they reached the curb, a light blue Studebaker pulled up alongside them. "Caleb! Come on, get in. We'll go pick up your mom, and I'll take you both home."

Caleb's face lit up with relief at the sight of the thin black man leaning over to open the passenger-side door. He dropped his books down on the seat and looked at Lily and Hal with a frown. "Can we take my friends home first, Uncle Vern?" he asked.

Caleb's uncle hesitated, and Hal offered him a tentative smile. Uncle Vern's gaze slid from Hal's hopeful expression to Lily's sniffles, and he sighed. "Come on the lot of you, get in."

"Thank you, Mr....." Hal trailed off because he didn't know the man's last name, but good manners compelled him to say something. "Mr. Uncle Vern."

"You're welcome, and it's Mr. Warner. Now be careful getting in. It's a madhouse out here." He had a rich voice that emphasized the slower rhythm of the south that reassured Hal.

They scrambled into the backseat with Lily on one side of him and Caleb the other. He rattled off their new address that he had finally memorized. Then the shock of the day's events hit him again. His world had gone topsy-turvy, and his stomach twisted unpleasantly in response. He found himself leaning against Caleb for comfort as Lily pressed against his other side. Caleb must've needed reassurance too because he slid his arm around Hal's shoulders.

Caleb's uncle had the radio on, and Hal listened with growing unease as grave voices interrupted to say there was no new news from the hospital about the president's and governor's condition. "He won't die, will he?" Lily whispered.

Hal wanted to reassure her, but he didn't know. From the sound of the voices on the radio, it sounded like he'd been hurt pretty bad. Hal hugged her close, at a loss for anything to say. If he felt unsafe, she had to as well.

The car pulled over to the curb, and Mr. Warner glanced back at them. "Is this it?"

"Yes, sir," Hal said and reached for his and Lily's packs. "Thank you."

Lily bolted out of the car and ran into the house, banging the screen door behind her. Hal glanced at Caleb whose eyes were wide with an apprehension that made Hal's heart pang in response. He reached back and squeezed Caleb's hand. "You're my best friend."

Caleb's expression brightened, and despite the scariness of the day, Hal smiled. Then his mom called his name from the porch. "I'm coming," Hal yelled and shifted Lily's and his rucksacks onto his shoulder. He waved to the car as it pulled off while his mom watched him with red-rimmed eyes.

"Hal, is that your new friend's dad?" She watched the car turn around the corner, her hands wringing the apron that hung around her waist. She caught his shoulder as he reached the porch and ushered him into the house. "That was kind of him."

"No. Caleb's uncle picked him up from school, and Caleb asked if he could drop us off first." Hal looked up at his mom. Lily had her blonde prettiness, but Stella Zimmer had none of Lily's fire.

"Is the president going to be okay?"

His mom patted her hair and glanced away, her eyes filling with tears. She never looked anything less than perfect, and Lily caused her no end of frustration with her knack of getting disheveled over the day. "I don't know, Hal, I'm sorry." She slipped an arm around his shoulder and hugged him to her side. "Now go on, get out of your school clothes. Your dad's coming home early."

A knot formed in Hal's stomach. "Dad's going to be upset isn't he?"

"You let me worry about that." Mom gave him a gentle push in the direction of his bedroom. As Hal started to leave, he heard the sound of a car coming into the driveway. He slowed, trying to get a glimpse of his dad's expression as he got out. Darren Zimmer was a tall, lean man with a stern jaw and a hard mouth. People said Hal favored him, but he didn't see it much. He liked to think he was more like his mom.

Dad's eyebrows were drawn tight in anger, and his motions were quick and jerky as he grabbed his briefcase from the car. He was angry an awful lot, and Hal couldn't understand why. After all, Lily and him were pretty good kids, at least they tried to be, and their Mom spent her life soothing him. She caught him lingering in the hallway and cast a quick glance outside before shooing him on. "Keep Lily out of trouble for a while. Will you do that for me?"

"Yes, Mom."

She flashed a harried smile before Hal scurried down the hallway, his heart beating faster. When Dad was in a mood it was like a dark aura settled over the entire house. Sometimes Mom or Lily could cajole him into better spirits, but Hal remembered all too well how Dad had erupted when Hal tried to hug him once, thinking it would be a comfort: Boys weren't supposed to hug each other.

That was only one of Dad's edicts, and it made about as much sense as most of them. Personally Hal thought that rule was especially silly. Maybe if Dad hugged more he wouldn't be so mad all the time. He'd been mighty upset when that picture of him and Caleb had hit the newspaper. Hal had argued that Caleb's arm around him hadn't counted because hugging involved two arms, not one, but Dad hadn't been convinced. Hal thought it was girls who had cooties, apparently Dad thought the opposite.

If hugging was so bad, then Caleb wouldn't do it. Hal had only known his friend for a couple weeks, but he'd witnessed enough to realize that Caleb tried his best to do the right thing, even when the right thing brought him personal discomfort. He never complained either. It made Hal want to try harder and tough out his own problems.

"Those goddamned communists have gone too far, Stella." Hal started at the sound of Dad's voice roaring from the living room. He hadn't been this angry in a long time, not since before the move when Hal had accidentally left his golf clubs outside. "There's going to be nuclear war, just you see. We can't let them get away with shooting a United States president, even if he was a godforsaken papist."

Hal hugged his arms around himself as his stomach jumped. He didn't want another war. They were already fighting in Vietnam. The images Dad painted of nuclear winter had given him more than one nightmare. A soft knock interrupted his thoughts, and before he could offer an invite, Lily slipped into his room. "Hal, I'm really scared."

Hal wanted to admit that he was too, but Lily looked like she was struggling not to cry, and this was a rare state for his sister. Normally Hal was the first to cry, much to Dad's disgust. "Want to help me put together my giant United States puzzle?" There were so many little pieces that it would take them a couple hours, even with both of them working on it, and distracting Lily would keep his own fears in the background.

Lily's face cleared, and her eyes widened with delight. Hal rarely shared his precious puzzles. "Can I? I promise I won't lose any pieces this time."

Hal nodded and dragged the box out from under his bed. He could hear Dad rumbling, but the words were muted, and Hal was grateful that he didn't understand. The world outside his room was crazy and dangerous. If he couldn't find a place outside the city to build a new secret fort like he had back home, then he would make his room their haven.

CALEB WATCHED Hal's house until they turned the corner, and then he climbed into the front seat next to his uncle. He already missed Hal's comforting presence and didn't want to be by himself in the backseat. He stared out the window and recalled the picture of Kennedy in his uncle's office. He'd thought it was weird that Uncle Vern would have a white guy's picture hung, even if he was the president, and he'd asked him about it. Uncle Vern had explained to him that President Kennedy was trying to help push civil rights forward. Maybe it was going slow, but it was more than any other president had done in a long time. Now he might be dying.

Sometimes Caleb would go into his office and look at the picture or Reverend King's and tell himself that one day he'd meet them. Now Kennedy had been shot, and Caleb felt numb, inside and out, as his vice principal's words kept echoing through his head.

"So that was your new friend?" Uncle Vern said, breaking into his thoughts.

"Yeah." Caleb glanced at his uncle, anxious to see what he thought of Hal. Though Uncle Vern never said anything, Caleb suspected he didn't trust white people too much. His uncle had white friends who occasionally visited, though it was rare, and he acted different around them, more reserved.

Uncle Vern smiled faintly, and one of Caleb's anxieties unraveled. "He seems real polite. If you want to have him over after school to do homework or listen to music, just ask ahead of time. I don't mind."

"Thank you." Caleb's heart swelled, and it eased the ache. There was nobody else like his uncle, and when he grew up, he wanted to be just like him. Caleb could talk to him about anything, and his uncle would give him a straight answer. "Uncle Vern, if President Kennedy dies, what's that mean for us?"

Uncle Vern took his eyes off the road long enough to shoot him a glance. "Well, it means we lose an ally, but it doesn't mean we lose hope. It doesn't mean we stop taking a stand, and it doesn't mean we quiet our voices."

Caleb tried to take courage from his uncle's conviction, but it was hard with the radio playing subdued music as they waited for more information. He tried to picture what had happened in Dallas and found that he couldn't.

He stared out of the window as the elegant homes transitioned to the historic buildings and warehouses of the oldest part of town. He touched the posters in his pocket and wondered what would happen to the Charleston Movement now and if he and Hal would ever get a chance to help. They'd pulled out the posters so many times to look at them that the fold creases were wearing thin. He'd have to see if he could get more copies so Hal would have his own.

It made him think of the meetings his uncle had and the conversations Caleb listened in on. Over the last two weeks, he'd shared those discussions with Hal and found him to be a good listener. It was one thing to talk these things over with his uncle, but Caleb found he liked sharing them with a friend his age even more. Somebody with a whole different outlook on all the changes that were happening. Sometimes it seemed like change came so slow, and other times, it seemed to spread like a lightning fire.

"Uncle Vern, does this mean Mr. Smith can stop the bill now?" Uncle Vern and his friends had been discussing the debate over Kennedy's Civil Rights bill the last couple of days. Smith's name had come up again and again.

"I hope not, Caleb." His uncle tried to keep the concern out of his voice, but Caleb knew him well enough to recognize it anyway.

A news alert came on the radio, and Uncle Vern turned up the sound as Caleb's stomach rolled with fresh anxiety. The president had to be okay; he just had to.

"This just in, a bulletin from Dallas, Texas. President Kennedy has died," a solemn voice announced.

Caleb's throat and eyes prickled as the announcer repeated the news. He looked at his uncle, saw his hands tighten on the wheel and his lips press together. Shock and grief spun Caleb's thoughts into a confusing whirl. It had to be a mistake.

He pulled his legs up onto the seat and wrapped his arms around his knees. Traffic slowed as cars stopped at signs and people spoke to each other through lowered windows. He watched a flag being lowered to half-mast, trying to make sense of it, and his thoughts only latched onto one fact, that nothing made sense anymore.

Normally when he was upset, his uncle would try to talk to him, but today he remained quiet. Maybe he was as confused and upset as Caleb.

"Uncle Vern? What's gonna happen now?" Caleb asked just to hear his voice.

"They'll swear in Johnson. He'll be the president now." The car slowed down again as they pulled up in front of the market.

"Why'd they shoot him?" Caleb struggled to understand how a person could do that. How you could be riding in a car one moment and then dying the next because someone had picked up a gun and decided they wanted you dead.

"I don't know, Caleb," Uncle Vern admitted. "I just don't know."

Caleb stared at his uncle with a frown. Uncle Vern always had an answer. Until now. It made his world less certain than it had been this morning. He wondered if Hal felt the same.

Uncle Vern squeezed his shoulder. "We can't control what's going to happen, but we can control how we react. There are going to be many upset people. Now is the time for extra patience and understanding. I may not be able to give you the answers you want and I'm sorry. What I can do is help your mom pack. I can take you home where we will be together as a family, helping each other out in times like these—that we can control. Do you understand?"

Caleb nodded as he pondered that. Uncle Vern was like Dad. His words often meant more than they seemed. He'd think it over and talk with Hal. For right now he'd take them to mean that helping out each other was a nice thing to do, and it made a person feel good when they did it. So it would make sense that when things were bad, being there for each other made everyone feel better even when they couldn't do anything to fix the situation.

"Okay, then, you go and tell your mom we're here to get her. I'll find a place to park, then come and help."

"Okay." Caleb jumped out of the car and dove into the crowd. The market buzzed with activity and low, distressed conversations. Many vendors were already gone, the rest were packing up. It was strange to see the large, open-aired pavilions half-closed at midday. Caleb darted through the crowd, without his usual greetings to those he knew, and headed straight toward Mom's spot.

"Caleb!"

His heart lightened at the sound of his older brother's voice. Caleb spied Rodney and put on a burst of speed. Today, more than ever, he'd wished Rodney had been at his school to wait outside his class the way Hal had waited for Lily. Though, even if Rodney had chosen to desegregate, he would've been in a different school anyway. He was a big guy now, in middle school, and he didn't let Caleb forget it.

Rodney caught him in a fierce hug. He'd gotten so tall over the last several months that Caleb thought he'd never catch up. "I was just about to go look for you."

Rodney must've run all the way from his own school on the outskirts of town to come check on them. "Uncle Vern picked me up," Caleb replied. "He's taking us home."

"Nobody gave you a hard time at that school, did they?" Rodney asked, checking him over with a frown. His face was thinner than Caleb's, his chin narrowing to a point, and a guarded wariness in his eyes that had been growing over the last couple of years. He looked extra on edge today.

"No, I think everybody was too scared and upset to start anything." Though Caleb wasn't sure what Monday would be like once people got over the shock. "Besides, Hal and I stuck by each other. They mostly leave us alone now."

Rodney shook his head with an expression of incredulity. He'd thought Hal was an imaginary friend Caleb made up, until he saw the picture of them in the newspaper. Rodney didn't believe Hal had punched James for him no matter how many times Caleb told him the story.

"Come on. Mom will be happy to see you."

Rodney led the way to her corner, and Effie Hudson greeted them with a relieved smile. She was often anxious about him living away from home during the week, and he suspected that if he wasn't staying with her brother, she might not have let him go. She hugged Caleb and smoothed his hair, though she didn't express her worry any other way. Her hands were rough from weaving the baskets, and Caleb had always found her touch to be soothing.

"Uncle Vern will be here in a minute," Rodney said.

"Well, then, we'd best be ready to go," Mom replied in calm, quiet voice. "We can have this packed up in no time." They went to work with the ease of long practice, nestling the baskets within each other as Mom gathered the tools of her trade.

"Mom, will Dad be home when we get there?" Caleb asked. All his emotions were roiling inside him in a tight whirl of confusion, worry and a terrible sadness. He wanted to be safe in his home with his family around him before he tried to make sense of it all, and every time he heard somebody crying, his chest tightened in empathy.

"I doubt he's heard the news out on the boat. I think we can expect him at dinner, same time as always," Mom replied.

Caleb envied his dad's ignorance. He'd rather be right there with him, working hard and oblivious to the chaos happening right now. A man had killed the president, right out in public in the middle of the day. Probably because they didn't like what he was doing. He couldn't see any other reason to take an insane action like that. If that could happen to Kennedy, what did that mean for Caleb and his whole family?

CHARLESTON, SC— DOG DAYS OF AUGUST, 1965

OTHER THAN the heat that smothered a body like a wet woolen blanket, what Hal hated the most about summers was that he only got to see Caleb once a week, twice if he was lucky. And on those rare days, he had to wait until Caleb finished all the errands his mom needed before she released Caleb to play. At this rate, by the time they finished putting the final touches on their fort, it would be fall, and they'd have to head back to school.

Middle school had to be better than the last two years. Caleb looked forward to the chance there might be more kids like him, and Hal hoped it didn't mean any changes for their friendship. It had taken him a while to figure out all the unwritten lines, where they could go together and where they couldn't without being harassed. That's why the fort was so important. It was all theirs, and nobody could tell them what to do there.

Too bad he couldn't come up with a reason his parents would accept that would allow him to hang out there in the evenings. Dad obsessed over the nightly news, complaining about the hippies and antiwar rallies in New York and Berkley. As an ex-naval officer during World War II, the protestors made him crazy. However, all the news of the war disturbed Hal. The image of Marines burning down Vietnamese huts with lighters was seared into his head. He didn't dare tell Dad that he wished the war would end. It would only lead to a lecture about the evils of communism that had ceased to make any impact on him.

He grabbed his lunch and canteen of water and juggled them with the big throw pillows he'd stitched together from Mom's scrap bag. They would give them something to lounge on and add color. Just because it was a fort didn't mean it couldn't have pretty little pieces. Maybe later in the week he could pot up some of the plants in Mom's garden too.

"Going to play," he shouted from the front door, knowing that Mom was busy folding laundry as she watched her morning shows. He didn't wait for a reply and instead ducked out onto the porch before she saw the pillows.

"I want to come," Lily cried scrambling after him, and Hal stopped with a groan.

"You can't. I'm going to the fort. It's outsiders only." Hal felt a little bad, because he could hear the desperation in her voice. He refused to look at her. He was a born sucker when Lily laid the big blue eyes on him. She knew it too and wielded it with a ruthless will. Besides, he had spent the last two days playing games with her when they'd been stuck inside because of all the rain and flooding. She had other friends she could play with. Now that he was twelve, sometimes the last thing he wanted was his baby sister following him around.

"Please, I'll help you carry your stuff. I have a lunch packed too." She sounded so hopeful that Hal squirmed as he steeled himself against her pleas. This was his time with Caleb, and he guarded those quiet afternoons where he could totally be himself with a jealous zeal.

"You'll ruin your dress, and Mom will be mad," Hal blurted out, desperate to find a reason to keep her behind. Immediately he knew he'd made a critical tactical error. Lily hated the pretty, frilly dresses she was forced to wear for her morning classes in deportment and etiquette. So far she'd behaved and saved her outbursts for him alone, but it was only a matter of time before Lily rebelled.

Lily's chin firmed, and her eyes flashed even brighter in anger. "Give me one minute."

Hal groaned again as she disappeared into the house, struck with a moral dilemma. Even if she could get ready in a minute, she didn't have any play clothes that would stand up to the work they'd planned for the day. When she came home a mess, there would be an argument for sure. He edged down the porch steps and took off as fast as he could while carrying everything. Oh boy, Lily was going to get him good for deserting her like this.

Several blocks away, Hal stopped to set his belongings down so he could take a drink of water and catch his breath. Lily would never find him now.

"Traitor!"

Hal choked, water spraying everywhere as he stared in disbelief at his sister. Lily ran down the road toward him, her face flushed, one hand holding up the waist of an old pair of Hal's jeans. She'd stuffed her hair under one of his ball caps, curls escaping in an unruly mess. She ran up to him and kicked him on the ankle. "You didn't wait, you big jerk."

Her appearance so astonished him that he couldn't be mad. She even had on a pair of his old sneakers. He was dying to know how she'd found him, but an even bigger question overrode that curiosity. "How the heck did you get past Mom like that?"

"I climbed out the window, but you're going to have to help me sneak in later." Lily jutted out her chin, daring him to deny her. Her audacity impressed Hal to the point that he couldn't offer an argument. There was no point in trying to send her back now, she'd just refuse, and taking her back would waste the rest of the morning.

"Fine, you can come with me," Hal said, and her expression brightened. "But you have to promise two things. One, you have to help out with the building and fixing, no whining. Two, you can't tell nobody about the fort or where it is."

Lily crossed her fingers over her heart before lifting her hand up. "I swear, I won't tell nobody. I can keep a secret. I didn't even tell you I already knew where it was."

"Okay." Hal had to be satisfied with that, and he hoped Caleb would be too. He doubted Lily would be able to sneak away most of the time, so it wouldn't hurt to let her come occasionally. He slipped off his belt and offered it to her. "You should've stolen a belt too. You're going to lose your pants."

"I couldn't find one." Lily slid it onto her skinny hips and then took Hal's lunch and one of the pillows. "I can help, see?"

They made their way out of town to a thicket of trees along the river. The ground was squishy from the flood, and by the time they got to the grove, Lily and Hal were spattered with mud and covered in sweat. The sound of voices and the banging of hammers on wood drifted toward them. At least he wasn't the only one who brought someone else to their fort.

As the trees thinned Hal saw Caleb and Rodney scrambling around on the roof. Caleb caught sight of them and grinned. "Look at what Rodney brought," he shouted to them waving a shingle in the air. "No more tarp. I think we can get a roof down that won't leak."

"Outta sight, thanks," Hal said to Rodney as they got closer. He was never sure what to think of Caleb's brother. Sometimes he was nice and helpful, other times he was aloof and rude. Hal didn't know if Rodney liked him or tolerated him for Caleb's sake.

Rodney glanced over and rolled his eyes. "Great, now there's two of them," he said loud enough for Hal to hear.

"Don't be a spaz," Caleb retorted. "Uncle Vern's got white friends, why can't I?"

"Uncle Vern's a lawyer. He has to have white friends," Rodney said. Despite his words he offered them both a smile. "Hey, Hal, who's the chick?"

"I'm Lily, and I'm not a chick, I'm me." Lily set their lunches down on a stump. "What're we doing first?"

"Well, the storm blew a mess inside, and we have to rig a better door," Caleb said as he slithered off the roof. "We were able to scrounge a piece of wood for the door. Did you find hinges?"

"Yep." Hal patted his pocket.

"Nice pillows," Caleb said to Lily, examining the one she'd carried. "Did you make them?"

"No, but I can make you curtains if you want," Lily offered, giving Caleb an adoring glance. She was so hung up on him, and seeing her look at his friend like that made Hal want to hide him away. He did not want to be competing with Lily for Caleb's attention in a few years. She had to be crushing hard to offer to sew. Lily hated that chore more than anything else.

"Why don't you make a screen instead," Hal cut in. "There's a frame in the fort and a scrap of screen big enough. Just nail it down tight." He was reluctant to admit he'd made the pillows himself with Rodney there. He knew his dad's firm opinions on women's work and men's work. It seemed silly to him and Lily, though Lily at least had the sense not to argue.

"Okay." Lily scampered inside the fort to get the materials. Hal figured if all four of them worked hard today, they just might finish it and have a few weeks to play before school started.

"You didn't rip these off from your mom did you?" Caleb asked, indicating the pillows. "I don't want you to get in trouble."

"No, actually, I made them," Hal admitted and glanced sideways at Caleb to see his reaction. "I've had lots of practice. Sometimes I do Lily's sewing projects for her."

"Far out." Caleb picked one up with a happy smile. "I bet you can make all kinds of cool stuff for the fort. Do you know how to do rag rugs?"

"I could try." He'd get Lily to ask Mom about the technique. "You don't think it's girlie that I made them?"

Caleb shook his head and set the pillow down on a dried off tarp. "I sometimes help Mom with her basket weaving. Maybe girls are normally the ones who do it, but you see some guys too. I don't have any sisters for Mom to teach, so why not me and Rodney?"

And that was why Hal loved Caleb. He wished they were brothers for real. He never felt defensive with him or like he had to explain himself. Caleb accepted him just the way he was. Well, so did Lily, but it was different with Caleb, Hal couldn't explain why.

Hal threw his arms around Caleb, giving him a hug, and to his secret delight, Caleb hugged him back. "Will you two cut it out?" Rodney called down with exasperation. "This roof isn't going to fix itself. I promised to help, not do it all myself."

IT PROBABLY wasn't the most weatherproof fort in the state, but by the time Caleb and Rodney finished fixing the roof, he was proud of their effort. He'd paid close attention when he helped Dad build their shed, and that had come in handy today. Even if it didn't last, the fun was in the building, and they could always put up a new, better one if they needed to.

Hal had tried to help and had proven he was clumsy when it came to using tools. Caleb had to give it to him, though, every time they'd come out here, he'd at least tried. Today after a couple of banged thumbs he'd given up nailing the hinges on the door and disappeared inside to clean out the mess of soggy leaves and debris blown in from the storm.

"Thanks, Rodney," Caleb said as his older brother stepped away from the door. It swung easily. Now all they needed was a latch hook and eye for each side. Or maybe find another method for keeping it shut. He'd have to ponder the problem. "We never would've finished it in time without your help."

"Hey, it was a chance to see you. No big deal." That was about as close as Rodney got to saying he missed Caleb during the school year, and he hated that it was coming up fast. He was so moody lately. Caleb didn't get what was going on with him. "You want to go to the beach with me, see if there are any girls there?"

"You know there's going to be girls." That was another thing, Rodney was girl crazy, and nothing sounded more boring than girl watching with his brother. Caleb shook his head and moved out of the way as Hal emerged with an armful of sticks and leaves. "No, Hal and I need to plan what we're going to do next. You can stay if you want."

Rodney's expression darkened. He glanced at Hal as he passed out of earshot and lowered his voice. "You always want to be with him instead, and he's always hugging you. Don't you think that's strange?"

"So?" Caleb stiffened, immediately on the defensive, though he couldn't say why. Caleb liked it when Hal hugged him. It felt nice. And Hal liked it when Caleb put his arm around him. It caused more comments lately, and Caleb was beginning to think they should be more discreet. It made him feel funny, like he was hiding what came natural to him, but he had to field enough questions about who he chose as his friends already. Sometimes it seemed like everyone was watching the two of them like they had nothing better to do.

"I'm just saying, it's weird that's all." Rodney shrugged and wouldn't quite meet Caleb's eye. "I guess I'm tired of hearing about how great he is. I mean he's okay; I'm not ragging on him or nothing. You two are just different around each other."

"Uncle Vern has a lot of guy friends." And to Caleb they'd always been affectionate with each other.

"Uncle Vern can't be the standard for everything you do," Rodney said with a roll of his eyes. "Besides, people think Uncle Vern's weird too."

This time Caleb bristled. Sometimes Rodney could poke too much. Taking swipes at him and Hal was one thing, they had each other's backs, but taking a swipe at Uncle Vern was a whole other issue. One that Caleb would not tolerate. He glared at Rodney, trying to come up with an appropriate putdown, but as usual, when it came to a confrontation, his impotent tongue tied up.

"Take that back," Caleb said, wishing he had Hal or Lily's fire to reinforce the weak demand.

Rodney eyed him and then held up his hands. "Wait, I don't think he's weird. I'm repeating what others in the family say. I think he's great. Come on, why are we fighting?"

"You started it," Caleb muttered, trying to figure out the same thing. More and more he felt like the odd man out in his family. Having Rodney call him out on his differences made him uneasy. They'd been arguing more than normal given Rodney's uncertain temper and Caleb's defensiveness. He hated it.

"I'm out of here. If you want to stay, go right ahead." Rodney gathered his tools and shot Caleb a bemused glance. "Just watch out for the little blonde. She's got her eye on you. If you bring home a white girl, Mom and Dad are going to flip their lids."

Caleb wrinkled his nose as Rodney left. He had to be joking. Lily? She was okay for a girl, but she was still almost a baby. Besides, she wasn't nearly as interesting as Hal.

"I hug you too much?"

Caleb turned with an inward groan at the sound of Hal's plaintive voice. It figured he would've overheard. Hal stood by the trees, his freckled face stricken, his hands shoved into his pockets. "I can stop."

"Rodney's crazy. I don't see how a hug ever hurt anybody." Hal didn't look convinced, so to prove his point Caleb went to him and slid his arm around Hal's shoulders. Hal leaned his head against Caleb's with sigh, and it confirmed what Caleb had thought earlier. He liked holding Hal. He liked it very much.

"Dad thinks boys shouldn't hug," Hal said with a hard note in his voice. "He thinks lots of crazy things. That I should find other friends, and I shouldn't read as much, all for stupid reasons."

That sounded like the absolute opposite of Caleb's dad. He was delighted Caleb liked to read and that he was exposed to new ideas and new friends at the school in town. He'd never had a problem with showing affection either. However, he had to admit that Rodney was right. While his parents didn't mind him having white friends, he was sure it would take them a long while to adjust to him having a white girlfriend. Not that he had any plans at all like that.

"Well if it's wrong for you, then it's wrong for me too?" Caleb asked. "And since I don't plan on giving up on any of it, I guess maybe it's okay if we keep it to ourselves."

"Which part?" Hal asked with a mischievous smile. "The hugging, the friendship, or the reading?"

Well the friendship couldn't be hidden since they pretty much did everything they could together. Since Caleb lived outside of town and Hal wasn't comfortable at his own house, they tended to roam around Charleston. The thought of hugging Hal in private made him feel funny, so he focused on the last problem and the easiest to fix. "You know, why don't we hide our favorite books in the fort? Your dad won't know how much you're reading if they're here."

Hal eyed the structure, his expression dubious, and Caleb couldn't blame him. It wasn't a bad first effort, but he didn't know how long it would last. They'd have to wait for the next rainstorm to be sure the roof wouldn't leak. "I suppose we could put them in tins to keep them safe. I have a bunch I'm not using."

The thought that Hal would trust his precious books inside something Caleb built filled him with pride. "First, though, we have to get a latch on the door. We don't want any critters getting in and messing with our stuff. Maybe next summer, after I've had a little more practice, we can work on a tree house."

"I'm not sure how much help I'd be." Hal held up his abused thumb with its makeshift bandage torn from the ragged end of Lily's jeans.

"You were plenty of help," Caleb assured him with a grin. "Just not with a hammer. Hey, where's Lily?" He hadn't seen her since she'd gotten bored with the work.

"She wanted to explore," Hal said, making a vague gesture toward the trees around them. "She promised not to go far."

Caleb frowned as he listened for her. Lily wasn't one to be quiet, that was for sure, but the only sounds he heard were the whir of insects and the trill of birdsong. His uncle teased Caleb about worrying about everything, but he couldn't help himself. Lily was only nine. "I guess we should look for her."

Hal grimaced. "Yeah, I suppose, though we'd better not let her think we're checking up on her." He cast a glance at Caleb as they headed into the surrounding trees. "Do you like my sister?"

Caleb pulled a branch away that threatened to smack him and waited for Hal to pass by before releasing it. "She's all right for a girl. Not to be rude, but it's more fun when it's just us."

A look of relief crossed Hal's face. "That's what I think. I tried to stop her today, but she's sneakier than I thought. Maybe she can come once a week. That's fair right? She gets pretty bored at home."

"Sure. I guess that would—"

A girlish, piercing squeal cut through what Caleb was going to say. He traded glances with Hal, and they tore through the undergrowth, ripping aside tangling kudzu, trying to get to Lily. The trees opened up near one of the many creeks in the area, and they found Hal's sister by the water hopping up and down with another squeal.

"Lily! You okay?" Hal shouted as he put on a burst of speed.

Lily spun around, her expression bright with excitement. "Hal, look, look! It's a snapping turtle. See how big it is?" She turned and pointed into the murky water. Sure enough, right where the water deepened, the turtle poked his head out from under a half-submerged log with a flopping fish in its mouth. Lily squealed again and capered. Hal pulled her back before she could fall in the water as Caleb took a closer look at her. Mud caked her legs, and more splattered the rest of her, flecks drying on her face until she was as freckled as Hal. Her hair had fallen from the cap, and bits of dried leaves and twigs were caught in the curls.

"Girl, you're a mess," Caleb said with a shake of his head.

Lily beamed in delight. "I know! It's wonderful."

Hal groaned and took Lily's hand. "Come on, I need to sneak you back home and clean you up. We'd better not get caught, 'cause if I get sequestered I'll be mad."

Caleb's heart sank. They'd just finished their fort, and he'd been looking forward to a long afternoon together. Lily looked crestfallen too, biting her pouting lower lip. "Why don't we find a watering hole that doesn't have a critter in it?" he suggested. "You can clean up there and it's hot enough to dry off. Then you don't have to go so soon."

Hal looked Lily over and then back at Caleb with a torn expression. "Please," Caleb said and Hal grinned.

"I can't say no to two pairs of pleading eyes." Hal laughed and gestured toward the creek. "Okay, quest leader, find us water that doesn't have a giant snapping turtle or a gator, definitely not a gator." He shuddered.

"There aren't as many of them as you seem to think." Caleb turned to follow the winding of the creek with buoyed spirits. They still had time together before Hal had to go. "'Sides, this time of day, most of them are sunning, and you can see them if you look. Trust me."

"I do," Lily said skipping along beside him.

"Of course I trust you." Hal fell into step beside Caleb and flashed him a smile. "You've never led me wrong before."

CHARLESTON, SC— JUNE 18, 1967

HAL RAN through the long, waving grass by the river, the strands whipping his legs and hands. He didn't care that the hot sun stole the air out of his lungs before he had a chance to catch a proper breath. He didn't even worry about the possibility of gators. He just wanted to get away from Dad and his mean words. No matter what Hal did, he just couldn't make the man happy.

"I refuse to have a sissy boy. You'd better straighten out fast, or I'm going to toughen you up. You're fourteen, not four. If you don't start acting like a man, I'll start whupping you like you're a little boy again."

He was plenty tough. He endured the bullies at school all year long and didn't whine. Of course, during the school year, he had Caleb by his side. Now Caleb was home with his family working over the summer, and he hadn't been confident that he'd be able to get away much. Hal had been bored and lonely. So what if he'd helped Lily with her embroidery. She'd been happy. He'd been happy. Until Dad caught them. Hal knew he was in trouble the second Dad's face went red. So he ran with Dad's shouts chasing after him like a junkyard dog after an interloper.

Caleb was out here somewhere with Rodney. Hal had sought out Caleb's mom in the marketplace, and she'd directed him toward this marshy area along the river. Winded, Hal slowed to a walk and drew in deep, heaving breaths. The soft lapping of the water on the river, the song of the insects in the tall grass, and the distant sound of voices eased away the memory of Dad's words. He would never come looking for Hal here, so at least for now, he was safe.

He didn't understand why people couldn't leave things alone and accept others for themselves. Everybody kept commenting on his intelligence, but if he was so smart, then why didn't Dad want him?

Being smart was supposed to be good. Books didn't explain why people called him girlish or a sissy. He liked things other boys liked. Just because he enjoyed pretty things too didn't mean there was any harm in it. If he was so smart, then he should be able to figure out why others were straight-up stupid.

He wasn't alone. Caleb and Lily felt his frustrations in their own ways. Caleb because he was black and Lily because she was a girl. They all had times when they felt like they didn't belong. They dealt with it in different ways. Caleb tried to follow the rules and make himself an example. Lily had her heroines and went out and did what she wanted to do while somehow making Mom and Dad think it was their idea. Hal tried to make himself heard in every way he could, but it always seemed like his voice was mute.

He climbed up on a pile of deadfall to search for Caleb and scanned the people gathering the tall grass. He spied him downriver, working by himself as his brother Rodney harvested a spot a little farther away. Hal grinned and jumped down from the deadfall.

Ooohh, Caleb was going to be so surprised. They hadn't seen each other since the last day of school. It felt like Caleb was always working now. Maybe Hal could get a job with him. It would be better than being stuck at home or even worse, working with Dad.

First, Hal had to sneak up on him. With that thought in mind, he crouched lower in the grass and made his way toward Caleb. It was hotter down among the grass with no breeze to temper the sun. Hal was dying for a swim by the time he caught sight of Caleb through the long stems. His friend concentrated on his chore, squatting down to tug grass up by its roots.

"Psst, Caleb, boo."

Caleb rocked back on his heels, falling on his rear end, and Hal laughed. He straightened from his hiding spot and grinned at Caleb as he twisted around to stare at him in astonishment.

"Warn a guy before you jump out of the grass," Caleb complained. Though there was irritation in his voice, his warm brown eyes lit up with happiness. He gave Hal one of his quick, one-armed hugs that made him want to lean against him in the hope that Caleb would leave his arm there longer. Caleb was so handsome with his broad cheeks and full lips, and he'd started to get muscle on his arms and calves. Sometimes Hal's heart beat a little faster when Caleb hugged him.

"Sorry. I didn't mean to make you fall over, though the look on your face sure was funny." Hal watched Caleb go back to work, overcome with curiosity. "What'cha doing? Is this something to eat?" It didn't look like any kind of grain that Hal had ever seen, but he liked the sweet scent of the grass, maybe it was a southern herb.

"You ask the craziest questions." Caleb picked up a partially filled basket and moved to a different clump of grass. Hal didn't see what was different from one type to another. "This is what Mom uses to make her baskets. Well, one of the materials. We also need to collect bulrushes and pine needles, but we'll do that some other day."

Hal looked at the long grass and tried to picture how they turned into one of the beautiful baskets he'd seen Caleb's mom selling, and he couldn't do it. "How much more do you have to get? Can I help?"

They could even make a game of it, pretend they were out on the prairie collecting grass to start a fire, or maybe there was a sickness, this was the cure, and Caleb and him were the only healthy ones left. Though at fourteen, they were getting a little too old to think about pretend games. They didn't hold the same endless fascination as they had before, and that made Hal even more restless and unhappy.

"It's going to take a bit. I have to fill this up." Caleb set the basket down and shot Hal a curious glance. "What are you doing all the way out here anyway? I didn't expect to see you 'til fall with the way things were going. As soon as I get one chore done, Rodney gives me another."

"I ran away. Well, at least for today. You weren't as far away as I thought you would be. It didn't take me long to get here at all." Hal watched Caleb and then tried pulling up a clump on his own, but the stems broke off in his hand. Caleb patiently showed him the technique and which plants he was supposed to be looking for.

He worked in silence for a few minutes, letting the rhythm and concentration soothe him. He looked over to see Caleb watching him, his dark face solemn and his eyes knowing. "Your dad getting on you again?"

"Yeah." Hal's eyes stung. Caleb patted his back, and nothing else needed to be said. Caleb was lucky. He was always talking about his family and how he missed them when he was at his uncle's during the week. Hal wouldn't mind having an uncle who he could stay with five days out of seven. "Have you heard the new Van Morrison song?"

"I like that one," Caleb said with a grin. "Maybe we can go by the house later. Dad bought new records. You'll love them, James Brown, Marvin Gaye. I bet we can talk him into breaking them out later. We can be dancing fools."

"Far out." Hal deposited his handful of grass into the basket after Caleb nodded his approval. This wasn't so bad. There were worse chores, and he'd rather be outside working than stuck inside, unless of course he had a new book. "So what do you do after you get the sweetgrass? Are you going to help make some of the baskets?"

"Maybe, though Mom is teaching my cousin because she knows Rodney, and I don't really have any interest in doing it for a living. She wants to pass it down another generation."

"If she had a daughter like my sister she wouldn't have much luck there either." Hal thought of Lily's annoyance with anything that appeared to be women's work and Mom's stubborn attempts to teach her embroidery. He thought it was relaxing, at least when Dad wasn't around. "Sometimes I think Lily and I are changelings."

"Like the fairy children from under the hill that you told me about?" Caleb shook his head. "You find good stories. How come Lily doesn't get as much grief as you do?"

Hal sighed and crouched down next to a similar clump. "She's sneakier." And more daring. Hal was learning to be more like her, though he felt a guilt that she never echoed. Even when he was doing something he liked, in the background there was always the sure knowledge Dad would disapprove. Which meant there was something wrong with him.

"I'm sorry," Caleb said. He touched Hal's hand as a lump settled in his throat. "You're always welcome to come see me."

"I know." Hal tried to smile and failed. He didn't know what he'd do if he didn't have Caleb. Caleb was perfect in just about every way. That belief sometimes aggravated his friend, but compared to the other guys in Hal's life, Caleb was the only one he could count on. Without him, he'd probably run away for real, and that was a terrifying thought.

CALEB COULDN'T believe Hal stuck it out with him. Harvesting sweetgrass was hot, boring work and they were both hungry, dirty, and sweaty by the time Rodney said they had enough and were free to enjoy the rest of the day. Caleb grabbed them lunch from the house, and then he and Hal headed off toward the shore. He didn't get why Rodney liked to watch the girls swimming, and his brother didn't get Caleb's disinterest, so they didn't talk about it anymore. Maybe he'd check them out today and figure out what all the fuss was about.

Hal followed him, his freckled face red from the morning spent in the sun and his normally inquisitive tongue quiet. It wasn't like him to be so silent, and it made Caleb feel all the more protective of him because he recognized Hal was still upset. He couldn't imagine his dad talking to him the way Hal's dad did. It wasn't right. Yeah, Hal was a little different, and sometimes it stood out more than other people's differences, but he was considerate and sweet, and Caleb loved him the way he was.

"I'm glad you came to find me," Caleb said as he caught sight of the glint of water in the distance. "I didn't think I'd get to see you all summer. I tried leaving a message with your dad to come meet up with me. I didn't realize how much I'd be working this summer."

"Big jerk didn't give it to me. I had to do something. I would've gone crazy if I had to spend every day at home. Besides it's not that far to your house, not if I head straight for the bridge. I could come just about every day. If you have chores, I could help, and then we'd have time together afterward." Hal talked even faster than normal, a sign of his desperation, and the hope in his eyes was painful to see.

"We could meet at the market on the days I help Mom," Caleb offered. There was more to do in the city anyway. Old Mr. Gensler had an ice cream shop, and he always made the two of them feel welcome at his counter. They could catch a double show at the movies or maybe hitch a ride down to Folly Beach Pier to scope out the hippies and listen to live music.

They paused on top of a low hill and looked down at the Atlantic, the endless waves racing up to kiss the shore. The sight of it never failed to make Caleb smile. Today the sun dazzled the water, making it mirror bright. It was a weekday, so there weren't that many people out, and Caleb lost interest in the thought of spying on girls. He'd rather get in the water.

"Want to go swimming?" Caleb asked. As hungry as he was, he wanted to cool off more.

"Oh yeah," Hal replied, his eyes intent on the waves.

They shucked their shirts and left them with their shoes and lunch, then waded out into the cool water. For the first time since school let out, Caleb wasn't lonely. He missed his family during the school year, but since he returned home this summer he'd been left with the nagging feeling he didn't quite fit in anymore. He didn't know how to fix it, though he'd tried. With Hal he could relax and be himself without the unmerciful teasing from his brother.

Caleb watched Hal as he dove into the waves. They both were getting taller and leaner, as if their bodies had decided to hit a growth spurt at the same time. Hal's features were a little more delicate now that his face had lost its childhood roundness. Otherwise, he didn't see anything at all girl-like in the way he appeared. Maybe if Hal talked his dad into going fishing with him one time and the man saw Hal with a wiggling fat fish between his hands, muck on his clothes, with an expression of pride and glee on his face, he'd forget his idiotic thoughts.

Hal looked better than most girls did. Probably why his old man sweated it so much.

Watching Hal swim compelled Caleb into the water after him. The cool wet flowed over him, invigorating and exciting as he slipped up behind Hal. "This is for sneaking up on me earlier," Caleb said with a laugh and pulled Hal under the waves with him. Hal wiggled from his arms and turned on him as their heads broke through the surface. He grinned, gray-green eyes sparkling and all traces of unhappiness gone from his face. Caleb's heart skipped a beat.

"I'm gonna get you," Hal said and chased Caleb through the waves. They played in the water until hunger drove them back to the beach, and then sat in the sun to eat and drowse. Caleb hadn't been this happy and relaxed since school let out.

Hal picked up Caleb's hand and turned it over to trace his finger over his palm. Caleb's hand tingled, and he became abruptly aware of

Hal sitting next to him, half-naked. "How come you're dark on one side and pale on the other?"

Caleb shrugged, he'd never thought of that before. "Don't know. God made me that way I guess. Why do you get brown spots all over your nose?" The hours in the sun had darkened Hal's freckles and begot a whole host of new ones.

Hal rubbed his nose, his expression falling. "Dad says I sat under a cow too long."

"What do cows have to do with freckles?" Caleb asked in confusion.

Hal flushed with shame in his eyes. "You know, when the cow goes…. Dad sees me as being flecked with cow shit."

Caleb pressed his lips together in hot anger at Hal's humiliation. He struggled to find something to say so Hal would understand the problem was with his dad, not him. "I think your dad's one of those people that has nothing nice to say about anyone." Hal remained quiet, staring down at his toes, and Caleb missed his quick, bright chatter and endless questions.

A group of girls a little older than Caleb and Hal walked by with towels draped over their arms. The girls shot them curious glances as they passed. Caleb realized Hal still had his hand, and he pulled it away with a confused flush of embarrassment. He studied the girls out of the corner of his eye, trying to understand Rodney's fascination. They had long legs, bathing suits that hugged their curves, and hair that swung with bounce as they treaded the sand. He had nothing against girls, and Hal's sister was fun to be around, but he didn't obsess over them.

He heard the other boys at school talk about girls too, and the girls his age were definitely boy crazy. But he couldn't see himself chasing after them, trying to impress them. Once again, he was the odd man out.

"Hey, Hal." Caleb nudged his friend and directed his attention to the girls as they laid out their towels on their choice spot. Maybe Hal could explain the attraction to him. At least Caleb didn't mind showing his confusion to him. "What do you think?"

Hal studied the girls for a few long seconds. "I think tomorrow we should bring our bathing suits. Drying underwear itches."

The unexpected comment and relief it brought sent Caleb into a fit of laughter. Hal joined in, snickering until he began hiccupping. It was good to know Caleb wasn't alone. He figured interest in girls would come. Right now he was too busy. He didn't have time during the school year to think about them, and frankly, the majority of the girls at his school were off-limits. Summertime was for fun.

He bet Hal started looking at girls first. Even though Hal was an oddity by being a Yankee, bookish, and friends with Caleb, he was cute and charming. He bet that next year Hal would be passing notes and holding hands in the hallway. The thought was depressing.

"Hey, we should make a pact," Caleb suggested.

Hal sat up with interest in his eyes. "Like blood brothers? I always thought that would be pretty neat."

"Yeah, like that. We've got to promise we'll never let a girl get between us. We'll always be best friends."

Hal wrinkled his nose. "That's crazy. Why would we let a girl do that?"

"Well, we're going to get girlfriends one day." Caleb gestured down the beach at the girls lying in the sun. Hal's eyes widened, then narrowed as he understood. "And unless we find girlfriends who are friends with each other I'm thinking we're going to find our time divided."

In fact, the more Caleb thought about it, the more he could see it unfolding. He'd seen the high schoolers, and except for a few, most stayed within their own race. He could see Hal being interested in a black girl, and he was sure Hal's parents would lose their cool over it. He and Hal were used to people treating them funny because they were friends. There was no reason why girlfriends wouldn't react any different about their relationship, so that would mean no double dates. They'd have less time for each other, that's the way the world seemed to work.

"I don't think that's going to be much of a problem," Hal said with a shrug. "I'm sure if we explain we're friends first, they'll understand."

Sometimes, Hal was incredibly naïve. He made Caleb shake his head and worry more often than not. He was in for a whole world of hurt one day if he didn't stop being so danged trusting. He wasn't sure how Hal got to be that way, considering his home life, but he insisted on thinking life was all sunshine. Caleb didn't think he was as cynical as Rodney was, but he was definitely more realistic than Hal.

"Hal...." How could he explain all that to him? Caleb shook his head, wishing his tongue wouldn't tie up when he groped for the right words.

"We should make a pact to be outsiders together for life. We're not going to let anything come between us," Hal offered when Caleb didn't say anything more, and the significance of that suggestion made Caleb warm and tingly.

"Now that I can agree to. Deal?" Caleb held his breath, feeling as if he was on the edge of something important.

Hal's grin stretched across his face. "Deal."

CHARLESTON, SC— JUNE 6, 1969

THE SCHOOL bell rang, signaling the end of the year, and delighted whoops filled the air as students scrambled to be the first ones out the door. Caleb shoved his books into his backpack, just as eager to get out of there. On top of splitting his time between helping Dad on the boat and Mom at the market, this summer he'd also be working in his uncle's law office. Now that he was sixteen, he wanted to earn money to get his own car, and he'd have to bust his butt to do that. So this last weekend was just for him, and it was all about cutting loose and having fun.

"Hey, Caleb. Some of us are heading down to the pier after dinner to get our kicks on. Wanna go?"

Caleb glanced up to meet Lou's dark-eyed gaze and grinned. "Far out, sounds like what I was looking for." He was sure his uncle wouldn't mind. He was always telling Caleb he needed to relax more.

"Theresa's going to be there," Lou teased.

Caleb flushed at the mention of Lou's slightly older, very foxy sister. To his surprise, she had indicated her admiration of him with bold eyes and flashing smiles. Rodney would be so jealous if he knew, and Caleb would make sure his brother heard all about it when he sent him his next letter. He wished Rodney were home and not in Vietnam. He would love to see the expression on his brother's face when he saw Theresa with her meticulously groomed afro and pride in her sense of style.

"That's good. She's fun to be around." At least she was when she wasn't trying to talk him into going on walks alone. His brother would definitely say there was something wrong with him for not taking advantage of the opportunity. Caleb just figured she wasn't the right girl for him. He felt a little bad about continuing to see her, but the idea of not having a girl hanging around him made him seem like even more of an outsider than he already was.

"Do yourself a favor," Lou said as he shouldered his bag. "Leave your shadow behind. He's not going to be happy being the odd man out."

Caleb looked down at his hands, searching for a reply, but it was too late, Lou was gone, and Caleb still didn't know what to say. In some ways, the start of high school had been easier. Six years of desegregation had brought a greater mix of kids, and he had many friends. But the feeling of being caught between two worlds was stronger when he only wanted to find a way to mesh them together.

They didn't understand Hal was different. They didn't get Caleb's friendship with him. And Caleb didn't know how to explain it without examining the long-established layers of his relationship with Hal. More than friends. Not quite brothers. Something else, something special, just between the two of them.

"Ready to get out of here?" Hal appeared in that quiet way of his, as if he hoped he'd be overlooked.

He'd gotten even more long and lanky over the year, a little bit clumsy, and his new glasses were forever slipping down the bridge of his nose. His freckles had disappeared, and his hair had darkened. There was something about his earnest gaze that made Caleb on edge at times.

"More than ready." Caleb slung his backpack over his shoulder. "Let's drop our books off at my uncle's, and then we can figure out what we want to do."

By unspoken rule they avoided going to Hal's place. His dad had only gotten crueler over the last few years. He said things that boggled Caleb's mind when he got the mean stuck on his tongue. The few times they'd tried to kick back at Hal's had been uncomfortable at best. Even when Hal's dad wasn't home, the shadow of his presence hung over the house.

Caleb figured the man had never taken the time to get to know Hal. Sure there was a gentle quality about him and there were times when people mocked him for it, still, sissified he wasn't. Sissies didn't make the stands that Hal did. Everybody at school knew that gentle or not, Hal wasn't going to let himself get shoved around. The funny thing was, he'd never hit anybody again after he'd punched James, but he was more than able to defend himself with words.

"Did you want to go to the beach tonight?" Hal asked as they joined the stream of kids heading out of the school. "We haven't been swimming in a while."

Lou caught Caleb's gaze and rolled his eyes with a significant glance toward Hal. Caleb shoved his hand in his pocket and shook his head in a silent message for Lou to let it go. Did it really matter if Hal came with them? Wasn't the whole point of desegregation, of him going through the hell of being one of the first, was so that they would learn to look past race and at each other?

Questions and thoughts like those were what set him apart. There was no point to it all if they kept to their own groups. Then there were days like today, the last few days before going home, when he just didn't want the argument. He was tired of it.

"Actually I'm going to be at the pier with Lou, Theresa, and some others," Caleb said, unable to meet Hal's eyes when he went quiet. Silently he begged him not to ask to come along and then felt ashamed for his thoughts. Hal didn't respond, and Caleb squirmed inside. Then the guilt flashed to anger. Couldn't they spend time apart without it being a big freaking deal?

"Okay." Hal hesitated and then flashed Caleb an odd look. He seemed on the verge of saying something, and then he shrugged. "We'll have time tomorrow right? I can come help you finish packing up your stuff."

Relieved that Hal wasn't going to make an issue out of it Caleb clapped him on the shoulder. "Sure."

Hal looked at him, and instead of the smile Caleb expected, he found Hal watching him with an intent expression. "It's Theresa, isn't it? You've got a thing for her, that's why you don't want me around."

Caleb's jaw dropped, and Hal's lips tightened as he turned his head away. Caleb couldn't figure out what was going on with him lately, but he wouldn't let Hal think he'd forgotten their pact. "Naw, man, it's not like that. Remember, no girls are going to get between us." Caleb nudged Hal, hoping to get one of his smiles. "Tonight's just a thing."

The corner of Hal's mouth lifted, and he nudged Caleb back. "Sorry, I know I've been clingy. I'm surprised you haven't run away screaming. It's not like you can't have other friends."

Caleb couldn't keep separating his life like this. He didn't want to feel like he had to defend Hal's presence, because it raised all kinds of uncomfortable questions. Like why he found himself drawn to the shape of Hal's mouth, or had the urge to wrap his arm around Hal's shoulders or take his hand. He didn't have those impulses for Theresa or any other girl. Those questions scared him, and he found himself pulling away.

He wasn't the only one either. There had been times when Hal had walled himself off or disappeared for no reason. When Caleb had asked him about it all he'd gotten were evasive answers that didn't tell him anything. Their easy friendship wasn't so easy anymore, not that Caleb wanted to give it up in any way. It was just that some days it took nurturing.

"I heard there was an antiwar rally going on tonight near the Citadel. Were you planning on going?" Caleb asked. If there was anything that would distract Hal from Caleb deserting him, it was a rally.

"I might, if I can get out. Dad's been acting weird." Hal rubbed his hand over the nape of his neck. "He's been keeping me close to home. I think he suspects."

Caleb laughed as they reached his uncle's house. The driveway was empty, so they'd have a couple hours before he returned home. "What? That you're a flower child on the inside or that you make a point of finding new ways to get under his skin?"

"Well, I was thinking of my anti-establishment sentiments, but now that you point it out, you're probably right about both." Hal dropped his book bag next to Caleb's by the door. "I need some means of retaliation, and so far getting under his skin is the only enjoyable option."

Caleb raided the pantry while Hal flipped through the LPs. Caleb loved his Uncle Vern's ever-growing record collection. By the time Caleb discovered the moon pies and poured them both glasses of milk, he heard the distinctive sound of John Fogerty's voice filling the living room.

He walked in, juggling plates and glasses, and found Hal lost in his own world, dancing to Creedence Clearwater Revival in his gawky, long-limbed way. His eyes were half-closed, his cheeks flushed, and his hair fell about his face in shaggy, soft waves that Caleb itched to brush back. The sight tugged Caleb's heart and made him flustered in a way that set him completely off balance. He just didn't know what to do about how Hal made him so mixed up inside. It was an internal tug-of-war that mirrored the frustration in the rest of his life. He wanted to go back to when life was at least semi-normal. That was the side that wanted to run away and hide, the other side wanted to cross the room and join Hal in his dance. Instead, Caleb stood there, frozen and watching, his heart beating faster until Hal glanced his way with a smile and Caleb's whole body flushed.

God help him. Life was too confusing.

HAL LEFT Uncle Vern's house knowing in his heart the whole reason Caleb didn't want him around tonight was because of a girl. He didn't want to go anyway, not if it meant watching Caleb moon over her. At the same time, he did want to go, just so he could see what he was up against. Jealousy was a living creature inside him, clawing to get out.

He stuffed his hands in his pockets and kicked a stone down the sidewalk as he reluctantly made his way toward home. Caleb had been acting weird the last few months, leaving Hal feeling like an intruder. Feeling like that with Caleb was just wrong.

Hal wanted to hold on to Caleb even harder, and he couldn't blame Caleb for seeking space. They had interests and friends outside of each other. It wasn't like Caleb had any desire to go to the meetings and rallies that Hal slipped off to. Hal didn't even try to pressure him. Caleb's brother was close to finishing a tour in Vietnam, and he didn't need to be reminded of how bad things were over there.

So if Caleb wanted to hang out with some girl tonight, this was Hal letting him go instead of being a pain in the ass. He shouldn't be so dependent on Caleb anyway. Hal just wished he knew why he got so distant sometimes. It wouldn't stop eating at him.

Hal's shoulders hunched in misery as his steps slowed. Caleb suspected. Hal had tried really hard not to feel the way he did about Caleb, but he couldn't seem to stop himself. He missed those times when they were alone and he'd take Caleb's hand or Caleb would slip his arm around him. He wasn't sure when they'd stopped.

Hal worried Caleb would realize how he felt about him if he indulged in those little urges to touch. Caleb probably picked up on his hesitancy because he hadn't put his arm around Hal in ages. The terror of losing Caleb's friendship kept Hal from telling him about his self-discovery, and for the first time since they met, Hal had a secret that he couldn't share with Caleb.

His house came into view, Mom's flower garden bursting with lilies, gerbera, and peonies. Hal ducked down the walkway between their place and the neighbors' and noticed Dad's car parked in the rear. He paused, reluctance dragging down his limbs. He wished he could figure out what kind of mood he was in. Hal slunk to the kitchen window and peeked in.

Mom stood at the stove, stirring and snatching glances at the clock. He could just see into the living room where Dad watched TV. His tense shoulders unknotted. That was a good sign. On bad nights Dad hid behind a newspaper with a glass of whiskey beside him.

The screen door creaked open, and Mom stuck her head out. "Hurry up, Hal. Come on and get cleaned up before dinner." There was an anxious air about her as she wiped her hands on her apron.

"I'm sorry I'm late," Hal said as he followed her into the kitchen.

"That's okay." She returned to the stove, fussing with lids and opening the oven door. The wonderful scent of roasted chicken set Hal's stomach to rumbling. He scrubbed half-heartedly at his hands, his attention more on Mom's meal. She'd made all his favorites: roast chicken and mushroom gravy, yeast rolls and mashed potatoes.

"I love you, Mom." Hal hugged her, and her hand smoothed over his hair in a quick, fluttering gesture. He'd grown so much over the last year and now stood several inches taller than her.

"I love you too. Don't forget that." She squeezed his shoulder and then pulled away. "Now go on, get your sister, and tell her to make up the table."

Hal knew better than to offer to set it for her. Dad was in a good mood. Better to keep it that way than to get into a ridiculous argument about gender and chores. Dad made up stupid rules just because he could. He wanted to control their home as strictly as he controlled cargo coming in and out of Port Charleston.

Dinner was animated with Lily's chatter about her plans for the summer that apparently involved tea parties with her friends. She was a born con artist. Hal gave her a secret wink and almost laughed when she beamed back at him. Just last week he'd found her climbing trees in a neighbor's yard, her knee skinned bad enough that he had to bandage it. Lily was better at showing Dad what he wanted to see. It was disgustingly dishonest and danged clever, and sometimes he hated her a little for it, but he also didn't want her to have to endure what he did.

"I have good news," Dad announced as he stacked his empty plate to the side and fixed Hal with a look that made his guts quiver with sudden wariness. He glanced at his mom who patted her hair and didn't quite meet his eyes. Hal ran through a list of his most recent transgressions, but none of them stuck out as something he should worry about.

"Good news?" Hal asked cautiously and Dad smiled. He looked so pleased with himself. As a consequence Hal's nerves sharpened to an edge.

"Very good news." Dad looked at everyone around the table in turn. "First, as your mother knows, I'm being transferred back to New York."

The words hit Hal with a profound, gut-wrenching shock. He barely heard the rest of Dad's words. "I know you all will be excited to return home. While Charleston has been good for most of us, it's time to return to where we belong."

Hal stared at Dad in dismay as Lily let out a wail of protest. "But I don't want to go back to New York. I don't remember it. All my friends are here."

"Nonsense, you'll adjust. After all, we did when we moved here." Dad patted Lily's hand reassuringly as he gestured toward Hal. "Hal can tell you all about it. He loves New York."

Hal stared down at his plate, pushing the remainder of his food around, feeling sick to his stomach. While that had been true once, his days of homesickness were long gone. Now he couldn't imagine leaving Charleston or Caleb behind. Maybe he'd had more friends up there than he did here, but that was years ago.

"The second bit of news I have concerns Hal."

Hal's head jerked up. "Me?" A quick shaft of hope struck him; maybe Dad didn't want him to return with them. He could go to a boarding school here. Dad had voiced that option more than once. Hal didn't like the idea of a boarding school, but if it meant he could stay in Charleston, he'd make that sacrifice.

Dad fixed him with a stern look that made Hal's heart wither with ice. The food he'd eaten became a rock, weighing down his stomach. "I have secured a spot for you at the New York Military Academy. You'll be starting in the fall."

For one long, dreadful moment Hal stared at the self-satisfaction on Dad's face as he tried to grasp the double blow pummeling him. He looked at his mom, but she had her head down, her hands fussing as she stacked the plates just so. He had the sinking, sickening realization she'd known all along, and she wasn't going to do anything to stand up for him.

"Don't make Hal go away," Lily cried out, shooting Hal an anguished look. "Please don't, Daddy."

"The decision is final," Dad said, with an uncomfortable expression as Lily turned pleading eyes on him. "They've already accepted him. You'll see him during the holidays."

"No!" Hal jumped up from the table, his hands balling into fists at his sides. "You can't make me."

Dad's face turned purple, Mom's lips tightened, and Lily's eyes widened in astonishment before she burst into tears. "You'll go, boy," Dad growled. "If I can't make a man out of you, maybe they can."

Hal glared at him, his hands tightening to hold off the burning in his eyes. Hal hated him. The emotion built up like a steamship, choking off his air. "You have to catch me first." With that he bolted for the door, Lily's wails and Dad's shouts chasing him down the street.

Tears burned in his eyes, but Hal refused to let them fall. He was not going to give anyone else the chance to mock him for being weak. He needed to find a place to hide. He was halfway to Uncle Vern's house before he remembered Caleb had gone out for the night.

Hal slumped down on a bench at a loss for where to go now. There were many piers and waterfront parks in Charleston. Caleb could be at any one of them. Hal could always go to the rally instead and find someone there who'd give him a spot on the floor for the night. When he didn't return, the first place they'd look for him was with Caleb. And Caleb would lose his mind if he didn't know where Hal was when Dad showed up searching for him. Hal had the half-hysterical image in his head of him and his parents converging on Caleb's house at the same time in the morning. He couldn't take the chance he'd run into them, so he needed to find Caleb now.

Besides, he needed him. The number of people he trusted to stand by him had just dwindled to Caleb and Lily. Hal needed his friend to help him figure out what he was supposed to do now.

LIGHT AND music from the pier danced across the sand. The gentle breeze coming off the ocean cooled Caleb and his friends as they celebrated the start of summer. Caleb had a belly full of shrimp and oysters, a beer in his hand, and Theresa hanging on his arm. School was over, and despite having to work this summer, he had plenty of things to look forward to. It should've been a perfect night.

But Caleb couldn't get into the scene. He felt like an imposter, and Lou's comments didn't help. Caleb had heard it all before from Rodney, and all the asides really meant one thing at the heart of it. *"Do you think you're better than us now?"*

Stupid bullshit that he'd thought he'd learned to disregard. He supposed it was a whole different vibe when it came from friends instead of family. Rodney he could ignore or irritate enough so he went away on his own. He didn't want it coming down to a confrontation. He'd rather just enjoy the night. So he tried to let it go.

Adding to his discomfort, he kept thinking about Hal dancing with a secret smile on his lips. It made Caleb's insides flutter and filled him with dread. Maybe there was a way he could get out of spending tomorrow with him. They had other days to hang out. Caleb wasn't sure when he started to get uncomfortable around Hal. He only wanted it to stop so they could return to their old friendship.

"Do you want to walk down the beach?" Theresa asked, her voice breathy against his ear.

Caleb's cheeks heated. He knew what a walk down the beach meant, and his hand felt clumsy around the beer. Any other guy here would jump on the chance to make out with a chick like Theresa. The thought just made him more nervous than a swindler facing Judgment Day. "Not right now," he said, scrambling for a reason. "I want to hear the band."

It was a sad excuse, and the look she gave him underscored that before she moved away to join her friends. Well, there went any chance he had to get with her. He should be more disappointed. Mostly, he just felt like a jerk for letting her down.

"So what is it with you and your shadow?" Lou asked, and Caleb bit back a groan. This was not a conversation he wanted to have, not now.

Caleb shrugged and took a sip of his beer. He was tired of ignoring it, though, so maybe it was time to meet it head-on, make Lou understand, at least try to anyway. "He's got a name. Won't kill you to say it."

A good-natured smile crossed Lou's lips. "You are touchy when it comes to him. Fine, Hal, better?"

Caleb wasn't sure if he'd scored a point or not. "Yeah."

"So, lay it on me. How'd the two of you become such good friends? I've been trying to figure it out. My cousin works with his dad, says he can be a real condescending dick."

"That sounds like Mr. Zimmer all right." Caleb had met him a few times over the years, enough to know exactly what Lou was talking about. He never said anything blatantly racist, but he was very aware that Hal's dad had a powerful dislike of people different from him. It didn't leave him much room to like anyone or anything.

"Well you know, like father, like son. You don't think that one day he's going to decide that—"

"Not Hal." Caleb shook his head, and Lou shot him a look of exasperation.

"Then what's so different about him? I know some of those rally cats he hangs out with. They say one thing to your face and something else behind your back. How do you know he's not doing the same?"

Caleb wasn't sure how Hal had turned out so different from his dad. Maybe it was because Mr. Zimmer's job took him away often, and his mom was gentle and quiet. Caleb also didn't know how Hal had held on to that sweet naivety so long, and Caleb had mourned its loss when it had started to fade.

Hal had a certain belief about the way the world should work, and he was hell-bent on living it that way until it came true. Sometimes it amazed Caleb, other times it made him crazy, and he just wanted to shake him. One day the real world was going to slap Hal in the face hard, and Caleb didn't want him to be hurt like that.

"When I met Hal there wasn't another kid at that school who would say hi to me unless it was accompanied with a sneer or a slur. He didn't have to be my friend. His first year at school would've been a lot easier if he hadn't been, but he stuck by me. And I stuck by him."

Lou raised a brow. "And?"

"And what?" Now Caleb was exasperated. "What else do you want?"

"Look, I'm not saying all white people are bad, but look around. Who gets hurt when it comes to problems between us and them? It sure isn't the white guy. If they're friendly they want something. They look out for their own, and we need to too. You guys get in a fight, and friends fight, you're the one who's going to end up regretting it, not him."

Caleb wished he knew how to explain it to Lou. He'd been trying to fight this fight for a long time. Still, he had to try again. "The only thing Hal's ever expected from me was for me to be his friend. My parents have high expectations for me. My brother thinks I'm betraying my roots."

He shot Lou a glance. "Even my friends, y'all think I need to act certain way to be cool. I should only hang out with black friends, listen to black musicians, and date light-skinned girls. The world is so much bigger than that. Hal just wants me to be me. You don't understand how relaxing that is. And I just want him to be Hal. He doesn't get that support at home. With us it's never been about race. I can't see Hal changing that drastically no matter what you say."

Lou watched him as he spoke, his head tilted. "Okay, okay." Lou held his hands up. "I dig. You don't want to talk about it. I'll leave it alone for now. But there's something about you two. Like you're both on your own little Caleb and Hal island." His gaze went from Caleb to Theresa with a look of speculation, and Caleb's cheeks burned.

"For a long time it was only the two of us. We used to call ourselves the outsiders." Caleb sent Lou a sharp look. "It doesn't have to be like that, though. You might try inviting him along. I bet he'll surprise you."

Not anytime soon, though, at least not until he'd stopped making Caleb so jumpy inside. He wanted to think his reaction earlier had just been a fluke, but that fluke had been happening with increasing, distressing frequency.

"Maybe he will." Lou tossed his bottle into the trash. "I'm going to get another beer. Want one?"

"No." Caleb stood there, turning his bottle in his hand. He was damn sick and tired of not fitting in, of not belonging anywhere. Right now it didn't help that Hal would understand where he was coming from. Lately it seemed that all this havoc in his life was because of him, even if Hal wasn't intentionally causing it.

"Caleb."

Caleb's head jerked up at the sound of Hal's voice, and he groaned. This had to be a joke. He must've hitched a ride from one of his rally friends and followed Caleb out here. He couldn't believe he'd done that when he'd said he was fine with Caleb going out for a night without him. Apparently, it was too much to ask for breathing room.

Hal stood just beyond the circle of light from their fire and didn't make any move to join the group. Caleb thought of his comment to Lou, implying Hal would be cool hanging out with them. Now he wondered if he was wrong. He sensed everybody's stares, measuring them. He knew the discomfort of joining a group of people when you were the different one and not exactly welcome.

"Can I talk to you?" Hal asked in a low, rough voice.

Caleb tried to bite back his disappointment that Hal wasn't joining them and his frustration that he'd showed up at all. The conflicting emotions unsettled him even more, on top of the very vivid memory of Hal dancing earlier and his urge to dance with him. Right now he didn't want to go off alone with Hal.

"Hal, later, I promise. Come on, man."

The outline of Hal's body went rigid. "But—"

"Tomorrow, for crying out loud." Behind them somebody snickered, and Caleb turned an irritated glance on the culprit. When he looked back, Hal was walking rapidly away his head down. Frowning, Caleb took a couple steps toward him, an inner warning jangling.

"Hal?"

Hal paused under a lamppost and glanced at him with an expression of furious betrayal on his face. Guilt and anger twisted Caleb's insides into a sickening knot. Hal had never looked at him like that, and Caleb's throat tightened as the anger fled. Before he could say anything else, Hal took off again, running this time, and disappeared toward the road. *Oh God, this is bad.*

"Wait, Hal!"

BY THE early hours of the morning, Hal had run out of places to go and landed right where he least wanted to be, staring at the darkened windows of his parents' home. After he'd bolted from Caleb, he'd sought sanctuary in their fort in the woods, but that had only made him wish even more that Caleb was with him.

Apparently Caleb only had time for him when he wasn't with his cooler friends. Deep down Hal knew that wasn't quite fair, but he didn't care. He'd gone from crying himself sick to raging. The hard, angry spark inside him had bloomed into an ugly, fierce fire, and feeding the fire was the only thing keeping his fear at bay. Every time he thought of going to military school, of being alone and different and isolated, that terror threatened to overcome him. So he concentrated instead on those who he should be pissed off with—Mom, Caleb, but most of all, his so-called Dad.

Hal continued to stare at the house, trying to figure out what do next. There was always an after-party when a rally ended, but the thought of trying to talk to anyone dampened the fire. He definitely didn't feel like trusting anyone else with his troubles at home, even if it meant he might have a place to crash for a few days. He could always sneak into his bedroom, grab the cash he'd saved and some clothes, and make his way to the bus station. Anywhere else had to be better than with his parents. But he didn't like that thought either. Somewhere in Charleston, there had to be a place where he could lie low until his family moved. What did it matter if they left him behind? They were planning to ship him off anyway.

"Hal?" Hal closed his eyes at the sound of his sister's voice. Lily had at least defended him when their mom hadn't even been able to look at him. Maybe making his favorite meal was supposed to make up for letting his dad send him away.

When he opened his eyes again, Lily stood on the sidewalk, looking like one of her porcelain dolls in her nightdress. "If you're running away, I'm going with you."

At that moment Hal knew he couldn't go, because Lily was stubborn enough to chase after him. It was one thing for him to be on his own, but Lily was barely thirteen. Though she meant it as a gesture of support, it only made him angrier because it stuck him right where he didn't want to be the most.

"I'm not running away," Hal said, struggling to keep the anger inside. "I've got no place to go."

"Caleb—"

Hal cut her off with a quick slashing motion of his hand. He was not willing to talk about Caleb. Besides, he realized that he couldn't ask his friend to take him in. It would open a whole world of trouble. And right now he didn't want to speak to anyone, least of all Caleb. "Come on, let's get inside before Mom and Dad realize I'm back and you're outside in your nightdress." Either one would mean an ugly scene, and Hal couldn't take another confrontation tonight.

Lily peered at him uncertainly, biting her lip. He didn't give her a chance to argue as he turned toward the house. With every step, he pressed down on his anger, until it was a hard, hot ball. It washed away his exhaustion and kept him going when the rest of him screamed to get away and stay away. He'd have to face Dad sometime, might as well be sooner rather than later. Then Dad could see that his days of trying to please his old man were over.

He made it as far as the hallway, Lily trailing unhappily behind him, when the light came on with a flick and a burst that stung his aching eyes. Hal flinched and cursed himself for displaying weakness in front of his dad who loomed at the other end of the hallway with a leather belt in his hand. "Boy, where have you been? Your mother has worried herself sick."

Hal hardened his expression, biting off the urge to say "good." He didn't care she'd been worried. Served her right. She could save her worries for the man she'd married, because from now on Hal was taking care of himself. Dad wanted to know where he'd been... well there was one answer that would piss him off. "I went to the antiwar rally down by The Citadel."

He had the immense satisfaction of seeing Darren Zimmer's face go purple with rage. If there was one thing Dad hated more than anything else it was hippies. Hal stood straight and tall, staring back at his dad with newfound belligerence. His hair had grown long since his last haircut, and his clothes were on the grungy side after the night he'd had hitchhiking to Folly Beach and back, then trekking through the woods. Hal knew exactly what Dad saw when he looked at him, a queer hippie, and Hal hoped he choked on his own anger and disappointment.

Mom came to the bedroom door, her face pale, with dark circles under her eyes. Despite his vow not to care, Hal felt a pang at the distress in her gaze. He glanced away and hardened his heart. Lily was the only one in his family who gave a damn, and he hoped she had the sense to stay true to her sneaky self and hide until this was all over. There was no sense in both of them getting an ass-whupping.

"God, you are a selfish fool." Hal closed his ears to the rest of Dad's words. They weren't anything new. Instead, he stared at his old man, letting the red wash of the tirade fuel his anger until Dad faltered midspeech and jabbed the belt at Hal's room. "Get in there."

Hal jutted his chin, steeling himself. It had been a while since Dad had taken a belt to him, but the tears and pain in his memories were fresh and sharp. At least Dad stopped after a few extra licks for being a crybaby. Well, damned if he'd give Dad the satisfaction tonight, or ever again. No matter what it took, no matter how many licks, he wasn't going to cry.

Mom laid her hand on Dad's arm. "Darren, please, not tonight. Let's all go to bed."

He took one look at the defiance in Hal's eyes and shook his head.

"No, this is between Hal and me. Stay out of it."

Hal crossed his arms and shot his dad an insolent look. "I thought the whole reason for a whupping was because I was selfish and worried her. She should have a say in my punishment." Hal was prodding the beast, but he'd lost any control over his tongue and any fear of consequences. "Be honest. It has nothing to do with Mom. It's because I defied you to your face. You know what, go ahead and smack me all you want, because you can't control me anymore like you do the rest of the family. I don't care what you think of me."

Mom gasped, her hand coming to her lips as she stared at Hal like she didn't know him anymore. Dad's eyes went dark and dangerous as he took one sharp stride toward Hal.

"No," Lily cried out, darting from her hiding place and holding her arms out in front of him in a fragile shield against Dad's advance. Hal bit off a groan. Dad stared at her in astonishment before he frowned, the line on his brow deepening. "It's bad enough you're sending my brother away. Isn't that enough?"

"Hiding behind girls now?" Dad sneered. Though Hal had decided not to care what Dad thought of him, it stung his pride. "Lilian, get back in bed right now, and don't let me catch you out of it again tonight. I've had enough lip from you today."

Lily stiffened, and Hal put his hands on her shoulders before she could argue. As much as he loved her for sticking up for him, he didn't want her getting herself into more trouble. Not when they wouldn't be able to stick together come fall. "It's okay, go on. It's a whupping, trust me, I can take it." He gave her a little push, and she looked over her shoulder at him, reluctance in her eyes as she made her way to her own room.

Hal faced down his dad and gestured toward the door. His obvious lack of fear seemed to take Dad aback. The fire inside him wouldn't let him be afraid. All he cared about was getting it over with so Hal didn't have to look at him anymore.

As Hal turned on the light in his room, he was confronted by all the little ways Dad had tried to paint a picture of who Hal should be. The majority of his books were hidden, tucked away in drawers or stuffed behind games on his bookshelf. All his craft supplies were in Lily's room. Hal had let him make his life a joke. He'd wasted all this time and energy on a man who would never be happy no matter what he did.

Dad caught his shoulder as he walked by him. Hal looked at him, meeting Dad's angry stare with one of his own. "Tomorrow you're getting your damn haircut, and if I find out you're hanging out with those hippies again there will be hell to pay. Do you understand?"

"Yes," Hal said from between clenched teeth.

"You sure don't know how to pick friends." Hal watched his dad walk out of the room with dull, aching astonishment. It took him a moment to realize that the threatened ass-whupping wasn't going to happen.

He sat on the edge of his bed, Dad's words ringing in his ears. He remembered the expression of impatient aggravation on Caleb's dark, handsome face when Hal interrupted his time with Theresa and his other friends. That compounded the hurt of the whole night and made it all so much worse. Hal had learned his lesson loud and clear, from now on he was relying on nobody but himself.

CHARLESTON, SC— AUGUST 1, 1969

"HEY, CALEB, your princess is here." Caleb flushed at the sneer in Rodney's voice, and it sparked the familiar slow burn of anger that had scorched him bare this summer. Caleb glanced up from his book to see Hal's long, lanky form and scarlet face. Rodney had scored two hits with his snide comment.

"I need to talk to you." Hal pushed his glasses farther up his nose and set his jaw in determination.

"Now you want to talk?" Caleb said with an edge he couldn't hide. He hadn't been able to get a grip of his emotions when it came to Hal. Not since the disastrous night at the beach. The anguish in Hal's eyes as Caleb brushed him off haunted him with gnawing guilt. At first he'd thought Hal was upset Caleb had turned him away, until he really started to think about it. Hal had searched him out for a reason, and Caleb hadn't even given him a chance to say what it was.

But when he'd tried to apologize the next morning, Hal had refused to see him. He could sure hold a grudge like nobody else. Caleb had visited every day after that, before finally realizing he had to wait for Hal to make the next move. And that made him pretty hopping mad. He'd been a jackass. Picking one friend over another was something he never should've done. Still, did that mean Hal had to cut him out completely? That hurt. That wounded him more than any torment Rodney could devise.

Hal's shoulders slumped as he looked down at his feet. He'd grown a few more inches over the summer, and he'd lost weight. Not that there had been too much to him before. Seeing how defeated he looked woke all of Caleb's protective instincts. His dad must've been at him pretty hard. He'd missed Hal, more than he could've ever imagined missing anyone.

"I'm sorry," Hal said, lifting his head. His gaze darted to Rodney and then to Caleb. "Not that it means much, but I did come to see you a few weeks ago. I swear, a couple of times, but you were always out."

Caleb set aside Kurt Vonnegut's *Slaughterhouse-Five* and gave Rodney a hard stare. His brother looked like their dad and had his pride, just not his kindness. Rodney just stared back at him with the mean edge that had been taking over him more and more. He'd come home on annual leave from the Army, and though he'd been a jerk sometimes before, it was worse now. There was a bitter ugliness in him that made Caleb wonder what had happened to his brother to change him so much. "I take it you felt you were above passing along a message?"

"I'm not the one who acts like he's too good for the rest of this family. Not like you with your fancy job, swanky home most of the year, and your dumb friend with your 'outsider' club." Rodney tossed Hal a sneering glance.

Caleb never should've taken Uncle Vern's offer to work in his office over the summer. Ever since Rodney returned from Vietnam, Caleb had faced his scorn. Caleb worked just as hard as Rodney, striving to save money. While their uncle's house in the city might be less crowded and had a few more comforts, it wasn't swanky. He didn't understand where Rodney got the dumb idea that Caleb thought he was too good for their family because he certainly never felt it. He hoped he didn't come off like a snob. His parents didn't make him feel like he did, and that was a small relief, but maybe their pride in him fueled his brother's anger. He didn't know.

Add the pressure from Lou, who'd taken Hal's silent treatment of him as behavior Caleb should've expected. Or Caleb's other friends who told him he needed to remember where he came from. As if he could forget. He wasn't ashamed of it, though they seemed to think that. His parents worked hard, day in and out, they kept a clean home, put food on the table, and knew what was going on with Rodney and him. But they were tired, and Caleb looked forward to one day being able to help them out beyond making and hawking baskets in the market or going out with his dad on the boat.

All that ran through his mind as Hal watched him with a solemn expression. Those strange feelings he stirred in Caleb awoke, and he wondered again when Hal had started setting him on edge. Maybe it was the way he'd look at him like Caleb had all the answers and could fix every wrong. Wasn't that a joke? He bet Hal didn't think he was perfect anymore. That thought brought forth a new aching pang along with relief. He'd always known one day Hal would see him as human and flawed as everyone else; he just hadn't expected Hal would take it so hard.

"Please," Hal asked with a naked plea in his voice, and Caleb felt a quick stab of alarm. Something was wrong.

"Let me ask Mom." Caleb tucked his book away with his mom's tools next to the tub of materials.

Mom gave them her blessing, and they walked down the old cobblestoned street, detouring around shoppers and tourists alike. Caleb shoved his hands in his pockets, unsure of what to say. There was a strain between them now that had never been there before, and it left him awkward and unsettled.

He watched people as they walked by, as always feeling like he was on the wrong side looking in. It was crazy, all those years they'd been friends, and except for when they'd first met, he'd never been so aware of the differences in their race until this year. It had never been a line between them until Caleb had put it there. "Don't you ever get tired of being an outsider?" he asked, startling himself by voicing the thought out loud.

Hal shrugged and kicked a stone as they turned onto Concord Street and made their way toward the park and its view of the water from the Battery. "Maybe sometimes, more so this summer. It wasn't so bad when we were together."

There it was, not quite an accusation, but the words were unsaid. *Why did you turn me away that night? I needed you.* Hal didn't say the words, but Caleb knew him well enough to get they were running through his mind. And he didn't have any answers for him. If he couldn't make sense of it himself, then he couldn't explain it to Hal.

"I'm sorry. I acted like a jerk. I felt pulled in ten different directions with people expecting me to act one way and not accepting me for me." Caleb didn't know how to explain it any more than that. It was no excuse, because if there was anybody who'd accepted him, it had been Hal. Caleb just didn't know how to say how Hal made him feel funny without hurting his feelings even more or thinking that Caleb had lost his mind.

"I know what you mean," Hal said with a quiet certainty in his voice that said he wasn't bullshitting. Yeah, he supposed Hal would understand.

They'd squabbled before, argued like brothers, but they'd never had a serious falling out. If they didn't want this slowly poisoning their friendship moving forward, they needed to get it all out now. So even though he didn't want to add to the tension, Caleb had to open up about everything.

"Hal, I came to see you every day. I showed up late for work or left early to try to make things right. I know I screwed up, but I don't think I deserved to be cut out like that. It… it really hurt. I thought we were closer than that. I thought you'd be willing to work things through with me." Just speaking of it brought back all that uncertainty, hurt, and anger.

Caleb shoved his fists in his pockets and wished that he could go back to that night. He'd punch himself in the mouth before he brushed off Hal with impatience. That was the moment when everything went wrong.

"I was so angry," Hal said, in a barely audible voice as he stared at the ground. "I was so pissed at everyone, even Lily, and she hadn't done anything. No matter what I did, I couldn't let go of that anger. It was wrong. I knew it was wrong, and it only made me madder. It was an ugly cycle I couldn't escape."

Hal looked at him, and Caleb expected many reactions, but not the glitter of tears in his eyes. Once again alarm hit him. This just wasn't Hal being upset because they'd fought and spent the summer doing their own thing. This was something else as well.

"What's wrong?" he asked, worry making his voice sharp. It was Hal's dad. It had to be. He'd hurt Hal in some way, even deeper than before. It wasn't right, the way he treated Hal, and Caleb was helpless to do anything to stop it.

"We're moving back to New York. Dad's starting a new job just after school starts." Hal's shoulders hunched together in a familiar gesture of misery as he looked away.

"What?" Caleb felt the bottom lurch out of his world. He stopped and turned to face Hal, trying to make sense of it. Hal couldn't leave.

"Yeah, I guess it had been in the works for a bit, but he sprung it on Lily and me that night after school." Hal quickened his step as they reached the park, aiming for the shade trees along the walkway. Caleb stared after him as reality dawned. Hal was leaving him behind. For one hot, spiteful minute, Caleb was furious with him. Then the ache of loss hit, and Caleb hated himself for missing his last summer with Hal.

HAL PAUSED when he realized Caleb wasn't beside him any longer. It was an agonizing reminder of the whole terrible summer and how he'd been utterly alone. When he turned to face his friend, the distance between them seemed wider than a few feet, and it wasn't because of the impending move. They'd hurt each other, and they could never take that back.

Hal stared at the sidewalk and the dappled pattern of shadows the leaves made as they blocked the streaming sun. His throat tightened around the lump of grief that had settled there, and his chest ached so much that he now understood why people called it heartbreak. They'd lost this last summer, and he didn't know where to begin to fix it, but he had to try.

His eyes burned and felt raw from the weight of the tears that he refused to let fall. In the back of his head, he could hear Dad's never-ending voice, telling him to man up. He'd cried himself out at the beginning of the summer. He wasn't going to let anybody do that to him again. It was all so wrong. He never expected to feel like an outsider with Caleb. Maybe moving away was the best thing for everyone. Maybe he'd do well at the military academy and finally get Dad to focus on something other than Hal's defects as a son.

Caleb's hand touched his shoulder. "Come on," Caleb said gruffly, "let's find a place where we can talk."

They walked out of the park, past the East Battery to where the water slapped up against the seawall. They took off their shoes and ducked under the railing to sit on the wall. The waves dashed against the stone, sometimes splashing up to kiss their feet. Despite Caleb's wish to talk, he remained silent as they watched the boats go by until the need to know why Caleb had looked embarrassed to see him that night outweighed Hal's fear.

"I messed up didn't I?" Hal asked, stealing a glance at Caleb's profile. The slight chubbiness of his youth had disappeared when Caleb shot up in height. Now he was a little shorter than Hal, though broader in the shoulders, but his eyes hadn't changed, neither had his smile. Hal missed his smile. "That's why you didn't want me being around your other friends. I embarrass you, like I do my dad."

Caleb shot him a look of confused disbelief. "That's just like you, thinking everything's your fault." He shook his head. "You've never been an embarrassment to me, and you didn't do anything wrong. I… it's complicated."

"Most things are." Hal kicked his feet, trying to skim them off the waves as a distraction from the ache. "Maybe you could try to explain it."

"You wouldn't understand."

Caleb often said that when their discussion touched on race. To be honest, Hal didn't get it most of the time. He didn't get why it was such a problem for people. This time, though, he wasn't taking his lack of understanding as an excuse to back off, not when it led to them both being hurt.

"Make me understand."

"I've been trying to figure it out myself. It makes my head ache," Caleb said slowly. He studied Hal as if trying to conjure the right words. "When we first met I was under serious pressure from my family to be brave and be one of the first to go to the white school. Rodney had wanted to do it too, but Charleston took its sweet time catching up with the rest of the country. I'm not sure it would've happened if Clemson hadn't been forced to admit a black student. By the time the lawsuit went through, Rodney was pretty mad and chose not to go. So I went by myself. I didn't feel brave. I was scared and lonely all the time. Until I met you."

Hal had known that, but he didn't think he really got what it must have been like. He'd thought he'd been the odd one as a Yankee, but he supposed if he'd gone to a school and been the only white kid where he wasn't wanted, that feeling would've been a thousand times more alienating. He knew what it felt like to be different, but he could mask his differences. He'd faced scorn, but not fear and hatred. He'd endured a thousand little slights day in and out from his dad, but not from complete strangers.

The idea of going to the military academy terrified him. He was different from other boys, and instinctively he knew they were going to pick up on that difference just the way his dad did. It made him look at Caleb's situation in a different light. "I'm sorry." It wasn't adequate, but he didn't know what else to say.

"You don't have anything to be sorry for." Caleb looked at him. "You're the only one I can be myself with. It's like everybody wants to us to pick sides, and I'm always on the wrong side of some dumbass line in the sand. It's like we fought for desegregation, right? Now years down the road as more of the schools mix up, it's like there is still an unspoken segregated wall. Whites should stay with whites, blacks with blacks, and people like you and me are looked at with suspicion by all. I'm sick of it."

Hal heard the frustrated anger in Caleb's voice, and he tried to understand, but he was sure he fell short of grasping it. His mom looked at his friendship with Caleb as a novelty, like he'd picked up an exotic doll. Dad had a few comments about finding his own kind, but usually he was too busy harping on other things to give him any grief over it. Some of the kids at school, James especially, came up with nasty things to say. But at least his few other friends didn't try to pressure him to stay away from Caleb.

"I broke a promise to you, and I hate that," Caleb said softly. "I won't do it again."

Hal nodded, staring at his feet again. The fight wasn't all Caleb's fault. He hadn't even given him a chance to apologize. Caleb hadn't even known anything was wrong that night. He bet if he'd told Caleb it was bad, Caleb would've taken the time to listen. But he'd been too hurt and angry to be reasonable. "I messed up too. You tried to talk to me, and I wouldn't listen. That wasn't fair. I'd like to think we'd never fight again, but I guess that's not realistic. Next time I'm mad, I won't shut you out."

They fell silent, letting the hot sun soak into their skin, and for the first time in months Hal felt some small measure of happiness, though it was bittersweet. Once he returned to New York, he didn't know if he'd ever see Caleb again. He'd missed Caleb over this horrible summer, and they only had a couple short weeks before Hal left.

"Being different is hard," Caleb sighed.

"Yeah."

Caleb slipped his arm around Hal's shoulders, and he leaned into him like he used to, like he'd wanted to do for months. In the dead heat of the afternoon, there was nobody around to say what they should and shouldn't be doing. Despite the sun hammering them, Hal fit right up against Caleb's rib cage and relaxed against one of the few comforts he trusted.

"Can I tell you something, a secret just between us?" Hal's heart pounded with sick fear. A part of him said he should keep his mouth shut, but if he couldn't tell Caleb his secret, then he couldn't tell anyone. Right now he needed to unburden his soul to someone, and a part of him wondered if holding on to this was part of the reason for the gulf between him and Caleb.

"Of course." Caleb looked at him with a curious expression. "What kind of a secret could you possibly have?"

"Dad's sending me to a military academy in the fall." The shock on Caleb's face underscored Hal's fear and misery. "I think he's afraid I'm queer and going there will fix me. I don't know."

"I take it your dad informed you of that the same time he told you about the move?" Caleb's fingers stroked his arm as Hal nodded. "God, no wonder you were pissed at the world."

Hal waited for Caleb to comment on the queer bit, staring down at his bare toes, sure that his friend would deny any possibility he could be attracted to other boys. Caleb's arm tightened around his shoulders, and Hal's eyes squeezed shut against the sudden sting of emotion.

"I don't understand your dad," Caleb said in a heavy voice. "And I don't think he knows you at all."

"But I am. I'm everything he says I am," Hal whispered, and as hard as he tried, he couldn't stop hot tears from welling behind his eyelids. He pulled away from Caleb before Caleb could withdraw and turned his face away to wipe his eyes. Dammit, he'd promised himself he wouldn't ever cry again.

"You are not," Caleb said fiercely. "You aren't weak or girlish and all the other mean things he calls you. And if you are queer, then so what?"

Hal stared at Caleb in astonishment. "But...."

"I messed up this summer. I forgot how we stuck by each other, and I'm not going to forget again." That old, stubborn light came to Caleb's gaze again. "So if you say you are, then I believe you, but it's not going to stop me from being your friend. We'll figure out a way to help you get through the school year. At least you won't be with your dad most of the time, right? That's got to count for something."

Hal grabbed Caleb's hand and squeezed it, unable to express the depth of his gratitude. He'd been an idiot to think Caleb would turn away from him because Hal liked boys instead of girls. They'd gone through too much together for that. He should've given Caleb a chance instead of wallowing in his hurt and fear. Though they would be apart the next school year, he wasn't alone. Caleb understood him.

"You wouldn't be weirded out if I told you I loved you would you?" Hal said, the words spitting out of him before he could censor himself. It was just such a relief to talk to Caleb again, to open up after being silent so long. Much longer than the length of their fight, if Hal counted all those months when he'd worried Caleb would realize that Hal was attracted to him.

Caleb touched the side of his head to Hal's. "Nah, man. I love you too. Brothers for life."

"Yeah," Hal said softly, a flutter of disappointment moving through him until he squashed it. Being Caleb's brother was much better than being on opposite sides with him. A brother was special, more than a friend, and even if it wasn't quite what Hal felt for Caleb, it didn't matter. He was leaving in a few weeks, and that was that. Hal would much rather leave with their friendship intact and strong than screw things up by alienating him again.

CHARLESTON, SC— AUGUST 22, 1969

CALEB AWOKE to the heart-wringing realization that the worst day of his life had arrived. Hal was heading back to New York this morning. Caleb ached all over with the force of the realization, but nothing hurt worse than his heart. He thought he'd been miserable the two months they'd been apart because of their stupid fight. This was worse. He might never see Hal again, and there were so many things he wanted to say, things he hadn't been able to find the words for.

The sun was just starting to rise as Caleb scrambled out of bed. He had plans to meet Hal by their old fort to steal a few moments before the Zimmer family hit the road. He didn't want to take a chance that he'd miss seeing him one last time.

"Hey."

Caleb tensed at his brother's soft call. They'd been fighting bitterly. Ever since Caleb found out Rodney deliberately chose not to give him Hal's message. He was supposed to forgive his brother, that's what Mom urged him to do, but it was hard when Rodney hadn't shown one spark of remorse. He glanced at his brother and for once didn't see that ugly acrimony in his eyes. If anything, Rodney looked sympathetic.

"Yeah?" Caleb asked warily as he shrugged into his shirt.

"Tell Hal I'm sorry his dad's sending him away, but he'll be okay at military school. He's tougher than he looks. It'll probably be rough at first, no lie. I think he can do it, though." Caleb stared at Rodney, wondering what brought this change but grateful for it nevertheless.

"I will, thanks."

"And grab my camera," Rodney said, pointing to the top of his dresser. "You'll want a picture."

Caleb nodded his thanks, not sure how to take this softer side of Rodney, and he didn't have time to figure it out. They'd talk when he returned. He grabbed the camera, put it around his neck, and retrieved his bike. Over the years he and Hal had worn out a path that made coming and going to the fort easier.

Their first fort sagged in dejected neglect in the clearing. Their second sat nestled in a tree, not far away. It made Caleb mournful to think that soon it would also start to fall apart. He couldn't see himself coming all the way out here without Hal.

As Caleb jumped off his bike, the ladder fell down from the trapdoor, and Hal appeared in its window. Caleb set his bike against the trunk with a wave of relief. He'd been sure Hal's dad would've found a way to keep Hal at home out of pure spite.

"I wasn't sure you'd be able to get away," Caleb said as he began to climb.

"I didn't take any chances. I got out of there before dawn." Hal moved out of the way when Caleb reached the trapdoor and helped him through. "I don't have much time. It's a long drive, so they want an early start."

Caleb's heart sank. He'd known it wasn't realistic, but he'd been hoping for a few more hours. They'd spent every minute together they could grab in the last few weeks, and the time had disappeared too fast. He wasn't ready to say good-bye.

"Well, in just two years you'll be eighteen," Caleb said, trying to find a bright spot so Hal wouldn't look as woebegone as Caleb felt. "Then you can come back." If he wasn't drafted, like Rodney, who was furious at the thought of possibly facing a second tour in Vietnam.

"True," Hal said with a smile that didn't touch his eyes. "We can do what we want then."

Caleb made sure no critters had come to nest in one of the big cushions Hal had made, then he settled back against it. They were nicer than the original ones, just as this second fort was better than the first. The cushion smelled musty, and the fort held a general air of neglect that made Caleb even sadder. This was their place, and neither one of them had looked after it much since last fall.

Hal leaned on the cushion next to him, and that trickle of nervousness from earlier in the year returned. He wanted to put his arms around Hal. Not because he wanted to offer support or comfort, like when they were younger. He wanted to do it because the thought of being closer to Hal made his pulse race in a thrilling way.

Caleb gave into the temptation to slip his arm around him, tugging him closer than he'd dared to in a long time. Hal settled against him with a sigh and pressed his face against Caleb's shoulder. The tension Hal carried hadn't disappeared in the last few weeks. He was quicker to anger than before, and those changes made Caleb's throat tighten because he blamed himself for being one of the causes.

"You don't think it's weird, hugging me now that you know I'm attracted to guys?" Hal asked, his voice muffled.

Caleb supposed he should. After all, he wasn't like Hal, even if he occasionally had thoughts about Hal that made him uncomfortable. "No," he admitted. "It doesn't feel weird at all. I just wish it wasn't the last time for a while."

They lounged in silence, the stuffy heat in the fort worsening as the sun rose higher. As hot as it was, Caleb didn't want to let go. If only they had more days together like this, more mornings when they could slip away to the fort to be alone. A thought flitted through his head. What would it be like to kiss Hal? His heart did a funny flip. He'd thought about kissing Theresa and never had that reaction, but then again, he hadn't had that reaction with another guy either. Just Hal.

"You know how strange I was acting toward the end of the school year?" Hal asked, lifting his head. Caleb found himself staring into his gray-green eyes, and the sense that there was only the two of them in the world grew stronger.

"I think we were both acting strange." Caleb remembered how he'd treated Hal with a wince of regret. They'd both been hot and cold, one minute pushing each other away, the next seeking each other out again. He wished now that he'd talked about it with Hal, even if he didn't know how to phrase all the conflicting emotions.

"I was afraid you'd notice I wasn't into girls, and I felt bad because I had a secret. I'd never had a secret from you before. I wanted to tell you, but…." Hal trailed off, and Caleb had a gut instinct there was more to it than Hal's attraction to boys, something unsaid. Caleb had to look away because he became vividly aware of Hal's body pressed against his own.

Caleb had never thought about it that way, but he supposed he had a secret too. Now with Hal getting ready to leave, Caleb wasn't sure what to do about it either. With the way Hal's dad screwed with his head and Hal's uncertain temper, how could Caleb tell him as his parting words, "Hey, you made me uncomfortable, so I thought the only way to handle it was by keeping my distance"? Just the thought of talking about it made his palms sweat and his stomach churn.

"I don't blame you for feeling like you couldn't tell me, not with the way I was acting," Caleb replied.

"I just wish…." Once again, Hal trailed off, but this time there was no doubt what he meant, because Caleb also felt it.

"I know; me too." He wished they had more time. He wished he had the courage to say what was in his heart, to hear what Hal had to say. He wished they could be free to be themselves without the world trying to dictate who they should be friends with, who they should love.

"Hal? Hal! I know you're up there." Lily's voice called from the clearing. "Dad's pitching a fit. He wants to go."

Caleb closed his eyes as his heart thumped painfully against his ribs. "I'll write you."

"I know," Hal whispered, his voice lost.

It wouldn't be the same. If Caleb had something he wanted to share with Hal, or if he'd had a bad day and needed to confide in him, it would be days before those letters would get to Hal and even more days before he got a response. Caleb wanted to comfort him with words, but his throat had tightened too much for speech. He hadn't cried in years, but the aching in his chest and eyes warned him he was perilously close.

"Hal?" This time Lily's voice floated up from the base of the tree. "Please don't make me go to New York without you."

Tears pooled behind Caleb's eyelids. He kissed Hal's cheek and let his arms fall away. Hal stared at him for a long moment and then his lips brushed near Caleb's, like the breath of a ghost, leaving them tingling. Before Caleb could react, Hal swung down through the trapdoor.

Caleb scrambled to follow, grabbing Rodney's camera as he went. He couldn't let Hal go without getting a picture of them together. "Hal, wait! Please."

HAL PAUSED just as he was about to bolt into the trees. He glanced back at Caleb who shimmied down the ladder with an unusual recklessness. Hal didn't want to go, but each second he lingered made it harder to leave. Lily waited by the tree with a look of dread in her eyes. She was worried he'd get into trouble with Dad, but Hal was of the opinion their old man couldn't do anything more to him than he already had. Taking him away from Charleston and Caleb had to be the worst thing that had ever happened to him.

"Yeah?" Hal asked, looking down at his feet. He didn't want to see what Caleb thought of that almost kiss. He wanted to touch his lips. He wanted to kiss him again. He'd been thinking about it as they lay together. Well more like obsessing over it. Maybe Caleb wanted to tell him never to do it again, or maybe he wanted a for-real kiss. Hal let himself linger on that wish for a fleeting second before dismissing it. Caleb would never suggest such a thing with Lily there. Hell he'd never suggest it when they were alone. Caleb wasn't like him.

"We need a picture together," Caleb said, waving a camera as he caught up to Hal. "Rodney lent me his new camera. I'll send you a copy."

Hal almost refused. He didn't want a picture commemorating this day of all days. But he didn't have many photos of him and Caleb. Most were years old. He may not want to remember this day, but he definitely wanted to remember Caleb as he was now. "Okay."

"I'll take it," Lily offered, coming forward. "Does it have a timer? Maybe we can take one of all three of us too."

"Yeah, see, it's right there." Caleb showed Lily how to work the camera. "Why don't we go take it up in the clubhouse? There's nothing to prop it on here." The three of them climbed back into the fort, and Hal was pathetically grateful for this extra five minutes.

Caleb stood beside him, their hands dangling next to each other, and Hal itched to take Caleb's. He must've been thinking the same thing because Hal felt a finger brush along his pinkie. He tried to smile, but no smile came as Lily took the shot. He just hurt too much.

"My turn," Lily said. She set the camera down on their improvised bookshelf and wiggled in between them.

Hal had to smile at her wide grin and happy eyes at being included. He couldn't deny she loved being with the two of them. If there was anyone who deserved to be an honorary member of the outsider club it was Lily. Her presence between them gave Caleb and Hal an excuse to huddle close. He caught Caleb's hand behind Lily's back and felt the reassuring press of his fingers in return as the camera flashed.

Lily turned, giving Caleb and Hal a regretful look as they dropped their hands. "We have to go."

The quick moment of camaraderie vanished as a shroud dropped over Hal's spirit again. "Yeah, I know. Give me a minute okay? I'll be right down, I promise."

Lily looked at Caleb and caught him in a fierce hug. "I'm going to miss you."

"Yeah, me too," Caleb said, hugging her back. "You take care of him for me, Lilygirl."

"I will. I promise." Lily sent one last warning look in Hal's direction and then disappeared through the trapdoor.

Hal stared at his feet. This had been hard enough a few minutes ago when impetus of that impromptu kiss had made him bolt. It was harder now. He would give anything for more time. Caleb took his hands, and Hal held on like he was clinging to a cliff.

"You know, we should've run away for a few days, gone to Woodstock for one last hurrah," Hal said, lifting his head. He'd thought about going himself, and if they hadn't had that fight and lost too much time together that summer, if he wasn't already leaving, he would've taken that chance. It would've been a hundred times more fun with Caleb by his side, though.

Caleb's dark brown eyes widened with shock. "Hal, seriously, I would've been killed by my entire family. They would've lined up to whup my ass. And you would've been running straight toward the state you're trying to avoid."

"True, all true, but we should've done it." More reasons why Hal hadn't considered it. Caleb did have a good relationship with his parents, and he couldn't honestly see his friend doing something so reckless. It would've been nice, though, just the two of them, alone together, camping out and listening to live music, maybe getting a little high. He bet nobody would've looked at them sideways there, whether they held hands or not.

Caleb's expression turned wistful. "It would've been fun, though, crazy, but… it's one of those things you only get to do once."

"Missed chances," Hal said softly, thinking of that near kiss, of those months they'd spent not talking to each other. It had been so stupid, and he wished he could take all of the anger back.

"Seems to be happening a lot this summer." Caleb stared at him a long moment, and Hal wondered if he was thinking the same things Hal was. "Promise me you're not going to do anything stupid in New York okay? I want you to return in a couple years."

"Define stupid," Hal said, knowing all too well Caleb had reason for concern. Hal found himself taking more risks than he would have before the reckless rage had grabbed a hold of him. All in the vain hope that Dad would change his mind about military school.

"You know, tying yourself to trains, breaking into draft offices to destroy records, getting arrested," Caleb said with a faint smile before his gaze turned serious. "Or running away."

Hal shook his head. "If I was going to run away, I would've been gone back in June. Don't worry. I'm not going to hitchhike out to California."

"Good, 'cause I'd have to look for you, and then we'd both have to answer to my mom."

Hal choked on a laugh at that thought, and then his eyes filled with tears and his heart wrenched as he realized Caleb wasn't joking. He would come looking for him to make sure he was okay, just as he'd kept coming by Hal's house to check on him after Hal ran off in anger. He was damned lucky to have Caleb as his friend, and he didn't want to forget that ever.

"Hey, God, don't cry," Caleb said, his voice turning husky as he tugged Hal into his arms. "Please don't."

Hal turned his face into Caleb's shoulder and tried to think about what Dad would say if he turned up late with red eyes, but all he could think about was this was good-bye. He was about to lose the one person who'd kept him steady for the last eight years.

"Hal?" Lily called up with desperation. "We're going to get it if we don't hurry. I'm sorry. Please, let's go."

Hal pulled away and dashed his hand across his cheek. "Yeah, I'm coming, Lily." He stared at Caleb who looked as if he had tears in his eyes too. In Hal's entire life he'd never seen Caleb cry. Hal was the one who couldn't keep it in, and if he didn't go soon they'd both end up a mess.

Hal kissed the tip of his fingers, on the hand they swore a blood oath on and held it out to Caleb. "Still outsiders, right?"

Caleb repeated the gesture and touched his fingers to Hal's. "Yeah, man, outsiders for life."

PART TWO

PART TWO

CHARLESTON, SC— SEPTEMBER 2, 2023

HAL TURNED a page in the memory book as Caleb finished another story. Mounted in the center of the page, the heavy paper yellowing and the edges worn, was the paperback cover of *The Outsiders* by S. E. Hinton. Hal smiled as he touched it. They'd passed that book back and forth for years before it disappeared. He couldn't believe it was the same cover.

He nudged Caleb, pointed at it, and Caleb grinned. "Oh wow."

Hal held up the memory book for everybody to see. "Who found this?"

Kendra raised her hand with a laugh. "It was in a trunk in the attic. You two need to go through there. It looks like you've saved everything."

"Was the book with it?" Caleb asked, his expression curious.

"Yeah, as soon as I picked it up the cover fell off. I almost tossed it when I saw all the notes written inside and realized how important it had been. I saved the cover and put the book back in the trunk."

"Writing in books, Uncle Caleb?" Drew teased. "You didn't have enough paper?"

"Uncle Hal started it," Caleb replied, neatly shifting the blame.

"I know I said books are sacred," Hal cut in as an indignant expression flashed across Kendra's face. "That's because you liked to color in them and scrawl the phone numbers of cute boys. I was making a commentary on the story as a message to your dad. That's different."

"Looks like scrawling notes to a cute boy to me," Kendra replied and everybody laughed.

Caleb flipped through pages of letters, all neatly stored in bags so they could be removed and reread. Hal was surprised by how many they'd kept. Letters had kept them connected after Hal moved back to New York. They'd kept him from going crazy at the academy. Letters that had kept Caleb grounded after he'd been drafted and sent off to Vietnam. There were short notes with guarded intimacies after they'd become lovers. Then back to the longer letters after their split when they struggled to find a balance between feelings that continued to linger and making sure their friendship stayed strong when Hal had run off to Ghana.

There were mementos from antiwar and gay pride rallies mixed in with letters of commendation from Caleb's superiors and Hal's letter of acceptance to the Peace Corps. Pictures from college days in New York City and Charleston. A coffee napkin from Greenwich Village and a cocktail napkin from a gay club in Charleston that had been closed down for decades. It just went to show how crazy their lives had gotten, and yet they'd made it through with their friendship intact. Hal and Caleb exchanged a glance and a smile with a wealth of years shared in that moment.

"Well, I think it's time for a game before you get all of us misty-eyed," Drew declared as he stood up. "I mean to wear the kids out so they'll pass out with no problem at the hotel."

"Can't we get more stories?" Zoe protested.

"Yeah, I want to know when Pawpaw realized he loved Grandpa," Abby said as she scrambled off the ground and dusted her shorts off. Drew's daughter had just discovered an endless fascination for boys and was always ready to hear stories of romance.

"Honey, I was always in love with your Grandpa. I knew before I left for New York," Hal said.

"You knew and you didn't tell him?" The look of horror on Abby's thin pixie face was comical.

"It wasn't the right time. We had plenty of things going on that summer. I was just happy we were friends again," Hal replied.

"We didn't really stop being friends," Caleb assured her. "We just needed to get our heads on straight."

"But did you know?" Abby asked, as the other kids ran off when the kickball was pulled out. "Did you know too and not tell him?"

"No, it took me a while longer," Caleb admitted as he took Hal's hand. "It took me a while to figure out a lot of things."

She looked toward her cousins playing and then at the two of them, obviously torn between hearing more and joining them. "Well, once you figured it out everything was okay, right? You told Pawpaw, and he moved back to Charleston, and you were happy."

Hal tugged on his ear as he tried to think of how to explain. Life didn't get tied up into a neat bow like that. "It took time, but once we figured it out we were happy."

Abby cut a sharp glance at Caleb as if she sensed Hal was holding back. "You have to understand, Abby, things were very different then," Caleb said gently. "It was hard enough for a straight interracial couple to be together. You'd think there wouldn't be that distinction if you were gay, but it was there for some. And when we first realized we loved each other, we couldn't be as open as we can be today."

Hal could see in her face that she didn't understand, and he couldn't blame her, things were so different now. Not perfect, nothing was perfect, but definitely better in many ways. She was growing up in a world where those differences didn't matter so much. Change crept forward, slowly, painfully at times, but still it moved. One thing Hal had learned was that they had to try to keep moving forward, keep trying to communicate and understand their differences. Pretending they didn't exist wasn't the answer.

"That's why you couldn't get married until you were grandparents?" she asked, shooting them both a look with thoughtful eyes.

"It is. We wanted it to be legal in our home state," Hal said, squeezing Caleb's hand. They'd considered having a ceremony at Lily's place in Massachusetts but ultimately decided South Carolina would turn around. They wanted to get married in Charleston, where they'd met and made a home.

Abby thought that over, and Hal could see a thousand other questions on her face. She reminded him of himself that way, always wanting to know how things worked.

"Abby, come on!" Joshua shouted.

"Coming!" Abby flashed them a smile and went running off to join her cousins.

"She's worse than the inquisition," Drew said as he held up a beer with a questioning look. Hal shook his head at the offer, but Caleb held his hand out for the bottle. "I noticed neither of you mentioned how hardheaded you both were."

"I wouldn't call it hardheaded," Hal cut in. "Like your uncle said, it wasn't easy then." It had taken a long time for both of them to be at a point where they were ready to trust, to risk everything they had to make that leap together.

"Uncle Hal, it's never easy. If love was easy it wouldn't leave its mark so deeply," Drew said.

"Look who's become a philosopher," Kendra teased.

Hal looked at Drew, touched by his insight. "You know, you're right. And when it has the power to mark you like that, it's very special indeed."

"You know, I was waiting for Abby to ask how your parents took your relationship," Kendra said with a glance toward the playing kids.

"I don't think Darren ever knew," Hal admitted. "We only saw him one other time after he kicked me out. It was at your wedding, Lily." She'd asked Hal to walk her down the aisle, and it had been a blow to the old man's pride. "We didn't say one word to each other."

Lily made a face and touched Hal's hand. "At least Caleb's parents never treated you the way Dad did. They accepted your relationship from the start."

"Well, it took Dad a while to come around. He was pretty upset when I came out to them," Caleb said. The memory of the break in Caleb's family still had the power to twinge Hal's heart, like an old bruise knocked on. If he could've spared Caleb that ache, he would have. "After he made up his mind that he could accept it, well, he treated Hal as one of the family."

"I didn't know that," Kendra said in surprise.

"You weren't even born yet. After it was said and done, we all wanted to move on and heal, not linger over it." Caleb took a sip of his beer and settled deeper into his chair.

"I remember the night Gramps came to see us," Drew said, his brow furrowing. "It wasn't long after Dad killed himself. I don't know what you said to each other, but I remember how relieved I felt because I knew there was tension. Nobody wanted to say why, but I knew it had to do with you and Uncle Hal living together. I had been so afraid the fight would continue over me and I wouldn't get to see some of my family no matter how it all fell out."

"We never would've let that happen," Hal said firmly. "Even if your gramps hadn't sought a reconciliation, your Uncle Caleb and I would've let you see him. Your grandmother never would've allowed anyone else in the family to try to take you away. You'd lost enough."

"Yeah, you didn't get in the way of Grandmother," Kendra said with a smile. "Or Uncle Vern. When those two collaborated things got done."

"How come she didn't knock everybody's heads together?" Drew asked.

"She made her stand," Caleb replied, "but she was also a big believer in allowing people to work out their own problems."

Hal stared down at their linked hands, thinking of the night when Caleb's dad, Thomy, had come to their doorstep looking far too vulnerable. Hal recalled how he'd cried, like he hadn't allowed himself to cry in a long time, when Thomy and Caleb had embraced.

Thomy treated him with respect after that, though there'd still been a bit of formal distance. Thomy had been a proud man who experienced too much discrimination, and though he'd never said anything against Hal's race, and he'd defended his friendship with Caleb when they were younger, there was a quiet barrier as if he couldn't quite bring himself to trust Hal completely. It had been such a nonintrusive barrier. Hal hadn't realized it was there until Caleb's mom passed and Thomy had come to lean on them more, and suddenly that last wall was gone. Hal and Thomy had grown close, and God how Hal had treasured that closeness. He missed that man. Thomy had become more of a father to him than Hal's father had ever been.

"What did Gramps say when he came to see you that night?" Drew asked. "I'd always wondered but didn't feel like I could ask."

"He said, 'I've lost one son. I can't lose another. Will you forgive an old man?'" Caleb said in a soft voice, and Hal tightened his hand around his. Caleb turned and looked at Hal, his dark brown eyes warm with years of shared affection. "And then he said, 'Hal makes you happy. He's always made you happy. I won't stand in the way of that.'"

The group fell silent, and then Kendra shook her head with sigh. "It's so sad about Uncle Rodney," she said and touched Drew's arm. "I wish I could've met him."

Drew's gaze grew distant. "I wish I remembered him more. War can screw a man up. I know some of the guys I served with, how much they suffered afterward. At least now there's help. There was no help for him."

Hal watched the look Drew and Caleb exchanged, the only two ex-soldiers in the gathering who'd both been to war. It was an experience Hal would never understand. Probably just as well, with as much anger as he'd had back then, war might've torn him apart. "I thought about talking your dad into dodging the draft," he said, seeking to change the mood.

"You didn't," Drew said with widened eyes.

"Of course he did." Kendra laughed and nudged her brother. "Are you really surprised?"

"Oh, I did… when did you call me? 1970?" Hal asked, turning to Caleb.

"1971. If I had just been one year younger, I would've missed it entirely," Caleb replied. "Do you want to tell the story or should I? This is a new one."

"I've got this one," Hal said, sitting back, recalling all the arguments he'd thrown at Caleb. "Let's see, I was on break from the military academy…."

DOBBS FERRY, NY—
APRIL 7, 1971

"HAL."

"Go away," Hal said to Lily as she knocked insistently on his door. He had three days left in his spring break before he returned to the hell school. He'd rather hole up in his room, reading a book and writing letters, than interact with his family. He didn't believe Mom's insistence that she missed him. If she missed him so much, then why did she let her husband send him away and then try to foist him off with the excuse that he knew best? Dad didn't know dick.

Lily opened the door with an expression of profound exasperation on her face. She was the only one Hal looked forward to seeing. At least he did when she wasn't intruding on his peace. He set aside his book, *The Quiet American*, with a glare. "Do you understand the meaning of go away?"

Lily rolled her eyes. "Fine, I'll just tell Caleb you can't talk." She turned up her nose with a sniff and turned to leave. Hal was out of the bed before she shut the door.

"Caleb's on the phone?" He hadn't talked to him since last fall when he manipulated Mom into allowing a call. He should feel bad for making her feel guilty. Dad had been super pissed when he'd gotten the bill, but Hal didn't care. He didn't care what they wanted or expected anymore. But for Caleb to call, that was serious. He needed to say something that couldn't wait for one of their constant letters.

"Yes." Lily followed him down the hallway. "Can you ask him to send me a copy of the picture of all three of us? The one we took before we left Charleston? I want one when you go back to school."

Caleb had sent a copy of both pictures. Hal had brought the one of the three of them to school, and it helped to keep the loneliness at bay. He supposed she wanted to remember that she'd been included too.

Guilt stabbed his conscience. He'd been isolating himself from her. "Okay, I'll tell him."

He peeked into the living room where Mom was crocheting, then picked up the phone in the kitchen. "What's wrong?" He wished he could reach through the miles and see Caleb in person, but at least he'd get to hear his voice.

"I got notice my number was picked," Caleb said, his tone hushed with tension, as if he was trying to keep himself from going to pieces.

Hal sat down hard on the kitchen chair as the words struck him with a breathless punch of sick denial. He'd been waiting and dreading this day since Caleb had turned eighteen and registered for the draft. Just as he waited and dreaded it for himself, his birthday wasn't that far off. Everywhere he looked it seemed like the walls were closing in around him. "What about college? It can't be too late to apply."

"Hal, we don't have money for college." Caleb's voice vibrated with all the arguments and reasons examined and discarded. Hal understood. Caleb would never cause financial stress for his family, but this was deadly serious. "I can't ask my parents for that. They would work themselves to the bone to give it to me, especially after how Rodney came back."

Hal couldn't deny that truth, but it didn't mean there wasn't a way for Caleb to get out of the draft. There had to be a way, Hal couldn't handle the thought of Caleb being drafted. His gut clenched with a sickening sensation. "What about your—"

"Uncle Vern has given me more than enough. I'm not asking him for nothing else." Caleb's stubborn conviction came through loud and clear, and it would be useless to argue. When Caleb made a decision like this, it was nearly impossible to change his mind. Hal clenched his jaw in frustration. "Besides, the Army will help me pay for college if I do my stint. It's the best chance I have to go. Good engineering schools aren't cheap."

Hal closed his eyes. There was no way in hell he was going to let himself be drafted. He'd spent the last two years living a quasi-military life. Once he graduated he was done. He didn't care what he had to do. If he couldn't escape through college, he'd find another way.

"Are you still there?" Caleb asked.

"Yeah." Hal twirled the phone cord around on his finger and grasped desperately for hope. "You know, being drafted doesn't mean you're going to Vietnam. You might get stuck on a base for a few years. That happened to a guy here in town. He got lucky, maybe you will too."

"Yeah, maybe," Caleb said slowly with no conviction. "I... I just don't want to end up like Rodney. Mad at everything."

Caleb had gone in-depth in his letters about Rodney, how he'd been worse when he came back from his second tour. Hal knew how worried Caleb was about him and his slow downward spiral. But Rodney had been angry at the world long before he'd gone to Vietnam. He'd had a whole pile of resentments that Caleb never carried. Hal understood Rodney and how that anger could carry a person away.

"You're nothing like your brother."

The thought of Caleb going off to war and maybe not coming home made him physically ill. It upset him even more to know that the Army was one place he couldn't bring himself to follow Caleb. It wouldn't matter if he was drafted or not, or even if a million strings were pulled and he ended up in the same platoon with him. Hal hated everything the military represented. And he hated it more each day. It felt like he was abandoning Caleb, like he wasn't there for him when Caleb needed him the most.

Living at home had been bad enough; the academy was much worse. It imprisoned his soul. He couldn't be himself, couldn't discuss his dreams. He had to pretend to be someone else to survive, and it carved him up inside.

He'd have to find a way of dealing with Caleb being drafted into the Army. Because even if he hated the military, he couldn't hate Caleb. He'd never get Caleb to consider dodging the draft, so he didn't even bother. Caleb barely ever broke a rule, there's no way he'd break a law.

"Promise me something," Caleb said, interrupting the circle of his thoughts.

Hal couldn't recall the last time Caleb asked him for anything. He was the one who usually needed reassurance and made those demands. For Caleb to ask now meant that it was important to him. The phone cord knotted between Hal's fingers. "Anything, what do you need?"

"When you sneak off to your antiwar rallies, remember that most of those guys don't have a say in whether they're going or not. Promise me you won't harass any of them coming home. Rodney's been getting it bad, and it's not fair. The people targeting him don't know what he did in Nam. They just know he's a part of a war they don't agree with, and they take it out on him. He didn't choose to be drafted. He didn't choose to go to Vietnam. Even if he had, it still wouldn't be right."

Hal shot a guilty glance toward the living room, but there wasn't any chance Mom could overhear. If he was caught sneaking out or someone recognized him at a rally and reported him, he'd be kicked out of the academy. Though, that might actually be a blessing.

He couldn't see Caleb yes sirring, no sirring, or obeying orders that went against his conscience, but it was hard to fight against a hierarchy that punished asking questions. He didn't want Caleb to go. He didn't want him to come back changed, to not be Caleb anymore. To not be the guy Hal loved even if he hadn't seen him in the last two long, miserable years. There had to be a way to fix this, Hal's thoughts scrambled desperately for a way out for Caleb.

"Okay, I promise," Hal said, at a loss for a solution. His gut churned. His throat tightened.

"Thank you." The evident relief in Caleb's voice made Hal a little ashamed. Hal knew how angry he was, and he poured it all out to Caleb in his letters. Between him and Rodney, he had to be bombarded with negativity all the time. "Did you get the book I sent you?" Caleb asked in a very welcome change of topic.

"Yeah, that one's a keeper." *The Catcher in the Rye* had spoken to that anger inside Hal and made him feel as if Caleb had reached across the miles to be with him. "I don't know why I haven't read Salinger before."

"I thought you'd like it," Caleb said. It was good to hear the tension ease out of his voice, to hear that rich southern accent that reminded Hal of better times.

"I have one I'm sending you, *The Outsiders* by S.E. Hinton. As soon as I saw the title I had to have it."

"I look forward to it." Caleb paused, and Hal heard the murmur of conversation on the other end. "I have to go. I'll write you this week."

Hal's spirits plummeted, and his concern for Caleb grew. "Okay. When you write, send another picture of the three of us for Lily. I think she's missing Charleston."

"I will. Hey, I've been meaning to ask you... now that I have you on the phone," Caleb's voice lowered. "Remember that secret you confessed to me before you moved?"

"Yeah, I was scared, but I had to tell you. There wasn't anybody else I could talk to that wouldn't freak out on me." Hal turned as he heard Lily's voice. She stood in the doorway to the living room, talking to Mom, no doubt running interference. Mom would unplug the phone on him before he had a chance to say he hadn't made the call. It made him think, though, maybe he could tell Lily. He trusted her to keep a secret, and it would be good to have someone in his family know and still give a damn.

"I wish you hadn't been afraid to tell me, but I get it. I can't imagine it's easy to admit, even to a friend you trust."

Though Caleb was cool with Hal being gay, he wasn't certain Caleb could handle his feelings for him. "I was an emotional wreck that summer. Any reason why you brought it up now?" Neither one of them had mentioned it in any of their letters.

"I... I was just wondering if you'd found anybody else like you."

"A couple who are stuck at the academy too and someone I met at one of the rallies." Mark was handsome, older, and definitely more experienced. He'd introduced Hal to a world he'd never imagined. If he ever saw Caleb again, he hoped to get a chance to talk about it with him.

"That's good. I don't like thinking of you being alone." Caleb sounded uncomfortable, and Hal couldn't resist teasing him.

"Liar, you just want to make sure I haven't scored before you." There was a startled silence, then Caleb laughed and Hal continued, "And for the record, yes I have."

"Bastard." Caleb laughed again. Hal closed his eyes and clung to the sound of Caleb's voice, the sound of home. "Look, I'll call you again before I head out to boot camp. Stay out of trouble."

"Yeah, yeah. Take care of yourself," Hal replied, trying to put the depth of how much he meant those four little words. *God, he'd better.*

Hal hung up the phone, the lighthearted moment gone as worry settled heavy on his heart. Caleb couldn't go into the Army, he just couldn't. There had to be a way out that Caleb would accept. Hal remembered how he felt when he moved back to New York, the fear he'd never see Caleb again. His hands clenched into fists. The disquiet was even worse now. People were dying every day in Vietnam. There had to be something he could do, some way he could help, but he was trapped at home, trapped at school, with no options or freedom.

CHARLESTON, SC— JUNE 18, 1971

CALEB PULLED a box of finished baskets from the back of the station wagon and carried it over to Mom's stand for her to set out. He had three more days before he left for boot camp, and she'd urged him to take the day off to pack and relax. The thought of being home alone with nothing to occupy his thoughts other than his impending departure depressed him. Caleb would rather fill his head with memories of a normal day. At least tonight he'd be out with his friends, saying good-bye and having a few beers. That would provide a welcome distraction.

"I only have a couple more of these," Caleb said as he set the box down at the corner his mom had staked out. "Then I'll start bringing in the supplies."

"Bring me my seat first, honey," Mom replied as she began to lay out the baskets with the smallest in the front. "My knees aren't too happy with me this morning."

He retrieved her padded stool, making sure she was settled before returning for the final boxes of finished baskets. The market came alive as more vendors arrived to set up in the relative cool morning air before the locals and tourists appeared. He loved the hustle of the market at opening and closing times, with long familiar faces checking on each other and grabbing gossip, or sharing new creations that had been dreamt up. He was going to miss this.

"Caleb!"

Caleb spun around at the sound of the familiar voice, his heartbeat quickening. No way. Hal waved from down the street, his glasses glinting in the morning light as his long legs ate up the distance between them.

"Hal?" With a great whoop of delight that had heads around them turning, Caleb ran to meet him and caught him in a huge hug, unable to believe what he saw. "What the hell are you doing here? When did you get in?"

Hal looked tired around the eyes, a little disheveled, but the grin on his face lit up his whole being. "Just now, I caught the overnight bus from New York." Hal hitched his knapsack higher up on his shoulder. He must've hiked over from the bus station. Caleb stepped back to take a closer look at what changes the last two years brought, and his pulse jumped hard. His hair was too short, in that military style. He'd lost the last of his freckles, and his eyes were harder, more defensive. Changes Caleb mourned. Other changes made his blood stir. The awkward gawkiness had disappeared, and time had refined Hal's features into one beautiful man.

"I can't believe your parents let you come down," he said, shaking his head, still trying to grasp the fact that Hal was in Charleston. Even after he'd turned eighteen and graduated top of his class at the academy, his dad kept him bound with more rules and regulations, threatening to withhold college, as if he knew what Hal feared most. It only proved he didn't know what his son was capable of doing when pushed. It worried Caleb. Hal was just waiting to explode, and Caleb had no idea which way the explosion would go.

"They don't know," Hal said with a careless shrug. "Lily covered for me. They think I'm attending an ROTC event at Columbia. They must be crazy if they think I'm going to join voluntarily. However, if it gets them off my back I'll be happy to pretend I bought into the whole thing. At least for a while."

Caleb shook his head but refrained from saying anything. It was too late, the deed done, and if their situation had been reversed, he would've made the same trek. He couldn't even say what it meant to him that Hal had come all this way to see him before he left. The moment Hal appeared, Caleb realized how much he'd needed to see him again. He gripped Hal's shoulder harder, and the defensive rebelliousness in his gaze faded to one of warm understanding.

"You didn't think I'd let you leave without seeing you?" Hal asked and cupped his hand around Caleb's neck. There was something about the stance, their closeness, that made Caleb's heart skip a beat and his face flush with warmth.

"I didn't dare dream." Caleb took Hal's knapsack. "Come on, we'll toss this in the car, finish helping Mom set up, and then go hit up all of our old favorite haunts."

"I'm not going to create any problems by showing up without warning am I?" Hal asked as they each grabbed a box. "I know there's not a lot of room at your house. I can find a place to crash if needed."

"It'll be okay, Rodney's gone most of the time, working nights and disappearing with his friends. Sometimes we don't see him for days, so you can take his bed. Besides, Mom will insist on feeding you, trust me." Hal had been skinny when he left Charleston, and he'd grown taller since then without putting on bulk. Caleb was never going to catch up with him now.

Growing up, Mom had always worried that her boys didn't eat enough, probably a holdover from when she was younger and Grandma had to scrape for every meal. Since Rodney came back from Vietnam, nothing but bones and haunted eyes, she'd taken her feeding regimen to another level. He had no doubt she'd want to try to get a little meat on Hal before he went home.

"Well, I made her a guest gift. I didn't want to come empty-handed."

Between them they juggled the two remaining boxes of baskets, Mom's stash of supplies, and Hal's little gift. Mom's eyes lit up when she saw them coming. "Hal? Oh my word, boy, look at you."

Hal grinned, gripped her hands, and leaned down to kiss her cheek. "It's good to see you again, Mrs. Hudson."

She got up, hugged him hard, and to Caleb's surprise, there were tears in her eyes. She'd grown fond of Hal once she got used to his constant presence, but he hadn't expected that reaction. She patted Hal's cheek, whispering to him, and Caleb's brows rose. She'd been more emotional the last few months as the time he had left at home ticked down. He didn't want her to worry about him, but it was useless to say so. Mom would worry no matter what he did.

"Where are you staying, Hal?" Mom asked as she picked up her unfinished project. "You don't have family around here, do you?"

"Well, ma'am, I hoped I could have a spot on the floor if it wasn't too much trouble. Though, Caleb mentioned the possibility of a bed in his room." When Hal wanted to, he could have such an expression of earnest appeal, it was impossible to resist.

Mom waved her hand, then began pulling dried grass through the outer rim of her basket, tugging it tight with quick, practiced motions. "Won't be any trouble at all. I'm just happy to see you."

She flashed Caleb another misty-eyed look that made him suspect her whispered words to Hal had involved him. She must have realized how much it meant to Caleb to have him visit. He found himself watching Hal as he produced the little present, much to Mom's delight. He couldn't believe Hal was here. It was probably going to take most of the day for it to sink in.

"It's just a little thing," Hal said as Mom unwrapped the embroidered placemats. "My sister made them up for me, but I supervised the whole project."

"You be sure to thank her for me." Mom smiled and tucked the placemats back in the wrapping. "Now go on, you two, don't fret about me. I have everything I need. Just check on in around lunchtime."

"You and Lily still playing that switching game?" Caleb asked as they walked back to the car. "You doing her needlework and she taking the credit?"

"Not as often as we used to. We don't have the time together to pull it off. She flat-out told Mom she wasn't doing it anymore not long after I went to school." A conspiratorial grin crossed Hal's lip. "I guess the quality of her work took a dive."

"I wish I'd been there to hear her talking her way out of that one," Caleb replied with a laugh. Hal's sister was something else. As much as she'd gotten on their nerves following them around, Caleb had missed her antics after she was gone.

They reached the car, and Caleb pulled out of the spot so another could unload their goods. "Tonight I'm supposed to meet Lou and some others for farewell beers. You in?"

"Sure. If they don't mind me coming along." Hal kept looking around and leaning forward as they drove through the city. "It's so good to be back home. Are there going to be any girls mooning over you tonight so I can tease you? Lou's sister still have her eye on you?"

"Naw, she gave up on me ages ago." Caleb parked in his uncle's driveway. "Besides now isn't the time to go chasing girls. I've had too much on my mind. You seeing Mark?"

"On and off. Right now off." Hal tucked his backpack behind the seat. "It's okay. There's a whole world out there and all kinds of men I haven't met yet."

Caleb envied Hal's bohemian view of life, taking each moment as it came without thinking of tomorrow, even if he was sure it would end up getting Hal into trouble. Caleb couldn't live like that. Hal needed the carefree attitude. It was probably the only thing that kept him from getting beat down.

Hal gestured to the house. "Is Uncle Vern home? I'd love to see him."

"He's at his office. We can stop by if you want. So back there with my mom, what was that about?" Caleb asked in a low voice. "What did she say to you?"

Hal's eyes twinkled, and a smile tugged at his lips. "Oh nothing."

"I'm still capable of dunking your skinny white ass," Caleb threatened, and Hal laughed.

"She thanked me for coming to see you. I guess you must've missed me or something."

"Or something," Caleb retorted. Their gazes met, heat sparked, and then the moment eased back to their old friendship as they both laughed. He hadn't realized how much he must've talked about missing Hal. It felt like a piece of him had come home right when he needed it most. "Mom... well it's been hard on her, on Dad too. She always wanted a whole posse of kids. She miscarried two babies, one between Rodney and me, and one after me. Rodney and I had an older brother, I don't really remember him, but he died from rubella. So she holds on to Rodney and me pretty tight."

"It must've been hard for her to let you live with your uncle during the school year," Hal said, and Caleb wondered if Hal thought of his own mom.

"I guess so, but she never said a word against it. Seeing Rodney struggle since he came home has hit her pretty hard. I think I'm worrying about them just as much as they're worrying about me."

"I can't even begin to imagine how your parents must feel." Hal took Caleb's hand. "And if it makes her feel better that I came down to see you, then I'm doubly glad I did. I had to be here. I couldn't let you leave without seeing you."

Caleb stared down at their linked hands. Hal was here. Caleb's chest ached and his throat tightened with emotion. "Come on," he said gruffly before he could embarrass them both. "Let's go see what's changed and stayed the same since you left."

HAL LAY in a limp sprawl on the borrowed bed, listening to the roar of cicadas and the whine of mosquitoes through the screen over the window. He was exhausted in that dreamy kind of way when his whole body was spent and his mind wasn't ready to sleep. He hadn't been able to get any rest on the bus the night before, and they'd been running from one end to Charleston to the other for most of the day.

They'd walked down along the Battery, taken a swim in their favorite cove, tramped through the woods to check out their old fort that was falling apart. Old Mr. Gensler had left his ice cream shop to his son, but he'd been there, sitting in a corner booth with his cronies. He'd invited them to sit with him for a sundae and conversation. They'd ended their adventure at Folly Pier with Lou, Theresa, and a number of Caleb's other friends who'd been astonished to see Hal but included him with a warm welcome that surprised him.

Hal's thoughts kept flitting over the perfection of the day and the realization that his memories and feelings had spoken the truth. He was crazy in love with Caleb.

Of course, nothing was ever going to happen. They were on opposite sides on too many things. Hal was gay, Caleb wasn't. Hal didn't want a damn thing to do with the military, and Caleb was going into the Army. His antiwar sentiments irritated Caleb, and they'd both been careful not to talk about the war. Heck, the only line that probably didn't matter at all was race, at least not between the two of them.

He supposed that if the impossible were to happen, and Caleb fell in love with him in return, people would be just as upset over them being a black-and-white couple as they would about them being gay. Which reaffirmed his growing belief that people were idiots. He was done with hearing opinions from those he didn't give a damn about.

"Hal, you awake?" Caleb's whisper floated across to him in the dark.

Hal closed his eyes, relaxing even more at the familiar sound of his voice. For the first time in years he had the feeling he was right where he belonged. "Yeah, can't quite sleep."

"Me neither." The bed creaked as Caleb shifted, and then Hal felt the grope of his hand as he reached across the short distance. His heartbeat leapt, and suddenly Hal was wide awake in every way. "I read that book you sent me, *The Outsiders*. I know you think I'm Ponyboy and you're Johnny, but honestly, I think both of them could work for either of us."

"Yeah, I suppose so." Hal rubbed his thumb over Caleb's fingers and dared to voice a thought that had lingered in the back of his head since he'd read the book. "Though, I think the two of them would make a more interesting couple than the girls they chased."

He suspected Caleb and him gave off some kind of vibe that showed how close they were. They'd gotten a few odd looks earlier when they were out with Caleb's friends. He'd seen it before, that sizing up and speculation, when he'd been out with one guy or another in New York.

"I hadn't thought of it that way," Caleb said, soft and low in the dark. Hal kept silent about how much Johnny and Ponyboy made him think of the two of them and the little private fantasy he had of the characters. "Have you met many people like you?"

"You mean queerer than a three dollar bill?" Hal wondered if he was making Caleb squirm on the other bed with his blunt talk. But Caleb didn't pull away, he squeezed Hal's hand as if he heard the defensiveness in his voice, the challenge he couldn't let go of anymore.

"I guess that makes me blacker than the dark side of the moon."

The unexpected retort made Hal laugh, and he had to bury his face in his pillow to smother the sound. The rest of the house was quiet, and Caleb's parents had to be up early to work in the morning.

It was no wonder he loved Caleb. There was nobody else who made him feel comfortable in his own skin like him. He could be himself, with all of his quirks and moods. He hoped Caleb felt the same about him. He realized then that he had to stop stressing about Caleb becoming a soldier. He had to trust that he would continue being the guy who'd become his friend.

He'd intended on seeing if he could talk Caleb out of this. It wasn't too late if he hadn't reported for duty, right? But maybe it wasn't such a good idea. Caleb had to do what he thought was right. He hoped Caleb understood that Hal had to do the same. He'd kept his promise about leaving the soldiers alone, and he'd continue to keep it, even when he heard news reports that made him sick inside.

"Caleb, I don't want you to go." The words slipped on out of him on a sigh, and he wished he could take them back. The last thing Caleb needed was someone else piling their worries on his shoulders.

Caleb was silent, and then the bed creaked as he rose and came over to Hal. He scooted over to make room on the narrow width, and Caleb slipped behind him. It was too hot to be pressed up against each other. They could get caught, and then how would they explain? However, Hal found it hard to care when Caleb wrapped his arm around his waist. When Caleb held him, it felt like home, or how a home should feel. Here he was safe, because no matter how much they might disagree on some issues it didn't change the bedrock of their friendship.

"Are you saying that because you're worried about me or because you disagree with the war on principle?" Caleb's breath ghosted over his ear.

"Can't it be both?" Hal looked over his shoulder at him, but it was too dark to get anything more than an impression of Caleb's face. He seemed more serious than upset. "I shouldn't have said anything. I don't want to mess with your head."

"No," Caleb replied firmly. "We should talk about it. The last time I held something in, we both ended up getting hurt. First, I may not go to Vietnam. They're looking at bringing troops home instead of sending more. I could end up on a base stateside for my entire service."

Hal bet Caleb tried that same line with his mom, and he believed it about as much as she did. Hal didn't know when he'd become so cynical. "Maybe you'll get to be an MP, going around base in your Jeep," he offered, playing along, and Caleb chuckled.

"I can't see myself as a policeman. Maybe I'll end up on a desk job. We'll see. I've got to make it through boot camp first."

This was real. Hearing Caleb talk about it so casually brought it home. Okay, so the US was bringing troops home instead of sending more over, but that meant whole units. It did nothing to stop new men from going over to replace the men coming back when they were injured or killed or when their stints were over. Hal laid his hand over

Caleb's and linked their fingers together as if by holding on he wouldn't have to let Caleb go.

"I know your dad put you through hell," Caleb continued, "and I know you were miserable at the academy, but you can't let that poison you against everybody in the military."

Hal stiffened. "That's not it." *Isn't it, though?* A voice whispered in his head. Every time he saw someone in a uniform, it was a reminder of how hard he'd tried to fit in, to measure up, just so he could get a little approval from his dad. It was a reminder of how far he'd fallen short.

"Then what is it?" Caleb asked.

"You've heard the news about My Lai and other atrocities. It sounds to me like we're doing more harm than good." He didn't want Caleb to be anywhere near that insanity. He'd seen Rodney tonight, how that anger of his had turned inward, the suspicion in his eyes a living creature. It scared him for Caleb.

Caleb was silent for a long time, and Hal listened to his breathing in the hot, sticky dark, waiting. "Seems to me there's ugly on all sides everywhere you go. I heard about horrors happening to soldiers too, not that it's an excuse. It's the way the world is sometimes. I remember when I was little, how grateful I was to be living here instead of Alabama or Mississippi where we were getting killed, our homes and businesses bombed or burned out because we dared to want equal rights. Not that long before you came to Charleston there were places I couldn't go because of the color of my skin. I know you remember the signs that lingered even after segregation was supposed to be over. And I remember my dad being called boy by men decades younger than him and wondering why he took it."

Hal turned his head again, his hand tightening around Caleb. He'd never talked about it much, and over the years, Hal had become much more aware of the hundreds of silent insults given because another person was different. He'd experienced it himself in questioning glances and sneers, the way a person would pull back as if he could somehow contaminate them by touch. "Did you ever find any answers?"

Caleb's lips brushed his temple, and Hal longed to press closer, to seek more, but he held himself still. "Yeah, don't answer ugly with ugly. Don't hate everyone because of the actions of a few. You taught me that. You showed me there are people who look past the surface to see who you are on the inside."

Hal bit the corner of his lip and blinked away the stinging in his eyes. Caleb made him so ashamed of every small thought, every bitter, angry memory that he held on to like it was some kind of shield. "I'm not sure how I taught you anything. You rescued me first from James. You didn't have to. I think you learned all of that from yourself." Hal wouldn't mind being a hero in Caleb's eyes, but Caleb was his sanctuary.

"You didn't have to become my friend but you did. This isn't one-sided, where you're getting everything from our friendship and I'm getting nothing. I didn't say it earlier, but I can't thank you enough for coming to see me, for risking your dad tearing into you. I… I needed you, and I didn't realize how much until you were here."

Hal's throat tightened, and he couldn't speak. So he turned to face Caleb and slid his arms around him as well. Caleb wouldn't admit he was afraid of possibly going to Vietnam. He never spoke of being afraid until after whatever was bothering him was over. Caleb also rarely admitted he needed anything, so for him to say he needed Hal made him want to do whatever it took to be there for him. He laid his cheek against Caleb's shoulder and prayed that this wouldn't be the last weekend they had together.

"I know too many people have let you down, but you trust me, right?" Caleb's asked.

"Absolutely," Hal breathed.

"Then just don't stop, and it'll be okay."

Hal's arms tightened around him, seeking to reassure Caleb in return. "Yeah, it'll be okay."

QUANG TRI PROVINCE, VIETNAM— APRIL 1972

CALEB LEANED out of the Huey door, the lap belt pulling snug against his body to keep him from falling as they flew low and slow. He studied the ground below with eyes gritty from exhaustion. It felt like he hadn't caught more than three hours of sleep a night in God knew how long. The fatigue underscored every other discomfort, physical and emotional, that had plagued him since he'd first disembarked. His entire body ached with the force of it, but at least it dulled the constant fear.

He'd told Hal once that when he grew up he wanted to be a soldier. *Fuck that.* Nothing had prepared him for this, not boot camp or his advanced training in the smothering heat of a Louisiana summer at Fort Polk's Tigerland. Nothing.

The roads were choked with refugees and deserters, clinging to what little they had as they fled the inexorable push of the Viet Cong that seemed to have sprouted from nowhere. One force came down across the DMZ. Then another rolled out from Laos, while a third moved south from Cambodia. The mood in the Huey held a grim urgency as they studied the ground, searching for both the downed surveillance plane and any sign of the enemy. All it took was one man with an RPG to bring them down. Just one.

As the sun sank, they spotted the telltale sign of black smoke rising from the wreckage, and Carlson brought them in lower. The steady thwap of the rotor blades filled Caleb's ears, and the rush of adrenaline burned off his exhaustion. The second Huey in their formation moved lower, skimming along the trees. Caleb caught sight of movement below. Two men burst out of cover, waving their arms, and Caleb's heart jumped as he recognized the flight suits.

"There, nine o'clock," Caleb barked, swiveling his body and M-60, hyperalert as they descended into the clearing. This was when they were most vulnerable. The bastards loved to target them in the middle of a rescue. Between the radio chatter and the plume of greasy smoke, they were bound to attract attention, even if the entire province had gone up in flames.

"Incoming, hot on their tails," Jimenez said, the undergrowth shaking as three Jeeps broke through, closing swiftly on the running men.

Caleb swore, the air filling with the sound of M-60s firing, his body absorbing the recoil. The world shifted focus, narrowed, to this one moment, the men running toward them, the blurred faces of the enemy behind them, the thud of his heart and rush of his blood.

The wind from the rotors whipped the clearing's long grass. It reminded him of home, harvesting sweetgrass in the summer with Rodney, or watching Hal trying to sneak through it. Thoughts like that kept him grounded and held him together by reminding him what he was fighting for.

They were close enough now that Caleb could make out the fear and determination on the airmen's faces, the blood on their suits, the pronounced limp of the soldier lagging behind. A hail of bullets ripped up the ground behind them, and Caleb answered with suppressive gunfire in return. The second Huey fired one of its rockets, lighting up one of the Jeeps.

The Huey touched down, shuddered as it was hit. Caleb strafed another Jeep, and it careened out-of-control before toppling over on its side. The final Jeep came to a halt, and a man rose up, rocket on his shoulder. Adrenaline surged as Caleb aimed in that direction and everyone fired at once. The rocket spit up toward the other team as another slammed into the ground near the Jeep sending men flying. Caleb caught sight of Jimenez on foot, coming around to help. For the moment it was quiet, but he didn't expect it to remain that way.

Caleb held out his arm and pulled the first airman aboard as Jimenez slung the other man's arm around his shoulders and supported him. Caleb scanned the downed Jeeps and limp bodies before looking toward the trees and brush. He couldn't tell in the fading light whether it was moving or if it was a trick of the eye. He trained the M-60 toward the trees as Jimenez helped the injured airman aboard.

"Anybody left?" Caleb called out, and the injured man shook his head, his eyes closed as his lips moved in a silent communication.

"They're all dead," the first man shouted back. Caleb tamped down the pang of helpless regret and muttered a quick prayer of his own for their souls and the chance that their bodies could be recovered and sent home.

The Huey lifted and then banked, heading toward the coast. The multihued greens of the trees and grasses gave way to the layered browns of sand and dust. Caleb leaned out to see what damage they'd taken. They looked banged up, and a thin line of smoke trickled out of the rear of the other Huey. Caleb would clamber over her with Royce, tools in hand as they patched up the holes with aluminum. At least putting things back together again made Caleb feel some comfort.

They landed at the field hospital, and the medics rushed the two airmen away. After they were gone, Caleb realized he didn't even know their names. That was happening more often. There were all these nameless faces filling his head and crowding him more every day. It ate at him, but he didn't want to know their names.

They hopped over to their base camp, and moved together with the ease of long practice to get the Huey settled. Jimenez swept out the spent ammo while Caleb tied down the main rotor blade. Carlson checked the rocket launcher as Royce looked over the damage and raised his thumb to Caleb. "Shouldn't take much."

Caleb nodded with a rush of divine gratitude. Now that they were back on the ground, he was exhausted. As much as he enjoyed the mechanical work, the insanity of the last few weeks had caught up with him. He needed to unwind and catch some sleep if it was possible.

He drifted with Carlson, Royce, and Jimenez toward their hooches as Caleb tried to decide if his body was begging more for food and a cold beer or skipping straight to his bed. The hot, humid air squeezed his lungs, clogged the throat, and made it hard to think. Hal had complained about Charleston summers profusely, but right now, they seemed like a cool and distant memory in comparison.

Caleb made himself comfortable outside his tent, listening to the murmur of conversation among the others and willing his muscles to relax. This was his home away from home, and at the moment, Caleb was damn glad to be back. Royce tossed him a C-ration and settled down next to him. Caleb glanced inside his box and grimaced, beans and motherfuckers again. He held up the cigarettes and looked at his companions. "I'll toss these in as extra if someone will trade with me."

"Done." Carlson handed over his ration and snagged the cigarettes from Caleb's fingers. "Smoking's killed my taste buds anyway."

"Nothing can kill the taste of those." Though the texture was worse. He dug into his pocket for the ever-present packet. The battered copy of *The Outsiders* Hal had sent him, complete with notes in the margin in his familiar loopy scrawl. The sweetgrass cross his mom made for him when he was deployed that smelled of home. And the latest letters from his family, Hal, and Lily. Everybody in camp carried something small that that they took with them, something that kept them going, and these were Caleb's talismans.

The sharp, acrid scent of cigarettes filled the air as Caleb dug into his meal. He didn't taste it, instead paying attention to the book as he sought out Hal's favorite scenes.

"Anyone care to lay money on the line?" Jimenez asked.

Caleb glanced up. Jimenez was shuffling a deck of cards with a questioning expression. Carlson and Royce chimed in and moved to set up space for a game. Caleb hesitated, as much as their camaraderie called him, he had too much going through his mind he needed to settle before trying to catch some sleep, and he needed the quiet to do it.

Royce's gaze lingered on him, reminding Caleb of the stolen moments they'd taken, the urgent release of stressed bodies and souls, and it only made him think of Hal more. Leaving home had taught him so much about himself, things he'd never had the courage to face before.

"I'll hold on to my money a little longer," Caleb replied with a quick grin, "and catch up on my letters."

Royce's mouth tightened, and jealousy flashed in his eyes as he glanced at the packet in Caleb's hands. He didn't get Royce's response. There was nothing between Hal and him but a loving friendship, just as there was nothing between him and Royce but occasional sex and the unique bond between men who risked their lives for each other. At least, there was no relationship that would last beyond them going home. Royce had a girl waiting for him, Caleb wasn't a fool. Besides, Caleb had no desire to admit he was gay or in living as openly as Hal.

And Hal never showed any interest in being anything other than friends. He was busy going to college, meeting other men like him, attending rallies and protests. Caleb forced his thoughts away from that before resentment hit him. He did not want to be like Rodney, angry at everything. The same way he had feared Hal would end up before he found his outlet.

Hal needed to feel like he had a voice, so he made sure he had a platform. The protests weren't against Caleb personally, or against the men he served with. At least he hoped to God not. He never asked Hal about what went on. He didn't want to know. Just as Hal never asked him about the war beyond making sure Caleb was okay. Sometimes their letters seemed edited as if neither one of them could fully open themselves up to the other. He missed the closeness they shared the weekend before he left for boot camp.

He wished he could understand better where Hal was coming from. Yes, he'd been sent to military school, and Hal hated the academy more every year. But some of those protestors did nothing but spew venomous hate. They rained abuse down on men who didn't deserve it as if they were the ones who made the decision to go to war. This war had been going on since Caleb was a kid.

Caleb had firsthand experience with hate groups. The thought that Hal could be involved in any way with one made Caleb sick. Hal was his childhood defender. He had to remember that Hal had been the one Caleb turned to when he'd gotten the draft letter. When he needed to talk to his best friend, Hal listened. He'd supported him even though he hadn't agreed with Caleb's decision not to pursue college. Hal had showed up unannounced so Caleb wouldn't go off to boot camp without seeing him again.

Most days remembering all that helped. It hurt, though, because there was a distance now that hadn't been there since the summer Hal moved away. Caleb didn't like that they weren't entirely open with each other in their letters. Sometimes he wondered if Hal held anger or reproach in between the lines. It could be so hard to tell with letters. Some things needed to be hashed out in person.

Caleb pulled out a picture of them that he'd tucked between the pages. He'd messed up the summer before Hal moved to New York. Maybe he was messing up now by not trusting him fully. He'd asked for Hal to have faith in him before he left, and Hal had promised he would. He needed to have faith in his friend. Hal had once entrusted him with a secret, one that had brought them even closer together. Maybe it was past time he confided the same in return.

His gaze lifted, seeking out Royce, who concentrated on the cards in front of him with a cigarette sticking out of the corner of his mouth. Hal had always known who he was, and he wasn't afraid of being himself. That was one of the things Caleb envied about him. It had taken Caleb far longer to admit he was attracted to men, not women. It had taken being shipped off here, cut away from everything he'd known, everything that had given him comfort, and every lie he'd told to himself.

He often wondered what would've happened if he'd kissed Hal before he'd left for boot camp. He'd thought about it more than once those days they spent together. Maybe Hal wouldn't be chasing every guy who had the same inclination as him. Maybe Caleb wouldn't be sitting here, making Royce jealous because he longed to hear another man's voice, longed to confide in someone else.

He recalled how they'd held each other that long night, too damned hot to sleep but neither of them willing to let go. There was an intimacy between them that had nothing to do with sex, something that Caleb had never felt with anyone else. If he'd kissed Hal… what if he'd responded? Maybe they could've taken a step toward a deeper relationship.

Then again, everything could've gone to hell, and Caleb might've lost his best friend. He couldn't tell his parents he was gay. Hal had pretty much already tossed his family to the side with the exception of Lily. Caleb couldn't do the same. Their ties ran too deep. He had spent years defending his friendship with a white boy. He couldn't imagine having to defend a relationship with another man, no matter his color.

All of this was getting ahead of himself, though. He was in Vietnam. Hal was in New York. When Caleb made it back home, he wanted to make sure there were no secrets between them. He'd have to write to Hal and hope he would not only understand what Caleb was trying to say, but why it had taken him so long to figure it out.

Caleb closed his eyes, clutching the slim book like he could reach across the distance and hold Hal's hands. He was worn down, heartsick, carrying too many things in his mind that he'd rather forget. He understood the expression in Rodney's eyes when he had returned home and wished to God he didn't.

NEW YORK CITY—
JUNE 25, 1972

THE CHANCES his parents would be in New York City were nonexistent, but Hal's nerves weren't listening to his brain's logic. It was Sunday. They were in Dobbs Ferry. They'd probably dragged Lily out to a fancy brunch and weren't even thinking about their son who came home as little as possible during the summer months. Through Mark, Hal had made a number of friends in the Village, and as a result, he always had a place to stay for the weekend if he wanted.

Which led him to his current state, heading out to march in his first gay pride parade with the firm conviction his activities were going to get back to his parents. In one way it would be a relief to have it all out in the open, though Hal would rather wait until he finished college. He didn't trust Dad to keep paying for school once he had proof that his son was gay. Hal didn't know what he wanted to do with his life yet, but he was pretty sure a degree would help.

Hal's gaze skimmed over the crowd of men and women who were preparing to march with him. He wasn't alone. He'd bet a good many of the others couldn't come out to their parents either. At least Hal had Lily. His sister knew him too well, and she'd drawn out his secret during a low moment. Caleb had just left for Nam, and Hal had been sick with worry and guilt. Who would watch over Caleb while he risked his life fighting a war that had gone on far too long?

"Worrying about your parents?" Mark said and took his hand.

Hal nodded and gave his reassuring grip a grateful squeeze. "Trying not to. After all, they never caught me once at an antiwar rally, and I did that for years."

"You'll always have a place with me," Mark said. "We'll figure out a way to keep you in school if you get kicked out. Or earlier if you decide you don't want to live with his conditions any longer."

Hal glanced at him and saw he was serious. The offer tempted him. Hal studied Mark's handsome, expressive face. His blond hair was starting to silver, and those bright blue eyes crinkled in the corners. It made him even more attractive than when they'd first met. There was something about an older man that made him hot and bothered.

They had a good time together. Mark was stylish, urbane, and endlessly inventive in bed. They'd been on-again, off-again for years. Mark wouldn't hesitate to take him back, and he'd remain true to his promise to help him finish school. While Hal didn't mind being Mark's pampered lover, the lack of exclusivity wore on him. Mark had many qualities Hal loved, but monogamy was not one of them.

Hal had come to the realization he wanted a long-term relationship with one man. Mark would say he was too young for such thoughts, to enjoy life and sex and not worry about settling down. But Hal couldn't help wanting more.

"I know." Hal gave him a quick, teasing kiss. "Thank you."

"Trying to keep your interest is like trying to catch a shooting star," Mark said with a regretful sigh and Hal laughed.

"I learned that from you." The crowd stirred, then moved forward as the parade began. Hal's heart jumped on a quick beat of excitement, a jolt of nerves. This was it. Hal had participated in many rallies, protests, and parades since he was fourteen. As much as he'd thrown his heart and emotions into the antiwar protests, that was nothing compared to how he felt now. Much of that had been fueled by anger and a need to rebel. This was much more personal.

Hal grabbed the signs he'd painstakingly lettered the night before and handed one to Mark. He turned it around and smiled. "Thank you," Mark said, taking his hand again. "What does yours say?"

Hal held up the second one with a little flutter. "All we need is love."

"That suits you." Mark tugged on Hal's hand and led him out into the thick of the crowd.

Hal's nerves faded into resolve once they were moving. He wasn't sure what to expect on this gray day. The last bit of rain from the lingering tail of Hurricane Agnes had petered out in the morning. It hadn't stopped demonstrators from gathering on Christopher Street or curious onlookers from watching as they moved down the route. He was expecting opposition.

He'd been to more than one demonstration that ended in a police raid. The only reason he'd managed to avoid getting arrested was because of long-honed instincts for recognizing when it was time to get out of a situation and the ability to winnow his way through a crowd swiftly without causing a stir.

He hoped they would be heard. The cry for equal rights took time and many voices lifted together. This was a start of a new era. One he was proud to be a part of.

Mark lifted their joined hands, chanting in his smooth baritone. Hal waved his sign, studying the throng around him. A man hopped up on a light post and urged the crowd on. Hal wasn't sure how many marchers there were, but the parade stretched out before them, and when he looked behind him, he found just as many people. Hal was swept up in the electric energy. This march was for Mark who had been arrested after the riots a few years ago. For Ginny who had been hospitalized after refusing a man's advances. This was for himself. For Caleb.

Caleb. Hal yearned to see him again. He would give anything to see him again. He needed him safe. He needed to talk to Caleb face-to-face.

He thought of the letter he'd received from Caleb a couple months ago. His friend certainly came out in a roundabout way. Hal wasn't sure if it was because Caleb was worried about censors reading his mail or if he had as much trouble writing down his feelings as he sometimes did speaking them. In reality Caleb could be quite eloquent when he stopped trying to overthink what he was going to say.

The letter awoke dreams Hal buried long ago and brought with them a whole flood of what-ifs. He knew why he'd really dismissed Mark's offer. It was because of the hope that maybe someday he might have a chance with Caleb, a chance for more than the friendship that had been the foundation of his life for the last nine years.

"You're thinking of him again," Mark said, leaning close to Hal's ear.

Hal felt the blush creep up the back of his neck. He couldn't be that obvious. He stole a glance at Mark who watched him with an amused and curious smile. "I don't know who you're talking about."

"Whoever's been putting that soft look in your eyes these last couple of months. Are you going to tell me who it is, or am I going to have to wheedle the information out of you?"

Hal shook his head. "It's not what you think." He wasn't ready to share his hopes and dreams about Caleb with anyone, especially since he wasn't sure he'd read Caleb's letter right. It could just be wishful thinking. And he was positive Caleb wouldn't want that information spread, even to those who didn't know him. He was a very private person.

"Hal, it's me. I recognize a smitten man when I see one," Mark said with a light laugh. "And I haven't seen that expression on your face in a long while."

Hal glanced down, torn by conflicting emotions. He wanted to confide in someone. Caleb didn't share much of what was going on in the war. Hal figured it was because he didn't want to worry him. Hal paid attention to the news, though. He'd heard about the increased air raids and the spread of the conflict when he had started to believe that maybe, just maybe the violence was over. Caleb could come home. With each report he wondered if Caleb was involved, if he was safe.

Mark didn't approve of the war or of the soldiers who fought in it. He'd been disappointed when Hal had stopped going to the rallies. He thought that Hal should've stuck to his convictions. But after Caleb had been shipped off, it was too upsetting to hear his friends plan on demonstrations against the soldiers. He had given his word, and Caleb was right, it wasn't fair. Those guys hadn't made the decision to go to war, that was the politicians. Hal took his campaign to them instead, focusing on writing letter after letter with a plea to bring the rest of their soldiers home.

"There may be someone, someday, but not right now." Hal shrugged and smiled. "It's complicated."

"You're such a hopeless romantic." Mark slid his arm around Hal's shoulders. "I hope it works out the way you want."

"Me too," Hal said fervently with a silent prayer for Caleb's well-being.

They turned down another street, and Hal heard a commotion, shouts of "thank you" and screams that didn't sound fear filled. Curious, Hal clambered up a light post to get a better look. A swirling knot of people surrounded a woman about his mom's age. At first he couldn't make out what all the fuss was about, but then the crowd parted for a moment, and he saw her sign. "Parents of Gays Unite in Support for Our Children."

A lump rose in Hal's throat. In another world with Dad out of the picture, he could see his own mom doing something like that. But twenty-five years of being married to Dad had worn down any self-expression that wasn't an extension of Darren's image of a perfect wife and mother. There were times, when he was away on a business trip, when Lily and Hal would see signs of the woman she'd been, flashes of humor that had them cracking up, affectionate moments of tenderness. As much as he wanted to deny it when he was angry, he couldn't. Mom loved them, but if she had to choose between her kids or her husband, he and Lily would lose.

"What is it?" Mark asked, looking up at him from the base of the lamppost.

"You have to see for yourself." Hal pulled Mark up beside him. "Over there."

Mark followed his pointing finger and raised one elegant brow. "Isn't that something?"

"Hey," Hal called out to a man who broke away from the throng. "Who is that?"

"That's Morty Manford's mom."

The name sounded familiar to Hal; then he remembered the letter written to the *New York Post* in the spring in defense of Morty. He had been blown away by it. Hal wanted to shake the hand of the woman who marched alongside her son. The selfless expression of love and support made him ache inside. As he was about to jump down he heard someone shout his name. "Hal Richard Zimmer!" The call came again, and Hal went cold inside. Only family would know his full name.

He clung to the post and searched the smattering of onlookers, a sick feeling churning in his gut. A slim young woman pushed her way through the parade, waving, and Hal's heart jumped.

"Lily?" Laughing he jumped down, picked up his sister, and swung her around. "Are you out of your mind?"

"Wouldn't be the first time you thought so." Lily hugged him hard and then squirmed. "Put me down you big oaf."

Hal set her down as Lily looked up at him with flushed cheeks and dancing blue eyes. He couldn't believe she was actually here. He wasn't sure he wanted to know how she'd gotten to the parade from Dobbs Ferry on her own.

"What are you doing here?" Hal asked, shaking his head.

Lily raked a hand through her curls. "I knew you were up to something big this weekend, so I looked into it. When I heard there was going to be a gay pride parade I knew you were involved." She glanced around her with wide eyes. "I thought it would be easy to find you. I wasn't expecting so many people."

"I can't believe you did," Hal said as Mark leapt down beside him. "Mark this is my sister, Lily." He hugged her to him again, stunned by her audacity and too grateful and happy for words. She'd come to be with him. "She is the most fearless, bold, troublesome, and just about perfect woman in the world."

Lily flushed and elbowed him in the side. "Stop it." She eyed Mark up and down. "Hey. Are you Hal's boyfriend?"

Hal coughed and shot Mark a pleading look. Lily was sixteen. He didn't care how precocious she was, she did not need to know they'd been occasional lovers since he'd been in high school. She wouldn't appreciate the distinction, but he didn't like the thought of her following his example, women's lib or not.

"Not anymore," Mark replied with a wink at Hal. "It's a pleasure to meet you Lily, Hal talks about you all the time."

Lily beamed up at them and then crouched to pick up a fallen sign. "I came prepared, are we ready to march or not?"

His heart flipping funny, the lump in his throat returning, Hal tipped the corner of the sign so he could read it. "My brother is gay and I love him."

NEW YORK CITY— FEBRUARY 9-11, 1973

AS THE bus rolled into the station in New York City, Caleb wondered for the hundredth time if he'd made the right decision. He'd been poised to spend his few days leave from Ft. Meade at home, but as he'd stood in line to buy his ticket he realized he couldn't go to Charleston, not until he got adjusted to being back. He needed time to wrestle with the things he'd done and seen without his parents comparing him to his brother and worrying. At least with the signing of the Paris Peace Accords last month, he didn't have to worry about doing a second tour.

All this went through his mind as the line shortened and he reached the teller. The next thing he knew he had a ticket for New York City in his hand. He hadn't even been able to get a hold of Hal to warn him. He could only hope that the message he'd left had been passed along and Hal was in town and not away for the weekend, or busy with a rally, or a lover.

This was insane. Caleb should've found a quiet place, maybe gone to DC or Baltimore for the weekend. There would be time for other visits later on. He didn't know if things were the same between him and Hal. He needed to know how Hal felt about his stint in Nam, how he felt about Caleb's revelation about his sexuality and hinted relationship with another man while he was deployed. He didn't want Hal to think Caleb hadn't trusted him. Yet even as he second-guessed his decision he knew he'd make it again. He needed to see Hal. Even if they had issues to work through, they would face them together as they'd learned to.

Caleb retrieved his duffel bag, tossed it over his shoulder, at a loss for what to do next. He needed directions to Columbia, and he should find a payphone and attempt to call Hal again before showing up. He turned, searching for a phone, feeling conspicuous being off base in his green coat with his Army issue bag. He couldn't help but notice the hostile stares pointed at him.

"Caleb!" Hal emerged from the milling crowd and caught him in a hug, his hands tightening on Caleb's coat. "I'm so damned glad you're back." Hal pulled away, looked at him intently, and then hugged him again.

Nothing had changed.

Relief flowed through him as all the fears he'd built up were broken down. Whatever Hal believed or thought didn't change his friendship toward Caleb. There were so many things he wanted to say, and every one of them seemed to be stuck in his throat, so he settled for inane and safe. "Thank God you got my message. I was afraid you were gone for the weekend."

"Are you kidding me? I've been waiting for you to have free time. I was prepared to come to your base in Maryland." Hal grinned at him and pushed his glasses up his nose. "Letters are nice, but I had to see you for myself."

Unspoken but clear was the sentiment that he wanted to reassure himself Caleb was safe and whole. He noticed the way Hal studied him, the concern in his gaze. Whatever he saw must've eased his worry because he smiled again and gestured toward the exit. "Come on. My dorm mate went skiing for the weekend, so we have the room to ourselves."

They discussed little things as they left the bus station, Lily's wish to go into nursing after high school, Hal's new round of classes and continuing search for a major. It was surreal. Caleb kept stealing glances at him to make sure he wasn't dreaming. Hal had let his hair grow longer, and it fell into his eyes in messy waves. Caleb liked it. It gave him a softer, sexier look, the simmering anger that seemed ever-present the last time they saw each other had faded.

The night air held on to them with a chill, raw grip as Caleb and Hal made their way toward the spill of light and sound coming from the dorms. He couldn't believe Hal used to say he missed having a winter. He'd bet good money Hal had changed his mind once he moved back north. Caleb shivered as icy fingers crept under his coat. He didn't see any appeal in freezing his nuts off for the sake of snow that got dirty and ugly only a few hours after it fell.

"You look like you could use a drink and a few days of doing nothing but lying around in a tipsy sprawl," Hal commented as they climbed the outside steps to his dorm. He held the door open for Caleb. "I have a bottle of whiskey in the room."

"I might take you up on that, though I'll be happy just to catch up and relax."

Students lingered in the hallway. Others had their doors open, listening to records and relaxing. The scent of marijuana drifted from one of the rooms, and he wondered how far Hal had taken his anti-establishment lifestyle. As they walked along the hall, Caleb noticed the startled looks and comical double takes. Then the odd picture they must make hit Caleb, and he began to laugh.

Hal glanced back in surprise, the corners of his mouth twitching. "What's so funny?"

"Us." Caleb laughed harder, leaning against the wall for support. He felt like he hadn't laughed like this in years, and the mystified expression on Hal's face made him laugh even harder. "What they must be seeing."

Hal took Caleb's hand, linked their fingers together, and lifted their joined hands. "Is it the black-and-white thing again? If so, they're just going to have to chill out."

Caleb shook his head. "Not this time." He gestured at Hal's wild print shirt, the matching vest and pants, the hair that brushed his shoulders, and full mustache. "You look like the love child of an ex-hippie and a disco dancer." Then he indicated himself in his scarred boots, distinctive Army green coat, and duffle bag.

Humor lit Hal's gray-green eyes. "The hippie and the soldier, yeah, I bet that'll turn a few heads. Good thing we're used to it."

He opened the door, and Caleb had to chuckle again because it was apparent which side of the room belonged to Hal and which to his absent dorm mate. A giant poster of a peace sign served as a headboard. A purple flag and an American flag stood in a small stand in the corner. That quieted Caleb's laughter. Hal had it there for him, and it touched him deeply. A picture of them sat on his nightstand with another one of Lily, and to Caleb's surprise, there was a smaller one of Hal's parents. He went over, picked it up, and gave Hal a questioning look.

"I followed your advice," Hal said with a shrug. "Don't fight ugly with ugly. Right now, we have a truce. I'm not sure how long it'll last after I introduce them to the love of my life, but for now we're in a better place than we have been in years."

Caleb set the picture down with mixed feelings. Hal looked more at peace than he had in a long time. Like he was finally living all the tenets he'd protested in the name of without the anger that fueled it. Though he had no trust Hal's small-minded father and weak mother would stick by him when that day came.

"You've finally met someone who's caught your wandering eye?" he asked with a pang at the thought of sharing Hal's heart. "Or are you with Mark again?

"Let's just say I hope the man I love will catch me at the right time. As for Mark, we're good friends. I'm forever grateful for his friendship and what he taught me. We may even hop into bed for old time's sake occasionally, but no, I don't see us ever committing to one another."

Caleb wasn't sure why that should make him feel better. From what he'd heard of Hal's first lover, he sounded like a good guy. Maybe it was the age difference. "I can't believe you've reconciled with your parents. Why didn't you write to me about it?" Caleb asked as he dropped his duffle bag onto the floor.

"I didn't feel like talking about them. Nothing to do with you, it's just writing you makes me happy. They don't. And I'm sure you don't give two figs whether or not they're happy. Besides I was more worried about you."

Caleb shrugged out of his coat, feeling like he was never going to get warm. "True, I don't care about them. But I would've loved to know you'd found some peace with them."

"Huh, never thought of it that way." Hal pulled out a bottle of whiskey and held it up with a questioning look. "Goes to show we need to see each other more often."

Caleb flashed Hal a smile as he took the bottle. "Your dorm mate's not going to mind me taking his bed?"

"Nah, we have an understanding." Hal sat cross-legged on his bed as Caleb settled himself. It felt so damn good to be in a place where he could just be himself. The knot of tension remained, but at least it didn't feel like he was being strangled. "How are you doing?" Hal asked in a softer voice. "Adjusted to being back?"

"Hell, no," Caleb admitted, unable to give Hal the same pat response he gave everybody else. He took a long swig of the whiskey and savored the slow, sweet burn of it before passing the bottle to Hal. "No, it's like my body's here, but the rest of me is still over there." He turned his head and met Hal's concerned gaze. "But I will be fine. Give me a little time."

"Do you want to talk about it?"

Caleb searched Hal's face and saw the offer was genuine. He trusted Hal to listen and not judge or preach, but he shook his head anyway. "Not yet. To be honest I came here so I wouldn't have to think about it, to be with someone who will just let me be. You know my folks won't."

Hal went silent and stared at his hands. "Okay, but there's one thing I need to know."

"What's that?" Caleb asked with a touch of concern about Hal's quiet withdrawal.

"Are you mad at me?" Hal lifted his head as Caleb protested. "Look, I know you were. We've been friends too long not to know when you're upset with me. I could read between the lines of your letters."

Caleb pressed his lips together and folded his coat neatly at the foot of his bed, taking the time to collect his thoughts. "We always stood together on just about everything. I didn't realize how much your involvement with the antiwar protests bugged me until I got over there. That war broke apart friendships and families, and I was scared that it could get between us."

"I think we learned our lesson the last time we let something get between us and didn't talk about it," Hal replied, and Caleb remembered how he'd distanced himself from Hal when his friend needed him the most. The memory shamed him, and he wondered if it still bothered Hal that he'd sequestered himself for most of that summer instead of dealing with him.

"That's why I didn't say anything. I didn't think I had a right to be mad." Caleb couldn't explain why his frustrations had turned in

Hal's direction. "I knew you'd keep your word, and I swear I tried to let it go. I—"

"I let it go," Hal interrupted.

"What do you mean?" Caleb asked, unable to stop staring at him. Part of it was the long absence and finding it hard to believe they were together, mostly it was far more elemental, the tug and pull he'd felt for so long to touch Hal, to hold him. Only this time, those little urges had a much hotter edge to them.

"I stopped going to those protests. There were people there who couldn't understand why I remained friends with you, why I put the flag up in my room. It got to the point where I wanted you safe at home more than anything else. Before it had been a cause, a way to tweak my old man's nose, and after you were drafted, after you left, it became personal. Scarily personal. I couldn't go to the rallies and hear hate talk against you and the other members of your unit. It wasn't right."

Caleb didn't know what to say. He felt like an idiot. He should've known Hal better than that. "I'm sorry. I don't know what was wrong with me."

"You have nothing to be sorry for. I just wanted to clear the air between us. What you said before you left, it made me think about a few things. About what was important and what I wanted. To be honest, if our positions had been switched, I know I would've been pissed too."

Their gazes met, and they both grinned. Caleb closed his eyes and shook his head. "So now you're a rebel without a cause. What are you going to do with yourself?"

"Are you serious? This is me we're talking about," Hal said with laughter in his voice. "I've found a new cause."

"I should've known. Let's see what is it? The legalization of psychedelics?"

"No, one bad trip was all I needed to keep me away from that." An expression of distaste crossed Hal's face, and he shuddered.

"The Black Panthers?" Caleb reached for the bottle and took another swig.

Hal snorted and shook his head, his eyes sparkling. "Wouldn't that be a sight? Nope, final guess, my friend, and if you get it wrong I'm leaving you in the dark."

Hal would too. He'd hold on to the information and tease him like a kid with an ice cream cone he didn't want to share. Caleb let his eyes wander over the room again, taking in the posters and photographs, all the little mementos that spoke of a person and what was important to them. His gaze lit on the flags again and he knew. "You know if your dad turns on the news and sees his son marching in a gay liberation parade he's going to lose his mind."

"True, but it'll save me from having that awkward conversation with him." Hal's eyes darkened with expected pain. They both recognized it was coming; it was just a matter of when.

"You won't lose everything." Caleb stretched his hand across the space between the beds, and Hal took it. He wanted to go to Hal, pull him into his arms like he used to, but he was afraid of what it would bring. Things were different. Hal was gay, and Caleb finally realized he was too. Touches could be interpreted differently, carry more meaning than comfort. "I doubt Lily will follow your mom and dad's lead."

A smile flickered across Hal's face. "Right on. She already knows and joined me in my first parade."

"That's my girl." Lily kept her promise to keep an eye on Hal, and her letters to him had been almost as frequent as the rest of his family.

Caleb ran his thumb over the back of Hal's hand and waited for that witchy gaze to meet his own. "And there's always me." They'd been through too much together for Caleb ever to abandon Hal. He was sure his own family would have something to say when they found out. He hoped they'd be willing to become Hal's second family, but if not, they would just have to learn to accept that Caleb wasn't going to give up being his friend.

Hal's hand squeezed his, and his voice roughened. "I know."

Caleb sought a way to lighten the mood. He was sure Hal didn't want to talk about his parents any more than he wanted to talk about Vietnam. This weekend was for them and them alone. "We need to discuss your dismal letter-writing skills, my friend, or come up with a secret outsider code only you and I know so you can put some of this shit down on paper."

Hal laughed and took the whiskey back. "That would be kind of fun, wouldn't it?"

HAL WOKE up with pounding temples, a sour taste in his mouth, and the sensation of a very familiar arm around him. It was a bittersweet feeling, so close to what he really wanted and so far away. He eased around to face Caleb, trying not to wake him. Though given how late they'd gone to bed and how much whiskey they'd drunk, it might be a while before he stirred.

Caleb's face was calm in sleep, the hard lines that Hal had seen the night before erased. He was less open now than before, more watchful and slower to speak. Despite that, Hal could read his friend, once he got used to the changes. He wondered what had happened to Caleb in Vietnam and if he'd ever be able to speak about it.

They weren't kids anymore. They'd grown up, were moving on in new directions, with different experiences that had changed them and would continue to do so. It ached. But Caleb was here. He'd turned to Hal first. Surely that meant something.

Hal traced his fingers over Caleb's familiar, dark face, the strong line of his jaw, the full lips, broad cheekbones, and the ache grew stronger. Before Caleb left for boot camp, Hal had no hope they could be more than friends. Then he'd gotten his letter with its implied confession, and now there was hope. Hope mixed with the fear that he'd read it all wrong, that he was only seeing what he wanted to see.

Caleb's warm brown eyes opened, and Hal's fingertips froze on his cheek. Caleb's gaze focused on him in a way that made Hal's heart trip, then beat faster. "Who was he?" he blurted out, and Caleb's brow furrowed.

"Huh?" His voice was rough from sleep, and the sound of it sent a shiver of awareness over Hal's skin. He was all too conscious of Caleb's body pressed against his, and he sat up before he embarrassed himself.

"The guy who made you realize that you weren't as interested in girls as you pretended to be." Hal turned his back to Caleb, afraid to see the expression on his face and more than convinced he'd mortify himself with a blush or a boner, or heaven forbid, both. He leaned over and made a grab for his discarded shirt. Thankfully they'd kept the majority of their clothes on. "Unless I misunderstood your letter and its references to our past conversations."

"Well it's not like I could write down that I realized I'm gay too."

He glanced over his shoulder at Caleb who studied him with mild amusement. "I'll give you that." Hal leaned on his hand and studied his friend. "So what was it? Did you have an 'aha moment' or just were afraid you might go out a virgin?"

Caleb's expression shuttered, and Hal felt like the worst jerk in the world. He touched Caleb's hand and said, "I'm a jackass. I'm sorry."

"No." Caleb smiled, a fleeting turn of his lips that lightened his expression. "It's okay. It was a little of both. Coming hot out of a combat zone tends to change your perspective on life."

"So are you still friends with him?" Hal should let it drop. He didn't want to know if Caleb was serious about the guy or not. He'd like to think he was a better man than that, that he'd be friends with whomever Caleb loved, but he knew himself too well. He'd despise the guy.

"I don't think it's the friendship that's on your mind." Hal stole a quick glance at him again at Caleb's dry tone. "Yes, we're friends, no we're not screwing, and it was never that serious between us. He's marrying some girl out in Iowa."

"Oh." Hal gave him a quick, nervous smile, feeling even more like an idiot than before. He needed to get away and fully wake up before he embarrassed himself further. "The dorm's quiet. Now's the best time to grab a shower if you want a hot one." He fled, knowing it was a retreat and inwardly berating himself for making things awkward between them.

The bathroom held its nighttime chill as Hal stripped. He didn't wait for the water to warm before he slipped inside the shower. The icy sting struck his skin, and Hal shivered, closing eyes to rest his aching head against the tiles. It was barely dawn, maybe Caleb would go back to sleep and forget all about this by the time he woke up again.

The curtain rattled, and Hal opened his eyes to meet Caleb's gaze. He was stark-naked. Hal found himself looking before he could stop himself, going weak-kneed. Caleb looked even better in the flesh than in Hal's dreams. All that time in boot camp and a war zone had added muscle Hal would never have. Caleb had always been heavier than him, but now he was built like a bear with rounded calves, heavy thighs, and a solid chest. A thin layer of black hair covered his dark skin, thickening into curls on his chest. He was fucking beautiful in every way.

"Was that an invitation?" Caleb asked, and Hal's face flooded with heat as he realized he'd been staring at Caleb's semierect cock. He hadn't realized his words would sound like a come on. But now that Caleb was here, Hal wasn't going to backtrack. He just needed to figure out how to make his vocal chords work again.

Caleb stepped inside, drawing the shower curtain closed behind him without waiting for an answer. Hal's heart pounded, and his voice clamped shut even tighter. Holding on to his gaze, Caleb reached for him, and Hal slipped into his arms without a second thought. He turned his face into Caleb's neck and clung to him.

He didn't need Caleb to say anything. It felt so right to be skin to skin with him, and he sensed Caleb needed the contact as much as Hal. "I'm glad you're back," Hal whispered. The words didn't convey everything in his heart. The depth of relief, the ache of loving him, and the uncertainty of not knowing what would happen when they returned to their regular lives.

Caleb's arms tightened around him, and he kissed Hal's throat. The intimacy between them was searing and laid Hal wide open. "I couldn't stay away if I wanted to," Caleb replied, just as low. "I need you, Hal."

"Me too." Hal pulled back and reached blindly for the soap, his eyes on Caleb's face. He looked so serious, so intent as his hand closed over Hal's. Caleb guided his hand as Hal washed him, and then Caleb touched him in return, his hands stroking Hal's skin, slick with soap.

Caleb kissed his shoulder, and Hal's throat tightened. He couldn't stop himself from touching Caleb again without the pretense of washing him. He ran his hands over Caleb's chest and broad shoulders. His fingers traced the scar on Caleb's bicep, a healing, bright pink, puckered line against the darkness of his skin.

"Don't worry," Caleb said with a soft chuckle, "that's the result of messing around off duty, not combat. Though after the dressing down we got, I almost wish it had been."

"Was this the mess-hall incident?" Hal asked in a hushed voice and Caleb nodded. "And you worry I'm going to cause trouble."

Caleb smiled, and then his expression became serious. His gaze left Hal's face and traveled down his body. Hal felt the path of that look like a caress on his skin. His body reacted, jumping from semi-aroused to full-on achingly excited. "I've thought about you so many times," Caleb said in a low voice. "I wondered what it would be like between us."

Pretty fucking hot in Hal's opinion, and they hadn't done anything yet. The thought that they might made him lightheaded, and a delighted shiver went down his spine. "I might've thought about it a few times," he admitted. More like a few hundred thousand. He had a moment, when the voice of reason suggested they might want to slow down and think the repercussions through, before Hal told that voice to go fuck itself.

Caleb palmed Hal's cock, and Hal leaned against the slick tiles with a soft groan as heat and want filled him. He couldn't believe Caleb was naked with him in the shower, that he was touching him. If it weren't for the lingering hangover, he'd be sure he was having a very vivid fantasy brought on by wishing for something he couldn't have.

Hal slid his arms around Caleb's waist, pulling him closer as Caleb's shaft slid between his thighs, hard and hot. Hal's chest ached, and it was hard to breathe in the steamy air. He slid his hands down Caleb's back, following the long curve of his spine to the tight muscles of his ass. Caleb kissed his throat and then his jaw and eyelids as Hal clung to him.

Slowly, Hal opened his eyes and smiled as he found Caleb staring at him. He didn't want to forget one moment of this, miss one second of seeing Caleb's pleasure. He slid his hand between their bodies and grasped Caleb's cock. Caleb half closed his eyes on a barely audible groan. It had to be the sexiest sound Hal had ever heard. He stroked the hard, heavy length of him, mesmerized by the expressive flickers that crossed Caleb's face, the desire in his eyes. It was so damned perfect.

Then Caleb caressed him with a sure grip that made it hard for Hal to remember they had to be quiet. He bit his lip, laid his head on Caleb's shoulder, and gave himself over the yearning joy of being with him. Caleb's soft pants filled his ear, and the heat that poured through him had nothing to do with the water pounding against their bodies. Hal turned his head and nipped Caleb's neck. Caleb groaned, his head falling back. "God, Hal."

"I know." His imagination had nothing on the reality. Caleb's touch, the taste of his skin on Hal's lips was so much hotter than anything he had ever dreamt. He wanted more and at the same time, he needed this sweet, tender moment to last just the way it was playing out.

They found a rhythm, stroking and rocking into each other's hands. Hal needed to kiss him so bad, to learn the feel of his mouth, and to discover how Caleb tasted, but he followed Caleb's lead and kept his kisses to Caleb's throat and jaw. This was a new territory for them both. Despite the fact that Hal had loved Caleb for years, he didn't want to upset the delicate balance of friendship and the hope of a deeper relationship. It had taken Caleb years longer to admit his attraction. This weekend was supposed to be a de-stressor for him, not a demand for more than he was ready to give.

Besides, it was pleasure enough to touch him, to watch his lips part and hear his drawn-out groan as Caleb came into Hal's pumping hand. Then Caleb's grip tightened on Hal's cock as he stroked him, and Hal followed with his own heady rush of an orgasm. With smiles and soft laughter, they cleaned each other again in the cooling water, then toweled off and snuck back to the bedroom to fall asleep in a tangle of damp limbs.

The weekend went by way too fast with Hal trying to hang on to every moment and make it last. Caleb didn't mention the shower they took together, so Hal kept silent too. Caleb didn't initiate any further contact either, but a couple of times over the next day he caught Caleb watching him with a soft smile on his face that made Hal tingle. He could be patient, wait for Caleb to make another move even if he was ready to jump on the next step.

As the weekend came to a close, Hal's chest tightened at the thought of their separation while he watched Caleb methodically pack his duffle bag. He remembered having to do the same at the academy. Clothes had to be folded just so and pass inspection. Hal wanted to roll his eyes, but he refrained because Caleb looked so serious about it. What harm could there be by stuffing it in willy-nilly? It wasn't as if the fate of the universe depended on properly folded underwear.

"How often do you get leave?" Hal asked as Caleb closed the duffle bag. He didn't expect Caleb to come see him every weekend. He hoped they could work out some kind of schedule once a month so they could visit each other. His base wasn't that far away.

"I need to go home for my next leave. Mom and Dad might accept me not coming home the first chance I get, but it had better not happen twice in a row," Caleb said with a rueful smile.

"True. If your mom has to come to Maryland to check on you, you'll be in trouble for a long time." Mrs. Hudson was not the kind of mother to be put off with letters saying Caleb was okay, she would want to see for herself. Hal tried not to be envious. Caleb had his own trials to deal with without having distant parents on top of it.

"Yeah, I'm still not an adult to her." Caleb straightened and took a final look around the small dorm room. "I'm not sure if I'll ever be."

Hal reluctantly grabbed his coat and shrugged into it. "Are you sure you don't want to hail a taxi? It's colder today."

"You don't have to walk me to the bus station. I can find it on my own." Caleb put on his coat as he gave Hal a pointed glance. "There's no reason both of us have to freeze our balls off."

"Don't be ridiculous." Nothing would induce Hal to miss these last few minutes. "Besides, I'm more worried about you with your thin Southern blood. I need to make sure the windchill doesn't affect your brain."

"Thin blood my ass. I remember your complaints all summer. There were times when you swore you would die if it got any hotter," Caleb retorted.

"Well, then, I guess we're even." Hal grinned.

Their gazes met, and the grin faded as Caleb held out his arms. Hal hated saying good-bye to him. He hated it more each time they parted. He should be used to it by now, but it never got any easier. At least now he'd have the chance to see Caleb again. One day, when he was done with college and Caleb was out of the Army, maybe they'd find themselves living in the same city.

Hal went to him and closed his eyes as Caleb's arms came around him. Maybe he wished for too much. That they didn't have to have their personal good-bye in private because they feared someone would see them. That he didn't have to hide how he felt for Caleb because people would judge them on so many different levels.

"I'm going to miss you," Hal said.

Caleb rubbed his hands over his back, then held him tighter. "Me too."

"You know if you need anything all you have to do is ask." Hal pulled back to look at him.

"I know. You too," Caleb said, his voice going gruff like it often did when his emotions ran deep. Then his eyes darkened, and Hal's heart skipped a beat as Caleb's mouth met his. At first he froze in stunned surprise while Caleb kissed him. His lips were warm and firm, and the pressure of his mouth on Hal's made it impossible to think. He tightened his hands on Caleb's coat and kissed him back on a dizzying rush of heat.

"Wow," Caleb said with a soft chuckle. "You had me worried there for a second. I thought I'd gone and stepped my foot in it."

"Now? You waited until now to kiss me?" Hal demanded breathlessly. "The weekend is over."

"Well, you could've kissed me first." Caleb looked so serious that Hal didn't know whether to laugh or groan. He supposed Caleb had a point. Given that he didn't know when he'd get this chance again, he wasn't about to ignore Caleb's challenge. He kissed Caleb like he'd been thinking of kissing him all weekend. Hell, like he'd been thinking of kissing him for years. The rush of freeing exhilaration he felt at finally acting on his urges swept him up as much as the heat between them, fanning it even hotter.

Caleb made a rough sound and kissed him back. Desire and need slid through Hal's body as their tongues tangled and their bodies pressed closer. When they finally broke apart, his lips tingled and his knees trembled.

"God, I am an idiot," Caleb said, staring at Hal's lips before meeting his gaze.

"Yes," Hal agreed. "Me too." He kissed Caleb again, a quick, hard kiss that he hoped would last until he saw him again.

"What are we doing, Hal?" Caleb's voice wavered between awe and worry.

Hal bit back the quick slice of hurt and gave Caleb a shaky smile. "We're figuring it out, wherever this road takes us. If it leads to something more, then I'm happy with that. If it doesn't that's okay too." If it didn't, Hal would find some way to deal with it and move on. At least he hoped so. Because now that this door was open, he wasn't sure if he could walk back out of it, and it was too painful to contemplate.

Caleb cupped the nape of his neck, and after a long, nerve-wracking moment, he nodded. "Okay."

ANNAPOLIS, MD—
AUGUST 25, 1973

CALEB AWOKE with a start, his heart pounding, his muscles stiff with remembered fear, and his gut churning. The dream took him back to where he never wanted to be again. Caleb could smell the stink of sweat and blood and spent ammo. He heard the screams, the roar of rockets pounding around him. He knew he wasn't there, that he was now awake, but the dream held him in its constricting grip.

Hal stirred against him, naked flesh sliding across naked flesh, and Caleb clung to the sensation like a lifeline. Vietnam was his past. These stolen weekends with Hal were his present, and Caleb wanted to hold on to that gift for as long as possible.

Long, familiar hands cupped Caleb's face as his ragged breathing eased. "I'm here," Hal whispered, touching his forehead to Caleb's. That was no less than the utter truth. Even when they were states apart, Hal had been reachable. He'd always had time for Caleb whenever he needed him.

Caleb closed his eyes and slid his arms around Hal, holding him closer. There were so many things he wanted to say, a jumble of emotions that didn't make much sense. He burrowed against Hal like a child seeking solace in the middle of the night.

The details of the dream began to fade. It embarrassed him that it affected him so much, even if the nightmares had started to ease off over the last few months. This one had been intense. Flashes of it went through his mind in a barrage of images and emotions. Caleb shuddered and winnowed his arms under Hal's body.

"It's okay, Caleb, you're home." Hal's hands rubbed up and down Caleb's sweat-slick back.

"I know," Caleb said roughly. Hal was home to him. He was everything that the word conjured: security, warmth, and acceptance. Caleb hated the time they were apart and counted down the days until he could see him again. The thought of anybody else seeing him like this, a shaken, scared mess on the verge of tears was a humiliation that Caleb wasn't sure he could bear. But Hal was different.

"Talk to me. What's been haunting you so bad?" Hal asked.

Caleb couldn't give voice to it, not with his throat tight with fear and sorrow. He knew it bothered Hal that Caleb kept so much in, and there were times in the dark of night when he was sure he could tell him, but these too quick weekends with Hal kept Caleb together as he adjusted to being back home. Hal was his anchor and sanctuary. Caleb wished he could find the words to tell him that without it coming out insipid and corny.

He kissed Hal, cutting off any further questions. One day Hal wouldn't be deterred by making love, but that was a worry for later. Right now Caleb needed to crawl into Hal's heart, to surround himself with Hal's kindness and loyalty and put his nightmares behind him.

Hal slid his hands from Caleb's face and embraced him in return as if sensing how desperately Caleb needed the physical contact. Hal's instant response awoke a deep hunger in him. As much as they saw each other, it wasn't enough.

They'd reconnected, taking time to check out different cities when they visited each other, the way they used to run around Charleston as kids. They spent hours in bed. Sometimes they just lay naked, holding each other and talking until they drifted off to sleep midconversation. More often those conversations turned sexual. They had discovered whole new chapters about each other in tender, intimate explorations. Caleb learned sex didn't have to be quick and furtive groping in a dark corner with the constant fear of being discovered lurking in the background. It could be sweet, heated, lingering encounters filled with breathless laughter. He ached in body and heart to think about it when they were apart.

"Caleb." Hal whispered his name with a soft groan.

Caleb loved the way Hal said his name like it was a prayer. "I need you," Caleb said, kissing the arch of Hal's throat.

"You have me." Hal turned on his side to face him and slid his knee over Caleb's hip.

Caleb closed his eyes with a shiver of pleasure as their cocks nudged each other. His shaft hardened even more, and Hal responded in kind as if they were in tune with each other. He kissed Hal again, harder and more insistent. His desire took on a sharp, greedy edge that Hal met with rough kisses in return. A fever settled in Caleb's blood. Hal got to him like that, from the familiar scent of him to the sound of his voice. All those details made him crazy.

Hal stroked both of their cocks in one hand, and Caleb let his head fall back as he soaked in the sensation. He slid his hands along Hal's body, following the long line of his torso. He recalled how he used to come up with any reason he could find to put his arm around Hal when they were younger, how much he enjoyed Hal's spontaneous embraces. That was nothing compared to how it felt to be able to touch him now.

He moved his head, lips searching, skimming along Hal's jaw until he found his mouth. He had waited far too long to kiss him for the first time. He should've done it before Hal moved to New York or found the guts before he left for boot camp. Hal cupped Caleb's face as they kissed, his tongue teasing. The mix of tender and wicked made it hard to think of anything other than the need for more.

"Your mouth is dangerous," Caleb said with a soft groan as they parted.

"You love my mouth," Hal whispered, hot against his ear. "You love it here." Hal's tongue swept over Caleb's lip, and then he moved lower before Caleb could capture it again. "And here." Lips nibbled along Caleb's sensitive jaw and throat, making him shiver.

"I can't deny that," Caleb said, trying to seek out Hal's mouth again, but he eluded him.

"Not yet." Hal pushed him until Caleb rolled over onto his back, then Hal straddled him. Caleb made out the bare outline of Hal's body in the spill of light from the hotel window. Hal's heat hovered over him, and his cock brushed against Caleb's stomach. It wasn't enough to feel; Caleb had to see him too.

He stretched out an arm and flicked on the bedside light. Hal shot him a smoldering glance between half-closed eyes. "I love watching you," Caleb said reaching for him.

Hal shook his head. "I'm not done." He moved down Caleb's body, and his warm breath ghosted over Caleb's nipple. It tightened in anticipation, and his breath caught. "You definitely love my mouth here."

"Hal...." The rest of what Caleb was going to say was lost as Hal's lips closed over his nipple with a hard suck that made his cock achingly stiff. Hal fucking knew what that did to him. Then Hal's fingers started toying with his other nipple, tugging and tweaking until Caleb couldn't stop his hips from circling against him.

Caleb never would've believed anybody would have the power to make him writhe in pleasure. Until he experienced the wicked power of Hal's lips and tongue. He remembered how wrong he used to feel, trying so hard to think about girls and not understanding why he couldn't feel what everybody else seemed to feel. This didn't feel wrong in any way.

Caleb knew how to make Hal tremble too. How to make him moan and ask for more in a breathless voice that made Caleb so fricking hot. Caleb slid his hands down to cup and knead Hal's ass. Hal complained about being too skinny, but Caleb liked the long bones of his body, the innate grace in the way he moved.

Hal moved his head to tease Caleb's other nipple into a matching aching peak. Caleb traced his fingers down the cleft of his ass, felt Hal pause his torment as he took in the sensation. Caleb slid a hand under him and rolled his balls gently. "I know you love this," Caleb said and rubbed the sensitive spot behind his sac. "And this."

Hal drew in a quick breath and caught his lower lip between his teeth. It wasn't quite a whimper, but almost. It fascinated Caleb how much Hal loved to be touched there, and he wondered how weak-kneed Hal would go if he licked him there. He'd have to test it out the next time they showered together.

"I'm not done showing off how dangerous my mouth is," Hal said, moving lower out of the reach of Caleb's hands. He rubbed his mouth against Caleb's stomach, his mustache tickling, and Caleb groaned as he realized where Hal was going. If Hal started sucking his cock this interlude would go too fast, and Caleb wanted it to go on longer than that. He wanted to be inside Hal, hearing his panted moans as they came together.

"Believe me, I know." Caleb tugged him up and claimed Hal's mouth in a heated kiss that left him hungry for more. "Your mouth is addicting, and I love the taste of you as much as I like watching you going down on me. But tonight I'm going to finger you until you're whimpering, and then I'm making love to you until neither of us can move anymore."

A quick, hard shudder moved through Hal's body. "Oh fuck."

"Not tonight." Caleb nuzzled his throat and pressed a kiss to his skin. "Slow, Hal, I'm going to take it very slow."

"You're killing me with words." Hal groped for the lube, his gaze hot on Caleb's face. "Less talk, more doing."

Hal pressed the bottle into Caleb's hand, and he didn't waste any time popping it open. Hal's eyes fluttered half-shut, and his mouth went soft as Caleb pushed his slick finger into him. Hal rocked his hips back with a breathy sigh. "More." Hal wore every emotion on his face, and it was beautiful to watch. There had been times when he'd paid dearly for that openness, but Caleb hoped he never lost that part of himself.

Caleb palmed Hal's hip, encouraging him to move by flexing that hand as he eased another finger into him. The lamplight gilded Hal's skin a pale gold that lightened to ivory and pink where the sun didn't hit him. Golden-brown curls covered his chest, though he didn't have as much body hair as Caleb did. He liked the way they looked together when they were naked and touching, so different and so alike at the same time.

Caleb stroked his fingers deep inside Hal, his cock aching even more as Hal circled his hips and their shafts brushed against each other. He couldn't resist kissing him again, long, lingering kisses until Hal began making hot sounds of need in the back of his throat. Caleb opened his eyes again to watch Hal's face as he brushed that spot inside him. Hal stiffened with a whimper, and then his body went lax as he pushed against Caleb's fingers.

Hal's eyes opened too, and the heat in his gaze set Caleb on fire. "More," Hal whispered.

"Like this?" Caleb touched him there again, and Hal shivered with another desperate sound.

"Yes…."

Caleb couldn't get enough, as much as he ached to be inside him, watching Hal get off mesmerized him. Then Hal took the lube and stroked it over Caleb's cock. "If you don't follow through with your promises, I swear I'm going to suck you dry."

Caleb's thoughts scattered, and his pulse jumped. Hal had a way of making a threat sound like a divine promise. Caleb couldn't get his tongue to work to form a reply, and Hal didn't wait for one either. He guided Caleb's cock and began to push back on him. Caleb groaned as he felt the slow give of Hal's body, welcoming him in.

Caleb caressed him, letting Hal set the pace and depth. It felt too damn good for words. Hal rocked his hips, sinking on him a little more with each motion with an expression of mingled pleasure and discomfort. Not for the first time, Caleb wondered what it would feel like to have Hal make love to him in return. The next weekend they spent together, they'd have to try because he didn't want to let another experience with Hal pass him by. No more missed chances.

Sometimes he couldn't believe that he was having sex with his best friend. Amazing, mind-blowing sex with the one person who knew him inside and out, who always had his back no matter what odds were stacked against him. He ached with awe and tenderness.

Hal sank all the way down on Caleb's cock and ground his hips against him. Caleb groaned again, and Hal laughed softly. "What was it you were saying about slow? I'm thinking fast and wild and crazy until our blood is pumping and—"

Caleb caught his hips before Hal started riding him. That would kill his intentions to go slow and deliberate for sure. Hal clenched around him with another chuckle, and Caleb's cock throbbed. Damn, he made it hard to think. Who would've ever thought that such a sweet-looking package would hold a devil once he lost his clothes?

"Not this time." He tugged Hal, lifting him off and missing the warmth of his body already. They moved, Caleb settling on top of him with Hal's legs wrapped around him. His breath caught on a sigh of pleasure as he began to push inside Hal again. He was so hot and tight…. Hal moaned and curled his fingers against Caleb's shoulders. Caleb paused, his body tense with the urge to continue, as he looked down at Hal with concern. They hadn't tried this position before. "Is it too much?"

Hal shook his head. "No… feels good." He slid his arms around Caleb's neck and brushed his lips over Caleb's. "I like it this way."

Caleb did too. He liked the way Hal felt underneath him, the throb of his cock against Caleb's skin, and the way he had unlimited access to

Hal's mouth. Caleb braced himself on one arm and slid his hand along Hal's thigh as they started to rock together. Hal's hands moved restlessly over Caleb's body, encouraging, teasing touches that made Caleb hungry for more. The slow slide and grind, the lingering kisses didn't last long. The scent of sweat and sex, the taste of Hal on his tongue, and the sound of Hal's pants and soft moans crumbled Caleb's resolve.

Hal sensed it and clenched around him, making Caleb groan. "Just a little more… harder." He dragged his nails down Caleb back, not painful, just enough to make him arch into Hal. "Yeah, like that."

"You make me crazy," Caleb said and stroked Hal's cock, trying to time it with the surge of his hips. The heat in Hal's eyes soon had Caleb thrusting faster, and still Hal clung to him and asked for more. The tension built to an unbearable ache, and then Hal's wicked mouth found Caleb's nipple again, and he came in a rush of heat and muscle-tightening pleasure.

"Oh fuck yeah," Hal groaned, grinding up against him and clenching rhythmically, prolonging his release until Caleb's head spun.

He kissed Hal hard, sinking his tongue into his mouth, teasing him as Hal squirmed underneath him with a desperate sound. He felt Hal winnow his hand between their bodies, and he broke the kiss.

He nipped Hal's lower lip and eased out of him as Hal moaned. He watched Hal for a split moment, enjoying the sight of him touching himself, and then he tugged Hal's hand away. "You're not the only one with a wicked mouth."

"Caleb…." Hal's eyes widened, and he clutched Caleb's shoulders as he slid down between Hal's thighs. His own scent mixed with Hal's arousal satisfied a deep inner need. He kissed the head of Hal's cock, and then it was in his mouth, and he was tasting him. The heavy, salty musk that he would hold in his memory all those long days when they would be parted until they had another weekend together.

Hal's hips rocked as he moaned, a low, drawn-out sound of need and pleasure that made Caleb's heart quicken. He sucked, and Hal's hands tightened, his hips thrust, pushing even deeper into Caleb's throat. "Oh fuck… oh fuck…. Caleb." Hal's voice was breathy, impatient, and pleading. It was such a sexy combination. He teased his tongue along Hal's shaft as he sucked and bobbed and listened to Hal's wordless pleas.

Their gazes locked, and Caleb couldn't look away if he wanted to. The connection between them was so strong. Hal's hand groped for his, and their fingers twined as Hal's eyes fluttered closed with an expression of intense pleasure as the first hot taste of him flooded Caleb's mouth. Caleb groaned as he continued to suck and lick until Hal's cock went soft.

"You know how sexy it is to watch you come apart?" Caleb asked, and Hal's eyes opened. Smiling, he tugged Caleb's hand and opened his arms to him as they settled against each other.

Hal kissed his temple, and Caleb felt his lips curve. "Who would've known you were such a voyeur?"

Caleb laughed and kissed him, their tongues swirling lazily together. "Only for you," he murmured against his lips. He may be attracted to men, but there had only been one who had made him feel as if he were never alone.

HAL STARED up in the dark, stroking his hand over Caleb's thick, rough hair as his lover nestled against him. He wasn't sure how long it had been since Caleb switched off the light. Long enough that his body had ceased tingling and slipped into that heavy laxness that came just before sleep. Caleb's breathing was slow and even, but Hal's thoughts wouldn't stay quiet long enough for him to nod off again.

It was hard to be patient when memories of the war tormented Caleb. He had experiences Hal couldn't hope to understand even if he wanted to. He knew he couldn't share every part of Caleb's life. They weren't the same person, and they looked at the world differently, so it wasn't like they had to be mirrors of each other. But at least before, they would talk about those differences. Caleb would tell him about what it was like to be a black man in the South, and Hal would talk to Caleb about the miseries of growing up with his dad.

Okay, not always. Hal remembered all too clearly how he'd kept silent about being gay when he first realized he was attracted to Caleb. And Caleb hadn't revealed the extent of the pressure he'd been getting from his other friends to fit in. Even now Hal had to admit he was holding back. He hadn't told Caleb he was in love with him. On one level, he recognized Caleb loved him, and Caleb had to know he felt the same. Some things needed no words. He just wasn't sure what the future would bring, so he didn't say the words out loud.

However, Caleb's silence was a whole different issue. No matter how much Hal tried to get Caleb to open up, he remained silent about Vietnam. It was a huge wall that Hal couldn't get through. And Caleb's nightmares worried him. They didn't come every weekend they spent together, but they came often enough. Hal knew from his own experience that talking to Caleb had been what saved him. If he hadn't had somebody to confide in, someone he trusted, with whom he could vent all that anger and fear, he wasn't sure what would've happened to him.

Hal hadn't expected Caleb to have the answers, and Caleb didn't try to pretend he could fix the problem. Caleb had just listened in that quiet way of his with his arm around Hal. It made him feel less alone even if Caleb had no way of knowing what it felt like to never measure up to his dad's expectations. He would never understand what it was like to know that his dad didn't love him. So now, Hal wanted to be there for Caleb in the same way.

Caleb stirred, his hand sliding down Hal's side. He sighed, the sound heavy. "It's hotter than hell over there. And so damn wet and humid you can't wear normal boots, they'd just rot apart in a couple of months."

Hal froze in surprise and then resumed his gentle strokes. He wasn't sure if Caleb was entirely awake or not, his voice sounded sleepy and far away, but he didn't want him to stop. "Your letters mentioned that it was nothing like Charleston," he finally said, to let Caleb know he was listening.

Caleb shook his head a fraction. "Not even close. I missed the breeze coming off the ocean, the smell of the grass by the river…." He trailed off, and Hal was beginning to think Caleb was going to leave it at that when he continued. "Carrying all that gear is hot, spent ammo is hot. I can't imagine going back there again like Rodney had to."

The thought made Hal cold inside. He knew how dangerous it was on the helicopters. Caleb had come out unscathed in body once. Hal didn't know how many prayers it would take if he had to do a second tour. "Do you have any idea if it'll happen or not? How long before you get your new orders?"

"Who knows? We've ceased bombing, and Congress banned further military activity. But there's so much chaos over there. Seems like it's spreading more than it's getting any better." Caleb turned his face into Hal's neck, his body tense.

Hal slid his arms around Caleb and hugged him. "Please talk to me. I know there are times when you want to. I swear, whatever it is you're worried about, I can handle it."

Caleb lifted up on one arm, pulling away from him, and Hal's heart ached at the withdrawal. "I've killed people." Caleb's stark words cut through Hal. "Does that make you feel any differently about me?"

Hal hurt for him. People often commented about how gentle Hal was, but in reality, that trait fit Caleb more. Hal had never seen him lift a hand in anger to anyone, no matter how much he had been provoked. He couldn't begin to imagine what it cost him, not just the reality, but also saying it out loud.

"No," Hal touched Caleb's chest. "I knew when you went it might come to that. Unless you lucked out and got an admin job. Even then it wasn't a guarantee you wouldn't see combat. I knew you'd be in a situation where it would end up being you against them, and I'm glad it was you. Does that change your feelings toward me? So much for my belief in peace and nonviolence right?"

To Hal's relief Caleb touched him in return, cupping his face and stroking his thumb along Hal's cheek. "No, Hal, it doesn't change a thing," he said, his voice rough.

They both fell silent, and Hal turned his head to kiss Caleb's palm. He didn't know what to say or do. Hal felt so helpless. He sensed the struggle Caleb was going through. He'd seen glimpses of it when they were out on the town and Caleb would get watchful and wary. He'd recognized the expression from when they were younger, the times when they ran into someone who made a snap judgment about Caleb before he said a word, based solely on his appearance. He'd seen the aftermath when he'd held Caleb after one of the terrible nightmares had finally loosed its hold on him.

"I guess real life has a way of messing with our ideals," Hal said. "You can talk all you want, but until you're actually in a situation you really don't know how you'll react."

"Isn't that the truth?" Caleb laughed, a short, rough sound that held no real humor. "Remember the conversation we had that night before I left for boot camp?"

Every moment of that night had been etched in Hal's head while Caleb had been away. He recalled the searing intimacy of being held by Caleb in the bed and the raw honesty between them that night. "Yeah, I remember."

"I had been so certain it would be easy to tell right from wrong. I had been so blindly sure I would always know what to do, but I was wrong. It was hard. It was ugly. You didn't know who to trust, and it wasn't just your life riding on the line; it was the other men with you. I wasn't prepared at all. To be honest, it scared the hell out of me. Even more than the thought of dying."

"Can you live with what you had to do?" Hal asked. He had no doubts about Caleb's answer; however, Caleb needed to admit it to himself.

Caleb didn't answer right away, and then he sighed. "Yeah, I think I can."

Hal thought he might have a real chance at getting Caleb to talk about what was haunting him. Get it out in the open so it wouldn't have such power anymore. "What do you dream about?" Hal asked, and Caleb stiffened before he drew in a long breath and relaxed against him.

"I dream about Dong Ha and the citadel at Quang Tri," Caleb said, his voice so soft that if they weren't lying right next to each other, Hal wasn't sure he would've heard him. "We were trying to evacuate before the VPA rolled over. Every time we'd land, we'd be swamped. The Huey can only hold so many people… we'd land, and all I could think was 'dear God' as all these men ran toward us, trying to crowd on all at once. They all looked so desperate, and you couldn't blame them because everyone knew time was running out."

Hal's throat tightened. He'd heard stories, but he realized he'd never taken the time to listen to someone who'd actually been to Nam. He'd only allowed himself to hear half of the tale. He sought out Caleb's hand and twined their fingers together.

"I dream about ambushes, coming in at night for a rescue, not knowing if we were going out to a legitimate call or if the Viet Cong were waiting to target our lights. They seemed to get a perverse pleasure in taking out teams like ours when we were on a rescue mission."

Hal closed his eyes and held on tighter. Caleb had to be just about the bravest soul he'd ever met. Not just for going on missions like that either. He remembered when he'd first come to Charleston and how he'd been the only black kid in their class. He got up every day and went anyway, knowing he'd be facing opposition on every side. The crazy thing was, Caleb wouldn't see it as bravery. He'd see it as another obstacle to be overcome with dogged persistence. It had to be done. They had to make a stand. So he was going to do it.

"I think that's what fucks with me the most," Caleb mused. "I can understand exchanging fire in a combat situation. But trying to down us when we're loading the injured or trying to recover a body so we can send them back to their parents… that I don't get at all."

"It's no wonder you have nightmares." Hal was just grateful they weren't a nightly occurrence. There had been times when confrontations with Dad had kept him awake, fearful and miserable. Times when bad memories would crowd his head, and he'd toss and turn, trying to replay what he could've done differently. He couldn't imagine dealing with Caleb's memories.

"I know you were upset and worried because I wasn't talking about it." Caleb lifted Hal's hand to his lips. "I needed these weekends with you. I needed the peace of not thinking about it. Coming home, it's hard to explain, it felt like I was returning to an alien place, like I didn't belong. You anchor me. You make me feel human again."

Hal swallowed around the sudden lump in his throat and burrowed closer. He loved Caleb so much he ached with it. As much as he needed these weekends as well, he lived in fear for when they would be over. They were in an interlude, waiting to see where Caleb would be stationed next or when he would go home. Hal had no illusions. The moment Caleb was out, he'd return to Charleston. He wondered if Caleb realized these weekends would probably only be a memory then. That normal life that Caleb wanted so badly had no room in it for a forever relationship with another man.

"I was upset and worried," Hal admitted. "You were hurting, and I wanted to do for you what you always do for me." It helped Hal to know that he did. Ever since they were little, he felt that he got more out of their friendship than Caleb did. It was his own insecurities talking—the need to measure up to an impossible goal—but sometimes it was hard to shake that belief.

"And what do I always do for you that you don't do for me? Be my friend? Listen to me when I need it?" Caleb's lips brushed over Hal's knuckles again. "Come on, Hal, you've always done that. You just talk a whole lot more than I do."

"When you get going you talk just fine," Hal replied. "It's only a matter of getting you to start. I don't know why you hold so much in. It's not like you were ever shut down when you needed an outlet." Hal tried not to sound impatient, not now when Caleb was finally opening up, but it was like all those months of frustration and worry had bubbled to the surface.

Caleb got quiet, and Hal cursed himself for screwing it up. He should've kept his fat mouth shut and listened.

"I guess I keep it all in because I don't want anybody to worry. When I started going to our school, my whole family was anxious. There wasn't anything they could do to help. I just had to tough it out. Same with going to Nam; everybody was already freaked out, especially with the way Rodney ended up, so I kept it in. I didn't think about it."

"Well, I can't speak for your family, but for me, I get more upset not knowing. Maybe it's because I know you so well, so I see when something's bugging you. You can put on a brave face for everybody else. You don't have to do that with me because I know the kind of man you are, and I'm not going to think you're weak because you let go a little."

Once again, Caleb quieted, and then he wrapped his arms around Hal. "You're the best thing that's ever happened to me, you know?" Before Hal could respond Caleb kissed him, a devouring kind of kiss that made Hal warm and achy. He was breathless, and his heart was beating faster by the time Caleb pulled away. "You don't understand how much it means to me to know you're always there. How much of a relief it was to see you again and realize that no matter what's going on with the both of us, our bond is still there. I was so scared when I got back...."

Caleb's voice trailed off, and Hal could hear it in his voice. Hal knew what it felt like, to worry he'd lose Caleb because he was going down a different path. They'd proven time and again it wasn't going to happen. Even if everything else failed, they'd still have their friendship.

"You and me, outsiders for life," Hal said softly. "Nothing's going to get between that. Not ever."

NEW YORK CITY—
MAY 10-12, 1974

"YOU KNOW, you don't always have to come to New York," Hal said to Caleb as they entered one of his favorite coffee shops in Greenwich Village. "I'm just as capable of coming down to you." He paused, letting his eyes adjust to the dim light and pall of cigarette smoke in the air. The room was filled with men sitting at small tables or grouped around the low-slung, faded couches. Hal spotted an empty table toward the back and led Caleb toward it.

"I know. Sometimes I want to get out of the area, especially now that I'm almost done. Damn, I can't wait until I get my papers and I can go home," Caleb said with a long sigh as he pulled out his chair.

Hal hated to hear Caleb talking about going home. That seemed to be his only topic of conversation lately. It made him feel small and petty that it was such an irritant, but no matter how much he tried to dismiss it, it bugged him. He had a year left at school before he could think of going anywhere. If he stayed in school. They'd only managed eight visits with each other while Caleb was stationed in Maryland. That would drop to maybe one or two a year when he left for Charleston.

He grabbed them each a cup of coffee, nodding to men he recognized as he made his way to their table. A man was talking to Caleb as he approached, cute and darker of skin with cool undertones. He moved away with an expression of disappointment when he saw Hal returning.

Hal set the mugs down and eyed Caleb as he sat. Sometimes he couldn't believe Caleb wanted him. Caleb could have any guy he wanted. He was so sexy with his slow grins and warm brown eyes that looked at Hal as if he was the only one who existed. But for all those looks, Caleb had never given Hal any indication that he wanted anything more than an occasional weekend together. It made Hal crazy, just fricking crazy. He didn't want to follow Caleb to Charleston only to find out he wanted to keep their relationship as it was, friends with benefits. And Hal was terrified to bring it up only to have his fears confirmed. It tore him up.

"Have you finally settled on a major?" Hal asked as he took a seat. "You know there are colleges in New York that have good engineering programs. You could move up here long enough to get your degree before heading south."

"I don't think I could survive several more winters up here." Caleb shuddered. "I don't know how you do it. Besides I'm not starting with engineering. I'm going to major in mathematics. I can find plenty of good jobs with that degree, and then after a few years, if I can find a program I like close to home, I'll look at civil engineering for a master's degree."

Mathematics? Hal couldn't think of a more unexciting degree. He glanced at Caleb to see if he was serious and found that yes, yes he was. "Why on earth would you want to do statistics for the rest of your life? Damn, Caleb, you'll die of boredom within a few years."

"You're exaggerating. It's a good field that'll give me lots of options. Jobs can be hard to find, and I want something stable. Exciting is for love and sex. I want to know that when I leave work on Friday, I'll still have a job come Monday," Caleb said, his expression earnest. Hal found that expression to be such a turn on. Sometimes Caleb was so serious. Right now, though, he wanted to go out of his way to lighten him up.

"I need to take care of my family," Caleb continued. "I don't want them working until their dying day. Engineering is good and all, but there aren't any programs close to home, and it'll take longer to get the degree I want. The Army's only going to pay for so much unless I re-up. After I've worked and saved for a few years, then I can go back for my master's."

Hal tried to understand where Caleb was coming from, but he didn't get it. It bothered him even more that it seemed like they were moving in opposite directions. Caleb was practical to the point of ridiculousness, and he tended to plan everything out. Hal didn't like to think ahead that often. It depressed him.

He didn't get why Caleb felt the need to be so near his parents that he couldn't take a few years for himself. They wouldn't begrudge him that. Neither did Hal understand the desire to put comfort and stability ahead of doing what he really wanted. Caleb stepped up to a challenge, not shied away. After all, he had agreed to go live with his uncle so he'd be one of the first kids to desegregate. He hadn't balked at being drafted. So why hedge now when it came to his career?

It was at times like this when he sensed the divide separating them in an ever-widening gulf. Hal's chest ached at the thought.

They both wanted different things out of life, and he wasn't sure if they'd ever find enough common ground to move beyond being friends and occasional lovers. Caleb seemed content with the way things were. Hal had tried. He'd thought he could live with what he was given, but as time passed, he felt more like he was convenient. He wanted to be so much more than that to Caleb. He wanted to be the man Caleb loved. The man he chose to spend his life with, and Hal had the sinking feeling that wasn't ever going to happen.

"I'm sure the Citadel has an engineering program," Hal argued. "That's right in Charleston. You can't get closer than that."

Caleb set his coffee down, folded his hands together, and gave Hal a penetrating look. "You are seriously recommending I go to a military college. You? The same man who protested that very same institution on more than one occasion."

Hal flushed. Okay, so Caleb had a point there. "That was different. You have an in with your Army experience. Henry Flipper went to West Point. You could go to their rival. Don't tell me that graduating from there wouldn't open doors for you."

"I'm not looking to become an officer, and the last few years taught me that emulating my childhood hero isn't what I want." Caleb touched their fingertips together. "What's got you so worked up?"

"I want you to be happy. You've always talked about wanting to build things, and now it sounds like you'd rather not pursue that because of a couple of lame excuses." Hal sat back, waving his hands for emphasis. "There are plenty of good engineering jobs. It's not like your parents are alone. They have Rodney, Uncle Vern, your cousins, and all the other insane amounts of relatives you have throughout South Carolina."

Caleb cocked his head and looked at Hal, his thick, black eyebrows drawn together in puzzlement. "What makes you think I won't be happy? Having a job isn't about happiness or enjoying what you do. It's about stability and providing for your family. If I can do that, then I'm happy. Let's be honest, Hal. Getting an engineering degree takes longer, and there is more competition for jobs. I can have a challenging career with mathematics, either with the government or in the private sector. It just makes more sense."

Hal started to argue, then shut up instead, mulling over Caleb's words to what he really meant. He hated that so much came down to race, that even now, eleven years after they'd met, Caleb still had to worry about how the color of his skin would affect his ability to get a job. God forbid if anybody found out he was gay as well. "It's not supposed to be like that," Hal said, knowing it sounded inane as soon as the words were out of his mouth.

Caleb shrugged and looked away. "Yeah, maybe not. Life isn't always fair. You sure have had your own crap to deal with. Maybe that's why you don't understand why I need to be near my family. I love Rodney, but I can't rely on him. Now he's gone and gotten some girl in a family way, and they ran off to get hitched. Things are crazy at home, and they need me."

"I need you too," Hal said quietly. "You're my family."

Despite saying otherwise, tension with his dad was building to a level he couldn't handle. Dad wanted him to major in business management and was unhappy with the classes Hal took. The thought made him ill. He refused to become a reflection of Darren. And Hal couldn't bring himself to trust his mom with his secret or his feelings. At least he had Lily. She was the only bright spot in his family.

"You know I'm always here for you." Caleb captured his hand, linking their fingers together. As always his touch sent the familiar double wave of comfort and heat through him. Hal brushed his thumb over their knuckles. "It's not like I'm choosing them over you. There's no reason why you can't find a job in Charleston after you graduate."

"I would never ask you to choose me over them." It would be a cruel request. He looked around at the crowded coffee shop, pictured the tree-lined narrow streets and old buildings of the Village, and the huge skyscrapers that clawed their way up to the sky in Manhattan. He loved it here, but it wasn't home. Caleb was right, there was nothing stopping Hal from moving south. He'd miss his friends here and his sister, but that was it.

He wasn't sure what was wrong with him. He'd been feeling homeless and adrift. A while ago, on a whim, Hal sent in an application to the Peace Corps. For years he'd had an urge to pick a destination and go explore the world. He hadn't expected the answer he'd received.

"Just promise me you aren't going to go completely practical on me, okay?" Hal insisted. "Pursue both; then if engineering falls through you have the math to back you up. Think of it as another one of those crazy challenges you'd never backed down from."

"Well, when you put it that way." Caleb took a sip of his coffee and smiled wryly. "I'll consider both. How about you? You haven't settled on a major yet, and your senior year is coming up. What was it last anthropology, sociology, education? All of them sound pretty boring to me."

"Well…." Hal took a deep breath and laid his hands flat on the table. "Hear me out and don't kill me until I'm done."

A look of alarm crossed Caleb's face, and he took Hal's hand. "What crazy scheme do you have going now?"

"I've been having problems settling on a major. I don't know what I want to do with my life. Do you remember Mr. Gibbons?" Hal noticed a group of men looking at their linked hands with disapproving expressions, and it added to Hal's aggravated impatience. This entire room was filled with people who had been discriminated against for being gay, and now they were silently judging him? Hal stared back in challenge until they looked away.

"How could I forget?" Caleb said with a groan. "He made your life miserable. I thought I had it bad."

"I'd been thinking that if I taught, I could ensure that my students will never experience humiliation like that. I can make a difference for a few you know?"

Caleb's expression softened, and he squeezed Hal's hand. "I think you'll be an amazing teacher."

"It's not enough." Hal leaned forward and tapped his finger on the tabletop. "I need to do more. It's been driving at me for a while. So… I sent in an application to the Peace Corps."

"That's you all over, always needing a cause." Caleb pulled back his hand, and Hal felt the cut of loss. Sometimes he wondered if he leaned on Caleb too much. Other times he reminded himself that he'd been going at life alone since he was fifteen. Letters, phone calls, and occasional visits were nice, but it wasn't the same thing as seeing Caleb every day and knowing he was there for him through everything that life would throw at them. Or knowing that Caleb wanted to same things that Hal did. "So what does that mean, after college you'd be gone for a few years?"

Hal bit his lip. "I applied for a two-year program. Afterward, I can reapply, but they don't want anybody volunteering for too long." Caleb looked thoughtful but didn't say anything. It made Hal a little crazy because he wanted Caleb to ask him to stay even though he'd resent it. Which only proved how screwed up in the head he was. "The thing is, I've been accepted. If I decide to take it, I'll have training for a few months, and then I can go."

Caleb's eyes widened. "Whoa, wait one minute. You mean to tell me you're thinking of leaving college when you only have a year left?"

Hal was afraid that would be the one part Caleb would jump on. "Chances are once Dad realizes I haven't been focusing on business, he'll cut me off. I figure going away, working, will give me a chance to get perspective and help me figure out what I want to do. I know you think a job is just a job, but it's not like that for me. It has to mean something."

"Have you thought about biting your tongue, doing what your dad asks, and then moving on after you have your degree? Even if it's a business degree, it's something."

"What's next?" Hal asked in exasperation "Do I let him pick my job too? Get married to some girl because he insists? When does it stop?"

A hand touched his shoulder, and Hal glanced up to see Mark standing by their table with a slight smile. Hal hadn't seen him in a year or so, not since Mark had taken up with a new lover. Not much had changed, though there was a bit more silver at his temples, but he was as gorgeous as he was the day they'd met. "Mark, it's good to see you."

"And you as well." Mark nodded in Caleb's direction. "Are you going to introduce me to your gentlemen friend?"

Hal saw Caleb sizing Mark up, and he hoped he wouldn't feel awkward. He'd never worried about introducing an old lover to a new one, mostly because he hadn't been too attached. This was different.

Mark had been his first, and well, if Hal had anything to say about it, Caleb would be his last.

"Mark, this is Caleb, my oldest friend in the world. We've been running around together since the fourth grade." Hal touched Caleb's hand in an affectionate gesture.

"Ah, the soldier," Mark said, and his hand tightened on Hal's shoulder before he held it out to Caleb. "It's a pleasure, Hal has told me all about the adventures you've had."

"Hal's mentioned you too." When Caleb shook Mark's hand, Hal had the oddest feeling they were measuring each other. Which was crazy because there hadn't been anything between him and Mark for a long while. "You've been a good friend to him when he needed one."

"Caleb's visiting for the weekend before he heads home to Charleston." The pang came again, the ache of missing him and knowing it was going to be a good long while before he saw Caleb again. Even longer if he took up the Peace Corps offer.

"Well, then, I'll leave you two to catch up." Mark leaned down, kissed Hal's cheek, and whispered in his ear, "Behave yourself."

"I always do," Hal said with laugh he didn't feel. Something was off about the whole encounter, but as he watched Mark walk away, he couldn't figure it out. Maybe it was the overall vibe of the coffee shop today. It didn't have its usual welcoming feel, not with the attention they attracted.

"Come on," Caleb urged. "Let's head to the Oscar Wilde Memorial Bookshop or somewhere quiet and kick back for a couple of hours. We can discuss your life plans there."

So Caleb felt it too. It wasn't the first time they'd gotten those looks, probably wouldn't be the last time. It rankled. He'd think they'd be welcome here. He tried to shake it off as they drained the rest of their coffee and rose. He didn't want to ruin a rare weekend together because he brooded too much.

"Have you ever asked yourself what you want out of life?" Hal asked as they left the coffee shop and headed down the street.

"You are thinking deep thoughts today aren't you? We're only twenty-one. Do we really know what we want yet?" Caleb asked with a good-natured grin.

"I think you're dodging the question," Hal retorted.

"I don't know. I guess to live the best life I can. All things considered, I think I've got it pretty good." Caleb nudged his shoulder. "How about you?"

Hal stared at a couple walking hand-in-hand and thought of others he'd seen in the parks, some with kids. He thought of the man standing next to him who he loved with his entire heart but who he couldn't have fully. "I want a family of my own, someone I can share my life with, have a home, maybe one day adopt a kid."

"I'm not sure that's in the cards for guys like us," Caleb replied in a low voice, and Hal's heart sank. "But it doesn't mean we can't be happy."

CALEB WATCHED Hal out of the corner of his eye as he packed up his duffle bag. Something was going on with him, but damned if he could figure out what it was. First there was the Peace Corp bomb, but it wasn't only that. Hal had been more mercurial than ever, one minute moody and withdrawn, the next clingy and emotional. Even the sex had been off, like Hal had been in his own world instead of in the moment with him. It made Caleb wonder if Hal had found someone else, that special person he'd been looking for.

It wasn't a scenario Caleb liked to contemplate. He'd gotten comfortable with the setup they had, and truthfully, the thought made him crazy jealous. He didn't like the reaction because Hal deserved to be happy. Caleb couldn't see him being content with quick relationships or friendships like theirs with a little extra on the side. No, Hal was going to find the guy he was looking for and shack up with him for the rest of his life. Caleb's hands tightened on the ties of the duffle as he shot Hal another glance.

"If you keep looking at me like that I'm going to start to wonder if I accidentally shaved off one sideburn," Hal said in a dry voice.

"I'm just trying to figure you out," Caleb admitted as he turned to face Hal.

"After all these years? Please, nobody knows me like you do." Hal picked up his roommate's tennis ball from the dresser and tossed it between his hands.

"I know you well enough to understand I should never let you brood because it makes you miserable and leads to more brooding." Hal rolled his eyes and continued playing with the tennis ball, but Caleb wasn't done. "I know you well enough to recognize that you're hiding something from me."

Hal dropped the ball with a guilty flinch as Caleb made a sound of satisfaction. Hal put his hands on his hips, his gaze focused on the ball as it bounced across the floor and then rolled under the bed. "Dammit." Hal scrubbed a hand through his hair, and his fair skin flushed. Another good sign that Caleb had hit the mark dead on. "What do you want me to say?"

"The truth for starters would be nice." Caleb sat on the edge of the bed, his instincts jangling.

"You don't want the truth." Hal sat down on the opposite bed and reached underneath to grope for the ball.

"That's a pile of crap. I'm telling you I want it. I'm not going to break because it's hard to hear." Caleb had the craziest feeling Hal didn't want to meet his gaze. "What is it? Have you found someone else? You think I'd be mad at you for that? If you've met someone, that's great." As he said the words, his throat tightened in denial.

Hal seemed to shrink in even more, and he shook his head. "You'd be happy if I found somebody else?"

Caleb shot him a look, getting the feeling that he'd stepped in it. Well, if he wanted Hal to be honest with him, then Caleb needed to do the same. "Well no, I'd hate it. But I know you're looking for that special guy who's going to give you everything you want, and I can't. So when that day comes, I'll hate it, but I'll understand."

His answer didn't appear to comfort Hal because he wouldn't even look at Caleb. "I... I feel like an idiot. I.... We can't have sex anymore."

"Why not?" Caleb stared at Hal in shock, his brain churning as he tried to figure out the reason for this sudden reversal. They'd never talked about being exclusive to each other. Caleb had always considered this to be more of a casual thing, even if he hadn't been with anyone else. The thought of Hal having another lover while being with him made him cold inside. "Are you afraid you might've picked up something?"

Hal shook his head again, his hands tightening on his knees. "No, nothing like that. I just need to go back to the way things were."

There was no such thing as going back, and perhaps that was something they should've considered before they let this get so far. It was too late now. Caleb sighed and ran a hand over his cropped hair. There was something else Hal wasn't telling him, and Caleb wasn't leaving until he heard him out.

"Okay," he said slowly, and Hal closed his eyes, pressing his lips together in a tight line. What the hell was going on? It was like everything Caleb said or did cut him up inside, and he didn't understand why. He wanted to go to him, wrap his arms around him, but he was afraid of the rebuff. "What is it? Is it not good for you anymore?"

Maybe Hal wasn't as attracted to him as Caleb was. That hit his ego because Hal turned him on like crazy, everything from the way he smelled, to the way he tilted his head when he considered a question, to his little laugh.

This time Hal did meet his gaze, and the last time he looked this upset was before the move. "Not in the way you're implying. It's nothing that you're doing, it's all me." Caleb started to go to him but stopped when Hal shook his head.

"Is it because of Mark?" Caleb said, and jealousy twisted into an ugly knot. He'd seen the possessive way the older man had been with Hal, angling his body as if he could shield Hal. It had pissed him off then, and it pissed him off now.

Hal straightened, his head tilting in confusion. "Mark? He has nothing to do with this."

"Have you ever told him we're together?" Caleb didn't think so. He had the impression Mark would've said something if he'd known.

"No."

The ache hit hard and fast. Hal wasn't holding back today. "Why not?" Caleb tried to hide his hurt, the sting to his pride, but from the look of sympathy in Hal's eyes, he'd failed.

"Well, for one, it would've felt like you were another notch on the bedpost, and it's not that way with us. I thought you weren't too keen on the idea of us being seen as more than friends. Maybe I was wrong. I'm sorry." Hal looked at him with cautious hope. "Was I wrong?"

Caleb sighed and shook his head. "No, I'm sorry. I'm jumping at things." Mark set his teeth on edge. "I got the impression he wasn't too happy about seeing us together, that's all."

Hal glanced away, disappointment evident in the downward turn of his mouth. Caleb felt like he was scrambling on a ledge, trying to keep from falling, and everything he said only made his grip loosen more. "What's going on? Talk to me. Why don't you want to sleep with me?"

"Look, you're heading to Charleston anyway, what's it matter?" Hal shrugged and picked at his jeans with nervous fingers. "You're not going to be able to come up every few months to get what you want anyway."

"What's the difference? I know you've been with other guys, and not all of them meant something to you. We're friends. At least we give a damn about each other. I don't see the harm in it. What's gotten into you?" Caleb asked, trying not to sound as desperate as he felt. They were friends who occasionally screwed. Everybody won all around.

"I'm sorry." Hal looked miserable with his arms wrapped around himself. "I tried; I really tried to keep it separate. I wanted to be what you needed, and I thought I'd be okay with that and nothing more."

The thought that Hal might be more accepting of someone else's touch instead of Caleb's hurt. It hurt badly like raw nerves that had been abraded and exposed. "Just talk to me, dammit Hal, don't shut down. How come you can go to someone else for sex and not me?"

Hal's head came up, and his chin stuck out at its most stubborn tilt. "I don't love them."

That didn't make one lick of sense. Of course Hal loved him. Caleb felt the same. He was all set to tell Hal that, but the expression in his eyes stopped him, an entreaty, a hope, that made him reexamine Hal's words. He loved Caleb. Not as a best friend kind of love. Not as a brother kind of love. This was a forever kind of love. The kind that spoke of a commitment above friends and family.

The kind that said "not only do I love you, but I choose you to keep that faith."

Caleb stood up as it all came together in a rush of exhilaration and terror. He'd grown up with a certain vision for his life, an ideal based on his parents. He'd get married, have a few kids, provide for them, raise them right. It had taken him a long time to admit he wasn't going to have that. That he was going to be a bachelor uncle to Rodney's kids just like Uncle Vern had been to them. It had been hard, but he couldn't ask any woman he cared for enough to be the mother of his kids, to live a lie.

His family was everything to him. They were the bedrock of his entire life. They'd known Hal long enough that Caleb was pretty sure they'd look beyond the color of his skin, but living in a committed, open relationship with another man… that was a whole different story. Dad was having a hard enough time coming to terms with Rodney's impending fatherhood. There was no way this wouldn't cause a new implosion.

As much as he cared deeply about Hal, as much as he loved him in his own way, he couldn't give him what he wanted most, what he deserved. Caleb didn't know what to do about it. He needed time to think, to figure it all out. Maybe he could let Hal off the hook while he did.

"Don't you dare lie to me." The harshness in Hal's voice halted the words before Caleb had a chance to say anything. Hal's hands had tightened around his elbows until the bones stood out on his skin. "If you can't tell me how you really feel, then don't make something up. It may make you sleep easier, but I know it'll be bullshit."

Caleb's lips pressed together and he nodded. No, he couldn't pretend with Hal, as much as it would make dealing with this easier. He couldn't say he didn't feel the same way when he did. "Okay." Caleb drew in a breath, trying to right his world, and only feeling hollow inside. "I'm sorry. I don't want to make you feel like that, and if you want to go back to the way things were, I… I understand." Saying the words made him sick inside, like he'd carved a piece of himself out.

Hal nodded too, though he didn't look any happier than he had a moment ago. Caleb started to reach out to him, to slip his arm around Hal's shoulders, and then it struck him. No more holding Hal, no more kissing him, or making love late in the night in the comfort of Hal's embrace… the loss cut sharply, and Caleb let his arm fall to the side. Hal blinked rapidly and looked away. Caleb wanted to yell "this is what you wanted."

But it wasn't, not really. Hal wanted to be honest with him, though it hurt them both. Hal wanted to be with him in every way, and he understood Caleb couldn't, so he'd accept that they'd be friends only. At least Caleb hoped he'd accept that and not distance himself or give him a silent treatment. That would just kill him.

"I do, you know," Caleb said, and prayed Hal would understand what he was saying. "But I can't right now, maybe I never will. I need time. I don't know. This is a lot to drop on a guy."

"You need time, and I need space while you figure it out." Hal gave him a sad smile. "What a pair we make."

Caleb wanted to return to the last kiss they shared and do it all over, knowing he might not ever get another. His entire being ached, and from the look of Hal, he was hurting just as bad. "Come here," he said roughly.

Hal hesitated, raw conflict in his gaze, and then he came over and let Caleb draw him into his arms. Ever since they were little Hal had fit against him like he belonged there. Caleb closed his eyes and drew in his scent as Hal relaxed. "Whatever happens, we'll always be friends right?" It scared him that it was even a question, but Hal was heartbroken, what if he responded by pulling away?

"Always," Hal said in a muffled voice and held him tighter.

"Okay." Caleb took a deep breath of relief. "We'll figure this out too."

DOBBS FERRY, NY—
AUGUST 18, 1974

"IT'S NOT too late to change your mind." Lily opened Hal's dresser drawer and began throwing socks and undershirts at him. She was pissed because every other throw hit him in the head. Not that he blamed her. Depending on how tonight went, they might not get to see each other again before he left the country. He wasn't holding his breath for a last-minute miracle.

"Oh it's too late, even if I wanted to, which I don't. I won't be able to get my housing back at school or the classes I need. I could always couch hop with my friends in the Village, but that would get old fast." Hal stuffed the clothes away into the battered trunk he'd been carrying around since his academy days. "Once Dad realizes I haven't taken one business class in the last three years he's going to flip his lid. I can't hide it any longer."

Lily didn't look convinced, and Hal felt like he was abandoning her. He wished he could find a way to explain to her that he needed to get away for a while and figure out what he wanted out of life. He needed to feel like he was doing something good and useful while he weathered his way through his self-discovery.

"Answer me this, what would you do if Dad decided he wasn't going to pay for you to go to nursing school?" Hal asked. "Would you sit meekly by and study something he felt was more suited for his daughter?"

Lily grimaced and didn't respond, but the last pair of socks sailed into the trunk, so at least she was listening. "But Ghana? That's halfway on the other side of the world." Lily flopped down on Hal's bed with a mournful expression. "I'm going to miss you."

"It's only for two years." Hal paused in the midst of his sorting and packing. He was having trouble deciding what had to go, what he could fit into the few boxes he'd brought for storage, and what he'd have to sacrifice if Dad went on a tossing spree while he was gone. Hal smiled half-heartedly at her and tugged on one of her wayward curls.

"I was expecting you to go to Charleston." Lily impatiently pulled her hair out of his reach. "I could handle that. I had been preparing for that day for years."

Hal turned away, pain lancing through his heart. "No, there's going to be no Charleston for me." He had no intention of letting his friendship with Caleb wither. He'd let himself tumble into a dream he couldn't have. It was time to wake up. He was sure that given time, he'd be able to visit Caleb without it hurting anymore, but visiting Caleb was totally different from living near him. Hal didn't trust himself to be sensible.

"Okay, what gives?" Lily asked, her voice sharpening. "Every time I mention Caleb or Charleston you look like an abandoned puppy."

Hal winced. He was afraid she wasn't exaggerating. "Nothing I didn't see coming." Hal's gaze fell on his battered copy of *The Outsiders*. Caleb had returned the book a couple weeks ago, and Hal hadn't been able to bring himself to open it. He hesitated, then grabbed it and tucked it away between the layers of clothes in the trunk. He'd look at Caleb's notes after he settled in. He couldn't avoid it any longer, not if he was serious about moving beyond this and going back to the way things used to be.

Lily handed him his small bag of toiletries and a sewing kit. "You and Caleb don't butt heads often, but when you do, you tend to make it spectacular. What happened?"

"It's not what you think." Hal shut the lid and turned to face Lily. He'd never confided in her about his relationships, and he'd never confessed his feelings for Caleb, but it was going to be a long time before he saw her again, and she was the only one in his family he could talk to. "I let myself fall in love with Caleb knowing it wouldn't be able to go anywhere."

Lily's lips formed an "O" of surprise, and then her expression softened into rueful sympathy. "Caleb does inspire that. I swear I was in love with him when I was younger, and he never noticed me." She gave Hal a searching look. "Only you."

"Yeah, well. It's a moot point." Hal sat back on his heels and looked around his bedroom. He'd managed to pare his belongings down to what was in the trunk and a few boxes he wouldn't feel too guilty about stashing at Mark's if needed. His stomach twisted. "I suppose it's time. Do you remember the plan?"

Lily raked a hand through her hair, looking as ill as Hal felt. "Yeah. If it looks like Dad is going to be completely unreasonable I call Mark who will come and get you."

Hal rubbed his palms on his jeans. It was crazy. He was twenty-one. He'd gotten used to the idea of being on his own. But this would upset the uneasy truce he'd found with Dad. He'd eventually accept Hal's open defiance over his major. He'd give Hal hell for dropping out of college, and nothing Hal could say would convince the man he'd finish on his own dime. But the real stumbling block would be the Peace Corps. There was nothing in Dad's personality that would understand Hal's desire to go.

He sighed and closed his eyes. He should've eased his parents into it. He should've told them when he first made the decision to go. It wasn't fair to spring it on them like this, but he selfishly wanted a few more months with the illusion of peace. Lily squeezed his shoulder. "Come on, we're being overly dramatic. Dad will yell, and Mom will cry, but it'll be okay."

Lily's little pep talk would have more impact if she didn't sound so doubtful. At least she'd be leaving for college herself soon. His sister would thrive at nursing school. She took to challenges with zeal and boundless energy.

Hal rose, helped Lily up, and went in search of his parents with a nervousness he hoped didn't show. Dad sat enthroned in his TV chair, watching the news with a beer near his hand. Hal studied Dad's bitter expression and wondered why he tried to please him. They kept playing the same game in a vicious circle, and neither was happy with the results.

Deep down Dad knew Hal was gay, and nothing was going to change the fact. His old man couldn't accept or acknowledge the truth. Therefore Hal couldn't win. His only option left was to stop trying to pretend he'd be the perfect son if he just tried harder.

Mom came into the living room, drying her hands on a towel and shooting him a nervous, pleading look. Hal sensed Lily hovering behind him, and he searched for a good way to start while his stomach churned. "Mom, Dad, I need to talk to you about school."

Dad's brows snapped together in a frown. "Did you get kicked out?"

"No," Hal replied evenly. This was going to be hard enough without rising to Dad's bait. "I've been thinking about majors—"

"There's nothing to think about," Dad interrupted and turned his attention to the TV. "You're majoring in business and getting your broker's license."

"Actually, I'm not." Hal took a deep breath as Dad shot him an irritated glare. Mom pressed her lips together and looked down at her folded hands. "I'm not sure what I want to do."

"Well I'm not paying for you to figure it out. I told you that." Dad pointed a finger in his direction. "Get your shit together or join the Army. They'll help you figure it out fast."

"You're right. It's not fair for you to continue to pay for college while I figure it out." Hal shoved his hands in his pockets and kept his gaze steady on his dad who looked pleased with that admission. Hopefully, it would ease the way for the second part. "So, I dropped out."

"Oh, Hal," Mom whispered, and Hal squirmed inside at the disappointment in her voice.

"What kind of a moron are you? How do you expect to get anywhere if you don't finish school?" Dad sat up straighter, and his face began to redden, always a danger sign.

"Wait, before you get too upset, I do plan on finishing, but in the meantime I've taken a job, and it starts in a week. Think of it as a two-year internship." Hal allowed cautious hope to sneak in when his parents exchanged glances. At least they were listening. "When I'm done, I'll go back to school and get my degree."

"What kind of job?" Mom asked. "How will it help you figure it out if school didn't?"

"It's intensive, and I'll be exposed to all kinds of fields." Hal hedged, and from the expressions on his parents' faces, they recognized the tactic.

"Hal joined the Peace Corps," Lily said, coming to stand beside him. She linked her arm through his in a show of support even as he groaned inwardly. "He's going to Ghana in a week."

Dad clenched his jaw. "Absolutely not. No son of mine is going off to do some hippie, do-gooder—"

"I am. I'm packed. I have my flight, all my shots. People are waiting for me in Accra." Hal silently begged Dad to shut up and listen for once.

Dad looked at Lily, then Mom, before his gaze landed back on Hal. "I want a word with you in private, right now."

Hal squeezed Lily's arm before she protested. If he didn't have it out with Dad, he'd never be able to stand his ground with him. Lily made a sound under her breath and walked out. Mom slowly rose and made her way over to Hal. She paused and studied his expression for a long moment before following Lily out.

"I'm only going to say this once," Dad said, rising from his chair. "If you go, I'm cutting off all support. You had no business quitting school and doing something as asinine as joining the Peace Corps."

"I know this isn't what you wanted for me, but I have to live my own life. If that means you're cutting me off I'm prepared to do it on my own." Dad didn't understand, but joining the Peace Corps had given Hal the first sense of pride he'd had in himself in a long time.

Dad's nostrils flared, and his lips formed a thin, white line. "You'll come crawling back. Just you wait."

"Never. Going. To. Happen," Hal replied, in a cold, quiet voice. Hal and his dad stared at each other in an echo of the confrontation years ago.

"You ungrateful little shit." Dad's eyes went flat with rage. "You've done nothing but mooch off this family since the day you were born."

"Bullshit." Hal clenched his jaw. "I did everything I could to make you happy when I was a kid. Straight As, standing up to the bullies at school, keeping my room perfectly clean, nothing I ever did pleased you. I even did well at that damned military school, and it wasn't enough."

"All I ever wanted was for you to man the fuck up, and you're a prissy little shit. Always fucking crying and whining. You make me sick." Hal stiffened under the onslaught, his throat tightening. "Every time I look at you, I think how the hell could he be my son?"

"Well I am. Anybody looking at me would know I belong to you. Even worse I inherited your temper, and it's something I have to fight against every day. So don't bother trying to deny me."

"I refuse to acknowledge a fucking faggot as my son."

There it was finally out. The truth they'd been dancing around since Hal discovered his fascination with boys. "What's wrong, Dad? Do I remind you of someone you used to know? Is that how you could look at me and know what I was when I was still a boy?"

Dad's face darkened even more, the red purpling to an ugly color. He grabbed Hal's shoulders and shook him hard. Hal's heart pounded, and his palms went slick with sweat. He'd never seen his dad this enraged. "Dad."

"I'm not your dad!" Darren shoved him back, and Hal's stomach twisted into a sick knot. "Get out of this house and don't come back. You're not welcome here anymore."

"Wait, don't do this," Hal said hoarsely.

"Get the fuck out of my house!" Darren grabbed the beer bottle off the end table and threw it at him. Hal flinched as it sailed just over his shoulder and shattered against the wall. "You have an hour. When I get back you'd better be gone, or I'm calling the cops and having them haul your pansy ass out of here."

"Dammit, will you just listen to me for once!" Hal shouted to Darren's back as he stalked toward the door. "You can kick me out, but it's never going to change the fact that I'm your son."

Darren slammed the front door, and Hal's hand tightened into a fist. He was overcome with the urge to chase him down and make him listen. But the image of the physical confrontation that would follow cooled some of the sick rage coiling in him. Chasing after Darren would solve nothing. It would only give Hal one more bad memory to add to the rest.

He turned away and saw Lily watching him, her face white, her eyes wide with shock as she spoke on the phone. Well, that was something. Mark would be on his way. Hal took the stairs to his room two at a time. Dammit, he didn't want Mark to come rescue him. Hal slammed his door open and dragged the trunk out into the hallway before returning to grab his boxes.

At the sound of a light knock, Hal spun around, biting his lip to keep from snarling at the intrusion. Mom stood there, her hands twisting together. She looked so old and her lost expression stole all his rage away.

"Mom—"

"Do you remember how upset you were when I sided with your dad about the academy?" she asked before Hal could say anything else. Hal nodded as she studied him with a penetrating stare. He would never forget that betrayal, and it had been a hard-fought battle to let go of that anger and forgive her. "Do you want to know why I agreed whole-heartedly?"

Hal sat down heavily on his bed and nodded again, unable to speak past the new quick stab of pain on top of his bruised and battered heart. He'd always assumed she'd stood by and allowed it to happen. He'd never known that she'd been in on the decision.

Mom came into his room and cupped his cheek. "It got you away from him. It gave you a chance to shine on your own. So go and shine, Hal. Just go."

Hal closed his eyes as a lump settled into his throat. He felt her hand fall away and heard her leave. The urge to talk to Caleb hit so hard that he moved before he thought about it. He bolted down the stairs, found the phone free, and dialed Caleb's parents' house.

"Hello?" The soft-spoken voice of Caleb's dad answered, and Hal had to swallow hard before he spoke.

"Mr. Hudson, it's Hal. Is Caleb there?" Hal eyed the clock. He had forty minutes left on his deadline, and he had no doubt Darren would carry through his threat and have him arrested for trespassing.

"No, I'm sorry. He's at his brother's." Hal squeezed his eyes shut on a wave of sick disappointment. "I can have him call you when he gets home."

"Yeah, he won't reach me here. I'm not welcome," Hal said roughly and then mentally kicked himself for whining. "Don't tell him that. I don't want him to worry. I'll try to get in touch with him again before I go."

"Hal...." Hal's hand tightened on the phone as Mr. Hudson hesitated. "I know you're getting ready to leave the country, and I hope you find what you're looking for. If you're anything like the boy I remember, you'll do fine. Take care."

Caleb didn't know how lucky he was. Hal couldn't blame him one bit for not wanting to upset the dynamic in his family. "Thank you, sir."

He hung up, sick with disappointment, and slammed his fist against the wall a couple times. It did little to cool the fury bubbling inside him, and it only hurt his hand. Hal gathered the rest of his belongings, setting them out on the sidewalk so they could move fast when Mark showed up. Mom was in her room, the door locked, and she didn't answer when he called her name. He trudged down the stairs, aching and wondering when he'd see her again.

"Hal, phone!" Lily called. "It's Caleb."

Hal hurried back toward the kitchen, his heart thumping. Caleb's dad must've tracked him down, and he'd never been so grateful for a bit of interference in his life.

"Thank you for calling me back," Hal blurted as soon as the receiver was to his ear.

"Hal...." Caleb's voice rolled through him, and Hal slumped against the wall. That was all he needed, just to hear his voice. It reminded him that everything would be okay. Because no matter how far apart they were physically, no matter how upside down and confusing their relationship got, they were there for each other. "Dad told me. I'm guessing your dad lost it over your news."

"Yeah." Hal closed his eyes, picturing the way Caleb would look, the worry in his dark brown eyes, and he ached so much for the chance to see him before he left. "The breaking point was the Peace Corps. Apparently wanting to help people makes me a weak pansy."

"Yeah, you're a real wilting flower. I wish I was there," Caleb said with frustration evident in his voice.

"There'd be nothing you could do." It comforted Hal to hear it said, to know that all he had to do was tell Caleb he needed him and his friend would come.

"You wouldn't be alone," Caleb lowered his voice. For a moment Hal was pathetically grateful Caleb wasn't there because he knew exactly what would happen. It would start out innocent enough, with Caleb holding him, but Hal didn't trust himself for one second to keep it platonic. It felt too natural, too right to be touched by Caleb and to touch him in return.

"I'm not alone. Lily's hovering, and I have a place to crash until I head out." Hal was reluctant to mention Mark's name given the way Caleb bristled whenever he was mentioned. "Then I have twenty-seven months to figure out my next step."

"I'm going to miss you." Caleb sighed. "When you get back don't even think about returning to New York, okay? Come here."

"I'll think about it." Hal wouldn't make any promises, but he'd entertain the possibility. He had time to wrangle his heart into submission. He glanced at the clock and winced. "Look, I have to go. I've got to get out of here before Dad comes home."

"Hal…. Man, take care of yourself."

Hal heard everything Caleb wanted to say in those words, everything he wanted to say in return. "I will."

When he went outside Lily was sitting on his trunk, watching his belongings. Hal took a seat beside her to wait in silence. She leaned against him as Hal tried to settle his thoughts. The two people who meant the most to him had reached out to him. He was leaving to fulfill a dream. Darren no longer had the power to control him. He tried to use those things as a counterbalance to the anger that beat inside him with an incessant drum.

"Boy, I told you to be out of here by the time I got back. Lily get inside."

Both Lily and Hal stiffened. "I am out of the house," Hal responded, not even looking in the direction of Darren's voice because he desperately wanted to make a scene. He wanted to make this as painfully embarrassing for Darren as possible, and he'd regret that display later on. "As you can see, I'm not even on your section of the sidewalk. If you want the Kittengers to evict me, then I suppose you'll have to knock on their door and ask them."

Headlights came down the quiet neighborhood street toward their house, and Hal breathed a sigh of relief as Mark's car pulled up. "I see you're all ready," Mark said as he got out. "Good to see you again, Lily."

Lily clung harder to Hal's arm, turning her face into his shoulder. Hal felt her tears wet his shirt. He smoothed a hand over her hair. "I love you, Lilygirl."

"I don't want you to go."

Hal's heart ached for her, for himself. "I'll write every week, and when I get back to the States, I'll visit you at school."

He untangled himself from Lily and moved his belongings into the car with Mark's help. "Who's that man?" Darren demanded with heavy suspicion. "Is he a friend?" The way he sneered the word turned it into a slur. It would serve him right if Hal kissed Mark in full view of the whole street. He was mighty tempted and only knowing how much Mark disapproved of such drama stopped him.

"You're a coward," Hal shot back.

"I'm not the one running away to chase a stupid dream."

"You sure as hell showed a fine bit of running away when you turned tail and left instead of talking with me." Hal shoved the last box into Mark's trunk and shut it. Hal turned toward Darren, who fumed from the safety of the front door, and flipped him a double bird. "You lost your chance for any answers then."

He blew Lily a kiss and slid into the front seat next to Mark, seething, his blood on fire from the confrontation.

"Well, Hal, you don't just burn bridges, you bomb the hell out of them as you go," Mark said as he pulled away from the curb.

"That's for damned sure," Hal muttered, keeping his gaze on Lily's slight figure as they headed away. He promised himself he would see her again and wished that it didn't feel so much like he was embarking on another exile.

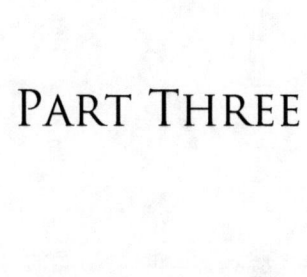

PART THREE

CHARLESTON, SC—
SEPTEMBER 2, 2023

"I CAN'T believe you just up and went to Ghana like that," Kendra cut in with a shake of her head as they looked through the photos of Hal's time there.

"Believe it," Caleb and Lily said in unison and then exchanged glances with a laugh. As much as Hal's abrupt departure had upset Caleb, he'd already been discharged from the Army and moved back to Charleston before Hal left. Their breakup was as much his fault as Hal's. Both of them running scared from what they wanted most. They might not have fought to keep that relationship, but they had fought like hell to keep their friendship.

All that meant Lily had been left behind in the ashes of her family. She'd written Caleb often, starting when he'd gone to Nam, and she'd continued the letters after Hal joined the Peace Corps. She'd become a sister to him during that time. He'd felt bad for her, but at least going away to nursing school had given her a life of her own. She'd needed to escape that environment as much as Hal.

"It was an amazing experience," Hal replied. "And if your dad hadn't talked me into moving to Charleston to finish college I would've served on another mission. I think everybody should do something like that at least once in their lives, serve somewhere. Caleb and Drew joined the military. Lily, you did Doctors Without Borders as a nurse. All you kids put in countless hours at the shelter with me. I think it's important."

"Ever the activist," Caleb squeezed his hand with a warm rush of affection. "Always helping people."

"You too, only difference is I'm loud about it," Hal said with a shrug. "You always did it quietly, never seeking attention for anything you did."

Caleb supposed that was true enough. Hal reminded him of Uncle Vern. He'd always been the voice of the family, calling people to action, whereas Caleb figured he'd led by example like Dad. He'd never been much for being the center of attention. He supposed the inclination had its roots when he first went to that white school. Last thing he wanted was to bring attention to himself. Some habits became a part of you.

"Whatever happened to your first boyfriend?" Drew asked with a frown. "I think I remember meeting him a few times. After you moved back to Charleston."

"Mark? We remained friends. We didn't get to see each other much. He had his restaurants in New York, and we didn't leave Charleston often. Life gets too busy sometimes," Hal said with a faraway look. "And then he got sick. I went to visit him in the hospital before he died. It was such a shock.... You think you have time, until suddenly you don't."

Caleb rubbed his thumb over the back of Hal's hand. That had been a hard time for Hal. He'd lost too many friends from the Village to the AIDS crisis. Hell, it had been hard on both of them. There had been so much fear and confusion at first. They hadn't known if they would get sick too. Then all the progress they'd made for gay rights took a turn for the worse. They'd had a family by then, and with all the fear and suspicion directed toward gay men, they'd worried more than once they'd lose the kids.

"I remember that. I went to see him too when I went home for a visit," Lily said. "You were his one regret, Hal."

"I know," Hal replied quietly. "Mark was fonder of the idea of commitment than actual practice. He tried. I'll give him that. But he loved a good chase, and it got boring for him after the chase was over." A smile flickered across his lips. "And boy could we butt heads. He thought he knew best. He had a hard time letting me make my own path."

"I'm sure his age had something to do with that," Lily said, with a prim twist to her lips.

"He wasn't that much older than me," Hal said with a laugh, though Caleb echoed her opinion. He didn't think it was much of a coincidence Hal met Mark after he was sent to the academy. Hal had desperately needed a father figure, and for a while, Mark had fulfilled that need until Hal outgrew it.

"Please, Hal. He was set in his ways enough to have a hard time changing," Lily retorted.

"I'll be the first to admit he wasn't a fan of our relationship, but I think most of that was fueled by having a hard time letting Hal go," Caleb cut in. Mark was enough of a romantic to recognize Hal and Caleb had a lifelong connection. It probably hurt him to know he'd never had all of Hal's heart. "If he'd been alive, I'd like to think he'd have come to our wedding."

"No doubt to try and take charge," Hal said with a laugh, and Caleb wondered if he recalled how Caleb and Mark had gotten so territorial over Hal's new apartment, each thinking they knew better how Hal should live. Hal had ignored them both and went on doing things his own way. It was pretty funny now that he looked back on it.

Shouts and cheers came from the field, and they all turned to see what the commotion was about. Abby and Joshua stood toe-to-toe, gesticulating and arguing. "And that's our cue to cut in," Caleb said, getting to his feet.

"Sit down, Dad," Drew said and stood up. "I'll referee."

"Your uncle and I were talking about taking a walk earlier," Caleb said with a glance at Hal to see if he was interested. "We'll see if the grandkids want to go with us. That'll give them a chance to cool their heads."

"I'd like that." Hal shut the memory book and carefully tucked it into the box. "It's been a while since we've had them all together. It would be a shame if the whole day went by with us sitting here talking about the past instead of enjoying being with them."

Caleb looked out at the grandkids, who were taking sides or ignoring the conflict, depending on their nature. He never got tired of seeing them together, and he didn't care how loud they got. He'd learned to tune out the noise unless it was something that required his attention. It was actually harder to get used to the quiet.

Parenting was a hard job, fraught with uncertainties and second-guessing. You had to build a framework of discipline and expectations for your kids and give them room to grow and test those boundaries. Grandparents had the pleasure of enjoying their grandkids with the freedom of experience. In his opinion, as a grandpa, his first concern was to love them, and the kids responded with an open heart. You couldn't beat that special bond of the heart between grandparent and grandkids.

Caleb and Hal walked out onto the field and were met with eight expressions ranging from embarrassed to excited. Caleb wanted to laugh; instead he focused on each kid before saying gruffly. "We don't need to step in, do we?"

"Step in what, Grandpa?" Zoe asked, examining the ground with interest.

"No," Abby said at the same time, snatching the kickball from Joshua's hands as he was distracted. "We're good."

"Your grandpa and I were going to go for a little hike," Hal said before Joshua gave voice to the indignation in his eyes. "Who wants to join us?"

"Ooohh I do, I do!" Zoe darted off the field toward them. "Do you think we'll see any warblers or kingfishers?"

"It's possible," Caleb replied and shot a teasing glance at Hal. "More likely than running across a gator these days. We'll probably see a coyote too." Humor flashed in Hal's eyes, and he shook his head.

Caleb wasn't surprised when all the grandkids chose to go with them. They saw Zoe every few days since she and Kendra were the only immediate family left in Charleston, and Zoe loved their walks. The others didn't get to see them or their cousins as often, and there was always something to see along the miles of paths throughout James Island.

"Can we go by the waterpark?" Abby asked, falling into step with Zoe.

Caleb was sure the waterpark was open for Labor Day, and it was warm enough that even if they got soaked through, they'd dry off before the sun set. Hal glanced at him, his eyes twinkling with a *why not* expression. He checked to see if he had his wallet as he considered all their options. "That's more of an all-day thing, and we'd need our bathing suits if we want to enjoy it," Caleb said, and before the disappointment could set in he continued, "But there's a splash fountain not too far from here. That'll be fun too."

The suggestion was met with enthusiastic replies, and they headed out in an uneven line with Caleb and Hal straggling behind. "Don't wear them out too much," Kendra's voice called out. "Then they'll really start fighting."

"By the time that happens, it'll be time for them to go home with you," Hal called back.

"Troublemaker," Caleb said with a chuckle.

"You were thinking it too," Hal replied as he took Caleb's hand. After spending so much of the day going over their past Caleb took such joy in being able to walk hand in hand like this. Disparaging looks were far rarer in their old age. Nowadays they were more likely to be ignored or given a sentimental smile, depending on a person's outlook.

Zoe and Abby skipped alongside them for a few minutes before darting off in an impromptu race. Caleb watched them go with a shake of his head. It would take more than a walk and a splash fountain to wear those two out. "Remember Drew at that age? He didn't know how to walk, everything had to be done full tilt running."

"Don't forget the jumping. If it could've been jumped off of, he would've tried it," Hal said with a rueful laugh. "My white hair started with him."

"I'd dreamt about this," Hal said, gesturing toward the grandkids. "I wanted it so bad, a family like this, but when I first wished for it, I never thought it would be possible."

"I never had that dream until you gave it to me," Caleb said. "I wanted you. You were my dream."

Hal paused on the path and turned toward him, his gaze softening. "You have a way with words, and you know how to make my heart jump."

Caleb smiled and squeezed his hand. "Thank you for giving me both our dreams."

"Pawpaw! Grandpa!"

They turned to see all the grandkids watching them with impatience, except for Abby who had a romantic look in her eye. "I think that's a warning to stop reminiscing and to move faster," Hal said.

"Seems that way to me." Caleb waved toward them. "We're coming. Don't mind us."

"Hurry up, Grandpa," Zoe called.

As soon as they started to amble down the path again, the grandkids got moving again except for Abby who walked toward them. "Can I have another story?"

"I suppose I could do one more," Caleb said with a smile. She was determined to get their love story. He could give her the quick version while they hiked. "Want me to tell you about when I finally convinced your Pawpaw to move to Charleston?"

"Yes." Abby beamed, falling into step beside him.

"Well, let's see," Caleb said, thinking back, "when Pawpaw came back from Ghana, I was living with your dad while Rodney was still alive."

CHARLESTON, SC— AUGUST 16, 1975

THE COMBINATION of a man's shouts and a high, piercing wail yanked Caleb out of a sound sleep. He sat up in the bed, his heart pounding, disoriented. For one terrible moment between the man's shouts and the feel of the hot summer air pressing down on him, Caleb had the unsettling notion he was in Nam again. Then the baby's cry cut through his confusion, and Caleb was right where he belonged, at Rodney's house in Charleston. The war had ended earlier in the year with the complete collapse of Saigon, and there was no danger of either him or Rodney returning.

Caleb yanked off the sheet tangled around him and trotted down the hall to check on Drew first. His nephew lay in his crib waving his fists and kicking, his little face scrunched up with the force of his angry cries. As soon as he saw Caleb, he rolled onto his side and pulled himself up by the railing so Caleb could pick him up.

"What am I going to do with you and your daddy?" Caleb said. He was getting used to the feeling of being overly large and awkward as he handled Drew. At least he wasn't stark terrified, as he had been the first time he'd held him as a baby.

Drew calmed down once he was settled against Caleb's shoulder, and his sobs turned to hiccups. "I can sleep through one of you making all this noise, but when you go at it together, it's another thing. Come on, let your uncle sleep." Caleb checked to make sure Drew was dry, then laid him in the crib with a soft toy. He rubbed Drew's back, silently willing Rodney to stop shouting. It was a useless wish. "I'll be right back, gonna check on your old man."

Drew whimpered as Caleb walked toward the door. "It's okay, Daddy's just having a bad dream. Uncle Caleb is going to sit with him until he wakes up."

Caleb discovered what worked for Drew was as effective on Rodney most nights. He stood in the doorway and watched his brother flailing on his bed, his shouts becoming hoarse as his vocal chords strained. "Rodney, it's me, it's Caleb," he said in a low soothing voice. "You're home. You're safe. Your son's down the hall. That's who you heard crying. Drew. It's okay."

He'd learned the hard way not to forcibly wake him. The one time he'd tried that he'd almost gotten his jaw taken off. He got why Rodney's wife took off. These last couple of weeks since he moved in had been terrifying and stressful beyond words. What he couldn't understand was why she'd abandon Drew as well. He was just a little guy, who had done nothing wrong. She left him in a situation that she couldn't tolerate herself. What kind of a mother did that?

The only thing Caleb could do when Rodney had one of his nightmares was talk to him like this. He found it calmed him down faster than anything else. He got what Rodney was going through. Maybe that's why he could stand it. He'd had his own share of nightmares when he'd come back from the war. However, Rodney's torments were on a whole other level. It gave him sympathy for the helplessness and worry that Hal had gone through with him.

"Rodney, whatever you're seeing, it's not real. You're in your own home. You're in Charleston. You remember Charleston?" Caleb continued, blabbing anything that came mind.

Eventually the shouts quieted, and then the thrashing calmed. Caleb was never sure if it was the sound of his voice or just a matter of Rodney running out of energy. All Caleb knew was that the nights he'd had those terrible dreams, like his brother, he came out of it much better when Hal had been there talking to him. Caleb had been able to put his dreams behind him and move on. Rodney seemed unable to do the same.

Caleb listened for Drew, but either he was happy playing with his toy, or he'd fallen asleep. "Hey, Rodney, it's me, Caleb." He took the chair next to the bed and dared to grasp Rodney hand. "You understand me? I'm right here."

Rodney's hand tightened around his to the point of pain. For a split second, Caleb feared he'd miscalculated and he'd have to fend his brother off again, but Rodney just held on like his life depended on it. "I'm not going anywhere. I know what you're going through."

Caleb continued to reassure him until Rodney's mind pulled back from its remembered horrors and he fell into a more natural sleep. Caleb sat there, straining his ears for any sound of Drew. He'd get up in a minute. The next thing he knew, someone was shaking him, and the sun made his eyes ache when he opened them.

"What?" He looked around, trying to place himself as Rodney gazed at him with a grim look in his eyes.

"You fell asleep in the chair." Rodney straightened, and Caleb noticed Drew tucked over the crook of his arm, his eyes wide open. He grinned at Caleb, showing off his two bottom teeth, one still growing in. "I take it I had another one of my episodes."

Caleb stood up, his eyes sandy and his neck aching from sleeping in such an awkward position. His heart ached for Rodney and the anger he heard in his voice, anger that was directed inward. Caleb had allowed himself to be hopeful when he'd met Rodney's girl. They'd been happy. Rodney had been so excited about the baby. He'd worked so hard to get them this home. Now he was struggling to make it on his own, constantly worried that he was going to fail.

"Yeah, but it wasn't too bad." Caleb admitted. "You went right back to sleep."

Rodney snorted and patted Drew's back as he began squirming and babbling. "Right. Not bad. Then why did you feel the need to watch over me as I slept?" He left the room, not giving Caleb a chance to respond.

Caleb went to his room to change and give himself time to think while Rodney calmed down. They'd had their share of misunderstandings growing up, and there had been a time when they didn't like each other very much, brothers or not. But ever since Caleb had returned home from the Army, there had been a new closeness between them. They'd both been to hell and back, and maybe it was past time to talk about it. He just hoped he could find the right words that would make a difference.

Rodney was in the kitchen getting Drew his breakfast as Drew banged on the tray of his highchair with his spoon. His attention was on his son, and his whole being softened as he spoke to him in a low voice. Caleb was grateful this was a day off for both of them. He could talk to him without Rodney having an excuse to run off.

"There's no shame in having nightmares," Caleb said quietly as he went to the coffeemaker to get it going. "I had plenty of my own. There were times when I thought I might never sleep normal again." He thought back on those nightmares with a shudder. Memories of the war had mixed with his worst fears come to life.

Rodney went quiet, and Caleb continued measuring out the coffee grounds while he waited his brother out. "They're not nightmares. I don't know what they are because I don't remember them. But between the screaming and the nights I can't sleep at all, when I'm just a restless mess, it's too much," Rodney finally said. "I thought it was over when I left. I thought it was all behind me, but I was wrong. I can't escape it, and it's fucking me over."

Caleb understood how he felt, and he suspected Rodney was carrying a whole lot more shit than Caleb could fathom. "You need to talk to someone. It doesn't have to be me if you don't want to, but it should be somebody you trust."

"I'm not crazy," Rodney insisted. "Who do you think I can talk to and not end up in a nut house? I'm not leaving Drew alone."

"I don't think you're crazy." Caleb turned to face him so Rodney could see he was serious. "I think you're carrying demons from what you've seen and the things you had to do to stay alive. You can find someone who's not going to judge you for it. But if you keep it all inside, it's going to chew you up until you're nothing but a shell. We've both seen vets like that, and I don't want it to happen to my brother."

Rodney's gaze flicked over him, considering, weighing his words. Well, at least he was listening. That was a start. Caleb glanced at Drew to gauge his mood, but he was paying far more attention to the bowl his dad was stirring than any tension in the kitchen. Rodney tested the heat of Drew's cereal and kept stirring. "Who'd you talk to?" Rodney asked.

"Hal." Caleb caught Rodney's surprised look and shrugged. "Come on, who else?"

"I thought he was an antiwar activist," Rodney said, sounding baffled. "I'll be honest, I never understood how you two became friends. You two are so different. Isn't he in Ghana, saving the world or something equally bleeding heart worthy?"

"Yeah, I can't say I'm too surprised now that I think about it. Hal's been heading toward something like that since we were kids," Caleb said, trying to think of how to explain the rest to Rodney. "We have much more in common than you think. We have the same interests in books, movies, music. We tend to balance each other out. I don't know. Hal's always been easy to talk to. Maybe because he's confided everything to me, or maybe because he's always taken me as I am whether he agreed with me or not." Caleb poured them both a cup of coffee and set one on the table for Rodney.

"But with the nightmares... I'll admit, I did have a hard time opening up to him at first. It was so raw when I got back, and it was pretty inhibiting with him being so against the war. But when I gave him the chance I didn't regret it."

"I don't know... you're lucky. I don't have anybody like that in my life." Rodney set the bowl of oatmeal on the table and gently took the spoon from Drew. Rodney began feeding Drew his breakfast with haunted eyes. "I don't know what I'm doing, and now I have Drew depending on me. I'm scared, man, I won't lie."

"You can talk to me, and I swear anything you say will be just between us." Caleb took his coffee to the table and wiped a smear of oatmeal off Drew's cheek. That boy loved his food that was for sure. "And you're not alone with Drew. Mom and Dad will help. I'll help. We're not going to abandon you like Drew's mom did."

"I'll think about it," Rodney said. Drew reached out, grabbed the next bite right off the spoon and slapped it against his mouth with oatmeal-smeared fingers. "Drew, if you'd be patient you'd get more in you and less on you." Drew grinned at him, his eyes dancing with mirth.

Caleb left the two of them to their morning battle and pulled out a saucepan and grits, his thoughts churning with worry. Damn, he missed Hal. It had been over a year since they'd parted, and it would be another year before he'd have a chance to see him again. Letters were nice, they gave him something to hold onto, but it wasn't the same at all.

He just needed Hal. There was so much riding him he hadn't expected. He'd planned on going to college and working a side job for the next several years. That was hard enough after Hal had planted the crazy notion of double majoring on him. He'd not counted on helping his brother with a baby too. And he was more than concerned about Rodney. He'd already been fragile before this whole mess with his wife happened. He'd been riding a high for a while after he'd gotten married, but then reality had crashed down hard. Caleb was watching his brother fumble through the chaos of his life, carrying a huge burden on his back at the same time.

He'd write Hal later on today. Even if he couldn't go into all the details about what was going on, it would be enough to know Hal understood. He'd be able to thank him for being there those nights when he'd wake up after a gut-wrenching nightmare, covered in sweat and shaking. Hal had been the one to talk to him softly, to remind Caleb who he was. He'd held him when he'd sobbed like a frightened toddler and didn't make him feel like he'd lost his manhood.

Caleb stirred the bubbling grits, but his mind wasn't on breakfast. It was thousands of miles east with Hal. It ached to not be able to admit he loved him. He wasn't going to lead Hal on, though, or ask him to wait. He couldn't give Hal what he wanted, and he didn't want to put him in a position where he'd try to settle for less than what he deserved. He wondered if Hal had moved on, found someone new. He'd been too afraid to ask because he wasn't sure he'd handle it well at all.

"Want some sausage with those?" Rodney asked, opening the refrigerator.

"You'll never hear me saying no." Caleb cast a sideways glance at his brother. He appeared calmer now. He truly enjoyed taking care of Drew. Maybe being a dad would be enough to help him work through his demons. Rodney had to stay strong for his son.

"So, how'd you come to confide in Hal?" Rodney asked as he tossed the package of sausage patties on the counter before grabbing a skillet. "I know you've been friends forever, but I can't imagine telling anyone there are nights when I'm afraid to go to bed because I don't want another episode. The only reason I'm mentioning it to you is because we're brothers and you've had nightmares."

Caleb set the grits to the side as Rodney laid the sausage patties in the cast-iron skillet. He'd been toying with the idea of telling Rodney that he was gay for several weeks now. Living together had strengthened their once-contentious bond.

He was tired of having pretend girlfriends or dating a girl for a short time because his family asked so many questions about his love life. If he wanted Rodney to open up about what scared him the most perhaps he needed to do the same.

A year ago the thought would have terrified him. Since he'd come home, he'd met other men like himself. Some whose families had cut them off, others who never revealed their preferences, and others whose families had accepted them in varying degrees. It had him reconsidering his own family and their reactions. There would be difficulties. He wasn't delusional, but would it be as bad as he feared? Caleb's parents were nothing like Hal's.

Still, this was huge.... Did he want to stress Rodney out by giving him another concern? Not just worry for Caleb, but having to keep the secret from their parents. Caleb couldn't put that extra pressure on him right now.

"Hal knows all my secrets, and I know his. We've trusted each other for years, so that helped." Caleb grabbed a couple of plates, pausing for a second to play peek-a-boo with Drew. "He was visiting me in Maryland when I had one of the nightmares. At the time I hated that he saw me in such a screwed-up state, but the way he responded proved to me I could talk to him."

Rodney turned over the sausage patties so they could brown on the other side. "It's good you had him. I'll think about it. But thank you for all these nights you've been here and dealt with me and not freaked out. It's helping me keep it together."

Caleb clasped his shoulder. "We're brothers. You know, I've seen the dark side of a family, and it's made me realize how lucky I am." He wanted to have faith in his family, to believe they would stick by him if they knew his secret, but he just wasn't sure. Even if they did, Charleston was a whole different world from New York City. He loved his hometown, but it was not the most ideal place for a gay, black man.

"Yeah." Rodney cracked a couple eggs into another skillet. "That's true. Our parents may not always agree with every decision we make, they may give us hell for it, but they do stick by us. The last year has proved that."

Caleb thought about Rodney's words and recognized the truth in them. If he had his family's support, he wondered if he and Hal could make it work despite the odds. It was such a seductive thought, because he didn't think anything would make him happier than spending the rest of his life with Hal.

Rodney nudged him, and Caleb moved out of the way to slide the sausages onto a plate as Rodney finished the eggs. "You okay, Caleb? You have a funny look on your face."

"Just dreaming." Caleb turned away and took a sip of his coffee. "Just dreaming."

CHARLESTON, SC— DECEMBER 22, 1976

HAL WAS coming. The excited thought kept racing through Caleb's mind in an exhilarated loop. They'd have almost a week together, and Caleb couldn't wait for it to start. The last time they'd seen each other, they'd both been a mess. Diving into an intense relationship straight after coming back from Nam had not been his wisest decision, no matter how good it felt. Hal had been struggling too, trying to find his place and break away from his dad's power trips. At first Caleb had hated the idea of Hal going into the Peace Corps, but after getting his letters, talking to him on the phone when he returned, he thought it had been the best thing in the world for Hal. It had given him a clean break, allowed him to regroup and move on.

Caleb watched the time as he ran through all the things he needed to do to make sure Hal would be comfortable. The couch bed was set up with fresh linens. The bathroom was clean. Maybe it wouldn't hurt to make sure he had enough towels. Hal had told him not to fuss, that he'd be okay with a pillow on the couch, but there was no way he was going to let Hal slum it.

He had a brief, wistful thought of the two of them wrapped around each other on his bed with desire and yearning. He couldn't ask for a dozen reasons, but damn it would be good to hold him, even if they did nothing else.

Caleb stirred the pot of greens and checked on the cornbread casserole in the oven. There was a little more time to go on it, but if Hal didn't get here soon he'd have to put it on the warmer. He wished he could get a hold of him to see if he'd been delayed on the road. The call from the nearest payphone after he'd set out wasn't enough.

Hal had been traveling since he returned to the States. He'd stopped in New York to visit friends and to get his transfer papers for next year. Then he'd dropped in on Lily in Pennsylvania. Before finally making his way to some bumfuck Kentucky town where he'd be working in a volunteer program until he decided on a school to attend.

Hal was crazy. Caleb had been saying it since they were kids, but this time he was serious. The man was going to work himself into a wraith.

Caleb wiped his hands on a towel and went to check on Drew to make sure the renegade didn't get into the Christmas tree again. Rodney would be home any minute, and Caleb was hoping Hal would get there first so they'd have time to catch up.

Jittery nerves had his hands trembling. Despite the craziness of their lives, Caleb wasn't sure he hadn't made a mistake by letting Hal walk away. He loved him, but he couldn't decide if it was a love between old friends or something more. Time and distance had a way of warping his perception, and he didn't know how he was going to react until he saw Hal again. Maybe they could slide into being just friends. He doubted it, though, because in the last two and a half years he hadn't found anyone who made him feel the way Hal did those short weekends they'd had together.

Drew sat next to the tree, pretending to ignore the shiny hanging balls. He gave Caleb an innocent look when he came into the room. "I'm not buying it, buddy." Caleb pointed a finger in his nephew's direction. Drew grinned back at him, not in the least bit bothered.

Caleb peered out the window, and his heart leapt with a jolt of happiness at the sight of Hal getting out of his car. Finally. With a whoop and a grin, he bounded out of the house. "Hal Zimmer, you crazy bohemian bastard." Hal spun around at the sound of his voice, and a smile lit up his face. "Get on up here."

Hal laughed and met him halfway. There was no hesitation as they hugged each other and the quick bittersweet pang washed away under the warmth of their friendship. "It's good to see you," Hal said, rubbing his hand over the back of Caleb's head. A quick tingle of heat raced through Caleb. Aw hell. Yeah, Hal still did it for him. Caleb longed to kiss him with an ache that hadn't abated one bit from their separation.

"Come on in," Caleb said, pulling away before he made this reunion awkward. "We've got catching up to do." Numerous phone calls and frequent letters weren't nearly the same as seeing Hal in person and having one of their all-night conversations.

They paused on the porch and looked at each other in the mellow light of the lamp. Hal had lost weight when he didn't have any to lose, and his hair had grown wild. Caleb felt a familiar tug of desire. "Damn, Hal, how do you manage to make scruffy pretty?"

"Please," Hal pushed him toward the door. Caleb couldn't tell if Hal felt that same exhilarated rush, that same pull of want and need to reconnect. "You'd better watch that smooth talk. I'm immune to flattery."

Caleb ushered Hal inside as his gaze swept the living room for Drew. The twerp was nowhere in sight. "Make yourself comfortable. I've got someone you have to meet."

"You'd better be fetching Drew," Hal called after him as he went down the hallway. "After all your stories, I'm dying to meet him."

Caleb heard a muffled giggle from Rodney's room. He made a show of looking in Drew's room first, then his own, knowing what was expected from the game. Then he peered into Rodney's room and saw a shadow move under the bed. Caleb crouched, reached under, and grabbed a leg. "Gotcha." Drew squealed and tried to scramble away as Caleb hauled him out.

"Come on, Drew, your uncle's best friend is here. You should come and say hi." He tickled Drew's ribs and the squirming, laughing boy tried to wiggle free as Caleb carried him to the living room. Hal stood by their Christmas tree, and he turned around with a grin as Caleb returned.

His nephew twisted in his arms and pointed at Hal. "Hey! Who dat?"

"That's Mr. Zimmer. He's the friend I was telling you about."

Hal grimaced and shook his head. "Don't listen to your uncle. Call me Hal, little man. No need to be so formal."

He held out his finger to Drew who grasped it for a quick second before pointing at the ground and looking at Caleb with laughing, dark eyes. "Drew down?"

Caleb set him on the floor and watched Drew make a beeline for the pile of cars he'd left suspiciously close to the tree. Caleb put his hands on his hips and tried to count the number of presents underneath and to see if there were any missing ornaments. Hal laughed, and Caleb glanced at him with a lifted brow. "What's so funny?"

"You… life." Hal shook his head and gestured toward Drew. "That kid has you hostage."

"True." Caleb took a stack of laundry off the couch and gestured for Hal to sit. He couldn't believe Hal was here, and he had a hard time not staring. He had to find a way to convince Hal to apply to college in Charleston and to move here next summer. He'd been waiting for Hal to return for good from the moment his dad took him away.

Caleb took a seat, watching Hal, trying to gauge how coming home had affected him. He seemed surer of himself, calmer. Even when they'd reconnected after Caleb returned from Vietnam and Hal hadn't been so angry, there had been a rebellious fire in him. Caleb sensed that fire had direction now. He liked this new side of him.

Hal studied him in return, and Caleb wondered what he saw. The last couple years had been challenging. Going to school, working, he was busting his ass on both ends. Still, Caleb felt like he was working toward something. His reconnection with Rodney made him very glad he had chosen to return home and move in with him. A little spurt of husky laughter caught his attention, and his gaze flicked toward Drew. And there was his nephew, another amazing reason to stay.

Of course, there was only one reason to leave, and that reason sat across from him. Caleb hadn't appreciated how strong his bond was with Hal. Maybe it wouldn't be such a bad thing to leave home to be with him. Caleb just didn't know.

"You look good. Coming home agreed with you," Hal said in an echo of Caleb's thoughts. Caleb met his eyes again, saw the ache that Hal couldn't hide no matter how hard he tried. Damn his parents to hell and back. His dad was bad enough, and frankly, no one was surprised when he proved to be a first-rate asshole. But for his mom to refuse his phone calls or a visit, that was far worse.

There was no way Caleb would allow Hal to be alone on Christmas. Not ever. And his whole family agreed with him. Thanksgiving had been bad enough.

"You look good too. As much as I hated you going so far away and despite your parents' idiocy, you look happier than I've seen you in a long time." A smile flickered across Hal's lips, and Caleb ached to touch him again. He seemed too far away on the opposite side of the couch. He remembered how it felt as natural as breathing to slip an arm around him or to take his hand, and Caleb no longer felt like he had the right.

"To be honest, I am happier. I know what I want to do with my life now, and I don't have to worry about Darren's approval or listen to his twisted opinions. I swear I feel free. My only regret is that Lily feels caught in the middle. I keep telling her she doesn't have to defend me, that this is for the best, but you know Lily."

"Yeah, I know Lily." Caleb hadn't seen Hal's sister since they moved, but it touched him that she'd kept in contact with him. During the war, he'd looked forward to letters from her as much as he had from the rest of his family. "She's going to make a wonderful nurse."

"She will. It's funny, you know how you always said my parents don't know me at all? Well it's the same for her. They'd expected her to find a husband and drop out the first year."

"So, lay it out for me. I'm ready to hear the Hal Zimmer life plan. Do you know where you're going to college?" Caleb asked, hoping Hal hadn't made a firm decision. "And what are you going to do after you get your degree? Another stint in the Peace Corps?"

"Lily would murder me," Hal said with a laugh, and Caleb joined in. He could picture Hal's sister following him and dragging him back. "No, I enjoyed my experience, but I want to make a difference closer to home. After school I want to get a job at a shelter and see about expanding youth services."

Hal was going to be poor for life, living paycheck to paycheck, yet he'd be very content. He'd never been one for coveting possessions or given much thought to shelter or food. Caleb had worried more than once that Hal would run away from home with no plan at all.

"How are you going to pay for school?" Caleb asked.

Hal shrugged and didn't look the least bit worried. Whereas money was something Caleb fretted about too much, though not as much as Rodney. "I have savings," Hal said, "not much, but some, and I've looked into student loans. I just need to settle on a school."

"College of Charleston," Caleb cut in as soon as he had the opening. Hal looked surprised, then thoughtful at the resolve in his voice. "Look, the cost of living here's not bad. The school is good. There are places you can work that'll give you the sense of helping a community that you need with the added benefit of it being a community you love."

Indecision warred with temptation on Hal's face. He took off his glasses and polished them on his shirt, lost in thought. Caleb decided to push the issue. He reached across the space and took Hal's hand in his, linking their fingers together. Hal's touch was warm and familiar, and to Caleb's relief he didn't pull away.

"Come home."

Hal stared at their hands a long moment, and then his gaze lifted to Caleb's. He looked torn, and Caleb took that as a sign that Hal wasn't as over their relationship as he tried to pretend. Caleb didn't want that to stop him from coming back to Charleston. "You don't have to be alone anymore. We're family. We always have been."

Hal shook his head with a tiny smile as his gaze warmed. "And you keep trying to say you don't have a way with words."

"I've had a long time to think about it." Caleb regretfully let go of Hal's fingers though he wanted to keep the contact. "And I'll admit I may have practiced the argument a few dozen times."

"I don't know… I was afraid it would be awkward, given the last time we saw each other." Hal worried his lower lip, and the action brought a wave of remembered heat and desire. It hadn't been just sex. Caleb could admit it now. Hal had been looking for his forever love, and Caleb hadn't realized they'd been that for each other. It had been right in front of him.

"We both promised we wouldn't let our friendship get ruined." He'd missed Hal, like crazy, even more than their separation when they were kids. He'd had a glimpse of what life could be like with him. Granted, it had only been long weekends only a few times a year, but those weekends had meant everything to Caleb. It had taken their friendship and deepened it into something very special and rare.

Caleb loved his family, and returning to Charleston had been for the best. But if he hadn't managed to convince Hal to relocate here once school was over, then Caleb would have to choose another direction. He was just going to have to get off his butt to follow Hal around the world until he talked him into giving them a second chance.

"True." Hal went quiet as Drew raced his car off the coffee table and onto the floor. When it flew off, he squealed and raised his hands. "I hope that's not a sign for a daredevil to come."

Well, if Hal wanted to change the subject Caleb would let him. He had four days to lay the seeds in Hal's mind that it was time to come home. He couldn't screw it up, and that meant giving Hal some space. He'd lived with the regret of letting Hal go for too long. He'd find a way to deal with being gay. He'd find a way to get his family to understand. Because the life he'd lived the last two years had been missing one huge, powerful part.

"You should've seen him after he discovered how the door worked. We had the damndest time. He liked nothing better than to wait until we weren't paying attention, then make a break for it." His nephew looked sweet as could be with his broad-cheeked grins and wild curls; however, the twinkle in his eyes gave it all away. He was a devil in diapers.

"There was this boy in Ghana, Yiri; he was so freaking intelligent. He made me feel dumb more often than not," Hal said with a laugh. "And he had too much energy for his body. If there was a ruckus, he was usually at the heart of it."

"So what was your favorite part? It sounded like you had your hands in everything." Caleb sat back and set his feet up on the coffee table. He was forgetting something, and the nagging sense wouldn't leave him alone.

"I thought it was pretty neat that many of the women wove baskets like your mom. They took full advantage of the fact I had experience collecting materials. It gave me a connection to home." Hal reached out a hand, steadying Drew as he climbed over him. Well, that was a hopeful sign. Hal thought of Charleston as home, at least subconsciously. "I brought her one back. Do you think she'll like it?"

"She'll love it, especially if she knew you had a hand in making them." Once again, the thought that he was forgetting something tickled his thoughts as the scent of food wafted from the kitchen. Then it hit him with a flash of chagrin, and he jumped up with a groan. "Grab the renegade and come in the kitchen. You can finish your thought there."

God, he hoped he hadn't burned dinner. Rodney would never let him live it down. The greens were fine, bubbling gently on the burner, the cornbread casserole had browned a little too much, and Caleb grimaced as he pulled it out. Dammit, he had wanted it to be perfect, not salvageable.

"Smells good. When's supper?" Hal asked, carrying Drew in on his shoulders. Drew strained his little arm upward, trying to touch his fingers to the ceiling. Seeing the two of them together made Caleb's heart jump with a pang. Hal fit in with his life as if he'd never been gone. Suddenly the next four days seemed far too short.

"As soon as Rodney gets here." Caleb covered the casserole and set it on top of the stove to keep warm. "Which should be any time now. He went out to get us beers." Sometimes he lingered, though, running numbers and talking to other vets.

"Up! Up!" Drew insisted, patting Hal on top of his head as he pointed at the ceiling. Hal lifted him higher, and Drew laughed when he touched the top. "Ag'in!"

"How's Rodney doing?" Hal asked, not appearing to be bothered by Drew's demands.

Caleb sighed and grabbed a pitcher of sweet tea from the refrigerator. "I wish he'd talk with somebody other than me, but every time I suggest it he shuts down. He's managing his anger better, but he gets these moods. I never know when they're going to hit or how long they'll last. He just seems so hopeless then. It scares me."

"How's he handling the holidays?" Hal set Drew down in a chair, and Caleb handed Drew a cup of his own before pouring himself and Hal a glass of tea.

"Good, better than last year. He's riding high actually. It's probably Drew's own excitement. He keeps trying to nab presents and bring them to his room to open early." Caleb fixed a look on his nephew as Drew brightened.

"Presents now?" He started to scramble down, and Caleb caught him with a laugh.

"Soon, I promise, three more days." He set Drew in his chair as those little brows drew together in aggravation.

"Dat's not soon."

Hal laughed and high-fived Drew. "I agree."

Caleb shot him a look that said *Don't encourage him*, but Hal smirked and did not appear at all daunted. "So come on, tell me more about what you liked in Ghana."

"Well, I liked being a part of the mediation, though I find it funny that me of all people was mediating. It definitely taught me a lot." Caleb had to chuckle at that. Debate was more Hal's style. He would've loved to watch him sweat through a mediation.

"However, my favorite part was working with the kids," Hal continued with a glance toward Drew. "I loved it. It made me think of possibly teaching again. Then I realized it didn't feel quite right. There are plenty of teachers. So after I got that position in Kentucky I thought of the shelters and working with youth in the cities."

"Teenagers aren't exactly kids," Caleb said and took a sip of his tea. "And if they've gotten to the point where they're in shelters they're going to be carrying a whole load of emotional baggage. Have you thought of working with younger ones, orphans in a group home?"

"Yeah, but I'd want to adopt or foster every last one," Hal replied softly, and Caleb could see that happening. He wondered how Hal would handle not being able to save everybody. He remembered the boy who'd been so naïve and sweet, taking everybody as they were, believing in the good first. He'd thought that boy had been lost. Maybe not.

"One day, when I'm settled down with someone, I can think about fostering." Hal focused on him again with a rueful shrug. "Teenagers need a safe place too, not stuck away with a bunch of adults. I'm hoping I can relate to them about problems at home."

So Hal was still dreaming of his one and only. Well, at least it meant he hadn't hooked up with anyone serious since he'd returned to the States. Caleb couldn't tell if Hal was in love with him the way Caleb loved Hal. He'd gotten better about hiding his emotions. As much as he wanted to test the theory, to push Hal into revealing his feelings, Caleb was going to behave until he had Hal back where he belonged.

"I think you're right, Hal. I'm glad you finally found what you were looking for." Caleb touched Hal's hand, and his friend looked away with a flush.

The sound of the front door opening had Drew scrambling out of his chair with a happy cry. "Daddy!"

"Yes." Hal said, pumping his fist. "Now we can eat." He got up and met Rodney with a grin as he came into the kitchen with Drew latched onto his leg. "Hey man, good to see you."

"Welcome home, wanderer," Rodney said, handing the beer off to Caleb and embracing Hal. "Now maybe Caleb will shut up about seeing you again."

Caleb's cheeks heated, and he looked at Hal with a shrug. "What can I say, I was excited."

"Like Drew in the candy aisle of the five-and-dime." Rodney tossed his son up in the air. "Right?"

"Candy." Drew patted his stomach. "Candy now?"

"No, buddy, dinner first. You'll get plenty of candy on Christmas," Rodney promised.

Hal glanced at Drew, and his face softened. Then he looked at Caleb, his gray-green eyes alight. "Thank you," he mouthed. Right then Caleb could read him just fine. He held his hand out to Hal as Rodney turned his back, and for a brief second their hands clasped.

"Love you, man," Caleb said in a low undertone, unable to stop the words, but hoping it conveyed the promise that if he had any control over it, Hal would never be alone again.

"Love you too."

CHARLESTON, SC— DECEMBER 25, 1976

AN EAR-PIERCING shriek of happiness jerked Hal out of a sound sleep. Heart thumping, he leapt from the couch, tangled himself up in the blanket, and almost fell on his ass. Drew paid him no attention, his eyes riveted on the new presents that had appeared under the tree overnight. How the heck Drew managed to see the additions in the dark, Hal couldn't tell. The sun hadn't even risen. Hal didn't even want to look at the clock to see how early it was.

"Daddy! Daddy, look!" Drew grabbed a brightly wrapped present half his size and manfully wrestled it out from under tree. "Daddy, Daddy, hurry!"

Seeing his excitement was more than worth the late night he'd put in with Rodney and Caleb. It was useless to try to urge Drew to go back to sleep, so he tossed his blanket on the couch and crouched down to turn on the tree. The lights made a spectacular show of colors and shadows on the ceiling, and Drew hooted his approval.

Hal couldn't wait until the kid noticed the stuffed stockings hanging from the knobs on the wall. Every time Hal looked at them and saw that Caleb included a stocking for him, it warmed him.

Caleb was right. They were family.

Rodney appeared, camera in hand, as Drew tore into the present. "Santa, Daddy, lookit what Santa gotted me."

"I see." Rodney crouched down and caught a photo of Drew's infectious excitement. Caleb's brother was grinning like a fool without any trace of the tension that came and went with him.

"Oh, for the love of God," Caleb said coming into the living room, looking like a sleepy, shirtless, sexy bear. "Drew, buddy, you're killing me."

"Uncle Caleb!" Drew ran over to grab his hand. "Come see."

Hal grinned to see the little smile on Caleb's face. He was often all growl first thing in the morning. Hal used to love teasing him into a better mood. From the expression on Caleb's face as he watched Hal, he also remembered those past mornings. "I'll go make us some coffee. We're going to need it."

Hal fled into the kitchen and attempted to regain his composure by measuring grounds into the pot. "Merry Christmas, Hal."

The sound of that sleepy, husky voice shook Hal to his core, and he almost spilled the coffee. The pull that dragged at him now had nothing to do with sex and everything to do with what Hal really wanted. He looked over at Caleb, and the warmth in his dark brown eyes eased the ache of loving him.

"Merry Christmas, Caleb." Hal flicked his fingers at Caleb's bare chest. "Go put a shirt on. It should be illegal for you to walk around half-naked."

The look Caleb shot him was pure heat and need, and Hal glanced away, his blood stirring. "Well, then, if we're going to be that way," Caleb replied, "you might want to think about wearing something other than those thin sleep pants. I can see—"

Hal touched his fingers to Caleb's lips to shut him the hell up, though it was too late because now they'd both acknowledged they were attracted. Hal shouldn't be so ridiculously pleased, because it would just complicate their situation, but he couldn't help enjoying knowing Caleb was pining too. And now his fingers were on Caleb's lips, and he was struck with the urge to trace his mouth, to kiss him.

Caleb's eyes darkened, and he pressed a kiss to Hal's fingertips that scorched the skin. Hal dropped his hand, shooting Caleb a quelling look, but Caleb just grinned, completely unrepentant. This was a playful side of him Hal hadn't seen before. It was like their roles had been reversed, and now Hal was the overly serious one, at least when it came to the two of them. Any other time he would've been thrilled at the thought that there were new layers to his friend that he could explore. But he had closed that door and intended on keeping it closed.

"Will you knock it out? Your brother's in the next room," Hal said in a fierce whisper.

The grin fell from Caleb's face, and he glanced over his shoulder at the empty doorway. Hal heard Drew's continued excitement as he pushed away the stinging reminder that no matter how they felt, they couldn't be open about it. This was a week for celebration, not regrets. He wasn't going to come between Caleb and his family. He'd witnessed this week how close they were and how much they were a part of each other's lives. If they hooked up again they wouldn't be able to keep it a secret for long.

Hal turned away to add the water to the coffee maker. Caleb stepped closer to him and Hal swore he felt the heat of his body. Damn him. There had to be an off switch somewhere. He shouldn't be exuding all those you-know-you-want-to-jump-my-bones hormones. "We have to talk about us at some point, Hal."

Caleb was right. Whether or not Hal moved down here, they needed to air things out. "But not now," he said firmly, feeling like a coward for ducking the issue.

Caleb took his hand and rubbed his thumb along it in a gesture that both soothed and made Hal desire him more. It seemed Caleb had been hesitant to offer those touches when Hal had first arrived, but then they slipped right back into it with ease.

Hal wondered how easy it would be to fall back into Caleb's arms. He wished he didn't feel that old tug of bone-melting want. He reminded himself that the last time they'd seen each other they'd been intimate. Surely the heat was normal and would fade the more time they spent together. Considering, however, Hal had felt that same tug since he was fourteen and it was just as strong ten years later, he wasn't holding his breath.

"Soon, okay?" Caleb said in a lower voice that sent a hot tingle of awareness through Hal. He had to be a masochist because he was enjoying this, getting all worked up and knowing Caleb was feeling the same.

"Yes, soon. Now go and take your distracting self elsewhere." Hal shooed at him, giving Caleb an aggravated look that only made him smile wider.

"You're cute when you're all bothered. I kind of like it."

"Will you two come on?" Rodney's voice had them jumping apart. He glanced over to see Caleb's brother in the doorway and turned back to the coffee pot as his face flushed scarlet. What he wouldn't give to have Caleb's skin tone at that moment. "You're going to miss it all."

"Hey, I needed coffee, or I was going to implode." Caleb followed Rodney out into the living room. "I'll slow the little bugger down."

Hal smiled as he heard a roar and a shriek that threatened to wake half the block. "Help! Uncle Caleb's gotted me." He knew Caleb had plans on being a bachelor for the rest of his life, and that would be a damn shame because he would be a great dad. He pushed away that wistful thought. Not today. And if he had his way, he'd avoid that conversation Caleb wanted too. Time enough for that during his next visit. He turned on the coffeemaker and went to join the fun before Drew got a hold of every wrapped package under the tree whether it was his or not.

The morning sped by as they exchanged presents and watched Drew pinball from one excitement to another. Then Caleb made a huge breakfast while Hal tidied up the living room, and Rodney wrangled Drew into a bath and the holiday clothes his grandmother sent him. Rodney even managed to get him down for a nap after they ate before it was time to pack them all up again to head to Thomy and Effie Hudson's house.

Hal quelled a spurt of nerves as they pulled up. It was one thing to spend Christmas with Caleb and Rodney. It was another thing to spend it with the whole Hudson clan. Caleb warned him they could be overwhelming. Hal wasn't used to large extended families, and he had no idea what to expect. The day was far different from any Christmas celebration he'd ever had. He and Lily wouldn't have dared wake up the whole house the way Drew had.

Dozens of cars were parked along the street, radiating out from Caleb's childhood home. Hal couldn't imagine how all the people would fit in there. Laughter and the hum of conversation spilled out of the door as they mounted the steps to the porch. Hal hung back, clutching the small gifts he'd brought for Mr. and Mrs. Hudson and wishing that he'd given them early instead of when the entire household was present.

"There's my baby." Mrs. Hudson beamed at them and reached out to take Drew. "Don't you look handsome," she said, smoothing the front of his holiday sweater.

"Lookit." Drew lifted his Evel Knieval figure up for Effie's inspection.

"Oh my, my, my." She fixed a look on her sons. "Whose bright idea was that?"

Caleb and Rodney pointed fingers at each other, and Mrs. Hudson shook her head. She kissed Drew's cheek and set him down. "Your cousins are in the bedroom. Why don't you go play?"

Drew ran off, clutching his new favorite toy as Mrs. Hudson watched him go with a rueful expression. "That child needs no more ideas than what's already in his head."

"Blame Santa," Rodney replied with a grin and kissed her on her cheek. "That jolly old elf's been causing trouble for a very long time."

"Now I know who to blame," she said as she hugged him and swatted Rodney as he disappeared through the door.

Hal missed Lily and his own mom. At least he'd had a chance to talk to Lily earlier. The happiness on Caleb's face brought a bittersweet ache, and he had to glance away.

"Hal, what are you doing back there? Get over here and give me a hug." Mrs. Hudson gestured at him to get moving and Hal smiled.

"I wanted to make sure you knew I had nothing to do with Drew's present," he joked as he hugged her. "So I stayed out of the line of fire before one of them pointed at me."

Mrs. Hudson framed his face in her strong hands and examined him. "It is good to see you again." She smiled and patted his cheek. "You've got a strength I don't think you appreciate."

Hal wasn't sure how to take that cryptic remark because he often felt more lost than strong. To cover his confusion, he handed her the presents. "I brought you and Mr. Hudson a little present back from Ghana. Merry Christmas."

"Hal, you didn't have to do that." Mrs. Hudson's teeth flashed in a delighted smile. "Come on, we'll just set this aside until later when things quiet down." With that she ushered him into the house and bedlam.

Hal felt self-conscious as he stood back and let it all soak in. The little house was crowded, every possible sitting place filled with a body. Caleb's relatives moved around the chaos with the ebb and flow of long practice. Two small tables had been set up in the living room. A spirited card game was taking place around one, while the other held bite-sized bits of food with even more wonderful smells coming from the kitchen.

Hal scanned the dark faces, looking for people he'd met before, some looked back with curious expressions, others welcoming, a few guarded. There were a couple he thought might've been cousins he'd met when he was younger, and he tried to place names from his memory with the faces that had changed over the years. Then Mr. Hudson was coming forward, followed close behind by Uncle Vern, and Hal grinned.

"Merry Christmas," Hal said, greeting both men with a handshake.

"It's good to see you," Mr. Hudson said with one of his slow, quiet smiles that reminded him of Caleb. "Traveling seems to suit you."

"It did, but I'm thinking of staying in one place for a while."

"So I hear," Uncle Vern replied, taking his coat. "Caleb told us he's trying to get you to come back to Charleston. I think that's a fine idea."

"I know it would make him happy," Mr. Hudson said.

Hal narrowed his eyes and glanced around the room looking for Caleb who had conveniently disappeared. Sneaky bastard. He was probably in the kitchen, avoiding him after getting his uncle and dad to corner him. Hal would find him and get him good for this.

"I want to thank you," Uncle Vern said, jerking Hal out of his thoughts.

"What did I do?" Hal asked.

"You managed to convince Caleb to not give up on the idea of engineering. I'd tried, but he can be amazingly hard-headed." Uncle Vern shot him a curious glance as he hung Hal's coat in the closet.

"That was you?" Mr. Hudson said with surprise and a pleased smile. "What did you say to him?"

Hal tried to think. He recalled being frustrated with Caleb, but at that time of his life he'd been frustrated by everything. "I gave him a hard time about it and wouldn't let it go. Caleb's never been a quitter. Maybe it hit his pride. He's quiet about it, but he's got it."

"That's nothing less than the whole truth." Uncle Vern agreed. "I'm just happy he's doing something for himself and not because he thinks he should."

Hal looked up as Caleb entered the living room. He looked so damn handsome and at ease. Hal had worried about him when he first came home and moved in with his brother. Caleb took on so much. Hell, he made Hal feel like a slacker. He thought Caleb should relax, take pleasure in the fun part of college, but he had to admit, Caleb appeared to enjoy his strengthened relationship with Rodney.

"Me too," Hal said, his gaze lingering on Caleb. Mr. Hudson excused himself and made his way over to Caleb. Watching the happiness on Caleb's face as he greeted his dad brought a quick pang. He couldn't jeopardize the bond between them, even if the last few days had stirred up longings he'd thought he'd put to rest. Hal turned away before he started thinking things he shouldn't. He had to let go of the dream of loving Caleb again, because he could never put himself between Caleb and his family. He never wanted Caleb to experience the pain of being forced away. It would be even worse for him than it had been for Hal.

"So what about you? Plan on finishing college?" The look Uncle Vern leveled at him would've had Hal squirming like a delinquent eight-year-old if he hadn't had a plan... of sorts. He'd had a hard time coming up with long-term plans beyond a vague idea of what he would like to do one day. But time was running out to make a decision if he wanted to start classes next fall.

"I do. I've contacted Columbia, and it shouldn't be too difficult to transfer with the bulk of my credits. I just need a school." Hal followed Uncle Vern over to the laden snack table. He caught a glimpse of Drew and an older cousin of his sneaking out from under the table with his hands full of half-eaten cookies. He was the cutest kid Hal had ever seen, and it was amazing to see echoes of Caleb and Rodney in such a little face.

"I can understand why you don't want to go back to New York. Have you considered Caleb's idea about coming here?" Uncle Vern poured himself a glass of cider as Hal filled his plate. "He probably wouldn't come out and challenge you like you did with him, but it wouldn't hurt to think of it that way."

"I promise. I'll give it some thought." Lily was pushing for him to move to Pennsylvania with her, and he'd looked at going to San Francisco as well. But California was too far away. As much as he loved the Peace Corps, it had taught him he didn't want to settle down that far from his loved ones. Kentucky wasn't too bad. It was sort of in the middle, but it didn't have the programs he was looking to get involved with after college. So right now his immediate choices were Philadelphia and Charleston.

"I'll hold you to that. Come on, since Caleb's tied up for the moment, let me introduce you around." To Hal's relief, Uncle Vern dropped the subject of his move and spent his own time getting Hal reacquainted with cousins he hadn't seen in years as well as many others he'd only heard of. It was a sad statement about his own family that Hal had immediately felt more comfortable and welcome here than he ever had at a celebration at home. Before Hal knew it, he was ensconced at the game table with a plate of nibbles near his elbow and a bottle of beer in hand, a part of the chaos instead of observing from the sideline.

Hal looked up as he felt the familiar weight of Caleb's hand on his shoulder. "Where'd you disappear to? I saw you talking to your dad, and then you were gone."

"I heard Aunt Tellulah's voice in the kitchen. I wanted to make sure she didn't touch the turkey or roast." Caleb dragged another chair over to the table and managed to make a space next to Hal. "She can bake like a demon, but she's a disaster with meats."

"Uncle Vern cornered me," Hal commented with a wry glance in Caleb's direction as he searched for any trace of guilt in his expression. "He also thinks I should move down here."

A surprised and pleased expression crossed Caleb's face. He rubbed his hand along his thigh, and his finger grazed Hal's leg. "Good. I need all the help I can get to convince you."

"So you didn't put him up to it?"

"Nope." Caleb held up his hands in an expression of innocence. "Though, only because I didn't think of it."

Hal felt strange knowing others in Caleb's family wanted him. Rodney had brought it up once too, and he supposed he wouldn't be too surprised if Mrs. Hudson did as well. It was weird in a good way, and Hal yearned for more of that sense of belonging. He couldn't remember feeling this relaxed and content in a long time. These last four days made him appreciate what it would be like to have a family that wasn't fraught with tension all the time.

"You're lucky you know," Hal said, leaning closer to him so only Caleb would hear. With a soft smile, Caleb looked around at his family gathered in the living room. "I understand why you came home instead of coming to New York."

"Yeah, I know I'm lucky. In many ways." Caleb smiled at him in a way that made Hal flush again. He wasn't sure if Caleb had ever looked at him in quite that way before. Back when they were sleeping together, Caleb had been closed off, contained, but it seemed as if the last couple of years at home had worn away the armor that he'd built while in Nam.

Caleb's cousin dealt a new round of cards, bringing the two of them into the game and saving Hal from having to make a response. He didn't get why Caleb always had the power to make him get all fluttery inside. He'd have to find a way to get used to it because when he weighed Philly with Charleston, there was no contest. His heart said Charleston every single time.

CHARLESTON, SC— JUNE 1977

CALEB EYEBALLED the next apartment on Hal's list and sighed. It didn't look any more promising than the last one. "You know, there are nicer places than the ones you've picked out. Don't you think you're taking this hippie thing a little too far?"

"Nicer means more money, and I'm on a tight budget." Hal got out of the car looking too cheerful considering the view of the apartment building. "I know you're all about them."

"I fully agree with sticking to a budget, but I'm sure we could find something better than these rat holes you've uncovered," Caleb said as they headed toward the outside steps. "The last one was a disaster."

"Considering I don't have running water where I'm at now, the last one looked like paradise in comparison." Hal took the stairs two at a time and greeted the landlady. She was in her seventies at least, her gray hair beehived up and shellacked in place. She puffed on a cigarette and eyed the two of them with a doubtful expression.

"Which one of you's interested?" she asked in a hoarse voice.

"Me." Hal peered into the open doorway and smiled. "I'm looking to rent for a couple years. Are you Mrs. Taylor?"

"Are you going to ask dumb questions? Who else would I be?" Mrs. Taylor gestured toward the apartment. "Well go on, have a look-see. It's got everything you could want."

Caleb decided he would be the judge of that. He didn't trust Hal's opinion on whether a given home was livable or not. Granted, right now he was volunteering in Appalachia after coming back from two years oversees, so his viewpoint was skewed. It was Caleb's job to look out for him, because it wouldn't kill his budget to have a few comforts.

The apartment was small with a boxy living room, narrow hallway, small kitchenette, a tiny bedroom, and even tinier bathroom off to the side. The furniture was worn and falling apart. The wood floors scuffed but salvageable, the linoleum in the bathroom peeling. There was a hole in the drywall in the hall, and a dozen other small repairs that needed to be done, but when fixed up it would do for a couple of years. And Hal was beaming. *Good God.*

"Is the price still as quoted?" Hal asked to Caleb's relief. He'd half expected his friend to sign a lease right there. Caleb at least had a few reservations remaining.

"If you're looking for a deal past what you're getting, go find another sucker" came Mrs. Taylor's testy reply.

"No, just wanted to make sure you hadn't decided to up the price." Hal turned around in a circle in the living room, his eyes far away, and Caleb tried to picture whatever it was that Hal saw and failed. "I'll take it."

Mrs. Taylor smiled, and Caleb shook his head. He didn't like starting anything, especially with old white ladies, but good rental price or not, he wanted to make sure Hal wasn't getting saddled with one huge headache after another. "Hold on a sec, Hal. I have a few questions before you settle."

"What's your problem?" The landlady turned her perpetually irritated gaze on him. "Who are you, his butler?"

Hal narrowed his eyes, but to Caleb's surprise, he merely replied in an even tone, "He's my friend, Caleb. He'll be vising often, so if that'll be a problem we can go." The Hal from a few years ago would've gotten defensive in a way that would've made hackles raise on all sides. But this new quiet challenge was far more effective.

"It was a joke, no need to be so sensitive, geez. What's got you in such a mood?" Considering her peevish response, the question was rather funny. "Just wondering why he was so curious. Need to make sure you're not subletting. Well, go ahead and ask your questions. It'll save me from having to answer them later on."

"This place needs handiwork before he moves in," Caleb said, indicating the flaking plaster on the ceiling.

"Do I look like I could handy anything?" Mrs. Taylor replied, setting her hands on her hips. "You make do, that's why I cut a little on the rent. I expect upkeep in return. It's all in writing." She reached into the bag at her side and pulled out a folder as she looked Hal up and down. "He looks as if he can wield a hammer just fine."

Which just went to prove that looks didn't mean a damn thing. Hal and a hammer was a disaster waiting to happen. "I know what you're thinking," Hal said. He must've seen Caleb's objection. "I've gotten better. I haven't hit my own hand in ages. I've got skills now."

Maybe if it meant putting an appliqué on a cushion or a pair of jeans, but Caleb kept that thought to himself as he turned to the landlady. "You don't plan on raising his rent once it's all fixed up?"

"Not a chance." She waved the folder in Hal's direction. "My boyfriend's cousin's a lawyer, and he drew up papers for me for two years, since that's what you said you wanted. You do the upkeep, the rent stays the same, even if I croak. After two years we'll renegotiate."

Caleb eyed the folder as Hal leafed through the papers. He should've brought Uncle Vern. Reading through a contract made Caleb's head hurt. He watched Hal scan through the agreement, his hair falling into his eyes. Hal disliked being called pretty because his dad had used it as a weapon one too many times. That was probably why he went the scruffy route more often than not, but it didn't take away from his long-lashed eyes or the almost delicate cast to his features. Caleb loved the way he looked, and sometimes, like now, just watching him made his heart ache.

He couldn't wait until Hal was back where he belonged.

Since Hal seemed to be intent on getting the place, Caleb returned to the bathroom and kitchen to check the water pressure and see if he could detect any leaks. The electrical wiring appeared to be okay too, so most of the changes were cosmetic, and Caleb felt better about Hal's excitement.

"I'm going to boot the current tenant. He's not keeping his end of the bargain," Mrs. Taylor was saying as he came back into the living room. She pulled out another cigarette and lit up. "And there'd better be no wild parties, drugs, and girls and all that nonsense. I don't want to get woken up by cops in the middle of the damn night. I need my beauty sleep."

"I wouldn't dream of it." Hal glanced at him and raised a questioning eyebrow. "Well, what do you think? Can I go ahead, and sign or did you want to look at the next one on the list?"

Mrs. Taylor puffed harder on her cigarette and eyed him warily. Caleb guessed she needed the extra income from rent, and having it empty would hurt her, but she didn't say anything. "Yeah, go ahead. There's nothing I can see that needs major work, and this place is a helluva lot better than the last one."

"Out of sight." Hal pulled a pen out of his pocket with a grin and signed both copies with a flourish.

A genuine smile crossed Mrs. Taylor's lips, and for the first time she looked kind instead of crusty. "You won't regret it. Thank you, young man. Are you sure you can't move in sooner? I can have the other guy out of here in two weeks. But you'll need to bring your own furniture. All the junk that's here is his."

"No, I have to finish my program in Kentucky. I plan on my move-in date being mid-August. Don't worry about the furniture. I'm pretty good at making do. Thanks again." Hal grinned at Caleb. "Ready to go? Looks like we have extra time on our hands before I have to head back."

"Sounds good to me." Caleb cast a look at the landlady as she led them out and determined he'd give her a call to see if she'd let him come by next month to fix it up before Hal arrived. He'd have enough to do to find a job and get ready for school. "You know, I can come up to Kentucky, help you pack up your place and move," he said as they headed out to Caleb's car.

"You don't have to. Mark's coming down," Hal said and slid into the passenger's seat. "I haven't seen him since I left for Kentucky and he volunteered."

Caleb's hands tightened on the wheel. If there was ever a name he was tired of hearing, it was that man's. It was bad enough he'd been Hal's first, even worse that Hal had been in a relationship with him more than once. He had no idea what qualities the other man had that kept Hal's interest, but it set Caleb on edge.

He started the car and pulled away from the curb. Hal had been avoiding discussing the two of them, and Caleb hadn't pressed him. He'd wanted to be damn certain Hal was really coming before he brought up their past. With the lease signed, Hal wouldn't renege no matter how much Caleb made him squirm.

"May I ask you something personal?" Caleb braced himself with a breath. Time for a reckoning for both of them.

"That's a dumb question." Hal slouched in his seat. "Since when have you felt we couldn't ask each other anything?"

"Since New York." Caleb glanced at him and saw how quiet and still Hal's expression had gone. Caleb struggled with whether or not he should push it and determined Hal was coming anyway, and they needed to have it out, or else it would always be the lingering shadow between them. "Since you decided you couldn't be my lover anymore."

"You didn't exactly fight to keep me," Hal said in a low voice.

Caleb's heart sank. Well, that was nothing less than the naked truth. "You're right, I didn't." And for Hal and the things he'd been through in the past, that would be a big deal. Caleb hadn't thought of it that way. At the time he'd been more concerned with making sure they remained friends, and that had been the easy way out.

"I'm sorry. I shouldn't have said that." Hal crossed his arms and bit the corner of his lip. "We wanted different things, and it wasn't going to change. Going back to being just friends saved us heartbreak in the end."

Maybe Hal was right. Then again, maybe both of them had taken the easy way out. Caleb was scared to tell his family the truth about himself, but he had to. Because Hal was right, it wouldn't take long for them to figure it out if he and Hal hooked up again.

He had to find a way to get the guts to face them and weather the storm afterward. They loved him, but it wouldn't stop them from freaking out. The thought of disappointing them in any way made him sick inside. The only thing he could count on was they wouldn't boot him from their lives. But it was going to be hell for a while.

The alternatives were either moving far away and taking himself out of their inner circle, which he did not want to do, or continue living alone and loveless. He'd tried weekend out-of-town flings and discovered pretty quickly it wasn't at all what he wanted. He wanted Hal. He wanted Hal's dream.

"You never asked your question," Hal said, breaking into Caleb's thoughts. "What is it you're so hesitant to ask?"

Caleb pulled up to a red light and looked over at him. Okay, this was it, time to find out whether or not Mark was serious competition, and he was more than a little nervous. "What is Mark to you? Do you love him? Why didn't it work between you guys? You seem like you have a genuine bond."

"Wow, that's a lot." Hal blew out his breath, his eyes widening in surprise. "Damn, and hard to explain. Mark's just a friend, and yes, I love him, but I'm not in love with him."

That sounded too close to comfort for Caleb. There were different levels of friendship, and he didn't want to think that Hal and Mark had anything like what the two of them have had for years.

Caleb waited to see if Hal would say anything else. He was uncomfortable about pushing for more answers. He stole another glance at Hal and saw that his lips had twisted in a sardonic smile. Caleb ached for him. Clearly there had been some hurt from Mark too.

"Mark has a dislike of monogamy," Hal said lightly, tapping his fingertips on the window frame. "I have no doubt he loves me, but unfortunately I'm not the only one he loves. I realized long ago that sharing someone's heart is not for me. I'm terribly possessive."

"And if he were to suddenly realize you were his one and only...." Caleb asked as the light turned green again. "Would that be what you wanted?"

He caught the slight, almost imperceptible shake of Hal's head as he stared out the window. "No, it wouldn't be what I wanted."

Caleb's heart lightened as he took Hal's hand. Well, at least that was one less thing to worry about. "Have you ever wondered whether or not we made a mistake by walking away?"

"No." Hal pulled his hand away, and Caleb recognized the lie. He had to bite the inside of his cheek to keep from calling him out on it.

"Well I have, just about every day," he said quietly. Caleb needed to know if he was too late or not, and Hal wasn't helping him out at all. He refused to believe he'd screwed up his one and only chance. "We were good together, weren't we?"

Hal continued to stare out the window, but Caleb saw the emotion in the tight line of his jaw. Then Hal looked at him, his eyes dark and moody. "Yeah, we were pretty amazing."

"We could be pretty amazing again," Caleb said, his heart thumping wildly.

Hal blinked rapidly and shook his head, then gave Caleb a rueful smile, but the expression felt off. "No, we couldn't. But we make real good friends, and I'm okay with that."

Well Caleb wasn't okay with that, but he wasn't going to dig for any more answers than he had. Before he went any further with Hal, he needed to figure out his own life and figure it out fast. Maybe he could talk to his uncle or Rodney first. Uncle Vern had always been an ally, and Rodney, well, he knew some of his brother's darkest secrets, and he trusted Rodney to stick by him in return.

God please let that belief be right.

CHARLESTON, SC— JULY 23, 1977

"TELL ME why the hell we're here again, sweating our asses off?" Rodney grumbled as he rubbed a damp washcloth over his face.

It was hot, and the apartment was stuffy despite all the windows and doors being open. The breeze coming through was fitful at best and did nothing to cool them down as they worked. Rodney and Caleb were stripped to their waists and covered in bits of flaked-off plaster as they fixed the ceiling. "Because Hal's going to be here in two weeks, and he's going to have enough to deal with without worrying about getting his home into decent shape too."

Rodney sighed and dropped the washcloth into the bucket of iced water. "And how did I get roped into this?" he asked as he examined the plastering job they'd just finished.

"Because you're his friend too," Caleb retorted, coming down off the ladder as he checked through his mental list of what else had to be done in between their days off. At least Mom had taken Drew for the day. It was impossible to get things done and keep an eye on him at the same time.

"I may be his friend, but not like you." Rodney folded up the little ladder and stuck it out of the way. "I could be at home watching *M*A*S*H.*"

"*M*A*S*H* doesn't start again for two months. More than likely you'd be chasing down your son while I sat back with a beer and a book." Caleb grinned at him as Rodney snatched the washcloth out of the bucket and threatened to smack him with it. As hot as it was, that would probably feel damn good.

"Okay." Rodney pulled his watch out of his pocket and checked the time. "I say you finish stripping the linoleum in the bathroom while I patch up the hole in the drywall, and then we call it a day. Fair enough?"

"Yeah, that'll cut down what's left. Then all we'll have to do is repaint and lay down the new linoleum. Dad plans on making the repairs to the cabinets sometime this week," Caleb said as he retrieved the tools he'd need for the job ahead. "Everything should be ready on time."

"We have to give ourselves a couple days leeway. You know Mom wants to come in and give everything a good cleaning before he gets here," Rodney said as he headed down the hall with a section of drywall in his hand.

"I can't wait to see Hal's face," Caleb said with quiet satisfaction. It was going to be such a load off Hal's mind. Rodney glanced at him in speculation, and it made Caleb skittish. Rodney had been looking at him like that more often lately, like there was something on his mind and he couldn't quite bring himself to say anything. It had Caleb questioning everything he did and said. Did he talk about Hal too often? When he did, were his feelings obvious? It was crazy making and kept him constantly on edge. "He's not going to believe we did this all for him," he continued by way of an explanation, though it left him feeling unsettled.

"He should know you better by now," Rodney said with a snort. "Hal's biggest problem isn't his family; it's that he doesn't believe he deserves any kind of consideration."

Rodney had a good point. Hal would be the first to go out of his way to help somebody else. And he had no problems asking for help when he needed it, but an unsought gesture like this, the idea that others would be thinking of him would completely throw him off guard.

"Well, he does know me. It's the rest of you he'll be surprised by. With the exception of Lily, Hal doesn't understand what a real family is like." Caleb knelt down in the hallway just outside the bathroom to check that the solvent he'd used had had time to work. It looked pretty good, so he began cutting and then peeling off strips of faded and cracked linoleum.

Rodney was family. Caleb's stomach clenched, and his hands felt clumsy. Hal was coming in a few short weeks, and Caleb hadn't gotten any closer to telling his family a damned thing. He hated this, because no matter how he looked at this, someone was going to get hurt. He wanted to keep pretending there was no need to tell them, but that was such a lie. Even if he didn't have a chance with Hal, even if he wasn't coming, Caleb needed to talk to them, because hiding who he was from the people he loved the most was eating him away inside.

Caleb sat back on his heels, staring blindly at the project in front of him. He sensed Rodney pause in his work with the drywall and look at him. "Are you okay?"

"Remember how scared you were to talk to me about your night terrors? It's like you thought that maybe I wouldn't want to be your brother anymore if I knew." It was a lame starting point, but Caleb couldn't get his tongue to say the words *I'm gay*. Two little words, and they weighed on him like a ton of iron on his chest.

"Yeah," Rodney replied quietly as he returned to measuring the hole in the wall. There was none of the bravado that Rodney sometimes showed, no denial. "I should've known better. You'd always been loyal, even when I didn't deserve it. Just thinking about it all scares me. Not because those nights are hell to go through for us all, but because they make me feel like I'm flawed. I'm terrified that one day everybody's going to see through me and realize it too."

Flawed. Yeah, sometimes that's how Caleb felt. Caleb looked at his brother who was now marking up the drywall where he wanted to cut it. "You're not flawed."

Rodney shot him a quick grin. "Well neither are you, in case you were wondering."

Caleb went back to work, mulling over Rodney's words. Knowing it and feeling it were two different things. Caleb didn't think there was anything wrong with Hal other than his occasional penchant for recklessness, and Hal was gay too.

He could tell Rodney his secret. He had to tell him, but the words stayed locked up.

"Whatever happened to that girl you were seeing last semester?" Rodney asked after several minutes passed. "The one you met in class."

"Nothing much, we had a few dates and realized we didn't suit." He sensed Rodney's gaze on him and grew cold. He'd tried the whole blending in and dating thing a few times, and it never worked out. He supposed if he didn't want his family to comment, he should've tried harder. Considering he lived with Rodney, his brother was far more likely to notice Caleb's lack of a love life than anyone else.

Caleb hated wondering about it. It made him ill, so he forced himself to concentrate on the task in front of him before he wound up cutting himself.

"Remember Theresa, that girl you used to see in high school?" Rodney asked, raising his voice slightly as he began to cut out the drywall piece. "I ran into her a couple weeks ago at the market."

Caleb's thoughts flashed back to the pretty girl who had been so into him. Damn, he'd been blind then. A straight guy would never have passed up a chance to make out with her. His lack of interest had been a sore spot. He'd known that, yet he hadn't recognized where his gaze had drifted off to. "I've seen her a couple times when I'm out with Lou. Her daughter looks just like her."

Rodney went quiet again, and then he set down his tools before turning toward Caleb. Caleb caught the movement out of the corner of his eyes and went still. He tried to tell himself it was ridiculous to be nervous. But he suddenly felt cornered.

"Can I ask you a question?" Rodney said quietly.

No. The word was on Caleb's lips, but he forced himself to meet Rodney's eyes. "Sure." *Please, God let it be something stupid, like could I take Drew tomorrow so Rodney could get in an extra shift.*

"Call me crazy," Rodney said slowly, his gaze intent on Caleb's face, "but I get the feeling you love Hal."

Caleb forced a chuckle and ran a hand over his hair as a white-hot shaft of panic hit him so hard it left him shaking. "Of course I do. We've been friends forever. He's almost like my brother."

"No, he's not," Rodney replied. "Not like a brother, not at all. I'm your brother, and you don't look at me the way you look at him. I couldn't miss it over the holidays or misunderstand the look in your eyes sometimes when you talk about him. You love the man."

Caleb's hand tightened around the cutter, and his stomach began to roil unpleasantly. He was never going to get a better opening than this, and denying it would just send him down a road he didn't want to be on. He closed his eyes, whispered a silent prayer, though he wasn't sure anybody was listening, and made himself meet Rodney's eyes. "Yeah, I love him," he said quietly. "I've always loved him. It just took me a very long time to face that realization."

His brother's expression wasn't shocked or disgusted; however, there was concern, uncertainty, and thoughtfulness in his eyes. Rodney went back to cutting out the drywall as Caleb watched him, wishing he could tell what the hell Rodney was thinking.

After a long moment, Caleb turned to his own work, hot and cold spells hitting him like he had a fever. He had to find some way of getting through to Rodney. "I tried dating women, and all I did was hurt them because I just wasn't interested. I tried pretending I was normal, and it only made me feel more not normal." He was such a coward. He couldn't look at his brother, and he couldn't say the words, couldn't admit outright that he was gay.

"When we were growing up, you always appeared uncomfortable when we talked about girls. I used to think it was because you were shy, though you never seemed to be shy about anything else. I used to wonder what you were waiting for." Rodney set the small saw down and turned to face Caleb. "Then I went into the Army, and I met guys who reminded me of you and Hal. I guess leaving home opens you up more to the world around you, people's differences."

Caleb couldn't believe he was having this conversation with Rodney and that his brother wasn't freaking out. It was surreal, but slowly the painful mass of knots in his stomach eased as hope took its place. "I'd gotten to be very good at lying to myself," Caleb said. "It actually took me going to Vietnam to admit how I felt."

It was awkward enough to dodge dates back home, but the pressure to fit in over there had been even more intense. Talk of sex had been open and ribald, and Caleb heard more than he'd ever wanted to know about the hooch girls. There had been pressure to join in on the conversation, pressure to visit the girls. Caleb managed to evade most of it with a fictitious girl back home even if it had given him a bit of a reputation for being too much of a mama's boy. Thank God for Lily's frequent letters, though if she ever found out Caleb had pretended they were from his made-up girl, he'd die.

"It's strange, I won't lie," Rodney admitted, "knowing that my little brother loves another man. It's hard to wrap my head around." A frown lined its way between Rodney's brows, and a fresh wave of fear and illness washed through Caleb. "I mean, I've always known about

Hal. I think anybody with any sense knew about Hal. And I knew you were closer than most friends, but I never questioned it until recently."

Caleb tried to say something, but there was so much crowding his brain, his tongue froze. He was torn between tension and relief that his secret was finally out.

"Is that why Hal was kicked out? Is that what you're afraid of, that we'll toss you aside too?" Rodney asked.

"I'm sure that's an underlying reason, though Hal never told his parents, just Lily." Caleb shot a measuring look at Rodney, relaxing a little more as the tension began to slide away. He was glad that Rodney had been the first to figure it out. "I think the ending factor was his dad figuring out that he couldn't control Hal."

"And what about you? Your first concern is always somebody else." Rodney frowned again, though this time Caleb could tell that it was a frown of concern, and his throat tightened. "You have to know that you're not going to be shunned."

"I'm afraid of disappointing Mom and Dad," Caleb replied with a heavy sigh. "Don't tell them, okay?"

"I think they'd take it hard. God knows they had a rough time dealing with me knocking up Drew's mama before we were married. They definitely don't approve of me raising him alone. But they came around, you know. I think they'd come around with you too. It's just a matter of weathering the storm. Because what it comes down to is, they love us. Sometimes I wonder why when it comes to me. You're the golden son."

"I am not," Caleb said with heat. He thought Rodney had given up all that nonsense. Then he saw the sly humor in Rodney's eyes and realized he'd said it just to knock Caleb out of his spiral of fear and worry. He shook his head with a little smile. "I need to think about it. I mean, I know I have to tell them, and I've been working myself up to it for months. It just… it's going to hurt them."

"Fair enough. I'm not asking you to run over there and confess. I'm saying there's no reason both of us should be lonely bachelors. If you have a chance at being happy with Hal, then you need to grab it and hold on to it. I love Mom and Dad, but this is your life. You have to live it for you, not them anymore." Rodney picked up his tools again. "I guess what I'm trying to say is that it's okay. You loving Hal, it's cool. How many people have a connection like the two of you do? That's pretty damn special."

Rodney was serious. Caleb could see it in his eyes. "Thank you," Caleb said gruffly as the full import hit him. His brother knew. He knew the secret Caleb had been trying to hide ever since he realized his sexuality. He knew, and he didn't care. His chest tightened as his emotions swam over him. He could handle Rodney being a little unsettled because Caleb himself had been unsettled when he first realized the truth. "I guess that means you don't think I'm a—"

"No," Rodney interrupted. "Whatever you're going to say, no. You've been looking out for me ever since you've gotten back home. You've helped me through some rough shit, and I don't know where I'd be right now if it wasn't for you. Dead maybe, on the street, I don't know. So I'm sure as hell not going to turn my back on you. And when you choose to tell our parents, if you want me by your side, I'll be there."

Caleb got up, went over to his brother, and hugged him. Thank you just wasn't adequate. Even if he wanted to say anything else, his throat was too tight for words, his relief too profound.

Rodney hugged him back and then gave him a push. "Go on, it's far too hot to be hanging all over each other. I don't plan on being here all evening. Let's get this finished and get out of here so we can relax."

CHARLESTON, SC—
AUGUST 3, 1977

JUST BEFORE sunset Hal pulled up in front of his apartment building. A porch light had been left on, which meant Caleb must've been here at some point, though his car was nowhere in sight. He was disappointed to be coming home to an empty place after just leaving another one, but he couldn't expect Caleb to wait around for him to show up. He had no doubt Caleb would be there within thirty minutes of finding out he'd arrived.

Hal felt battered after the long day of packing and driving, but damn, it was so good to be back in Charleston. For a long moment, he sat there in the car with the window rolled down, taking in the scent of summer flowers and the breeze from the ocean. This was home. His wandering days were over.

He dragged himself out of the car and pulled out his beanbag chair. Out of all the furnishings stuffed in the car and strapped down on the hood, other than his books and bookshelf, the beanbag was the most important. He'd need to get the remainder of his belongings before he fell asleep, but right now, he didn't have the energy. A quick nap would be just what he needed. In the morning he'd drive over to Caleb's job to surprise him.

Hal had only himself to blame for his exhaustion. He should've started packing and organizing sooner than he had, instead of cramming and tossing last minute. He trudged up the stairs, anxious to get into his own place. A welcome mat had been set out on the doorstep, just as Caleb promised, and Hal fished underneath it for the key. He stepped inside, flipped on the light, and stood there blinking in astonishment at the freshly painted and spruced-up living room.

He stepped outside, checked the number over his door with a sense of unreality, and felt his heart catch. He'd been prepared to live in a mess as he got the apartment pulled together, and he'd had no doubt Caleb would've helped him with the repairs. But he never expected to arrive and discover they'd started without him. The place even smelled like it had been freshly cleaned from top to bottom.

Hal entered again and dropped the beanbag off to the side. The orange stood out as a bright splat of color against the buffed floors. Without the dingy furnishings, it looked as if there was more room than Hal recalled. The walls had been repainted and the ceiling fixed. In a daze Hal went down the hallway to find that the work hadn't stopped with the front room. The hole in the hall had been filled. The bathroom had a new floor. Clean towels hung on the rack, a shower curtain over the tub, and basic toiletries had been laid out in case Hal didn't want to unpack anything before he showered.

Swallowing the lump in his throat, his pulse thumping wildly, Hal's exhaustion vanished as he continued to explore. He'd never felt so welcome in his life. He leaned against the door to his bedroom, his heart aching with a bittersweet pang that brought a smile to his lips. Damn Caleb for making him fall in love with him all over again. Not that he'd ever fallen out of love with him. The last two visits had proved that.

And to make it even crazier, Caleb didn't plan this for that response. He did it because he was that kind of a guy, because he was kind and decent and he gave a damn about Hal.

He was in serious trouble.

Hal went into the kitchen and found similar repairs. In fact, there was nothing left to do but move his things in, have the rest of his furniture sent from New York, and go shopping for what he needed next. He was going to have to find some way to repay Caleb for all this.

A package of Dixie cups and paper plates sat on the counter, and a note was taped to the refrigerator door. Bemused, Hal picked it up and scanned Caleb's precise handwriting.

> *Hal,*
> *Mom left sandwiches and a pitcher of Kool-Aid in the fridge. She put some basics in the pantry. The phone line is on, so call me when you get in. No excuses about how late it is. Call me or else. I have a key to your apartment and I will retaliate.*
> *Caleb*

Hal stuffed the note in his pocket and peeked inside the refrigerator. Sure enough, there were the sandwiches, neatly wrapped in wax paper stacked next to a carton of eggs, some milk, and the promised Kool-Aid. His stomach growled, reminding him how ravenous he was. Hal grabbed a sandwich and tore off the wrapping. He couldn't remember how long it had been since he'd last stopped for food. Curious, he opened the pantry and found a box of Twinkies. Oh yeah, even better. Hal raided the box before making his way over to the phone on the wall.

"Hello?"

Hal swallowed a bite of Twinkie at the sound of Caleb's voice. "I've found the woman who would make me consider marriage." He paused with a grin, imagining the shocked expression on Caleb's face. "Your mom is the most wonderful woman in the world, next to Lily."

"That is true, but you and my mom, no, just no."

"She left me Twinkies, Caleb, a whole box of Twinkies." Hal's grin widened, and he took another bite of his sandwich. "That is love. Seriously, I don't know how to thank you. I can't believe what you did here. I don't know what to say, man."

"You don't have to say anything, and before you say any nonsense about repaying me, shut it down. Most of the stuff we had in the shed and the linoleum I got on a deal. It's not like you had a lot of square footage."

It would be useless to argue, so Hal would just have to find another way of showing his gratitude. "Seeing all of this woke me up again. I was half-tempted to stumble upstairs and pass out till tomorrow. Now I actually feel like I can get this done before crashing."

"When did you get in?"

"About ten minutes ago. I got a later start than I wanted, and it took too long to get to the main road." Hal balled up the wax paper in his hand and made a mental note to get a new trashcan tomorrow. He needed to start a list.

"Mark didn't keep you on track?" There was a tone in Caleb's voice that made Hal take notice. He didn't see why Caleb was so bothered by Mark, but clearly he was. Hal thought he'd settled this the last time he visited.

"Well, Mark sent me a letter backing out. Not that I blame him. I couldn't really see him in the middle of nowhere, so I'd been prepared. The letter came late, and the waiting gave me far too much of a chance to ignore reality." Hal leaned against the counter and considered a second sandwich. The first one hadn't even begun to fill the hole in his stomach. "He promised he'd make it up to me."

Knowing Mark it would be a grand gesture. Hal couldn't picture him physically toiling, so he'd been surprised by the initial offer. He was curious to see what Mark would do to fulfill his promise. He hoped Mark remembered Hal didn't like to have money waved around and spent on him. He appreciated the gesture, but he liked to pay for things on his own and not feel beholden to anyone.

"Well, get something in your stomach and hold tight. We're on our way over to help you get unpacked." Caleb hung up the phone before Hal could reply, and he set the receiver on the wall with a shake of his head. Caleb and his family had done enough for him, but calling him back would be useless. Besides, Hal wanted to see him, and with a little help, the car would be unpacked in no time. So he grabbed another sandwich, poured himself some Kool-Aid, and walked through his apartment again.

He couldn't believe this place was his. This wasn't a dorm room, or a made-up bed on a friend's couch, or a place set aside for him in a host home. This was all his. He could walk around buck-naked, and nobody would be there to care. He could have as many books as he wanted cluttered all about. He didn't have much to fill up the apartment now, even with as small as it was, but he had plans to make it entirely his own space.

Hal had finished his sandwich and was hauling up boxes when two cars pulled into the lot. He heard Drew first, his voice bright with excitement, then he saw Caleb walking toward the apartment, and his heart stuttered. It felt like he'd been waiting the last nine years for this moment, returning to Charleston for good and knowing he didn't have to be Caleb's friend from afar.

"Hey there," Hal called down softly from his landing, and Caleb paused to look up.

"Welcome home." Warmth swept through Hal at those words and the gruff, husky sound of Caleb's voice. Hal left his box on the doorstep and went to greet him. As he moved to hug Caleb, he held up a hand to Hal's chest stopping him. "You shaved your mustache."

Hal brought a hand to his bare upper lip. It felt strange to him after having facial hair for so many years. "Yeah, I figured it was time." It felt like a fresh start, and Hal wanted to embrace that idea.

"Man, I liked your mustache." Caleb pulled him close for a quick, tight hug, and then Hal stepped back as Drew ran up, calling his name.

"Who are you?" Hal asked Drew as the boy hung on his leg.

"Andrew Vernon Hudson." Drew tipped his head back with a smile. "And you're Uncle Caleb's white friend."

Hal laughed and bent down to hug him as Rodney walked up with a groan. "Sorry about that. He'll say whatever's on his mind."

"Nothing to be sorry for, it's true." Hal straightened and greeted Rodney. "Thank you for everything. I thought I'd walked into the wrong apartment."

Rodney smiled and caught Drew's hand before he could dart off. "Trust me, Caleb organized the whole thing. Dad and I just showed up when we were told to with tools in hand."

"I helped too!" Drew said, waving to get his attention.

"Is that right?" Hal asked, and Drew nodded, his face serious. "Well thank you, little man. You must be better with that kind of stuff than me. Did you come to help unpack too?"

"Uh-huh," Drew snuck a glance at his dad. "Don't wanna go to bed."

Hal laughed and opened the trunk of his car. "I admire your honesty." He pulled out his pillow and handed it to Drew. "Stick that on top of the orange beanbag chair for me, and I'll find other stuff you can carry."

Drew wrapped his arms around the pillow and trotted off, trying to keep his chin over the top so he could see where he was going. "All the boxes are marked for the room they belong in," Hal said as he hauled out a box.

"Is it legible?" Caleb asked, lifting his brow.

"You've had plenty of practice deciphering my scrawl. There are only so many options," Hal called after him as he walked away. "Oh, and watch the box by the door." He tucked a lamp under his arm and sprinted past Caleb to get it before they tripped in the dark. He set the lamp inside his bedroom, moved in the box and found Drew buried in the beanbag chair, his arms around the pillow.

"Comfy?" he asked, and Drew nodded.

"Can I keep it?" Drew asked, laying his cheek on the chair.

"If I let you keep it, where am I going to sleep?" Hal asked, curious to hear Drew's response. The little boy cocked his head and then patted the floor next to the beanbag.

"Right dere," he said with a toothy grin, and Hal laughed. Damn, as tired as he was, he bet he could sleep on the floor and not notice how hard the ground was until morning.

"What the hell is in this?" Rodney asked as he came inside. "Lead bricks?"

Hal glanced over as Rodney set the box down. "Some of my books."

"Just some?" Rodney shook his head. "You and Caleb. How did you two ever learn to talk to each other when your noses were always in books?"

"We talked about what we read," Hal said with a laugh as he followed Rodney out.

It didn't take too long to empty the car with all three of them going at it while Drew occupied himself by opening every box that came through the door. Hal wished he'd hidden a toy in one as a surprise.

After the last box had been brought up and Hal's two bookcases were situated in the living room and bedroom, he collapsed down on the now empty beanbag chair and closed his eyes. He never would've been able to bring all that stuff up himself. He would've given up a quarter of the way into it and prayed that his belongings were there in the morning. "I owe you all a steak dinner and a movie."

"You don't owe us anything," Caleb said.

"Speak for yourself," Rodney retorted. "Just say when and where, Hal, and I'll be there."

Hal held up both thumbs. Sitting down had been a mistake, closing his eyes had been a bigger one. His whole body was weighed down, and he just wanted to sprawl here a little longer.

"You're staring," Rodney commented in a low voice, catching Hal's attention as he was about to drift off. "I promise, he's not going to disappear if you turn away."

"He looks dead on his feet. I want to be ready to catch him if he passes out," Caleb replied sounding embarrassed.

Hal cracked open one eye to find Caleb watching him and Rodney looking at his brother with an amused expression. A stab of alarm hit Hal's gut. He'd seen the considering looks Rodney shot them the last two times he'd visited, and now, not even a day into him being back in Charleston for good, they'd already given reason for comment.

"Too late. There's no need to catch me. I'm laid out." Hal propped himself up on his elbows and watched Rodney snag Drew as he ran by. "Thanks for your help, guys. It would all still be in my car if it was up to me."

"All joking aside, you don't need to buy me a steak. If you want to repay me, you can be on the babysitting list." Rodney laid Drew over his shoulder and clapped Caleb on the arm. "See you at home. I've got to get this one down, or he'll be a terror tomorrow."

Hal crossed his arms as Rodney left, taking the munchkin with him. He wanted to ask about the little exchange between Caleb and Rodney, but he wasn't sure if he was reading too much into it. It might lead to a conversation about the two of them, and Hal was not up to that. As worn as he was, he'd probably blurt out something and give Caleb the wrong idea.

Caleb crouched down next to him and opened a box. Incredulous, Hal watched him pull out a stack of his books. "You do realize you're probably on an FBI watch list right?" Caleb held up battered copies of *Howl and Other Poems*, *The Autobiography of Malcom X*, *Giovanni's Room*, and *Fahrenheit 451*. Hal was too hard on his books. He carried them with him for weeks rereading, sharing, and marking them up.

"You might be right." Hal shook his head as Caleb set the books on a shelf. "It's too late for that. I'll unpack tomorrow. If you start I'll feel obligated to help, and I don't want to do shit."

"I was thinking about all those weekends when we'd stay up talking about activism or philosophy or whatever craziness went into our heads when we were punch-drunk tired at three a.m." Caleb fished more books out and smiled at *Brave New World* and *Native Son*. Hal remembered Caleb introducing him to those books. "Don't you miss it?"

"Yeah, it's been a while." Hal nudged Caleb with his toe. "I've been reminiscing. You know you're the one who got me started on this whole crazy life, thinking I could make a difference. Remember when we used to pass out those Charleston Movement posters?"

"Oh yeah. Uncle Vern had kittens when he found out you were helping me. He was sure your parents were going to find out and cause trouble."

"Don't you get mad? Get tired of trying to fight the bullshit?" Hal asked as he sat up and took out another stack of books. Caleb appeared to be hell-bent on getting this organized tonight, and he was making Hal feel lazy. At least it offered them an excuse to talk longer.

Caleb tilted his head and looked at Hal for a long moment. "Yeah, all the time. It's maddening, infuriating…. Sometimes you just want to pound sense into a person. And when I feel that way, I know I need to step back and let it go, because it'll eat me up inside."

"That's the part I have trouble with," Hal said with a sigh as he shoved books onto the bookshelf. "Letting go."

"You know, what gets to me isn't the outright hatred. That's scary, because I never know when I'm going to be a target. But what really digs under the skin is the day-after-day little slights. The way people look at me like I'm an unknown dog, and they don't know if I'll be friendly or if I'll bite. Or the assumptions they make that make me shake my head in disbelief because it's so damned backward and ignorant, yet they think they're being supportive, and they expect me to nod and agree because any other response offends them. Then people say I'm imagining it or being too sensitive, and part of me wants to believe it, but deep down I know it's just another symptom that affects us all."

"This got deep," Hal said with a sideways glance. At least, most of the time, people didn't look at him and immediately peg him as gay and treat him according to how they felt about that. It had happened, but not as often. There was no closet for being black.

Caleb grinned at him, easing the frown lines that had worked their way around his mouth. "Well, that's one of the best things about you, Hal. When it gets deep, you dive right in with me."

Hal wanted to catch Caleb's hand and kiss his fingers. Hell, if he were honest, he wanted to curl against Caleb and kiss him for real. He ached to feel Caleb's arms around him, to have the pressure of those lush lips against his own. He was too tired to have any of his defenses up.

"You know what one of the best things about you is?" Hal asked turning toward him. "I know no matter what, you're going to be there for me. For anybody you love."

Caleb's eyes darkened, and Hal's heart skipped a beat. Caleb was going to kiss him, and Hal couldn't understand how his inner voice was shouting *no* and *yes* at the same damn time. He looked away, breaking eye contact, and mashed his pillow into a comfortable lump.

"Is that all you have to sleep on?" Caleb closed the empty box and indicated the beanbag as Hal yawned wide enough to make his jaw pop. "When does the rest of your furniture arrive?"

"Should be next week. I'll give Mark a call and get the ETA. Maybe I'll hit up a few yard sales this weekend." Hal sank down on the bag, fighting another yawn. He needed to get more furniture because Mark only stored Hal's bedroom set. He couldn't have Caleb come over with no place for him to sit.

"He really left you hanging in Kentucky?"

Hal's eyes flew open. He hadn't even realized he'd shut them. He recognized that tone—not quite overprotective but edging there. "Go easy on him. He's as city bred as you can get. He's not built for Appalachia country. He'll make it up to me." Hal squeezed Caleb's hand with a smile. "You did more than enough. So don't worry about not making it to Kentucky, okay?"

Caleb leaned down and kissed Hal's cheek. "I'm glad you're here. I'll see you tomorrow, and we can see about getting more of these boxes unpacked. Unless you want me to stay?"

Hal shook his head and curled deeper into the chair. "I'm not fit company. I think I'll just lay here for an hour or so." He smiled at Caleb. "I'll see you tomorrow."

He watched Caleb head for the door, through half-slitted eyes. His friend paused and looked back at him, then shook his head and flipped off the lights. Hal curled his arms around the pillow, closed his eyes, and let his body go limp.

CHARLESTON, SC— AUGUST 6, 1977

CALEB HOPPED out of the truck he'd borrowed, excited to tackle the day ahead. He grabbed the classified section of the local newspaper off the dashboard and slapped it against his thigh as he headed up Hal's steps. He'd circled all the promising yard sales, and if they hit them up early enough, they might have first pickings.

He couldn't stop grinning even if he looked like a fool. Hal was home. His whole body sang with that knowledge. And once the errands were out of the way, they'd have the entire weekend to kick back and relax. Caleb had been looking forward to this all week.

He knocked on the door, mentally going over the list of yard sales and mapping out their route. The door opened, and his good morning died unspoken. Mark stood in Hal's doorway, handsome in a Hollywood kind of way that Caleb had never gone for. Caleb's gaze slid to a love bite on his throat, and a hot stab of jealousy hit his gut. Hal had only been in town three days. When the hell had Mark arrived to stake a claim?

"Caleb?" Mark stepped back to let him in. "Come in, Hal's expecting you."

"When did you get to Charleston?" He glanced at the bruise on his throat again and noted with relief that it appeared to be a few days old. His equilibrium had not needed a scare like that, but relieved or not, he couldn't say he was happy with Mark being in Charleston in Hal's place so early in the morning.

"Last night. I brought Hal's furniture down from New York. I wanted him to have a proper place to sleep, now that he's settled here for a few years." There was something in Mark's tone that made Caleb wonder if the other man wished Hal had moved to New York instead. Too bad. Because even if Hal decided that he'd rather be in New York, Caleb would follow him.

Caleb stepped inside and noted the new boxes in the living room to replace the ones Hal had emptied and broken down. Hal stuck his head out of the bedroom, shirtless and sexy, even with his hair an unbrushed mess. "Give me five, and I'll be ready," he said and disappeared into his room. "Grab a cup of coffee."

Caleb didn't steal a look in Hal's room. He didn't want to know if Hal's bed had been set up or not or wonder if he'd slept in it alone last night, platonic or not. He believed Hal when he said that nothing was going on between him and Mark, but he also recognized Mark was interested, and it made him more than a little grumpy and territorial.

"How long are you in town?" Caleb asked, crossing his arms. He supposed Mark would be going along with them to the yard sales, and that put a definite damper on Caleb's morning. It would be rude to not include him, and Caleb wished he could conveniently forget the manners his mom had drilled into him.

"For a week. I decided I deserved a holiday, and I've never been to Charleston. I'm looking forward to Hal showing me around. I've heard it's got a quaint, old-world kind of charm," Mark said over his shoulder as he went into the kitchen. "Coffee?"

"No thanks." Boy, Mark was making himself right at home in Hal's place. It didn't matter if the same could be said about himself or that Hal invited that kind of intimacy. Hal was the kind of person who lived by the mantra his place was yours. Caleb just didn't want Mark anywhere near Hal's place. It was jealousy talking and maybe insecurity, but knowing it didn't change his feelings.

Maybe Caleb wouldn't be so bothered if he knew what step he was taking with Hal next. Hal liked to tease him about being too much of a planner, but when it came to the two of them, Caleb found himself at a loss. Romance was a concept that left him feeling even clumsier than when he got all tongue-tied talking about his feelings. He suspected that Hal would absolutely love being romanced. Where was he supposed to begin?

Every scenario Caleb came up with, he second-guessed to death. The last time they'd slid so easily into the relationship without all the angst of how they felt as teenagers. It wasn't going to be so easy this time.

"So, Hal tells me that you surprised him by fixing up his apartment," Mark said, his back to Caleb so he couldn't see the other man's expression. Something about his voice made Caleb think Mark wasn't all that pleased about it or felt like he was in competition with Caleb. That wasn't why Caleb had done it, but he didn't mind if it put Mark on the defensive.

Caleb looked around the kitchen. It still looked worn, but it was an improvement over what had been there before. "I guess we both like to surprise him. I know Hal's grateful to have his furniture back." At least he'll get a decent night's sleep. It couldn't have been comfortable sleeping on that beanbag the last few nights. "I'm sure he's happy to see you again."

"So yard sales?" Mark said with a pained expression as Hal entered the kitchen. "Don't you want to get matching sets instead of whatever's available?"

"Not really." Hal shrugged and poured himself a cup of coffee, then upended the sugar container over his mug in a steady stream. He was going to be wired today. "I just want a place for us to sit, a place to eat, though that's optional, and maybe some extra dishes."

Caleb lifted the newspaper with a wave. "If we get moving we can accomplish that."

Hal saluted with a mocking flip of his hand, his gray-green eyes sparkling. "Yes, sir, Gunnery Sergeant, sir."

Caleb had a crazy urge to wrap his arms around him and kiss that mischievous smile. He was very conscious of Mark's gaze on him, and it was inhibiting. He recalled the innocent time when he didn't care if anybody saw him with his arm around Hal or not. Before he realized what his feelings meant. Of course, he wasn't in any position to give Hal a kiss anyway.

Caleb caught Hal's hand and squeezed. Hal squeezed back as he took a sip of his coffee, and the look in his eyes went from teasing to warm.

"Break it up, you two." Mark set his mug in the sink. "Let's go look at some secondhand furniture."

"Don't be a snob," Hal said with a laugh as he nudged Mark playfully. He gulped down the rest of his coffee and straightened away from the counter.

"Can I help it if I want you to have nice things?" Mark replied with no trace of offense. Hal was right; Caleb couldn't picture Mark in the backwoods of Kentucky in a cabin with no running water. He must not have believed the extent of how much Hal had been roughing it when he offered to help Hal pack. Heck, Caleb hadn't believed it at first until they'd gone apartment hunting together. He could only imagine how appalled Mark would've been if he'd seen some of the places Hal had been checking out.

"I borrowed my cousin's truck in case we get lucky and find something. It'll be a tight squeeze with all of us, but we can manage." Maybe it was rude of him, but Caleb hoped Mark took one look at the battered truck and opted out. To his disappointment, Mark didn't say a word. Hal slid into the seat between them, and Mark casually stretched out his arm over Hal's shoulders with a quick look at Caleb like he was daring him to object.

Caleb clenched his jaw and pulled away. It was going to be a longass day. He'd have to keep it together because he didn't want Hal to notice the tension between him and Mark and get upset. Hal was very good at noticing when something was bothering Caleb.

"Since you're going to be around a week, we should show you around," Caleb said. He thought of the club down on King Street but squashed that idea. He wanted to take Hal, just the two of them. If Mark came along he might end up seeing them dance together, and he didn't want that any more than Mark probably wanted to see him and Hal dancing with each other.

"Hal promised me the grand tour. I'm eager to see the old mansions with their gardens. And I wanted to take him to Perdita's and The Colony House. I hear Charleston is turning its culinary atmosphere around. It might be a good place to invest in a new restaurant."

Even if he'd been invited, Perdita was definitely out of Caleb's budget range now that school was getting ready to start again and his hours would be cut back. Mark made the kind of money where he didn't have to think about the expense of coming down to Charleston for a week of wining and dining.

Now that he thought about it, he bet Mark was in a fancy hotel, not slumming it with Hal in his tiny apartment. Caleb narrowed his eyes. Probably trying to talk Hal into shacking up with him for a week. His comment about investing here hadn't escaped Caleb's notice. If Mark opened a new restaurant in Charleston, he'd be in and out of their lives. He didn't want to begrudge Hal a friend, but he also didn't want to worry about Mark trying to get back in Hal's bed either. If he didn't respect commitment to Hal now, why would he respect it when Hal made a commitment to someone else?

"You like history. We can take you to plenty of places around here that you'd enjoy," Hal said, and Caleb relaxed inside at the *we*. "We can walk by the Old City Jail and go through the newly dubbed French Quarter. They're starting to restore the old warehouses down there, build up the area into something nice. There's Ft. Sumter and museums, all kinds of things."

Caleb pulled up to the first sale on his list, a multi-family affair, and saw to his satisfaction there was furniture out as well as several tables of items just for the kitchen.

"Oh, look at that bookcase," Hal said, leaning forward in excitement. "It's beautiful."

"Focus, Zimmer, you need a table and chairs first," Caleb said as he clambered out of the truck. He held the door open for Hal who shot him an exasperated look as he slid out.

"Your priorities are skewed. There is always room in the budget for more bookcases and books," Hal retorted. "I can eat on the couch if I have to."

"You have to have a couch first," Caleb called after him as Hal made a beeline for the bookcase, bypassing the kitchenware.

"You're not going to win that one," Mark commented as Hal was distracted by the boxes of books nearby.

"Don't I know it." Caleb watched his friend for a long moment. He could admit that he was tempted to check out the books himself. Hitting yard sales might not have been the best strategic move. This wasn't likely to be the only place where they found books. At the next stop, if they didn't see more furniture out, they were moving on.

"You should know I tried to talk Hal into moving to New York after his program in Kentucky. I suppose the time wasn't right. He has too many dissatisfied memories," Mark said slowly. "But he also has many friends. I think he could be happy with me there."

Caleb stole a glance at Mark, surprised by his candidness. "I'd admit he has friends there and he liked the culture he found in the city, the ability to be himself. But Hal has a home in Charleston, a sense of family that New York can't give him."

"Maybe, but it's not going to keep me from trying to convince him to move back when he has his degree. You know what he wants to do with his life. Where better to help homeless youth then the biggest city on the East Coast?"

Mark may have a point, but it didn't change the fact that Hal belonged in Charleston. If Mark waited that long before making a move, he was going to find himself on the definite losing side. That is if Caleb ever got his ass into gear. Mark showing up like this had shaken him up.

For a second Caleb considered being just as candid and decided against it. He couldn't go announcing his intentions without revealing them to Hal first. He'd just be stroking his own ego and engaging in a figurative chest-bump match with Mark, which would do nobody any good.

"I have no doubt Hal will make a difference no matter where he goes," Caleb replied and went to check out the stack of dishes and box of mugs on one of the tables. His gaze strayed to Hal who crouched before the books, the early-morning sun glinting off his light brown hair.

Mark joined him at the table and picked up a spice rack with an expression of mild amusement on his face. He set it down on the table with shake of his head. "Please tell me you have a list of what he needs, or we're going to be at this all day."

"Right here," Caleb tapped his temple. "This morning we're mostly looking for big items, a couch, kitchen table, and chairs. If we see other things he can use at a good bargain, then we're grabbing them as well."

"Allow me to take care of some kitchen items. I know them well, and I've seen what's sadly lacking in his." Mark pulled a box of kitchen implements to him and began going through them. "This is more fun than I thought. You don't know what you'll find."

"I guess this is not how you'd pictured you'd be spending your stay in Charleston," Caleb commented as he left Mark with the kitchen boxes and went to examine a nearby table. It was too big for his kitchen, and the heavy style didn't suit Hal at all. Caleb turned to check out the used tools instead. He needed a smaller Phillip's head screwdriver.

"No, I wanted to ask for another chance," Mark murmured, just low enough for the two of them to hear. "Though the object of my affection seems hesitant to take me up on my offer."

Caleb went cold inside, and his vision went blurry with shock. The situation was more serious than he'd thought. He glanced around at the people milling about the yard. Hal was occupied in the middle of a haggle and not paying them any attention. The few other die-hard browsers were occupied at other tables stretched out across the lawn.

"To be blunt, you're not going to get a second chance as long as this person is not your first and only choice." Caleb set down the tool in his hand and turned to face Mark who was studying him with a thoughtful expression.

"I'd be willing to try an exclusive commitment with them." Mark was very serious, and that alarmed Caleb even more.

"They deserve more than a try." It irked Caleb to know that the truism applied to himself as well.

Mark also looked toward Hal, who noticed their attention and waved with a guilty smile. He'd bought the damn bookcase. Caleb hoped it didn't put too much of a dent in the money Hal set aside for this morning's purchases. Though Mark would probably buy whatever the hell Hal wanted if Hal would let him.

"You influence him too much." Mark gestured around the yard sale, though Caleb was sure he meant more than this. "When I first met him all he could talk about was you and missing here. You talked him out of the antiwar protests. Then there was the insane idea to join the Peace Corps. Now moving to Charleston. What else do you have in store for him?"

"That's an awful lot to lay on a guy. You should know him well enough to understand Hal has his own mind, and once it's made up it's pretty difficult to sway him." Caleb wasn't sure whether to be amused or offended. "I don't have any more influence over him than he does me."

"I don't like it." Mark frowned, his expression darkening. "Things are difficult enough for… you know. This situation makes it even more difficult."

Caleb picked up a screwdriver, turning it slowly in his hands as he tried to pick apart all the nuances of what Mark was saying. He could be talking about the little triangle between the three of them, or being a gay man in South Carolina versus New York, or the fact that Caleb was black and Hal was white. Whichever way, Mark was right, they all made the situation more difficult, but that wasn't about to stop him anymore.

"I know you care about him, and I know he values your opinion, Mark. But I'd be careful not to think you know best for him. He's had enough of that with his dad, and he'll push back. You'll wind up hurting each other, so don't." Something in the way Mark's expression darkened made Caleb think he'd hit a nerve. "And if you think you can drive a wedge between our friendship, you're wrong. You won't be the first person who's made that mistake, and Hal doesn't have any patience for those kinds of games."

Mark took a step closer to him, his gaze intent and spoke in a low voice, "But you're looking for more than friendship aren't you? Here, in a place where everybody will notice and comment. You're going to put both of you in danger."

"You aren't saying anything we don't already know. Make no mistake, above everything else, Hal's my friend first, and he always will be." Caleb stared at Mark, hoping he'd hear him. "Neither one of us plan on doing anything that will change that fact."

Mark studied him a long moment, then stepped back and returned to the kitchenware. Caleb let out a breath and raised his head to see Hal watching him, his head cocked and brow lifted. He took a quick glance around, but nobody else appeared to have noticed anything out of the ordinary. He looked at Hal, grinned, and shrugged. "What?"

Hal shook his head with a roll of his eyes and went back to shopping.

CHARLESTON, SC— AUGUST 12, 1977

THE FIRST time Mark had taken Hal to a restaurant like this with its hushed and fancy décor, they'd only known each other a few weeks. Hal had felt out of place and awkwardly young in the rich surroundings and low candlelight, but Mark had been witty, charming, and he'd captivated Hal's senses. It had been so easy for him to tumble into desire and adoration. It was sobering to realize how desperate he'd been for affection. Now he was content with the friendship that had blossomed from that unlikely beginning.

He straightened his dinner jacket, grateful that he had one remaining suit, or he would've felt as awkward now as he had then. The maître d' checked their reservation and handed the menus off to a hostess with a smile and a murmured, "Enjoy your meal, gentlemen."

Hal and Mark followed the hostess to a table in the corner that offered them a little privacy. Hal had noticed all the extra attention Mark had shown him this week, but he was no longer a horny seventeen-year-old boy in need of responsiveness from a father figure. He loved Mark, but only as a friend. The infatuation had died long ago. If Mark were honest with himself, he'd admit that he was more interested in the chase and capture than in the keeping.

"This wasn't necessary," Hal said as they took their seats, and Hal shook out his napkin. "We could've spent your last night in Charleston at Folly Pier or relaxing at the hotel bar."

"Nonsense, the pier was enjoyable, but a place like this is where the people who make the rules come." Mark looked around at the occupants of the other tables, glittering and spiffy with their jewelry and tailored clothes. "Schmoozing may not be your style, Hal, but considering what you want to accomplish, knowing who the movers and shakers are and becoming part of the circle will help you get the grants you need to establish your own youth shelter."

"Does this mean you've accepted the fact I've chosen to make Charleston my home?" Hal asked as Mark studied the wine list.

Mark waited until he'd given their waiter the order for a bottle of Merlot before responding. "I hoped the prodigal son was going to return home after school was over, but I can see from our time here how much you love this town."

"I do. Don't get me wrong, I loved the Village too, but this place always called me home." There was something about the slower way of life, the historic homes hugging the river, the heat and charm of Charleston that drew him. He'd been aching to return here ever since he'd left. It hadn't taken much persuasion from Caleb at all.

"Though, I do have to know one thing. When are you going to take me up on my offer to run away with me to San Francisco?" Mark asked in a teasing voice and Hal laughed.

"When you're serious about it, give me a call." He took a sip of water as the waiter returned and presented the bottle of wine for Mark's inspection. He watched the familiar ritual with a smile. He couldn't see Mark leaving New York for anything or anybody. He had his restaurants, his friends, and his reputation among the local politicians. He'd worked too hard to get where he was to start over on the other side of the country.

"Order whatever you want," Mark insisted as the waiter hovered with an expression of expectation. "College students do not get many opportunities for a fine steak dinner."

That was certainly true, and Mark had been disappointed Hal hadn't let him spoil him this week like he used to. One night couldn't hurt, and Mark was leaving in the morning.

"I'll take the rib eye, medium please," Hal said and handed the waiter the menu.

After Mark ordered, he lifted his wineglass toward Hal. "Here's to second chances. After this last week, I can see how that restlessness in you has calmed. As much as I don't want to say it, I think moving here may have been the right idea."

Hal clinked his glass to Mark's, sorry to see their week together coming to a close, but more relaxed now that the pressure to change his mind was gone. He'd hoped Mark would finally accept Hal's decision to move south. Now if he could just get Lily to see that it was the right decision. "Thank you." Hal took a sip of the smooth, dry red. Mark did have excellent taste in wines.

"Caleb pointed out that you knew your own mind, and I had to admit, after looking at our past, he was right. I'd never had much luck swaying your decisions once you'd decided on a plan."

Hal lifted a brow in surprise. Caleb and Mark had a few encounters, and though they seemed friendly enough in a reserved kind of way, he hadn't missed that there was a certain amount of tension between them. He'd wanted to ask about it but didn't want to stir things up when Mark was only going to be visiting for a week. "Caleb has complained about that tendency of mine more than once. So tell me, did you enjoy Charleston?"

"It has its charms," Mark replied. They discussed the highlights of the week and the possibility of Mark visiting again. "You should come up to New York again sometime soon."

"I'm not sure about soon. I just got settled. Maybe next spring, I'll see if Caleb would be interested in a road trip." Though, that might not be the best idea. Alone in a car with Caleb for hours, sharing a hotel room, yeah, no road trips for them.

A slight, polite smile flickered across Mark's face. "May I ask you a personal question?"

Hal sat back with his wineglass as the waiter returned with their steaks. "Go right ahead."

"You and Caleb were lovers once?" Mark asked in a low voice after the waiter left.

"For a short time, but it didn't work out. We decided we made better friends," Hal said with a renewed ache of loss. Caleb was not helping him let go, not with the way he'd been bringing up their past. Hal's heart may not be broken anymore, but it didn't mean he didn't sometimes mourn the past and torture himself with what-ifs.

Mark smiled with sardonic humor. "The same decision we came to?"

"That was a completely different situation, and you know it." Hal set down his knife and leaned closer. "You agreed that you weren't interested in being exclusive."

"You don't share, I know. And I know in my heart that as much as I might want to try a commitment, I don't see it lasting." Mark sighed and cut a piece of his steak. "I did come down here with the intention of having another wild romp, but I realized I'd lost my chance long ago. I might be out of place, but I think your friend might see you in a different light than you see him." Hal frowned, sensing disapproval in Mark's voice. "I think he's looking for more, and I'm not entirely sure you find the idea unwelcome."

Hal remained silent as he cut his steak into small pieces and tried to gather his thoughts. He'd often gone to Mark with relationship woes, though he'd never admitted his feelings about Caleb. Some inner warning had always made him hold back.

"It was kind of crazy how it all came together," Hal said slowly. "I'd waited so long for Caleb to see me as more than the best friend who followed him everywhere. His other friends used to call me his shadow. Then I found out Caleb was like us, and I began to hope something might happen. I'd always loved him, as a friend, as a brother, and I wanted more. It was good, you know. It was really good between us, but we needed different things, and we made our friendship the priority."

"I'm not a fool. I can see you still love him and he loves you too," Mark said. "Let's just say he's not as over you as you think, and he wants to give it another try. Would you be able to say no?"

Hal thought of Caleb and his family, the respect and love between them all. He wasn't going to be the cause of souring that relationship. "Yes, I'd be able to say no."

Mark watched him with a thoughtful expression. "I almost believe you."

"You don't understand. I will always love him. I have always loved him. But Caleb knows what I want and need, and he won't open that door again. It goes the other way too. If we hook up again, it'll ruin him, and I won't let that happen." Mark nodded, his expression relaxing. "I will find someone for me," Hal continued. "Caleb can choose the bachelor route. I sure as hell am not."

Silence fell and Hal relaxed, enjoying the steak and Mark's company. Mark and Caleb's mutual jealousy of each other would almost be amusing if it didn't emphasize the fact that currently all three of them were single. That sucked. Though the thought of Mark taking up with another lover didn't make Hal want to stab his half-finished potato.

"Well, I'm glad to hear that," Mark said, cutting into his thoughts. "You and Caleb... would've been a monumental mistake. I'd considered saying something in New York the first time I suspected you were more than friends, but then he was out of the picture, and you were making plans to leave the country."

Hal frowned, trying to understand where the turn in the conversation had come from. "What do you mean?"

"You're so naïve," Mark said, his expression pinched in exasperation. An uncomfortable feeling crept over Hal. He laughed it off as Mark being Mark, but it put him on the defensive.

"I haven't heard that in a very long time, but when I did, it was never in connection with my love life." Hal took a last bite of his steak, his stomach protesting how full he was. "So what about it bothers you so much you feel you need to comment on it now?"

As soon as the words were out of his mouth, Hal wanted to snatch them back. From the sinking sensation in his gut, he wasn't entirely sure he wanted to hear Mark's answer.

"I can't believe you had a relationship with him at one time," Mark said, looking as uncomfortable as Hal had started to feel. "Friends is one thing, but really, Hal."

Hal frowned. Once again there was that note in his voice that sent warning jangles up Hal's spine. Hal narrowed his eyes. "What do you mean by that? Come out and say what is on your mind because clearly, you're dying to voice it."

"I think it's obvious," Mark said in a stiffer voice.

"No, it's not." Hal's fingers tightened on the napkin in his lap. "Explain it to me."

"Not to be indelicate," Mark said, a flush staining his cheeks, "but he is a Negro."

Hal bristled and glared at Mark. It took an effort to remember to keep his voice low. "What has that got to do with anything?"

"Be realistic," Mark said with a pained expression. "You're now living in the Deep South. It will be hard enough for the both of you as gay men. Sticking to your own kind will make it easier." Mark's tone was reasonable, but Hal wasn't going for it. He could not believe he was hearing this. He'd expected opposition, but not from Mark.

"You're kidding me, right?" Hal's dinner began to weigh heavy on his stomach as he saw the grave expression in Mark's eyes. He wasn't joking.

"No, I'm quite serious. This isn't against Caleb. I've had the chance to have a few conversations with him, and he seems like a fine man. It's obvious he cares for you a great deal, but I'm not sure either of you are capable of seeing the whole picture because your feelings are too wrapped up. I'm just looking out for you. It could be dangerous."

"Let me remind you that as naïve as I might appear, it's not like I haven't lived in South Carolina before. I went to school with Caleb when desegregation was just starting in the city. People were against our friendship, didn't understand it, tried to pull us apart. We were bullied, had our asses handed to us a couple of times, and yet we stuck together. Yes, the problem exists, but as long as we stick on our sides and ignore it and don't fight, it will always exist." Hal tossed his crumpled napkin on his plate, sick to be having this argument with Mark. Especially when it was a moot point, because there was no chance in hell he would let him and Caleb move past friendship again.

"Hal, please don't be upset," Mark soothed. "I'm just concerned."

"Is this really because I'm living in South Carolina?" Hal asked in a hard voice. "Or is it because he's black and I'm white? What if we had stayed together, and he'd moved to New York, where it might be safer? Would you have given us your blessing then?"

Hal should leave it alone. He wasn't even sure he wanted the answer, but he couldn't stop himself from poking at it. Better to know where Mark stood than to be constantly wondering whenever he talked to him.

Mark was silent a long time as he turned his wineglass in his hand, and then he sighed. "I'm sorry, Hal. I don't see a relationship working when you're of different races. Some things are meant to be kept separate. Relationships are difficult enough without such a huge difference."

Hal pushed back his chair, but the sick, twisting in his stomach made his legs feel unsteady enough that he didn't stand up. Mark didn't know a damned thing about long-standing relationships. "I can't believe I'm hearing this," Hal said in a low, furious whisper. "After everything we did together. After everything you taught me. You marched with me for gay rights, for equal rights for women. You told me you believed in civil rights for God's sake."

"And I do," Mark insisted, leaning closer. "That's different. Just because I don't believe in mixing races doesn't mean I don't believe they don't deserve equal rights."

"No." Hal's fist thumped the table, and nearby diners looked in their direction. "No, it's not different. We're all in this together. You of all people should understand that. How many times have you been arrested for what you say you believe in? I thought you would understand. It's not about the color of our skins, or our gender, or who we fall in love with. It's about how we make each other feel, about ourselves, about life." Mark winced, and Hal realized that his voice was rising, but he couldn't seem to make himself lower it. "Caleb and I are friends, totally, unconditionally, and I trust that friendship. Now you're trying to tell me I should back away because it could be harder on us? Because we might hook up again and you don't approve?"

"Hal, calm down, please. You're making a scene. I'm sorry. I shouldn't have said anything. You'd respected my advice in the past. I hoped you would continue to do so," Mark said, his voice going from soothing to slightly censorious. "I am looking out for you both."

Hal couldn't believe this was happening. Hal's eyes burned, though he'd learned tears served no purpose. He saw his old friend in a new light, and their relationship would never be the same. He tried telling himself that Mark was older, that he'd grown up in a different era. He tried telling himself it was a nonissue because he and Caleb weren't going to get back together, but neither argument helped. He'd thought he and Mark had known each other better than this.

His thoughts reeled as he stood up, and all Hal could say in response was, "I'm sorry too."

"Hal," Mark called out after him as he walked away. Hal couldn't leave it like this. There was too much history between them, but he needed to get away and clear his head. There was a hard, ugly knot inside his chest, and he was worried about what else he might say if he stuck around.

He counted on the fact that Mark had to pay the tab and that he wouldn't dream of chasing him out of a fancy restaurant. The expression on Mark's face at the end, that mix of fatherly righteousness and concern stuck in his brain. Not that Hal's dad had ever looked at him with concern, but he wondered if he'd looked at Mark as a substitute and because of that, he was here, with Mark thinking he could dictate who he loved. Well, Hal was done with changing his life to suit others.

And damn Mark for making him think about Caleb and stirring up his feelings for him. That was the last thing Hal needed.

CHARLESTON, SC— AUGUST 19, 1977

"I'VE MISSED this." Hal leaned his chair back and breathed in the night air. "I can't believe how much." The day's heat had cooled off with the setting of the sun and the breeze coming off the ocean. Folly Pier was alive with diners, couples dancing, and the heady beat of live music.

"It's definitely a different scene from New York." Caleb grinned and tipped his glass in Hal's direction. "How're you handling the heat?"

Hal laughed and sipped his drink. "By avoiding the apartment during the day and sleeping in damp shirts chilled in the fridge at night. I'm probably going to wind up with a cold before school starts next week."

Caleb was right, it was a different scene, more laid-back and courtlier in an old, nostalgic way. The dancing couples were all the same race and opposite sex. Definitely not like some of the discos up north. But then again, the clubs in New York didn't have the sensual pleasure of the hot southern air on their skin and weren't open to the tang of the Atlantic scenting the air.

He glanced at Caleb and found his friend watching him. Sometimes it seemed like Caleb was afraid he might disappear again. Hal had told him not to worry. Returning had felt like a piece of his soul had fit back into place. The only problem was that he couldn't take his thoughts off Caleb, even when he wasn't around. He was having an even harder time controlling his hormones. Whenever he caught Caleb watching him in that quiet way of his, he'd get a tingle that reminded him how hot they were in bed together.

Hal had such an urge to lean across the table to kiss him, a craving that struck him in both the heart and the gut. It would be one thing to lust after him if his feelings weren't all tangled up with the desire.

Once again he cursed Mark for making him remember how good he'd had it with Caleb.

"So what are you thinking about so hard?" Hal asked. Probably wasn't the wisest question. Caleb might take the opportunity to bring up the conversation Hal had been avoiding. Still, he was feeling too content to worry.

"I was thinking about how Theresa Drayton used to try to talk me into walking down the beach whenever we came here." Caleb glanced out at the water, and Hal followed his gaze, looking at the moon shining on the water and the path it made to shore. "I never did go, but I'm wondering how I would've reacted if you'd asked me instead."

Hal wondered about that himself a few times. That year of high school had been so difficult. Caleb had struggled with his friends' expectations and what it meant to be black in a world that was changing pretty fast. Hal had realized girls held no interest for him, and his biggest fear had been Caleb would freak out if he knew. If they hadn't had those fears driving them apart, that summer might've been filled with stolen kisses.

That was definitely not a thought Hal needed on his mind right now. He took another sip of his drink and met Caleb's gaze. The heat between them jumped and made it even harder to think. "I'd thought about kissing you before I left town, but I never worked up the courage."

Caleb smiled, and there was something in the curve of his lips and the glint in his eye that made Hal's pulse jump. "Would you like to go for a walk with me now?"

Heaven help him, was Caleb trying to make him crazy? Hal couldn't tell if he was flirting or teasing. Caleb had never been a flirt. He was too straightforward and said what he meant outright. Still, Hal couldn't escape the notion that Caleb was trying to court him. Somehow, that was even sexier. For all the time they had spent together both as lovers and as friends, they'd never dated.

"Ummm," Hal tried to get his tongue around a thought that wouldn't come out all wrong. "I was thinking how much I'd like to dance instead."

They both glanced at the lit-up square crowded with gyrating bodies where they couldn't join in for several reasons. "Yeah, that does sound nice. If we want to dance, I know of a place where we can go."

Hal was eager to explore more of Charleston now that he was an adult. They had gone to a few bars when he'd visited at eighteen, but he didn't know what the nightlife had to offer around here. "Where's that?" and so help him if Caleb mentioned another walk down the beach he didn't know what he'd do.

"It's a place down on King Street called the Garden and Gun. I've been there a couple times. Trust me, you'll love it," Caleb promised and put money down on the table for a tip. "It's a place for people like us."

"In Charleston?"

"Low country doesn't mean backcountry," Caleb replied with a smile. "Come on, nothing I say will paint the picture. You have to see it. We'll take my car, and I'll drive you back after."

A good twenty minutes alone in the car with Caleb and multiple places where they could pull over and indulge in another missed teenage opportunity. Necking. Hal thought of the backseat of Caleb's car with a shiver. He really needed to get laid, but the thought of a quick fling left him feeling cold and empty.

He was such a fool. He wanted Caleb. He loved Caleb. Dammit, the sex was good with Caleb. Maybe they could sneak around and keep it a secret. Hal wasn't sure if it would matter that much to have the world think of them as just best friends if they had each other behind closed doors.

Then he remembered the hurt and the restless wanting in New York. A part of that had been because he didn't know if Caleb had been in love with him in return. If that made him miserable, how would he handle Caleb leaving in the middle of the night or him going out on dates with women to throw off suspicion? He wouldn't handle it well at all. He was a needy, greedy lover, and he'd want Caleb to be with him all the time, which would bring them right back to the fear of being discovered. Hal was realistic enough to know a situation like that could lead to resentment on all sides. No, this was better. They'd made the right decision.

Caleb caught his hand as they reached the car. The parking lot was swamped in shadows, but Hal heard the laughter and conversation of other people as they headed to and from the pier. "Hey, don't look so sad."

"I'm not." Hal squeezed his hand and smiled. "Truly, I'm not. Come on, show me this dancehall of yours." He wasn't sure how he'd gone so fast from being convinced he'd moved on to knowing he hadn't, but he needed to figure it out. Maybe refusing to talk about it when Caleb brought it up had been the problem.

But not tonight. They both were starting school soon, and it would be hectic. They would have homework to do, exams to study for in between their jobs. Caleb had the additional responsibility of helping out Rodney with Drew. Their evenings would be busy as they settled into their routines. Tonight would be one last summertime hurrah before the madness began.

Caleb reached over and took his hand again. "Something has been bothering you ever since Mark left. Care to spill your guts? I can tell when you're upset."

Hal closed his eyes with an inward wince. He was still pissed at Mark, and Mark was furious Hal had embarrassed him in front of the Charleston elite. That had not been the time or place for him to vent his feelings. Hal selfishly wished he'd never seen this side of Mark. He didn't let too many people into his heart, and Mark had been one of them. He couldn't believe he'd been so unaware, and he wondered if he'd missed the signs. He supposed everyone had to have a narrow blind side.

"Hey, talk to me. What's wrong?" Caleb asked with concern. Nothing soothed his battered spirits like the sound of Caleb's gruff voice in his slow drawl.

"You were right about Mark and how he felt about our past relationship. In fact he was so concerned there was a possibility of a repeat that he felt it was his duty to warn me we'd be putting ourselves in danger if we dared, but what it came down to was he didn't agree with it, and since I was his dutiful junior, I should fall in line."

"Ah," Caleb said softly. "I'm sorry. I'd hoped he wouldn't go down that road."

"Mark's sorry too, but it doesn't change his opinions." Hal sighed and wished he had Caleb's arm around him right now. "Am I as naïve as everybody always says? I never saw it, and I should've, right?"

"What it comes down to is that for some reason, despite everything you've been through, you continue to try to see the best in people, not the worst. It's what makes you special, and I hope you never lose it," Caleb said.

"I feel like a fool." Hal leaned his head against the window.

Caleb was silent a moment. "If there's one thing I've learned it's that even when there are lines dividing us, it's up to us whether or not we we'll allow them to keep us divided. You and Mark have learned things about each other that you don't like. Maybe you have a chance to change his mind. I think you two have been friends long enough that it's worth a try."

"I thought he irritated the hell out of you. Why're you encouraging me to talk to him?" Hal asked in disbelief.

"Because I think you'd regret it if you didn't. Because I know he's not going to be able to sway you from our friendship. What got under my skin about him was that I was terribly jealous and felt threatened because I knew he wanted you back." Caleb ran his thumb over Hal's knuckles. "I'm trying to let go of that because you two are friends with a long history. Remember when Lou was against the two of us being friends? He was sure I was going to wind up getting hurt because I trusted a white guy, and eventually he came around, but if I hadn't given him a chance to change his thinking he would've never known that it could be different."

Hal supposed Caleb was right. He shouldn't hold on to his anger too long. He knew what it did to him. But the problem of Mark would have to wait for another day. Hal was not ready to talk to him, and he highly doubted Mark would want to hear from him until he got over the sting of his public embarrassment.

"I'll call him in a few weeks. That'll give both of us a chance to calm down."

"Both of you, or just you?" Caleb asked with a squeeze of his hand.

"Trust me, both of us. I went off on him in front of the gentry at a very swanky restaurant." Hal couldn't help his smile when Caleb choked back a laugh.

"Oh my."

"It was a nice speech about right being right and loving who you love. Very impassioned," Hal said earnestly. "It definitely caught the attention of diners around us."

"Oh God, Hal." This time Caleb did laugh. "Yeah, separate corners for a few weeks."

Hal glanced down at their hands with a smile. Caleb had been touching him for as long as he could remember, holding his hand or putting his arm around him. In fact, now that he thought about it, Caleb had initiated all their first contacts. He'd been the one to crawl into Hal's bed so they could hold each other, he'd come into the shower that morning, he'd kissed Hal first.

Again, all thoughts he should not be having. Still his curiosity was stirred. He had never considered himself to be shy about initiating sex ever. Caleb was the one who hid his sexuality. How was it that he had the guts to start anything when Hal hadn't been able to do the same? It wasn't like he hadn't dreamt of hopping into a shower with Caleb or he hadn't rehearsed kissing him so often that it was seared into his head.

Hal traced a circle on the back of Caleb's hand. "Can I ask you a question and you not take it the wrong way?"

"Shoot."

Hal laid his other hand over Caleb's as he struggled with how to phrase it. "You're always touching me. You always have. Even before you realized you were gay. It never made you nervous? Or made you question yourself? I mean, there were times when I'd thought of kissing you, but I don't think I ever would've gotten the guts to try it with you. It didn't stop me with other guys. I don't understand how you could when I couldn't, when I was the one who knew exactly what I was."

Caleb lifted their hands and kissed Hal's fingers, then the inside of his wrist, and his senses tingled. "Okay, looking back... when we were little, you were starved for affection, and I felt protective of you. I'd put my arm around you, and you'd cuddle into me like a kitten. It made me feel good. I could always tell when you needed that contact. It was all over your face and your body language. As we got older, I knew there were places where we couldn't do it, but I was never afraid you would reject my touch. There were times when I had thoughts about you that did make me nervous, made me question why I had those feelings and urges. Those last six months before you left were bad. It was one of the reasons why I kept backing away and needing space. But even then I wasn't worried about losing you if you found out I had thoughts like that."

"I knew you wouldn't reject me either, not really. At least I kept trying to tell myself that, but I didn't want to risk it." Looking back on it, the times Hal hadn't had any inhibitions were when the encounters had no driving emotion behind them other than desire.

"In your head you might've known you could trust me, but what about in your heart? Think about it, Hal. How much experience have you had with people who were supposed to love you rejecting you instead? It would make anyone afraid to take that risk. Even when we had never done anything sexual, and I went to join you in the shower, it didn't have as much weight for me as it would have for you. If you'd said no, it would've stung, hit my pride a bit, but I would've gotten over it. Not because I didn't care, because I did, don't get me wrong, but I've never had your experiences with rejection."

Hal hadn't thought of it that way, but before he could comment, Caleb continued, "You knew you loved me. I didn't realize how deep my feelings were at that point. That's another factor. You had been rejected too many times, and I had been very blessed when it came to my family. So no. I don't think it's all that strange."

Hal's heart swelled to the aching point. There was no one else who knew him like Caleb, and despite the fact Hal was an emotional mess more times than he wanted to be, Caleb wanted to be near him.

"You're pretty amazing, you know that?" Hal said, finding his voice again as Caleb parked along the street.

Caleb leaned over and dropped a quick kiss right on his lips that left him yearning for a deeper contact. "I think you are too."

CALEB WAS both excited and nervous as they neared the club. So far Hal had not shot down any of his overtures, and though Hal thought of this as a night out between friends, Caleb considered it an opportunity to woo him. Hal had been worried he'd take those questions wrong, but in reality Caleb took them as a good sign. Hal wasn't over him, which meant that Caleb had a chance at convincing him to give them another shot.

Mark's sudden appearance had made Caleb realize that he needed to make a move. He couldn't expect Hal to stay celibate, and he just might lose his cool if Hal started dating somebody else, so he had to do something. He ended up broaching the subject with Uncle Vern. His mother's brother had always been a mentor to him. Part friend, part older brother in many ways, and always easy to talk to. Even then, Caleb had been terrified to tell him that he was gay.

He had walked away from that conversation a little freer, a little wiser. He wouldn't get the same kind of acceptance from his parents that he'd gotten from Rodney and Uncle Vern, but he wouldn't be alone either. He'd have advocates, and that made a huge difference.

"You weren't kidding were you?" Hal asked, breaking into his thought. Hal gestured to the line outside the Garden and Gun. Couples lined up, some of them men with their girls, others who were clearly together despite being the same sex. The quiet unspoken rule that races couldn't mix socially didn't exist here as it did in too many places. Caleb had always felt comfortable at the club, and Hal would love it. They joined the end of the line, and Hal turned toward him. "So you come here often?"

"I wouldn't say often." This was more Hal's kind of scene. Caleb liked to dance too, but he was more of a sit back and listen kind of guy, especially if there was good company, good food, and good drinks. He loved going to the pier. But here, he could dance with Hal. "A few times."

"You're not going to subject me to a whole bunch of ex-lovers are you?" Hal asked with a teasing smile. "Just to get back at me for a few uncomfortable moments in New York."

"You're the only guy I've brought here." Caleb reached over and took Hal's hand, enjoying the shy look that entered his gaze. He didn't have any experience with wooing or lover's talk. Even when they were together before, even loving each other, it had been more like friendship with an added hot dimension at night. But he thought that Hal deserved that extra attention, and it might give them both something they'd needed.

"Aren't you worried you might be seen by someone who knows you?" Hal asked as the line moved forward. "This is quite a mixed crowd."

It was nerve-racking when Caleb thought about it, but it wasn't something he could dwell on either. Except for his parents, the most important people in his life knew the truth. This week he was going to gather all his courage and tell them.

As for everyone else, if he got the chance to live the life he wanted with Hal, then it was going to get out eventually. He'd probably lose friends over it, the way Hal might lose Mark. But the alternative was living without Hal and knowing that Caleb had been the one to give up on any chance they might have.

"Not as much as I once would've been," Caleb admitted.

Hal pulled his hand free and looked away. "What are we doing?" he said so softly that Caleb almost didn't hear him. The tense withdrawal in his body said more than any words.

"Do you trust me?" Caleb asked, refraining from putting his arm around Hal though he wanted to. He was pretty sure that would send him running.

Hal hesitated, and that hurt, but then he turned to Caleb and looked at him with a steady gaze. "Of course I do."

Which pretty much told Caleb what he needed to know. Hal trusted him with everything except his heart. Maybe he wanted to, maybe he even believed he did, but he wasn't ready. That was okay. It wasn't as if Caleb had shown him this was going to be any different than the last time. One way he could do that was to let Hal dictate the pace instead of diving in without thinking first.

"Then we are here to have a good time, dance our feet off, just be ourselves and how we are with each other." Caleb leaned closer to whisper in his ear, "I promise to behave like a gentleman the entire night."

"And I suppose that a part of behaving like ourselves involves me cuddling into you like a kitten?" Hal asked with a wry smile.

"Well, I certainly wouldn't turn it down," Caleb admitted seriously. One of the things he truly missed was having the right to hold Hal as long as he wanted and having Hal curled up against him like there was no place on Earth he'd rather be.

Hal laughed, shook his head, and held out his hand again to Caleb. Caleb's heart skipped a beat, and he smiled as he took it. Music, the intelligible roar of conversation, and laughter washed over them as they stepped through the door and into the club. Gyrating bodies packed the dance floor, and knots of people gathered around small tables and the bar.

Hal moved to the side to let others in and paused to drink in his surroundings. Caleb remembered when he'd first discovered this place and how stunned he'd been over its inclusiveness. His immediate thought had been he wanted the chance to bring Hal here.

Caleb wasn't surprised when Hal headed straight for the floor. He loved to dance, and when he did, it was like he was off in his own world. The disco lights made his glasses glint, and his lean body moved in rhythm to the music before they even reached the pack of bodies. Hal pulled him right into the center and turned to face him with an expression of joy.

For a moment Caleb forgot to dance. All he could do was watch until Hal threw his arms out with a laugh. "What's wrong? Forget how to move?" he asked as the music changed from Donna Summers to the Bee Gees.

"Too busy watching you," Caleb replied over the steady beat.

"It's more fun to dance with me," Hal replied, and Caleb couldn't disagree. He caught Hal around his waist and moved in closer. It had been years since they danced together, and after a few missteps that had them laughing, they began to move in sync.

Caleb tried to recall what he'd said about being a gentlemen and how this was an evening to go out and have fun as friends with no pressure. It was damned difficult with Hal's body moving against Caleb's before dancing away again and leaving him wanting more. He couldn't figure out how Hal seemed so unaffected by their closeness because he was making Caleb's pulse jump and his blood hot.

Their eyes met, and the sound of music fell away. Everything Caleb wanted to see was stamped on Hal's expression. The love that had been there for as long as Caleb could remember shone the strongest and underneath it, a desire and need that had Caleb's hands shaking to touch him and his mouth aching to taste him. He pulled Hal close to him. "I love it when you look at me like that."

Hal shivered and slipped out of Caleb's arms. "Behave."

Behave. Yes, that's what he was supposed to be doing, but Hal tempted him beyond reason. They remained on the floor until they were breathless and thirsty before retreating to a table with a couple of drinks, then pulled their chairs close to each other so they could talk over the music.

"You know, I remember the first time I wanted to dance with you," Caleb said. "It was in high school. We were at my uncle's after classes, and you were dancing by yourself in the living room to 'Born on the Bayou.' There was something about you that day that made me crazy."

"I can't believe you remember the song." Hal took a sip of his drink and looked at Caleb thoughtfully. "I never realized how much you thought of me like that."

"We never talked about it. Not even during New York." It was strange when Caleb considered it. After all the hundreds of hours of conversation covering just about everything, they had never really talked about their deeper feelings except for that one aborted too short talk in Hal's dorm room. "Hell, there were too many things we never talked about. You never admitted you loved me until you were saying good-bye."

Hal stirred his drink, staring down at the cubes of ice as if they held a divine fascination for him. "I didn't want to push you into saying something you weren't ready for. I kept telling myself if you felt the same way, you'd say so."

"Sometimes I'm incredibly dense," Caleb said, and Hal flashed him a look of protest. "When I'm comfortable, I don't often explore any deeper even if I should. You made me happy, you made me comfortable and at peace again during a time when I needed it. I was too busy enjoying that peace to question why I felt so comfortable and happy with you."

"You were happy, and I snatched that away because of my own insecurities." Hal sighed. Caleb shook his head, slipping his arm around his shoulders.

"No, you shook me up, reminded me I shouldn't take things for granted. For the first time, when it came to us as a couple, not us as friends, you told me how you really felt and what you needed. I had to hear that." Caleb hadn't intended on the conversation getting so serious and open, but since Hal wasn't pulling away or changing the subject, Caleb wanted to take this chance. He'd been trying to get Hal to talk about them for a long time now. "Remember when we were little and we made that vow that we'd never let somebody else get between us?"

Hal's gaze went far away, and a soft smile crossed his lips. "You were worried about girls. I guess that turned out to be a rather baseless fear didn't it?"

"Yeah," Caleb admitted with a laugh. "I've been thinking we should make a new pact."

Wariness darkened Hal's eyes, and he remained silent as he played with his straw. "What kind of a pact?" he finally asked.

"That we're honest with each other about how we feel. No more hiding. We lay it out in the open and deal with it together no matter where it takes us." Caleb held his breath, waiting for Hal's reaction. This was dangerous territory, and if Hal was going to duck and run, this would be a trigger.

"Fine, you want the truth?" Hal's jaw jutted out at its most stubborn angle. "I need you to be my friend. I'm not at a place where I'm willing to risk losing that."

Despite Hal's answer, Caleb was encouraged because at least Hal wasn't shutting him down anymore. He squeezed Hal's shoulder as he searched for how to express his own feelings. He'd never felt the need to say these things, he'd always assumed it was known, both with his family and with his friends. But history had shown him Hal needed the words as much as he needed the physical affection.

"Our feelings for each other aren't going away. We've tried spending time apart. We've tried ignoring them. Unless we plan on doing something to make us hate each other—"

"I could never hate you," Hal cut in.

"And I couldn't do anything to make you hate me." Caleb let his arm slip from Hal's shoulders as he finished off his drink. "Maybe we should think about that. Because I don't think pretending we're just friends is going to work, so we're going to have to figure it out."

"We are just friends, and that's how it's going to remain. I'm serious. You've got too much to lose," Hal insisted.

Caleb wasn't risking anything more than Hal. Yes, they could lose friends or future jobs. Yes, it would be hard at times, but they were both used to that. Hal wasn't backing down from that challenge, and neither was Caleb.

Caleb pushed back his chair and stood up, holding his hand out to Hal. "We'll argue about it another night, okay?" He smiled at Hal's look of relief. "Dance with me?"

Hal took his hand with a shake of his head. "I'm onto you, Hudson. That's a wicked agenda you've got. First you get my heart and head going and then distract me with dancing only to do it all over again."

Caleb hadn't thought of it that way, but Hal had a point. "There are worse plans."

"You're impossible, you know that," Hal replied as he followed Caleb out toward the floor. Then he stopped, halting Caleb with him and jerked back his hand. Caleb turned toward him, a question on his lips, but Hal didn't give him a chance to voice it. "I thought I saw...."

Caleb's gaze followed Hal's pointing finger and saw someone who may have been Lou before he was lost among all the people crowding the club. He shrugged, took Hal's hand again, and tugged him closer. Surprise flashed across Hal's face, and Caleb dropped a kiss on his lips. "It's okay."

"But...."

"No, it's okay," Caleb assured him. "Think of it this way if it makes you feel better. Just say you did see someone who knows us. They wouldn't be here unless they were comfortable around gays or gay themselves. This is who I am. It's not going to change. I've come to learn that if I want to be happy in my own skin, then I need to accept myself. Being gay is as much a part of me as being black. I can't hide from it and pretend I'm something else. That's no way to live."

Hal didn't say anything. He just slid his arms around Caleb's waist and held him tight. Caleb loved the way he offered empathy and comfort without Caleb ever asking. He always seemed to know when he needed him. Caleb closed his eyes and held him close in return. He hoped that Hal would be ready to hear him say *I love you* soon, because Caleb was finding it very difficult to hold back and give Hal the time to adjust to the idea that it was far from over between them.

CHARLESTON, SC— SEPTEMBER 6, 1977

CALEB STARED unseeingly at the stack of dishes as his hands worked without thought at drying and putting them away. He could move around his parent's kitchen with ease, even blindfolded, which was a help now as he tackled this simple chore while trying to rehearse the conversation he needed to have with Mom and Dad.

It should be easier this time right? It wasn't like he hadn't faced this moment twice already. Though, Rodney had practically pried the words out of him, so Caleb wasn't sure that counted. Uncle Vern had been the only family member who had never once pressured him about dating, and that made it easier to face him. This conversation was going to be with his parents, and that was distressing on a whole other level.

"Are you okay? Sure you don't want me to stay?" Rodney asked, coming up beside him.

Caleb's heart skipped and squeezed. He hadn't even heard his brother enter the kitchen. He was pretty far from okay. This was the most terrifying moment he'd ever faced in his life. Because he knew, without a doubt in his heart, that Mom and Dad were going to be hurt. They were going to be disappointed, and he'd never consciously, deliberately done that in his life.

"Thanks, but this is something I need to do on my own," Caleb replied. Uncle Vern had offered too, and it was so very tempting to have them beside him. Instead, Caleb let himself take comfort in knowing they supported him. This was between him and his parents. He didn't doubt Rodney and Uncle Vern would have their say later on. Besides, Rodney was stressed out enough. Caleb could tell he wasn't getting enough sleep, and he had gotten to be jumpy lately.

"Have you thought about not telling them?" Rodney asked in a low voice. "They've gone this long without figuring it out. You wouldn't be the only unmarried bachelor in the family."

Caleb rubbed his hands on his jeans, trying to quell the nervous flutter in his stomach. A few years ago, he would've jumped all over that suggestion. Now he knew it wouldn't work. "I want to be with Hal," he replied just as low. "That might work while we're finishing up school, but what about when it's over? I want to share my life with him, get a place of our own. I don't want to lie and say we're just friends. Not anymore. I owe them the truth, right?"

"I didn't realize you two had made that much of a commitment to each other." Caleb looked over sharply at the sound of discomfort in his brother's voice. Rodney smiled ruefully and shrugged. "Like I said, it'll take getting used to. I think you're right. Give them a chance to come around before you shack up together, unlike me who announced a pregnancy and shacking up at the same time."

Caleb wished Rodney would stop comparing the two of them. He had enough to deal with without talking himself down all the time. He'd taken responsibility for the situation. Couldn't he see that? Or how happy and secure Drew felt?

"Are the leftovers put away?" Mom asked as she came into the kitchen. "Do you want to take some home for tomorrow?"

"Are you kidding?" Rodney grabbed the paper bag he'd packed up off the counter. "I've already portioned it out. Come on, Drew," he raised his voice. "Time to get home."

Caleb's stomach lurched. It was cowardly of him, but he wanted Hal there. However, if Hal knew what he was about to do, he'd have a fit. He hadn't missed the hints Hal had thrown out over why they should remain just friends. Hal was concerned Caleb's parents would discover them, which meant he was worried about how they'd take it.

He slid his hand into his pocket and touched the photo of him and Hal. It didn't make the nerves any easier to deal with, but it did remind him why he needed and wanted to talk to his parents.

"Bye Gam'ma, bye Gam'pa," Drew shouted as he barreled past the kitchen. Caleb heard the front door open with a squeal of springs on the storm door, and then his nephew was gone. The look of exasperation on Rodney's face broke some of Caleb's tension and let him take in a breath.

Rodney punched him lightly on the arm with a murmured, "See you at home" and then chased after his son. Caleb turned around and faced

Mom. The smile on her face faded, replaced by a look of concern. Before she could ask what was wrong, Caleb shoved his hands in his pockets and gave her a nervous smile. "I need to talk to you and Dad."

Mom's head tipped to the side, and she studied him for a long moment, as was her tendency when she was trying to figure out if he or Rodney were guilty of a misdeed. He stared back at her steadily, his stomach churning in agitation. She smiled and smoothed the front of her dress. "Well, come on, then, don't just stand there. Your dad's on the porch with his pipe. I'll call him in, and you can tell us whatever it is that's got you so serious."

Caleb retreated into the living room. The fireplace mantle was crowded with mementos, some silly, some serious, the memories of a close-knit family—a plaster of Drew's tiny handprint, pictures of Caleb and Rodney as kids, and then in their Army dress uniforms, the little basket Hal had brought from Ghana, and his dad's Beatles bobblehead set. Poor Ringo, his head didn't sit quite right after Drew had gotten a hold of it.

He heard his parents come into the living room, the rich, spicy scent of Dad's pipe lingering in the air as he passed. Caleb gently tapped Lennon's head and set it bobbing. Strangely enough, all of his inner turmoil quieted. Caleb turned around and met their curious gazes. "Mom, Dad, first off, I love you, and I need you to hear me out." Caleb sat down on the edge of the hearth and then stood up again, filled again with the restless, nervous energy. "This isn't going to be easy for any of us, but you need to know the truth about… about me."

Caleb stole a quick, nervous glance in their direction. Dad stared straight at him with stoic resolve as Mom reached out to take his dad's hand. "Oh my God, Caleb, are you sick?"

"No," Caleb assured her.

She sank back in her chair, relief in her eyes, followed quickly by resignation. "Another grandbaby?"

"No, Mom, please, hear me out," Caleb insisted, before she could come up with more scenarios. He rubbed his palms on his jeans and abruptly sat down again. "See, there's no chance of me getting a girl pregnant, ever. I'm gay."

There. It was out. He couldn't believe he'd actually spoken the words. The living room fell silent as Caleb looked at his parents with pleading eyes, feeling more raw and vulnerable than he ever had in his life. Suddenly he was no longer the ex-soldier who'd been to war, or the confident college student. He was a little boy desperately hoping that his parents wouldn't be too mad at him. Their expressions went from stunned, to confused and then finally disbelief.

"You're not gay," Dad said, breaking the uncomfortable silence.

"I am, Dad," Caleb replied with quiet insistence. "I've always been gay, ever since I started noticing boys instead of girls."

"I don't understand," Mom broke in. "You've been dating girls since high school. Where did you ever get such a crazy idea in your head?"

"I've dated very few girls, and not one of the relationships went well. Every one of them figured out pretty quick that I wasn't attracted to them. After I realized I was gay, the only reason why I went out with a girl is so that people wouldn't suspect I was different." Caleb clasped his hands together to keep them from shaking.

"You're just shy," Mom said with a nervous laugh. "You haven't found the right girl. When you do, you'll see the difference."

"There is no right girl for me." Caleb drew in a breath to steel himself for the next part. "But there is a right guy, and I… I love him."

Dad's graying brows came together in a fierce frown, and Caleb held his breath. "Hal?" Caleb nodded and tried to smile, but failed. "So you're telling me you think you're in love with Hal?"

Caleb tightened his grip on his hands. "I don't think I love him. I know it. I've loved him for a long time."

"Caleb, son, we both know Hal's different," Dad said, the pinch of his mouth looking pained. "You two have been inseparable since you met, but I think you're confusing missing your friend and the excitement over having him back in town with being in love. Just because Hal is the way he is, doesn't mean you are too."

"You're going through a phase," Mom said gently, her expression dark with concern. "You'll grow out of it."

"Mom, come on, seriously. Anybody who's ever known Hal since he was a child has known he wasn't growing out of it. It's the same with me. It's who I am. It's how I was born. I can't change it, or grow out of it, or pray it away."

His parents exchanged glances, and Caleb flinched back from the disappointment in their eyes. Dad looked at him like he didn't know

Caleb anymore, and it shriveled him up. He stared down at his hands, his chest aching.

"When did you start thinking you were gay?" Dad asked.

Caleb wished he wouldn't phrase it that way. "When Rodney got all girl crazy, I knew I was different, because I didn't see what he saw, and it made me very uncomfortable. I tried to ignore it. I've known for sure since Vietnam. I realized that I'd been running from myself since I was a teenager, and I made the decision to stop running."

"Well what happened to make you think—?"

"Nothing happened the way you seem to think it did. I'm not traumatized like Rodney. I'm not confused. I'm gay. I love men." Caleb tried to calm the frustration boiling up. "It took me a very long time to admit the truth to myself, and it took even longer for me to accept that I deserve a real relationship with someone I love. I ran from that too, and I ended up hurting myself, hurting Hal."

Dad's jaw tightened as his lips pressed together in disapproval. Even worse, Caleb could see tears welling in Mom's eyes. "I tried to keep it a secret, and I pushed people away, choosing to be alone instead. But I don't want to be alone for the rest of my life. Can't you see that?" Caleb asked. "I have a chance to be with someone who's always loved me for me. My best friend who will stand by me through anything. I can't let that slip by."

"Caleb, what will people think? And what about a family of your own?" Mom asked. When he didn't answer, she began to cry in earnest. "Why must you always pick the harder way?"

"I didn't choose this, and I don't know why it chose me. All I know is that I love him. I want to be with him, and Hal loves me too." Caleb tried telling himself that their pain and anger would be worth having Hal. He tried telling himself that they'd get over it, come to understand it. But right now those assurances felt very hollow.

"I just don't know how to accept this," Dad said in a slow, heavy voice. "Maybe if you try—"

"I have tried," Caleb interrupted, frustration and fear leading to impatience. "I've tried and tried. I've pretended I was like everyone else. All it left me was feeling like I didn't fit in and very lonely."

"What do I do?" Mom asked, looking toward Dad like he could give her a divine answer. "What am I supposed to do?"

You could love me. "You could think about it and ask yourselves if I'm any different now than I was before. You can give us a chance, stand by us, 'cause Hal and I are going to need all the backup we can get."

"No," Dad cut in, his eyes flashing in anger as Mom cried harder. "No, I cannot support you in this. I cannot. It's not right, son. It just isn't. I love you, but this is asking for too much."

Caleb stared down at his hands, his throat tightening as hot tears slipped down his cheeks. He'd known it was going to be like this, but oh God, it hurt far more than what he'd prepared himself for. "I understand," he said hoarsely. He couldn't look at his parents. He couldn't handle it if he saw outright rejection. "Maybe we can talk again later when you get a chance to calm down and think about it. You could talk to Rodney and Uncle Vern too. They know."

"There's nothing to talk about," Dad insisted.

Caleb blew out his breath, his heart so heavy that it felt like it was sinking right out of him. "Okay. I guess... I guess I'll go, then." He dashed the back of his hand across his cheeks and got up. The time for arguments was over, and as much as it ached, he had to leave them to think about it, discuss it without him, and wait out the adjustment.

Neither one of them made a move to stop him as he made his way toward the door, and the sound of Mom's tears and Dad's stony silence followed him all the way out to the car. He'd have to warn Uncle Vern and Rodney that he was likely to be a very sore subject for a while.

Caleb leaned his head against the headrest, at a loss for where to go next. He wasn't up to another emotional encounter, and if he went home, that's what he'd get. If he went to see Hal, he wouldn't be able to hide how upset he was, and he didn't want to trigger any bad memories. When he confessed his love to Hal and asked for a second chance, he wanted it to be a happier occasion than it would be if he went over tonight.

He shoved his key in the ignition and pulled out. Before he even realized it, he'd turned the car in the direction of his Uncle Vern's house. No matter what ever happened, he'd always be welcome there.

CHARLESTON, SC—
SEPTEMBER 16, 1977

HAL PULLED up next to Caleb's car in a deserted side lot of a new neighborhood. There was something that appeared vaguely familiar but different about the place. He looked around, got his bearings, and realized they were near the section of woods they used to play in all the time when they were kids. Only it wasn't so wild anymore. A good portion of the trees had been knocked down for more homes in the process of being built.

He shook his head as he got out of his car. He hadn't seen Caleb for over a week. He'd barely heard from him on the phone. If it weren't for quick glimpses in the distance on campus or the little notes that appeared in his books, Hal would've thought Caleb was avoiding him.

Caleb grinned at him over the top of his car. "I was getting worried you'd gotten lost."

"I should ask you the same. Did you forget where I live?" Hal asked as he smiled back at him. "I haven't seen you since before school started. Rodney can't even pin you down."

"I've been taking care of a couple of things," Caleb replied and opened his trunk.

Hal looked at him in confusion. It wasn't like Caleb to be vague, and normally it would make Hal think he was wrestling with a problem, but obviously, Caleb was excited. It also wasn't like Caleb to avoid him, yet Hal had the impression he'd been doing just that. He wondered if Caleb was regretting taking him to the club or if he needed some distance to get perspective because there was no mistaking the heat between them had only grown hotter.

Hal had been thinking of Caleb constantly, dreaming of what they could have if he was willing to give them a chance. Of course, Caleb hadn't actually said he wanted a relationship again. He'd merely pointed out that neither of them had moved on. Hal could hardly deny the truth of that. The time they'd spent apart had only made their bond stronger.

He was still trying to figure out whether Caleb was wooing him or not. If he was, Hal didn't know how to shut that line of thinking down without hurting him. One thing was for sure, Caleb was trying to make him crazy; that's all there was to it.

"Like what?" Hal asked, moving toward him as Caleb straightened from the trunk and handed him a picnic basket. Hal raised a brow as he hefted it. What the hell had Caleb packed for them to eat? A whole friggin' cow?

"It's a surprise." Caleb stuffed a flashlight in his pocket and grabbed another box. "Come on, the path's still there."

"You've got to be kidding me." Bemused, Hal followed Caleb into the trees. Their tree house had been on the verge of falling apart when he left Charleston. He couldn't imagine anything remaining. The air was still and hot underneath the trees, and the scent of green and growing things brought back a hundred happy childhood memories. "Are you feeling nostalgic?"

"Something like that." Caleb glanced over his shoulder. "I want no interruptions tonight."

"My apartment's private." Hal said. For the love of God, the basket was heavy.

"Not nearly as much fun. Aren't you the teensiest bit curious?"

Hal had to admit he was. The walk to the clearing didn't take long, and Hal laughed when he saw the sturdy shack, nestled on its old branch. "I see you've upgraded." The new clubhouse was bigger and had shutters over the windows and a solid ladder descending from a familiar trapdoor.

Caleb grinned and set his box down on the ground. "After I moved back I figured Drew would need a place someday, so I've been working on and off at it some weekends. Then I hurried up and wrapped up the final touches over the last week. Can't wait for you to see it."

Hal eyed Caleb suspiciously. It was no secret Caleb loved projects like this and working with his hands the same way Hal loved to sew. That was Hal's thinking alone time. Caleb, on the other hand, viewed work like this as a social occasion. The only time he went at it alone was when something was bothering him and he needed a project to occupy his thoughts and give him peace.

"Are you okay?" Hal demanded.

Caleb dropped a kiss on Hal's mouth, scattering his thoughts and making his lips tingle. "Yep." He turned and started up the ladder, leaving Hal with their supplies.

"I hope you remembered our old net trick," Hal called after him as Caleb climbed. His gaze lingered on the bulge of Caleb's arms as he hauled himself up and the way his backside filled out the jeans he wore. Hal jerked his gaze away when he realized he was staring.

"Oh ye of little faith. Please, remember who you're talking to. I've designed something better. Come around to the side," Caleb called as he disappeared through the trap door. Curious, Hal walked around the side to see what else his friend had been up to. The little house looked much more secure than their old one. Not that Hal had noticed at all when they were younger, but now that Drew was going to inherit it, Hal was glad that it was snug and solid up in the tree.

A pulley system was attached next to a wide window. Caleb opened it and stuck his head and shoulders through. "What do you think?" Caleb hooked a large basket, then lowered it to Hal.

"I wish you'd thought of this a decade ago," Hal responded as he set the box and picnic basket inside. Caleb had even attached bungee cords to the sides to make sure nothing would fall out. "It would've made hauling our equipment so much easier." He watched Caleb pull the basket up with no effort. "A lot easier."

He clambered up the ladder, feeling like a young teenager again. There had been few places they could go where they felt they could totally be themselves without worrying about unwanted attention. This had been their favorite haunt.

Hal straightened, the top of his head almost brushing the ceiling. A small table and a few chairs occupied half the space, and shelves had been built into one of the walls. There was even a good-sized nest of old blankets and worn-out pillows that made a perfect spot for reading or daydreaming. "Wow, if we'd had all of this as kids we never would've left this place."

"You know?" Caleb knelt on the floor, opened the box, and handed a camper's lantern to Hal. "Hang it from the hook in the ceiling." Then he pulled out a small battery-operated fan and clamped it to the open window.

"You've thought of everything," Hal said with a shake of his head as he turned around in a slow circle. "You know what this place needs, right?"

"I know exactly what you're going to say, and that's your job." Caleb shoved the box out of the way before Hal could see what else was in it and turned to the picnic basket. "I can't sew worth a damn, so if you want rag rugs or curtains, you know where the fabric store is."

Hal helped him unpack, his stomach rumbling with hunger. "So this is what you've been up to? Fixing the clubhouse? You should've told me. I would've loved to help."

"There's more to do," Caleb replied. He shook out a tablecloth and set a fat candle in the center of the table. "I'd planned on having this all ready, but I ran out of time."

Hal paused while unwrapping a set of wineglasses. He glanced from the table to the nest of blankets as realization struck him like lightning. Caleb was planning a seduction. He set the glasses down with a thump. This was his fault. He should've made it clear earlier. Now he didn't know what to do. He hated the coward inside him that urged him to find an excuse to leave.

It wasn't Caleb's fault Hal had gotten hurt in the past. Hal hadn't told him how deep his feelings ran. Hal had been the one to break things off. It wasn't fair to punish Caleb because he was screwed up in his head and heart. He had to face it, as much as he wanted a happily-ever-after, he wasn't sure he was even capable of giving someone that level of trust. Even Caleb. He'd been stung once, pulled back because it got scary, and now he was afraid to dip his toe in the same waters.

Caleb pegged him right. He was an emotionally insecure child. He just didn't know what to do about it. He had to figure out something, or they both were going to get hurt. He couldn't do that to Caleb again.

"Caleb, we need to have a serious talk."

Caleb looked at him sharply as he pulled out a bottle of red wine. "What's wrong?" His expression fell as he caught the look in Hal's eyes. "I messed it up, didn't I? I should've had it all ready before you came."

Hal shook his head. He could only imagine how he would've raced down that ladder if he'd seen the table already laid with its romantic setting. He felt terrible because it was obvious Caleb had put so much thought into this evening, even going so far as to finish fixing up their old clubhouse. No one ever did the thoughtful and loving gestures for him like Caleb.

This was harder than he thought possible. Harder than the last time he had to let Caleb go. He'd only been in town a few weeks, and they hadn't taken that next step, but it felt like another breakup.

"We can't slide back into being friends with benefits, Caleb." Hal couldn't look at him. "We just can't."

"Good thing I wasn't planning that, then." Caleb returned to organizing the table for dinner as Hal's head jerked up and he stared in confusion. He wasn't sure if he was disappointed or relieved. Could he have read the signals all wrong?

"Okay… what are you planning? Because I'm lost." Hal couldn't believe he was the one urging for a conversation instead of trying to duck and cover. "One minute we seem like we're just friends and that's what you want; then another minute it feels like you want something more. I don't know what to think anymore."

Caleb abandoned the picnic basket and stood before Hal. He took Hal's hands in his own and stared down at them for a long moment, his thumbs brushing tenderly over Hal's skin. "Can I ask you something?" Caleb lifted his head and met Hal's gaze.

Hal's heart skipped a beat, and even as his nerves began jangling, he found himself holding tight to Caleb's grip as if he was afraid of letting go. "What?"

"If you could have anything you wanted out of life, what would it be?" Caleb asked in a soft, urgent voice.

Hal's stomach plummeted. "That's not fair."

"Why isn't it fair?"

"I can't have what I want, so what's the point in saying it?" Frustrated, Hal tried to pull his hands back, but Caleb wouldn't let go.

Hal turned his face away, his throat tightening, his heart aching. He couldn't do this. He couldn't wake up that dream again.

"Because we've only danced around the issue since we broke up. If we don't talk about it and voice how we feel it's going to continue to haunt us." Caleb lightly squeezed Hal's hands until he lifted his gaze. Hal drank in the look of his familiar face, the rich brown of his eyes that conveyed such warmth and hope. "Do you want to know what I want?"

Hal should say no. The safe and smart thing to do would be to say no, and Hal found that he couldn't. "Yes," he whispered.

"I want you." Caleb released one of Hal's hands and cupped his face. "Come on, Hal, tell me it's not too late. Tell me you love me like I love you."

Oh God, he said it. Caleb actually said it. Hal looked at Caleb, his eyes slowly filling with tears until Caleb blurred before him. Dammit, he'd promised himself he wouldn't ever cry again, and a few words from Caleb had dissolved him into a quivering mess. "We can't." Hal closed his eyes, felt the hot drip of tears spill down his cheeks. "Don't you see? We—"

Caleb's mouth touched his, and Hal's heart lurched. He brought up his hands to push him away, but couldn't stop himself from kissing Caleb back. He tasted the same, like home, like Hal was right where he always wanted to be. All those feelings he'd buried came alive again. All the time he'd spent convincing himself he wanted nothing more than friendship had been for nothing because one kiss changed everything. Hal needed Caleb in his life in every way.

He was so screwed.

Hal pushed him back, his body tingling, his heart hurting even more. "I do love you, but I… we can't do this."

Caleb brushed away Hal's tears. He looked so anxious, so hopeful that it brought a renewed ache. "What if I said you could have everything you ever wanted with me? We can be together all the time not just occasionally. I was an idiot to let you walk away, to let my fears rule me. I don't make the same mistake twice."

Caleb was saying all the things Hal wanted to hear, everything he'd dreamt of. The two of them, together, maybe getting their own place. Who knew, maybe one day a chance for a family… but that was the whole problem. Family. Hal had resigned himself to never having a relationship with his parents. Once it got back to Mom and Dad that he was living openly with a man there would be no chance of repairing the breach. He was prepared for that. At least he had Lily. He had his friends in New York and here. But Caleb's family meant too much to him to risk the same estrangement.

"Rodney said something a while ago that got me thinking," Caleb continued when Hal remained silent. "I need to have a life for myself, not for anyone else, not him, not my parents. You are the life I want."

Hal's throat closed on a choked-off sob as he fought a new onslaught of tears. Nobody could lay him open, strip him bare, and make him want so deeply like Caleb. Hal had no defense against his words. "I can't let you lose your family over me. You don't know what it's like, to know you're alone, and if things go bad, you have no home to return to. You're so lucky. I watch you all, and I can see how much you respect and love each other. I don't want to be the cause of you losing what matters most to you."

Caleb pulled him close, and this time Hal didn't resist. He'd didn't know how many times they had comforted each other by holding on just like this. Hal pressed his cheek against Caleb's shoulder, hating himself for being so weak when he needed to be strong. He had to let Caleb go.

"My family knows." Caleb kissed the top of his head. "I told them I was gay. And they know that I'm crazy in love with you."

Hal pulled back, his mind reeling as he stared at Caleb. "You did what? When?"

"Well, Rodney figured it out while we put your apartment together. He confronted me about us," Caleb said. "He's cool with it. Then I spoke with Uncle Vern because I figured if there was anyone in the family who'd support me all the way it would be him, and he did."

Hal tried to get his scrambling, racing thoughts together. "What about your parents?" Hal asked through numb lips. "What did they think?"

Caleb winced, and a cold knot blossomed in Hal's stomach, freezing him. The set of his jaw said he was angry, the turn of his mouth sad. This could not be happening. No. There had to be a way of fixing this. "They're pretty upset," Caleb admitted. "They don't understand I didn't choose to be this way. They think it's something I can fix if I just will it away. Look, I know what you're thinking. I've met your parents. I know what they've done to you. Because of that I know you don't get how real families work. Mom and Dad just need time to process it. They love me. They may not like this decision, but they aren't going to throw me away."

Hal wanted to believe him, but he wanted it too much, and he didn't trust himself to make the right decision. Hal took Caleb's hands again and stared at them as his eyes stung anew. He pushed the sensation back, swallowed it down. He stared at their linked fingers, black and white, outsiders forever right? Only he didn't want that for Caleb. These were the hands of the man he'd always loved, but he couldn't let his own selfish needs ruin Caleb's life.

"Caleb, I can't be with you," Hal whispered, and Caleb's hands tightened over Hal's.

"So this is your answer? You're walking away? After everything we've been through. Dammit, don't do this to me. We love each other. This is about us, not my family or yours."

Hal forced himself to look up during Caleb's impassioned plea. He was killing him inside, knowing he was making Caleb feel worse. Knowing how much Caleb was hurting because it mirrored his own feelings. He didn't know what to do because every solution looked like it was heading toward more heartache. He could feel himself wavering. God he was so weak. He couldn't take Caleb looking at him with his heart in his eyes and not respond.

"I... I need time to think." Hal squeezed Caleb's hands as his eyes darkened with pain. "Just a couple days. This is a lot to take in. You've been planning this and have had time to consider every angle. I'm not jumping in this time, not without thinking it through."

"Okay." Caleb pressed his lips together and let go of Hal's hands. "You need to know two things before you start your thinking time."

"What's that?" Hal watched Caleb with a new wariness. He wasn't sure he could hear any more words of love without his will crumbling into nonexistence.

"One, I didn't tell Mom and Dad for you. I told them for myself. I'm tired of dodging questions about girlfriends and tired of feeling like I'm constantly lying to them. I won't say that knowing there was a chance we could be together wasn't a motivation, but when it came down to talking with them, it was all about me telling them who I am and where I am going with my life. I want them to be proud of me for me, to love me, not some ideal image in their head."

Hal tried to rationalize that, but his thoughts wouldn't stop spinning. Had he felt the same when he'd told Lily the truth? Had he needed her to accept him for himself?

"I'm not the only one who believes they'll get over the shock and come around," Caleb continued. "Rodney and Uncle Vern believe it too."

Hal's heart twisted. He'd believed that once. He'd kept telling himself that if he'd tried harder or played by the rules, Dad would come to accept him or Mom would defy Dad for him. All those wishes wasted on something that was never going to happen.

"I hope you're right," he murmured.

"There's something else you need to know. Maybe the last time we were lovers, it was the wrong time for us. And it took me longer than you to realize a few things. But I'm not going to let you walk away without one hell of a fight. So you might want to keep that in mind too."

There was a promise in Caleb's gaze that made Hal's heart beat faster and his mouth dry up. "Okay," Hal said faintly.

Caleb kissed him again, a hard, demanding kiss that sent a hot lick of desire through Hal's body. Even knowing he shouldn't encourage him, Hal kissed Caleb, gripping his shirt as if he was afraid to let him go.

Caleb looked at him, his gaze soft, and Hal swallowed the lump in his throat. "I love you," Caleb said, and Hal nodded. "Did you still want to have dinner with me?" Caleb gestured toward the table.

The urge to run away warred with the wish not to hurt Caleb any more than he already had. Caleb had gone to so much trouble to make this night special.

Hal hesitated, then nodded again, the daze starting to lift. Caleb smiled, the ache in his eyes easing as he turned away to finish unpacking. Hal dragged his hands through his hair, trying to still their trembling.

Lord help him, he didn't know what to do. He closed his eyes. He wasn't going to be able to resist Caleb, not if he truly intended on fighting for him. Hal had waited too long for this and given up on them once. He couldn't give up on them again. But he wasn't going to stand by and let Caleb lose his parents either.

CHARLESTON, SC—
SEPTEMBER 17, 1977

HAL LEANED against his kitchen counter, silently willing the coffee maker to hurry up and finish brewing. His eyes were gritty, there was a faint headache throbbing at his temples, and he was dying to crawl back into bed. Only it wouldn't do a damn bit of good. He'd barely slept. His thoughts kept lingering on the evening with Caleb, how perfect it had been despite the painful ache of reawakened hope.

He loved Caleb…. Caleb loved him.

The fact that their feelings remained this strong, for so long appealed to Hal's instinct that they were meant to be together. But the shadow in Caleb's eyes when he talked about his parents hurt. It hurt worse than the final night in New York when Hal left, furious and sick inside. They'd all known it was coming. It had only been a matter of time before the stress lines fractured their family into shards. This whole situation with Caleb's mom and dad was different. It was wrong and unnatural.

Hal loved Mr. and Mrs. Hudson too. He respected them. They'd opened their doors to him, gave him a sense of belonging when he'd needed it. Though they'd never discussed it, Hal suspected they'd known his preferences, and still they'd welcomed him for the holidays. It made him sick to think he might not be welcome anymore. To know Caleb had left their home angry and upset. It woke up too many memories. Caleb didn't deserve this.

Hal poured himself a cup of coffee and burned his tongue. Restless, he set the cup down and went to get dressed. He couldn't believe Caleb had come out to his family. Well, maybe not Uncle Vern. He'd always been open-minded and fought passionately for fairness. Rodney though…. Hal was surprised he'd been so accepting. However, that reaction was based on the angry, bitter man Hal had known years ago. He sensed that the angry bitterness remained, only directed inward. How would Rodney handle this tension? That worried him too.

He sat on the edge of his bed, socks in hand. He couldn't fault Caleb. He understood. He remembered making the leap to tell Lily. He'd wanted her to know the true him too. They were so close that it felt dishonest to hold that crucial bit from her. While he'd been afraid, Hal supposed deep down he'd known that, even if she'd been upset, she wouldn't stop loving him.

There had to be something he could do for Caleb…. He had to talk to the Hudsons. He couldn't hide from the situation and pretend it didn't exist. There was too much history between them for him not to try. He owed it to Caleb.

Hal grabbed his car keys and headed over to their house. Mr. Hudson was off on weekends now, and Mrs. Hudson only worked the afternoons on Saturdays, letting her niece take charge. So there was a chance they'd both be home.

The little house was quiet when Hal pulled up, but the old station wagon was parked in the driveway. Hal steeled himself as he got out of his car. Caleb's parents had always been good to him. And now, they might never want to see him again. Could he face that kind of rejection a second time? Then he remembered the look on Caleb face last night as he told Hal that he'd never stop fighting for him, and his resolve firmed. Hal couldn't do any less.

He knocked on the screen door and tried without success to quell the jangling of his nerves. Mrs. Hudson came to the door but didn't open it to let him in. Hal's stomach sank. It had already started before he'd even said anything. Her eyes were rimmed red, and she looked as if she had aged since he'd seen her last, as if her bones were too heavy for her body to carry. "Morning, Hal," she said in her soft voice.

Hal shoved his hands in his pockets. "I just want a few minutes."

"Is Caleb okay?" she asked, and the immediate question gave Hal hope when there had been none before.

"He's hurting and angry. He might not show it, because he loves you, but it's there." Mrs. Hudson glanced away, and her lips trembled. "May I come in and talk to you and Mr. Hudson?"

She hesitated, then pushed open the screen door and motioned him inside. Mr. Hudson sat in the armchair in the living room, his expression set and unreadable. He got up slowly as Hal entered the room. "Please leave. You're the one who sent my son down this path he's taken. Who's convinced him he's something he's not," he accused, his gaze pained.

"Thomy, don't," Mrs. Hudson said. "He just wanted to talk to us about Caleb."

"It's okay," Hal said. He faced Mr. Hudson, seeing the same grief and anger that Caleb had. They carried it in the same way, hiding it with lifted heads and straightened shoulders. "I haven't infected him or led him astray, if that's what you're thinking, sir. Caleb is far too stubborn and strong willed for that. But I am the man Caleb loves. He didn't chose to fall in love with me, and I can't help but love him back."

"It's not right. It's not natural," Mr. Hudson said, and Mrs. Hudson made a soft sound of distress.

"All I know is I've always been this way for as long as I can recall. Dad tried to beat it out of me, and it didn't work. I tried to be a good kid, and that didn't help. Caleb tried to pretend he wasn't like this, and it changed nothing. He'd been prepared to go through the rest of his life alone and loveless because it would make you two more comfortable," Hal said with quiet insistence. Mrs. Hudson met his eyes and then looked away, hugging her arms to herself.

"Caleb's your son. He's still the man you've always thought he was. He tries so hard to do the right thing, to do what's expected of him. Don't ask him to choose between you and being loved by me." Hal felt his composure start to break, and he struggled to hold on to it. "Because I do. I've loved him my whole life."

"I won't," Mrs. Hudson replied, and when Mr. Hudson shot her a look, she straightened and glared back at him. "I can't let this tear us apart. He's our son. We have to figure out a way to come to accept it or ignore it. I don't know, but something. Thomy, for God's sake, that boy has never asked us for anything, and I can't remember the last time I saw him crying, but he stood right here and pleaded with us, and we let him walk out. That's what's not right."

Hal's heart ached anew because he could picture it too well. But her words made him think Caleb was right, maybe given time his parents would come around. He remained silent as Mrs. and Mr. Hudson regarded each other in a silent argument.

"I'm not sure what you or Caleb are thinking, but telling him we don't approve and not accepting your... relationship, isn't the same as kicking him out of the family," Mr. Hudson said, turning his attention to Hal.

"If you could reach out to him, call him, talk to him, please. You're too close to not try."

"Caleb doesn't want to hear anything I have to say, and we don't want or need your judgment. This is between our family, not yours," Mr. Hudson said in a heavy voice. "Now, I need you to leave. Don't come back unless you're invited."

"Thomy, this is my house just as much as it's yours, and—"

"It's okay, Mrs. Hudson," Hal cut in. "If staying away helps, then I will. All I ask is don't exclude Caleb. I can't watch him be hurt like I was. Work it out with him. Invite him to your Sunday family dinners. I promise, I'll stay away."

Mr. Hudson's jaw tightened. "Caleb won't stand for that. Not for long anyway."

"I'll tell him it's okay." Mr. Hudson was right, though. Caleb might let it slide for a little while, but not long, and Hal didn't want to be the center of a stubborn feud. Hal hoped it was a sign Mr. Hudson was wavering. He could see Caleb's parents were hurting as much as Caleb. If they just talked and worked at it... maybe this hurt could be healed. This at least was a start and Hal didn't want to destroy the headway he'd made by pushing them too far. "Thank you for listening."

He turned to go, feeling as if he was leaving a part of himself behind. In many ways, they had been a second family to him, and once again, he was choosing to cut himself off. It hurt so much, he was shaking inside.

Mrs. Hudson followed Hal to the door and stopped him with a hand on his arm. He couldn't look at her. He'd lose it if he did. So he stared at her hand instead, gnarled and work worn from years of weaving baskets into art. "Hal, please be patient. I'm trying to understand."

Hal nodded but found he couldn't speak as she continued, "When you're a parent, you picture a certain life for your children. Often you forget those children have minds of their own, and they constantly surprise you. I don't want this kind of relationship for Caleb or for you.

Life is hard enough without being so different. But what I want isn't going to change anything. If he has to be this way, at least he's this way with you." She squeezed his arm and let it go with a pat. "Now you tell him when he's ready, he can come see me at the market and we'll talk."

Hal looked at her then and saw the hopeful entreaty in her eyes. He tried to smile, but he couldn't get his mouth to work. He leaned down and kissed her cheek. "Thank you, Mrs. Hudson. Good-bye."

He was almost to his car when she called his name. He turned and looked at her standing on the porch. Behind the screen door, Mr. Hudson watched them and stayed silent. "Maybe after a bit, you both can come see me. You hear?"

This time Hal did smile. His own mother would've never defied his dad like this. Not for anything. "Loud and clear, ma'am."

Hal pulled out of their driveway and picked a direction. He was restless, though not as bad as before. He expected Caleb later on in the day, and he wanted to be ready. Last night, Caleb had laid it all out on the line, and Hal hadn't had the courage to cross it. That wasn't going to happen again.

His breath came out in a wondering rush as he realized that without even thinking about it, in his heart he'd already made the commitment to Caleb. Now he just had to show him that he didn't have to worry about Hal hiding anymore.

CALEB SAT in his car and looked up at Hal's apartment. Hal's Buick Skylark was parked outside, and the living room windows were open. That was good. Caleb had been half-afraid he'd scared Hal into avoiding him, and he was too worn out to go searching for him again. Not that it would stop him for one minute.

He'd handled it badly yesterday. If Caleb hadn't been so wrung out from his argument with his parents or so damned nervous over getting the dinner just right, he wouldn't have been so clumsy with his words. Maybe he shouldn't have told Hal about his parents' reaction…. No, he couldn't start lying to him or keeping secrets. Especially when Caleb was trying for a fresh start.

He hadn't seen Hal cry like that in a very long time. It underscored how much Hal's parents had wounded him. It hurt to see him fall apart like that. Last night, after they'd parted, Caleb had wandered all along the Battery, staring out at the dark water, trying to figure out how he could've done it differently. He came to the conclusion that the reason Hal was so upset was because of how much he loved Caleb. Otherwise it wouldn't have mattered so much.

That gave him the faith he needed to go home. Tonight he'd find some way to make Hal see they belonged together because as long as they were together, they could handle anything. They'd proven that again and again. It had taken them fourteen years to get to this point, where they both fully admitted they were in love. He hoped it wouldn't take another fourteen years before they could find their happiness together.

Caleb took a deep breath and headed up to Hal's apartment feeling silly and nervous at the same time. He should've brought flowers. That's what lovers did. No, flowers didn't suit Hal. He should've bought him a book or a new record. Caleb almost turned away to do just that, but what if Hal had seen him from the window? He'd be confused, maybe upset if he saw Caleb leaving again without a word. Next time he came over, he'd bring him a little gift.

He knocked lightly, and Hal opened the door with an exasperated expression. "I don't know why you bother knocking. What's the point?" He grabbed a handful of Caleb's T-shirt and tugged him inside. "I've been trying to get a hold of you all day. I was beginning to think I'd have to hunt you down."

That had to be a good sign, and Caleb figured it would be better on his nerves if he took it as such. "Well, I stopped by this morning, but you were gone. So I picked up an extra shift at work." Hal looked a disheveled mess with his hair sticking out in tuffs and waves. He was barefoot, shirtless, and his jean shorts were worn out to threads, but he looked damned beautiful, and Caleb itched to kiss him.

As he reached for him to do just that, Hal sidestepped him and held up his hand. "Wait. If you start kissing me. I won't be able to think, and there are a few things I need to say."

Caleb lifted Hal's hand to his lips and brushed a kiss over his knuckles. A little smile crossed Hal's lips, and then his whole expression became serious. It was worrying. Caleb reminded himself that Hal had just about promised him there would be kissing, so whatever he had to say couldn't be all that bad.

"I…." Hal dragged his hands through his hair and fisted them, which explained the state it was in. Then Hal dropped his arms and gestured toward the couch with its colorful throw. "Okay, sit, you're hovering."

Caleb sat, and this time it was his turn to shoot Hal an exasperated look. "And you're dithering. Just tell me."

"I talked to your parents this morning." Hal paused and bit the corner of his lip.

"You did what?" Caleb stared at him in disbelief, and once it sank in, he searched Hal's face for any sign of new grief. That conversation had to have been rough on everyone. "You didn't have to do that."

"I did, for your sake. For their sakes. For my sanity. I can't know your family is hurting and not try to talk them into at least reaching out to you." Hal faced him, his fair skin flushed with emotion, his eyes bright. The picture he made warmed Caleb inside, and he stared at Hal in wonder.

He couldn't believe Hal had done that for him. He knew how much courage it had taken for Hal to face that kind of parental disapproval. It brought it all home, right there in the sudden thumping of his heart. He loved Hal, and Hal loved him back. He couldn't quite believe he'd finally made the leap that brought them together again. He'd rather focus on that truth than the pain that throbbed every time he thought of Mom and Dad.

"I went over there sure I was going to face a scene like the one my parents gave me too many times," Hal said, starting to pace in front of him. "With Dad raining abuse and Mom standing back, looking at me with pleading eyes like I could fix it all if I could just be better."

Though Caleb absolutely couldn't see his family doing either one of those things, facing their disappointment and shame had been hard enough. He'd carry that memory with him for a long time. "I hope they didn't hurt you too," he said quietly.

"Not intentionally. I think that's the real difference. They definitely spoke their mind, but they didn't do it cruelly or to demean." Hal knelt in front of him and took Caleb's hands. "They don't understand, but I think maybe you're right, maybe they just need time."

It helped to hear that, especially coming from Hal. If he saw it, believed it, then it couldn't just be wishful thinking. "Thank you. I… don't know what else to say. Thank you for talking to them for me."

"Your mom wants you to come see her in the market when you're ready," Hal said, as if he knew just what a gift he was handing Caleb.

A lump hurtled itself up into Caleb's throat. "She does?"

"Yeah," Hal said, his gaze wistful. "That's what I wanted to tell you earlier. They do love you. I don't think Dad ever loved anybody but himself in his life. I know Mom does, but she loves peace more than me. I suppose, maybe I shouldn't blame her so much. If I had married a dick like that I'd probably be craving peace too."

Their eyes met, and Caleb's heart skipped a beat at the look in Hal's eyes, love without reservation or fear, without the adoration he had when they were younger that Caleb felt he could never live up to.

Caleb tugged on his hand and Hal rose. He sat back against the soft cushions of the couch as Hal straddled Caleb's hips. "I promise not to turn into an asshole if you say you're willing to be mine for the rest of our lives." Caleb cupped Hal's cheek. "I know too many people let you down, even me sometimes, but I won't ever walk out on you. Tell me you're willing to give us a chance."

Hal closed his eyes and leaned his cheek into Caleb's hand. "You love me." He opened his eyes and stared at Caleb with a smile. "Say it again."

"I love you. I'll say it as many times as you need me too," Caleb said fervently.

Hal's eyes got misty, and he blinked it away. "I'm yours." Those two words made Caleb's heart jump. "And there have been times when we both let each other down. I think the difference is we never let it stay that way. So maybe we will again, but I think I trust us to make it right."

Caleb slid his arm around Hal's waist and tugged him closer. Their lips met in a kiss both heated and tender. Caleb couldn't believe this was real, after all that time hoping and wishing… dreaming of this moment. He pulled back and watched Hal's light gray-green eyes flutter open, trying to memorize every second of this moment.

Hal touched his forehead to Caleb's. "You and me, we're going to be okay."

"Yeah, we're going to be just fine." Caleb slid his hands up the length of Hal's spine, marveling again at the differences in their bodies, Hal's long leanness that should make him appear skinny if it wasn't for his broad shoulders, and Caleb's bulk. He loved the way they fit together, how Hal felt pressed up against him.

"So… I couldn't help notice you're half-naked," Caleb murmured. "Were you planning to kill what self-restraint I had when I showed up?"

Hal's mouth widened in a wicked grin. "Actually, I was cleaning and trying to distract myself, waiting for you to show up or return my call. Now all my weekend chores are done, and I'm completely free."

"Is that right? Well, then, we'll have to take advantage." Caleb figured there were going to be many distracting days in his future if Hal made that a habit. He kissed Hal again, little fluttering kisses along his jaw and down to the pulse of his throat. It had been so long that it felt almost like the first time all over again only without the nerves.

He didn't care if they screwed or didn't screw. He just wanted Hal naked and in his arms. He'd missed that intimacy, the closeness that had come so easily to them both.

"I was hoping you'd say something like that." Hal sighed and let his head fall back as Caleb continued to nuzzle along his throat. His hands tightened on Caleb's biceps, then slid down to pull up the hem of Caleb's T-shirt. Caleb lifted his arms, his heart pounding harder. He couldn't believe he was touching Hal again, tasting him. His cock swelled and began to ache, pressing up between Hal's thighs.

A quick, teasing smile flashed across Hal's lips, and he circled his hips against him, making Caleb catch his breath at the hot zing of excitement. Hal slid his hands over Caleb's chest, leaning back to look him over. Caleb found himself doing the same, his gaze drifting over Hal's body at the pale skin tanned from the summer sun, the golden-brown hair on his chest and long legs, pink nipples tightened into buds.

Caleb pressed a kiss to the notch on Hal's breastbone and then turned his head to rub his cheek against him. "So now that we're officially a couple and not just friends with benefits, does that mean I get to give you a pet name?"

Hal pulled back with a dangerous gleam in his eyes. "If you even think about calling me kitten, I'll bite."

Caleb choked on a laugh. "I'll keep that in mind." He cupped Hal's ass, the worn denim thin and soft enough for him to feel that Hal was wearing nothing underneath. This reminded him so strongly of those long afternoons they used to spend together naked, sometimes playfully wrestling to see who'd top, or just talking and touching until the mood heated again. "Forget the nicknames, I just want to take you to your room and get naked."

Hal shivered and slipped his arms around Caleb's neck. Sharp teeth nipped Caleb's earlobe, Hal's breath hot and promising. "Race you there. If I win, I'm going to blow you." Blood rushed from Caleb's brain straight downward, and before he could recover his wits Hal had scrambled off his lap and was running down the hallway snickering.

Caleb groaned and pulled himself up to chase after him. Hal had better not already be naked, or there would be a reckoning. He wanted to strip those nonexistent shorts off Hal's long legs. Whether Hal got to his bedroom first or not didn't matter, because Caleb fully intended on getting his mouth on Hal too.

He paused in the bedroom doorway, staring at Hal, sprawled out on the bed, cheeks flushed, eyes laughing, looking happier than Caleb had seen him in ages. Caleb's heart tumbled and fell all over again. Everything that had happened up to this point, everything that would happen going forward would be worth it, just to know that at the end of the day, Hal would be waiting for him.

CHARLESTON, SC—
SEPTEMBER 2, 2023

CALEB OPENED the front door to their house, grateful to be home. It had been a wonderful day and so much fun to catch up with their extended family, especially the grandkids. But he was wrung out from a day full of emotional highs and nonstop activity. He felt his age tonight, in the stiffness in his joints and the aching of his knees. Sleep would wash most of the exhaustion away, a good thing, because Lily and her daughter were coming over for breakfast. It would be nice to catch up with them when it was quieter. Today they'd been pulled in all directions.

Then tomorrow afternoon there would be another get-together here in their backyard with the kids and grandkids. A chance to be together one last time as a family until the holidays arrived. It sure seemed echoingly quiet now without all the chatter. It wasn't the first time Caleb thought their home was too still.

Caleb shut off the house alarm and stretched, joints popping as Hal shut and locked the door behind them. Maybe it was time to get a dog. Hal was always urging him to exercise more, and Caleb couldn't bring himself to try the yoga and tai chi that Hal practiced in the courtyard. Hal had never left his hippie days behind. He'd just channeled it in a whole other direction. But a dog would be nice, and there were plenty of beautiful places to walk around Charleston.

"You're awfully quiet," Hal said, touching his shoulder. "You okay?"

"Yeah, just thinking about how quiet it is. Our family is one wild bunch," Caleb said with a rueful grin, and Hal snorted.

"That shouldn't surprise you." Hal moved past him into the kitchen and poked his head in the refrigerator. He couldn't possibly be hungry. They'd stuffed themselves silly over the day.

"I forget how much energy those grandkids have. I don't remember our kids being like that," Caleb mused.

"You're kidding me right?" Hal straightened and stared in disbelief at Caleb. "Drew never walked anywhere if he could run. The foster boys were inventive twin demons, and Kendra—I don't even want to get started on Kendra. Zoe is one hundred percent her mother's daughter."

"True, you got me," Caleb said with a laugh as he went to check the kitchen door to the garden out of long habit. "They were a handful too. It's funny how time changes your perspectives."

He stood at the back door and studied the flowers lining the courtyard, buds closed tight for the night. It was a nice evening to sit out by the koi pond and talk. He wasn't quite ready to haul himself up the stairs to go to bed. He was about to suggest that when Hal came up beside him with the delicate long-stemmed wineglasses that Drew had given them as a wedding present.

Hal handed one of them to Caleb, half-full with a chilled white. Must be the Riesling, then. "A toast?" Hal asked. "To celebrate the last sixty years and to salute the next decade to come."

"Just a decade? Why aim so low?" Caleb slanted him a look with a slight smile. "At least another thirty, come on, we're not that old."

"Good point. To another thirty years and the hopes that they are as full and rich as the rest of our lives have been," Hal said, and they clinked their glasses together. "I love you."

"I love you too." Caleb took a sip of the delicate, sweet wine and savored the intimate moment with Hal. After all these years, he still marveled at their relationship. Maybe the hot fire of falling in love had faded, but the insecurities also went with that disappearance. He wished more people experienced the joy and warmth of being with their best friend for so long.

"So this day has got me thinking," Hal said, turning toward him.

"Always a dangerous prospect," Caleb teased. "Anything in particular?"

"Well, for starters, we never had a real honeymoon. If I recall things right, you were working on the final phase of that jetty project, and I was in the middle of writing the grant proposal for the sustainable garden at the shelter." Caleb thought about it and had to admit Hal was right. They had been so busy going off in different directions that Caleb wasn't sure how they'd managed to squeeze in a wedding. "I think it's past time we do something about that," Hal continued and nudged Caleb's arm with his elbow.

Caleb contemplated his suggestion for a moment, and then a slow smile crossed his lips. The idea of running off to an exotic and romantic place with Hal for a few weeks greatly appealed to him. "Why not. Since you've been thinking on it, do you have any place in mind?"

"Machu Picchu," Hal said, with an innocent smile.

Caleb closed his eyes and shook his head with rueful exasperation. "I'm remembering why I stopped letting you plan our family vacations. You have no idea of what it means to relax." That trip had been enjoyable when they were younger, and the view at dawn had been life changing, but Caleb wasn't sure he wanted a repeat performance at seventy. His knees ached thinking about it.

"I'm teasing. I want to go somewhere we've never been before." Hal slipped his arm over Caleb's shoulder. "Something cultural and picturesque that appeals to both exploring and relaxing by a pool or beach."

That reminded Caleb of a place he'd considered more than once, but they'd never settled on it for a vacation. "Something like Amalfi Coast?" Caleb suggested.

"I like the way you think." Hal finished off the last sip of his wine. "We've spent the entire day reflecting on our past, and it was fun, but I think it's time we look to our future. We've been retired a couple of years now and caught up on our rest. We should be crazy for a while."

"I'm not sure I'm up to your definition of crazy," Caleb said.

"Liar." Hal brushed a kiss over Caleb's lips and set their wineglasses on the counter. "I'll see you upstairs. Don't brood out the window too long. We have honeymoon plans to make."

"I'll be along in a few minutes," Caleb promised.

"Don't make me come looking for you," Hal called over his shoulder.

Caleb listened to the sound of Hal moving up the stairs to make sure he didn't stumble and smiled. Caleb got testy when anybody hovered over him, and now look at him, guarding Hal's steps like he was a toddler. Maybe Hal was right. They'd gotten restless these last few years. They should shake things up, go out and do all the things they couldn't do when they were working and raising the kids. They had the money. They sure as hell had the time.

After his surgery Caleb felt better than he had in years. He continued to stare out at the garden, plans wheeling in his head. When they were younger, Hal had wandering feet, and Caleb always wondered if he'd take off to explore the world. But he never had, at least not long-term, except for Ghana. They'd gone to exotic places as a family. Still…. Caleb couldn't shake the idea that maybe it was time to move along and rediscover his husband. His husband. Damn he loved the sound of that.

Why not give them both a chance to wander? He didn't want to wait until it was too late. He grinned as the idea came together in his head. Hal was going to love this.

HAL HAD changed into a comfortable pair of loose cotton pants and was stretched out on his bed, looking through the memory book when Caleb called up the stairs. "Don't let me catch you with your nose in a book with just the bedside lamp on."

"What do you think you're going to do about it?" Hal asked with a snort in his voice.

"Oh, I'm going to do something." The threat was empty, but it was part of a ritual that had been going on for so long that Hal wasn't exactly sure when they started. Probably when his eyesight took a turn for the worse. God knew he harassed Caleb enough about his diet, so he supposed they were even, and that's what allowed them to keep their sense of humor about it.

Now Hal was stuck with large-print books or his e-reader, but e-readers just weren't the same. He'd admit, he did love the convenience of being able to carry so many books when he was traveling. Still, nothing beat the feel and scent of a book heavy in his hands.

Hal smiled at Caleb as he came into the room and pointed at the overhead light. "See, your fears are for nothing."

"Don't even play innocent." Caleb shot him a look of fond exasperation. "I've caught you too many times."

Well, Hal couldn't deny the truth of that. He turned the pages of the memory book, finding new things he'd missed before. This was a gift that would keep showing them wonders, and he was touched to his core over the gesture. They had an amazing bunch of kids.

He pulled out one of the letters Caleb had written to him while Hal was in Kentucky. So much had changed.... Hal lifted his gaze to Caleb who was brushing his teeth in the bathroom... yet Caleb still had mighty sexy calves, with ankles that looked slim again now that his hypertension had eased. Wouldn't Caleb laugh to know what he was thinking?

"So I was giving some thought to your proposition," Caleb said, rinsing off his toothbrush.

"Our belated honeymoon?" Hal asked, tucking the letter in the pouch Kendra had crafted.

"No, to your notion that we needed to do something crazy with our retirement years." Caleb stuck his head into the bedroom with an avid expression that told Hal he had a plan. He couldn't wait to hear this. Like Caleb said downstairs, his notion of crazy was vastly different from Hal's.

"Give it to me." Hal set the memory book on his nightstand.

Caleb turned off the bathroom and overhead light and joined Hal on the bed, dragging out his revelation. Hal had learned over the years just to let him have his fun, though that didn't stop him from lifting his brow in an expression of expectation.

"Remember after college, before Drew came to stay with us, when you suggested we do a tour of all fifty states?" Caleb asked, folding his hands over his stomach.

A shot of excitement raced through Hal's blood, and he tried to squelch the reaction. Caleb couldn't be suggesting that. It wasn't practical. "I know you're not thinking of jet-setting from one end of the country and back." As much as he hated to admit it, that much traveling would be exhausting... but shitballs... he wanted to try. There were so many places he wanted to see—the Olympic National Park, the Painted Desert. He wanted to explore the remaining covered bridges in New Hampshire and the Amish country in Lancaster, Pennsylvania. The possibilities were endless.

"God no. That would require too much organization." Hal stared at Caleb, wondering what the hell had gotten into his husband. Too much sun maybe because Hal and Caleb definitely weren't speaking the same language. "Will you stop looking at me like I've grown another head," Caleb said.

"You said 'too much organization.' So stop acting like you have," Hal retorted. He had to have a plan. Caleb never considered anything seriously without one. "What're you thinking?"

"A motor home," Caleb said with quiet satisfaction. "The ones they have today have just about anything we could ever want. We pick a destination and head out. Then we can stay in any one place for as long or as little as we want. We can sell this place or get something smaller if we want a home here to come back to instead of bothering Kendra. What's keeping us here? We're retired. The kids are scattered."

"You're crazy." Hal shook his head, but he lingered over the idea.

"You said you wanted crazy." Caleb brushed a kiss on Hal's mouth, then lay down and tucked himself into the sheets. "Give it some thought."

"You drop a plan on me like that, and now you're going to sleep?" Hal asked.

"Yep." Hal watched in bemusement as Caleb tucked the pillow under his arm and closed his eyes with a smile playing around his mouth. "Lily will be here early, and I want my sleep. We can talk about it tomorrow night."

Hal shook his head as Caleb promptly began snoring lightly. Even after all these years, Hal didn't understand how he could fall asleep so fast. Caleb said it was a holdover from the Army when he had to grab what rest he could, when he could. But Hal was more inclined to think it was a family trait.

He considered going through their book again and decided that lying down next to Caleb was much more appealing. Now that he was stretched out in bed, the excitement of the day was catching up to him. He yawned as he shut off the lights and put his glasses in a safe spot. He'd learned the hard way that he couldn't see well enough to find the damned things if they weren't where they were supposed to be.

Hal listened to Caleb's breathing, as he tried to relax his mind. It was hard. So much kept whirling through his head, and as he got older, he slept less because of it.

His thoughts jumped from picturing how they'd been as boys when they'd first met, with not one damned clue that when they'd rescued each other they'd made a friend for life. Then he surged forward to the future Caleb had suggested for them. A motor home... at least it would be bigger than their old clubhouse. They should call it the Outsider Express, just for the memories alone. The thought made him chuckle quietly.

They'd have to scale back their belongings, but they'd been talking about doing that anyway. Hal loved this home, and Caleb did too, but it was too much for just the two of them. Kendra would protest. She was sentimental like that. After the excitement of the reunion was over, they'd have to make plans. He liked Caleb's suggestion... it was crazy... but it was a good kind of crazy.

Hal rolled onto his side with a sigh. Even as tired as he was, he couldn't settle down. He reached out and laid his hand on Caleb's arm. It always amazed Hal how just touching him, acknowledging Caleb as a permanent part of his life always stilled his thoughts and calmed him down, even when he was at his most anxious. To Hal that feeling went beyond love, and family, and friendship... It was like they shared a soul.

He felt himself relax, and his breathing began to match Caleb's as the fog of sleep started to wash over him. Then just before he drifted off, he felt Caleb take his hand, and the last of his scattered thoughts quieted. Hal was right where he belonged.

MARGUERITE LABBE has been accused of being eccentric and a shade neurotic, both of which she freely admits to, but her muse has OCD tendencies, so who can blame her? Her husband and son do an excellent job keeping her toeing the line, though. Marguerite loves to spin tales of stubborn men with smart mouths, working toward a deep and lasting love, no matter what else she throws at them.

She has won the Rainbow Award for Historical Romance with Fae Sutherland, as well as the Rainbow Award for Paranormal and the Rainbow Romance Award for Excellence, also in Paranormal.

When she's not working hard on writing new material and editing completed work, she spends her time reading novels of all genres, enjoying role-playing games with her equally nutty friends, and trying to plot practical jokes against her son and husband. Unfortunately for her, her son is learning her tricks very fast.

Website: www.margueritelabbe.com

ALL
BETS
ARE
OFF

MARGUERITE LABBE

It only takes one night with Ash Gallagher to make Eli Hollister think he's finally met the right man at the right time. Good thing he doesn't bet on it, because Ash turns out to be a student in Eli's class at the local college. Eli can't deny he's attracted, but now it's complicated. He's already in enough trouble with the department head, a man who would like to see Eli denied his tenure and fired.

Ash is looking forward to taking his life in a new direction. After serving one active-duty stint in the Marine Corps and another in the Reserves, he's ready to put his military life behind him. The last new experience he'd planned for this semester was to fall in lust with his English professor, but the more Eli resists, the more Ash is determined to have him. Then he discovers Eli's playing for keeps, and Ash is only interested in a fling... or is he? Between these two, when it comes to life and love, all bets are off.

www.dreamspinnerpress.com

Andrei Cuza and Dean Marshall celebrated their tenth anniversary only to have their happiness shattered by a random, insane event: On his way home from closing a business deal, Dean stops on the parkway to help a young mother with her flat tire, and her ex arrives, murders them, and takes off with his two kids.

Ghosts have haunted Andrei all his life. He bears the guilt for his sister being stuck in limbo, because ghosts are frozen at the moment they died, unable to adapt to the changes in their living loved ones. When Dean returns to Andrei as a ghost, the double punch of losing him and having to watch him founder if he doesn't move on is almost more than Andrei can bear. Despite dangers in limbo—Jackal Wraiths that devour souls are hunting him—Dean isn't going anywhere until he helps Andrei track down the missing children. Andrei is in danger as well when he pays dearly to feel Dean's touch one last time. Time is slowly running out as Dean and Andrei try to say good-bye while they track a killer who's more than happy to kill again.

www.dreamspinnerpress.com

After a grueling battle in ancient Greece, lovers Dexios and Lykon committed their lives to each other in the name of Goddess Cythera. After the war, fearing the strength of his love for Dexios, Lykon abandoned his vow and returned home. Heartbroken, Dexios called on Cythera, who changed him into four unfinished statues. In that form he would wait for his fickle lover to return, break the curse, and make him whole.

Thousands of years have passed when Galen Kanellis finds the disassembled pieces in the storeroom of a Seattle museum and makes them the focus of his new exhibit. Needing information, he contacts his ex-lover Nick Charisteas. Nick has a lifelong dream of finding the Dexios Collection, and the last thing he expected was for it to wind up in the hands of the man who broke his heart. As both men search for answers about the statues, worries of abandonment and fear of loss test their renewed relationship, threatening to separate them again—this time permanently.

www.dreamspinnerpress.com

Death is never the end and love is only the beginning

My Heart is Within You

Marguerite Labbe

Triquetra Trilogy

Book One of the Triquetra Trilogy

The power of heart and soul holds the key to the survival of the last of the ancient vampires. Kristair is running out of time. His race has faded away, prey to delusion and deterioration, and his only chance to live long enough to find a cure is to bind his psyche to a human vessel in a long forgotten ritual.

Kristair's chosen vessel is Jacob Corvin, a man of passionate stubbornness and fierce loyalty; he has captured Kristair's fantasies so completely that he is both the vampire's greatest strength and most crippling weakness. Drawing upon Jacob's spirit and Kristair's resolve, they each bind a portion of their souls to one other. For as long as Jacob carries Kristair's heart within him, the vampire can continue his quest.

Just when they have hope, their mission is threatened by The Syndicate, a group of younger vampires who attempt to force Kristair to teach them his secrets before he disappears like the rest of the ancients. Battling both The Syndicate's attacks and his unexpected need and love for Jacob, Kristair's strength begins to fade, forcing him to make a decision that will change his and Jacob's lives forever.

www.dreamspinnerpress.com

Book Two of the Triquetra Trilogy

Heartbroken by the death of his vampire lover, Jacob Corvin finds himself embroiled in the intricacies of vampire hierarchy. He is consumed with rage after Kristair's torment and death, and when The Syndicate returns he is more than ready to personally destroy every one of the power-hungry vampires.

That anger and pain cannot be soothed, because before he disappeared, Kristair transferred all his memories and a piece of his soul to Jacob. So as hard as Jacob tries to move on— he can't. Kristair's heart still beats in his chest, and Kristair's memories whisper to him.

As he gets dragged further into a war between the vampires, Jacob starts to believe he's losing his mind. Those whispers and a feeling of Kristair's presence are growing within him, and he starts a desperate struggle to retain his own sense of self and sanity. But Kristair is not so easily silenced when he's determined to return to where he belongs.

www.dreamspinnerpress.com

They've fought to be together, now they have to learn to live with one another

Our Sacred Balance

Marguerite Labbe

Book Three of the Triquetra Trilogy

Lovers Kristair and Jacob believe they're done with the supernatural and on the road to a new life. But the supernatural isn't done with them. A stalker is targeting vampires, tearing them from their sanctuaries and leaving them to burn in the sun, and when the vampires of Pittsburgh call upon the ancient Kristair, he cannot refuse them aid despite Jacob's objections.

While their quest becomes more dangerous, tempers flare when Jacob tries to make Kristair understand the limitations of being human again. As they struggle to reach a balance between them, the other vampires become restless, eager to find the person responsible for the deaths of their own so they can vent their rage.

But the enemy is closer than they ever imagined and carries a personal grudge against them. Their mental link gone and spiritual strength halved, Jacob and Kristair must conquer Kristair's newfound helplessness and learn to communicate with each other before their enemy destroys everything they've fought so hard to win.

www.dreamspinnerpress.com

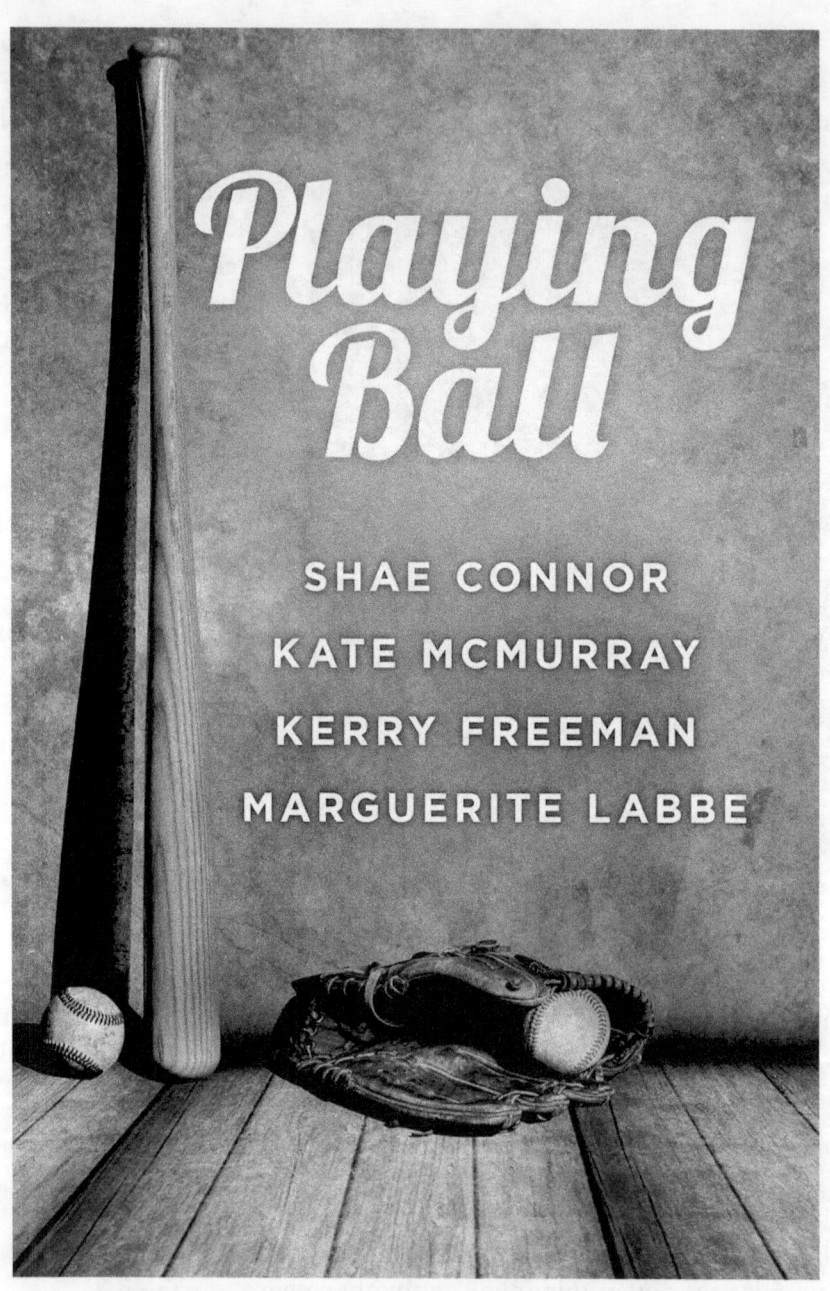

Playing Ball

SHAE CONNOR

KATE MCMURRAY

KERRY FREEMAN

MARGUERITE LABBE

www.dreamspinnerpress.com

SERPENTINE SERIES

Sex, Love, and Videogames

CJane Elliott

www.dreamspinnerpress.com

RENAE
KAYE

SAFE
IN HIS
ARMS

www.dreamspinnerpress.com

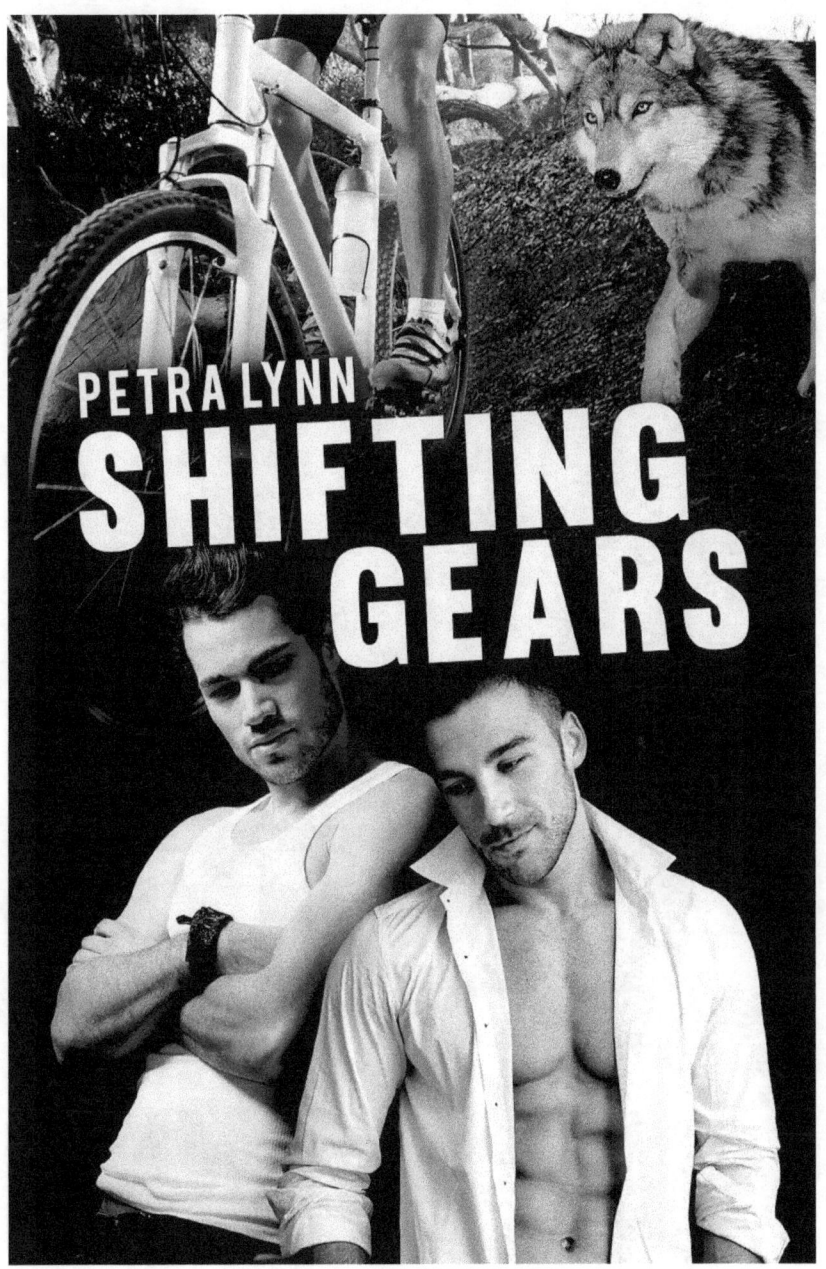

PETRA LYNN

SHIFTING GEARS

www.dreamspinnerpress.com

CANNING THE CENTER

TARA LAIN

LONG PASS CHRONICLES

Kate Sherwood

IN TOO DEEP

www.dreamspinnerpress.com

Buchanan house

CHARLEY
DESCOTEAUX

www.dreamspinnerpress.com

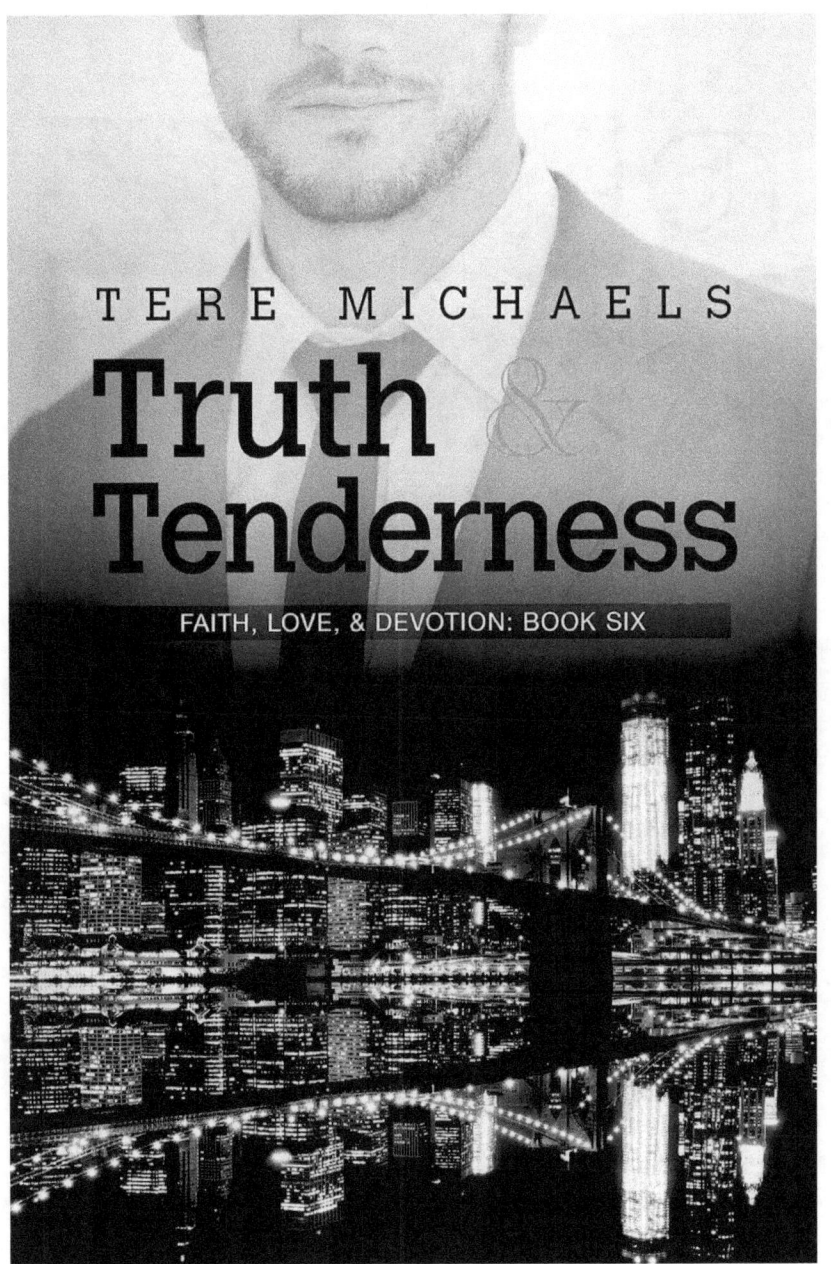

TERE MICHAELS

Truth &
Tenderness

FAITH, LOVE, & DEVOTION: BOOK SIX

www.dreamspinnerpress.com

www.ingramcontent.com/pod-product-compliance
Lightning Source LLC
Chambersburg PA
CBHW070045030726
47506CB00002B/355